MY MOTHER'S HOUSE

Also by Lily Tobias and available from Honno

EUNICE FLEET

MY MOTHER'S HOUSE

HOUSE

LILY TOBIAS

With an introduction by
Jasmine Donahaye

Welsh Women's Classics

First published by Hutchinson in 1931
This edition published by Honno Press
'Ailsa Craig', Heol y Cawl, Dinas Powys, Wales, CF64 4AH

1 2 3 4 5 6 7 8 9 10

© The Estate of Lily Tobias, 2015
Introduction © Jasmine Donahaye, 2015

ISBN: 978-1-909983-21-2 print
ISBN: 978-1-909983-22-9 ebook

Published with the financial support of the Welsh Books Council.

Cover image © Flik47/Shutterstock (Stained-glass window inside
the Great Synagogue, King George Street, Jerusalem) Cover
design: Graham Preston
Text design: Elaine Sharples
Printed in Wales by Gomer Press, Llandysul, Ceredigion SA44 4JL

INTRODUCTION

Lily Tobias was, first and to the core, a nationalist. She believed absolutely in the right to self-determination of small nations, believed that placing primary value on one's own culture, language, traditions and collective identity was a human right, and a fundamentally progressive liberal idea. Her nationalism underpinned her socialism and her committed pacifism, and equally informed her feminism. She was all those things – feminist, socialist, pacifist, nationalist – not only in principle but also in deed, and in uniquely Welsh-Jewish ways. Consequently it's no surprise that *My Mother's House* should be a uniquely Welsh-Jewish work – not because it is alone in the cultural hyphenation of its setting, but because that cultural intersection, the exploration of ethnic and national identity which so often proves inescapable for Welsh people and for Jews, is not just incidental to the work but is its subject and focus.

The 'mother's house' in the title of the novel derives from the Song of Songs – 'for I held him, and would not let him go, until I had brought him into my mother's house', as it is given in the book's bilingual epigraph. The title points to the central plot, in which the idealised heroine Edith brings the wayward Welsh Jew Simon back to himself, and to her. To Tobias, there was no boundary or distinction between the personal, religious, cultural and national aspects of one's identity, and the mother's house of the title also points to a central argument of the novel: the necessity for Jews to find a home in Judaism and Jewish identity, and a national homeland in Zion.

The world of *My Mother's House* – of the protagonist Simon's upbringing and roots – mirrors that of Tobias's upbringing. Orthodox, traditional, but, at the same time, politically radical, her father decided to leave Swansea, where Tobias was born in 1887, and shortly after her birth move with the family twelve miles up the valley to Ystalyfera, a coal and tin-plating town (at the time a village), where he opened a shop. Simon, like Tobias, grows up in a Welsh-speaking industrial community in the Swansea valley (although the place-names are fictionalised), and his early progress beyond a tradesman's life, through access to grammar-school education, echoes that of Tobias's brother, Joseph, who went on to Cardiff University and training as a doctor. But although there are some family parallels, Simon is a fully realised fictional character who has very different aspirations: to be neither Welsh, nor Jewish, both of which he finds constraining and shameful social burdens, but to be English – and, further, to be an English civil servant.

In the course of his flight across the Severn, that mystical border both of the psyche and of language and culture – away from what he feels is a debased and primitive Wales, and towards the giddy, enlightened opening out of English life to which he aspires – Tobias mocks, but she mocks sympathetically. With poignant humour she presents him as a fool for seeking to deny his 'true' nature; we know he will have a come-uppance. We see, building, his embarrassment at his mother's butchered English, and her 'jargony' Yiddish, and his contempt for Welsh-inflected-English, and for Welsh. By contrast, English, in the person of Lady Hafod, and in her granddaughter Edith, both of whom he encounters for the first time as a child, is something pure. It is the seduction of English, and of Englishness, of course, that defiles him; it creates in him a doubleness that he cannot resolve, and that predicament is the lesson of the novel, if it has one: the attempt at assimilation, the 'betrayal' of your roots, is not only doomed to failure, but dooms you to a miserable alienation from yourself.

The novel is, thus, centrally concerned with the boundaries and limitations of assimilation – both the kind of assimilation that is desirable for Jews, and the kind of assimilation that is possible. In parallel, and as illustration, it is also concerned with the limitations and consequences of attempted Welsh assimilation, which, Tobias suggests, will also inevitably fail.

Tobias's ideas of Jewishness were blood-based, racial, and essentialist – a Jew couldn't *not* be a Jew. As a consequence, Simon's marriage to the wild Patagonian-Welsh girl, Jani, cannot be sustained: even the product of that union ends in miscarriage, Tobias here making absolute in biological terms the Jewish edict against 'marrying out'. This might now carry all the resonances of a racist disquiet over miscegenation on the part of the author, but Tobias's essentialist formulations of Jewishness were typical of the period (a formulation that derived from within as much as from outside Judaism), and that miscarriage perhaps constitutes more an extreme presentation of the Jewish religious law against exogamy than fear of miscegenation.

By contrast, Tobias does not render Welshness in racial terms so much as in moral ones: she depicts as traitors those who seek to be English by abandoning the Welsh language, repudiating the heritage and culture of Wales, and anglicising their accents in an attempt to 'get on' and disguise their origins. They are in her terms traitors to their people, to the past and to themselves, and it is among this treacherous class of anglicising or anglicised Welsh that she locates hostility to Jews, a corruption of what here and elsewhere she presents as the fundamentally warm and welcoming embrace by Wales of its Jewish population.

Simon cannot be whole until he accepts his Jewishness, and he does eventually find a middle ground in which he sees the value of his parents' quiet, faithful traditions, can take pride in his people and the Jewish past, and can repudiate the shame of otherness that he has internalised from a hostile and suspicious dominant culture. He has encountered that hostility both as a Jew and as a Welshman: his is a doubled internalised self-hatred, and though he does not in the end embrace his own Welshness, he does come to have a more sympathetic understanding and appreciation of its value.

In returning to his Jewishness, Simon understands that true 'Englishness' can never be his: it is something to be born into, not gained by accent or attitude or attribute – it is an inaccessible privilege to which he is not entitled. Consequently – though his use of the terms 'English' and 'British' are slippery – he does, finally, find more inclusive, broad possibilities in a formulation of British-Jewishness, and of a British nationalism. It is therefore as a British Jew in military service in Palestine in the First World War that he is reprieved, redeemed in the end by his love for Edith, that 'English' girl of his childhood, who brings him back to his Jewish identity, and to 'Zion'. Edith, of course, is no English girl at all: it turns out that she, too, is a Jew – for she is a female version of George Eliot's towering fictional figure, Daniel Deronda.

Eliot's novel *Daniel Deronda*, with its Zionist theme, was, to Tobias, a powerful validation and affirmation of Jewish national aspirations. Like her younger sister Kate, she had read Eliot in her early teens – illicitly, in the outhouse, it was said, to escape their mother's fearful edict against unkosher literature – and she would return to the author at regular intervals through her long life. But her deepest engagement came during the course of writing *My Mother's House*, for it was interrupted by a commission to dramatise *Daniel Deronda* for the London stage – and it was that dramatisation that gave her the shape for her own novel.

Tobias's adaptation of *Daniel Deronda*, the first such dramatisation, was staged at the experimental Q Theatre (in Kew) in 1927, and at the Palace Theatre in 1929 (there were also plans for a West End run that did not materialise, because Tobias wanted to focus on finishing *My Mother's House*). To anyone who knows *Daniel Deronda*, the inversion in *My Mother's House* will be immediately apparent. Edith, the sophisticated heroine, is Deronda: like him, she discovers belatedly that she is Jewish, while Simon, at odds with himself, marrying the wrong person, is Eliot's Gwendolen, looking to Edith/Deronda to rehabilitate or rescue him from an internal wrongness and self-betrayal (however Simon's marriage to the

Patagonian-Welsh girl, Jani, has none of the extraordinary vicious abuse in Gwendolen's marriage to Grandcourt in Eliot's novel).

Tobias's dramatisation of *Daniel Deronda* followed not long after the staging at the Q Theatre of Caradoc Evans's controversial and provocative play *Taffy*, but even if her own portrayal of Welsh people had something of Evans's Welsh primitives, undoubtedly she would have found his literary 'treachery' towards his own people abhorrent. By contrast, Tobias sought to repudiate popular hostilities and prejudices about Jews – and, at the same time, to make a case for self-worth among Jews, too. As Leon Simon wrote in the foreword to her first book, a collection of stories called *The Nationalists and Other Goluth Studies*, Tobias's message to the assimilated Jew was to 'abandon the somewhat servile tendency … to keep his Jewishness as much in the background as possible; it bids them behave on the assumption that the Jew has the same right as another to love his own people, to take pride in its history and its literature, to feel a vital interest in its future, to go about among his fellow-men as one who, in so far as he is different from them, is entitled to be different without being therefore thought inferior.' The stories, he went on, were 'neither argument nor pleading, but just a presentation of the way in which the Zionist spirit gets hold of Jews of various kinds, lifts them in some degree out of themselves, gives them a new sense of pride and dignity and responsibility, and makes them feel that to be a Jew is worth the cost.'[1]

My Mother's House develops the themes sketched in that earlier book (in which the nationalists in question were both Welsh and Jewish), and takes in the full range of British and British-Jewish attitudes to Zionism and to Palestine (including Welsh sympathy for Jewish national aspirations). Nevertheless, the novel is not a treatise on Zionism or

---

[1] *The Nationalists and Other Goluth Studies* (London: C. W. Daniel, 1921), pp. 9–10.

nationalism so much as an exploration of the uneasy predicament of Jews and Welsh people as national minorities.

Coming to political consciousness at the very end of the nineteenth century, Tobias was shaped by the atmosphere of cultural pride fostered by the Cymru Fydd movement. She grew up in a period of intense cultural and political hope and commitment – to Home Rule, to Welsh national aspirations, to support for a threatened culture and an increasingly embattled language. At the same time, in Ystalyfera, and then in Swansea and subsequently Cardiff, she was actively involved in the rising Independent Labour Party, and immersed in the early organisation of the Zionist movement. Her Zionism was progressive and principled and, until much later in her life, definitively anti-militarist: 'The authentic voice of Israel pleads for "Peace – Peace – Peace,"' she wrote in an article in 1920 in the *Zionist Review*. 'It is not for us to hush a single note of that compelling cry. For, unless we fulfil its message on the soil of Palestine, we shall be false alike to the most vital teaching of our past, and to the greatest present need of racked mankind.'[2]

Nevertheless, though progressive in principle, at the time of writing the novel her Zionism was not informed by the reality of conditions in Palestine, nor was Tobias well informed about the impact of Jewish immigration. By the late 1920s, she had only briefly visited the Middle East, and until she moved to Palestine in 1935 she relied on information that was, of course, largely sympathetic to Jewish aspirations. In her view, typical of many Zionists at that time and since, Jewish interests and historic claims took precedence over concerns for the existing population – indeed it was believed that Jewish immigration and economic development and 'redemption' of the land could only bring much-needed benefits to Palestine's Arabs. In places, the attitudes to Arabs in

[2] 'Zionism and Militarism: some other considerations', *Zionist Review* 4.5 (September 1920), p. 90.

the novel therefore make uncomfortable reading in the present. Largely expressed through the heroine Edith, who travels to Palestine before the First World War, they smack of the simplistic, 'primitive native' formulations typical of British imperial attitudes of the period.

Tobias envisaged the Jewish homeland in Palestine – promised by Lloyd George in the now infamous Balfour Declaration of 1917 – as a form of British colony. Later, her view of the British Mandate would change radically, and she explored its complexities in her 1939 novel, *The Samaritan: An Anglo-Palestinian novel* (the sequel to *My Mother's House*). But in the late 1920s, when she was shaping *My Mother's House*, she saw Jewish settlers and 'colonists' in Palestine in reduced and simplistic terms as beneficent redeemers in the British colonial mould.

While in *The Samaritan* she sought to unpick the British-Jewish-Palestinian triangle of identity that she herself later lived, in *My Mother's House* she was concerned with Welsh and Jewish tensions within a British context. In its original form, this would have been more evident, but parts of the novel were cut, allegedly for reasons of length, but very likely for reasons of subject matter at the behest of her English publisher – for they were overtly Welsh, and overtly nationalist. One excluded excerpt was published in Welsh translation in the magazine *Y Ford Gron*, and another in English in a short-lived Cardiff magazine called *Kith and Kin*. Both excerpts concern Lloyd Patagonia, the father of Simon's first wife, and the forms of nationalism he espoused, in particular the cultural nationalism behind the establishment of the Welsh colony in Patagonia in 1865: 'In Wales our nationality was being crushed out of us,' he explains to Simon. 'We were not free to worship as we wanted, we were not allowed to own the soil that belonged to us, we were not able to elect men of sympathy to represent us, and we were even punished for talking in the language of our fathers … Inspired we were with the vision of an independent community, the creation of a new Wales. Our government would be carried on in Welsh, all the offices of state, as well as the religious services, the schools, the courts, and trade... At last our own language, our own dear language.'[3]

Had that material been included, the intertwining and comparison of Welsh and Jewish national aspirations that are a central concern of the novel would have been clearer. Those parallel and intertwining threads wove through all Tobias's work, as they wove together through her life.

A note on the text

Lily Tobias was a Welsh speaker, but her education was through the medium of English. As Welsh reviewers in 1931 observed, there are mistakes in some of the Welsh words and phrases in the text of *My Mother's House*. It is impossible to know whether they were hers, or her publisher's editorial intervention, and so in this edition these – and the Yiddish words and phrases – have been retained unchanged and unnoted.

Jasmine Donahaye is a Senior Lecturer at Swansea University. Her books include a biography of Lily Tobias, *The Greatest Need: the Creative Life and Troubled Times of Lily Tobias* (Honno, 2015); a memoir, *Losing Israel* (Seren, 2015); a monograph on Welsh and Jewish cultural and political interactions, *Whose People? Wales, Israel, Palestine* (University of Wales Press, 2012), and two poetry collections: *Self-Portrait as Ruth* (Salt 2009) and *Misappropriations* (Parthian, 2006).

[3] 'Kin, if not Kith', Kith and Kin 1.1 (March 1933), pp. 21–23.

MY MOTHER'S HOUSE

I

ON THE day when he came home from school, and found a carriage and pair standing outside his father's shop, Simon Black made a discovery that disturbed profoundly his relationship with his mother. That she remained unconscious of it did not relieve the torment of his awakened mind. At the age of eleven, mental suffering, intense if short-lived, is impervious equally to ignorance or knowledge on the part of its object.

At first it was merely a pleasurable excitement to know that a rare commotion in the village street was centred at his own door. Little boys and girls stood, either with noses pressed on the window-pane, or as near as they dared to the shining equipage with its pair of lively greys, and its rotund coachman commanding his dignity and the reins. Grown-ups stared as eagerly from their doorways, or behind the geraniums on their front-room sills. Lady Hafod, the great dame of the countryside, had not been seen in the district since Christmas. Her annual distribution of gifts to the poor from chapel and parish church (proof of her wide-sprung benevolence, of her own tolerant creed, and perhaps of the indiscriminate composition of her huge rental) was followed by frequent shopping visits to the village when in residence at Hafod; increasingly rarer, since Sir Gwilym's death, than her occupation of her Devon home. But never before had her ladyship been known to patronise the picture-framer's shop.

Simon's nostrils carried a delicious perfume into his brain and the pit of his stomach, dissipating the desire for tea and lots of bread-and-butter: his eyes, goggling, drank in a scene of surfeiting charm. Lady Hafod was leaning over the counter towards his father, holding up an object in her white-gloved hands. It was a small picture, the glass of which was cracked across the middle.

Although a grandmother, and twice widowed, Lady Hafod had barely passed her fiftieth year, and even to the adult eye looked not quite forty. Slimly shaped under dove grey silk, her fair hair edging a flowery toque, the blue of her eyes lighting up a skin still smooth and delicate, she was a beautiful woman who had lost nothing but the dewiest freshness of youth. To the little boy sliding in from the narrow door, she was an ageless being from some superlative realm, remote in every aspect from the measures of village life. Of heaven and angels he did not think, for such imagery was not his natural fare: but into his mind's eye flew a figure of poetry already familiar there.

The lovely lady and the cracked glass! – irresistibly the conjunction was linked with the verses instilled that very afternoon by an enthusiastic teacher. Miss Credwen Hopkins had led the class a weary canter in shrill sing-song, to bring out what she conceived to be the musical values of the Tennysonian lines. Her youngest pupil alone seemed to rejoice equally with herself in a clear vision of the glittering knight—

"And as he rode, his armour rung"—

but neither he nor his older fellows heard anything incongruous in her emphatic Welsh enunciation of the magic syllables. Perhaps it was because the r's and the broad a's were particularly strong and vibrant in her favourite verse, that Simon remembered it now so vividly—

> "Out flew the web and floated wide
> The mirror *crracked* from side to side
> The *currse* is come upon me – *crried*
> The Lady of Shalott."

The Lady of Hafod, unconscious of doom or romantic comparison, was saying vivaciously—

"Very well, Mr. Black, – I rely on you to take the utmost care of it. You see—" she hesitated,— "it is the only photograph of my first husband that I possess. My little granddaughter dropped it this morning, and she is so upset by the accident that nothing will console her but seeing the glass whole again. It is so kind of you to promise it for tomorrow – I particularly want it before she leaves. Her nurse takes her to London in the afternoon. Can I send for the picture in the morning?"

Wings had sprouted in Simon's ears, and were bearing him up – up – to the ceiling on a rushing air of delight. The nightingale's song poured suddenly on tuned senses could not have moved them more. It was not the voice alone, melodious though it was in pitch and volume; but the accent – the accent was sheer revelation. For the first time in his life Simon heard English perfectly spoken by an Englishwoman.

"Ah, is this your little boy, Mrs. Black?" Till then Simon had not observed his mother standing back near the counter's edge. She moved forward and nodded her head jerkily.

"Yes, lady – mine son – Simon – he is now just from school—"

"So I see. Tall, like you, is he not? And do you like school, little man?"

The music, shot with discord from another source, ebbed in gentler waves round a submerged head. "Shy? – ah, well—" A gracious glance, a gesture of farewell, and the lady was gone, the equipage rolled away, the staring crowd dispersed.

Simon stood as if stricken, and looked dumbly at his parents, who had bent their heads intently over the picture. It appeared to excite in them an unusual interest, but Simon was not listening to their talk. Strange pangs were searing his late delight. Never before had he felt such joy in the spoken word: but never, too, till now, had he realised how inadequately the English tongue was uttered by those around him. His mother's voice, in particular, responding to that perfect music, had given him a shock. Surely it was harsh? – it was empty? – Certainly it malformed intolerably the simplest structure of sense and sound.

His head hung in bitter shame and confusion. His mother to be so gross a culprit! It seemed incredible. Yet he had always known in a vague way that her use of language was deficient. But, then, the deficiencies of all the village women were at least equally marked. It was from them that Mrs. Black had learned to speak English, and it could not be surprising that she reproduced their native accent in addition to their grammatical errors. But this consideration, even if it occurred to Simon, had no power to modify his grievance. That Welsh women should speak English badly was, to him, a matter of indifference: that his mother should speak it badly, and in the presence of an English lady, was anguish and mortification in the extreme.

Over the tea-table Simon continued to suffer, as he listened, not to the actual conversation, but to the broken accents that recurred in his parents' haphazard use of English. He did not try to decide whether it was fortunate or unfortunate that they used it so little in the family circle; the other horrid tongue, already impatiently endured, only now suggested itself to him as a factor in the mutilation of the true speech.

Somehow his father's shortcomings did not offend him so deeply: partly because his father never had mattered in anything so greatly as his mother, whose passionate love had clamoured round him all his life; and partly, perhaps, because the short, fairish man, sitting awkwardly in the Windsor chair which he had bought at a sale, was a quiet, meditative, abstracted sort of person, who seemed to speak as little as possible, and used a soft, pleasant voice that minimised the most disturbing of jargons. It was lamentable that the contrast with his mother's tones should deepen the painful emphasis of faulty volubility. Simon squirmed as he looked unhappily at his gaunt, restless mother, sallow of skin, black of eye and hair. The critical sense within him, awakened in such disquiet, was baffled at the familiarity of her appearance. Does one ever, at least to the age of twelve, really see one's mother? How is one to tell what she looks like to the world, how detach the indefinable image that is part of one's unseen self? Simon struggled, but could not get a clear visual impression of Devora Black, though he had gazed illuminated on the Lady of Shalott and the breathing Lady of Hafod.

"Well, what is the matter? – but the child eats nothing! Come, my Shimkele, drink your tea, – and you, maiden," (the term was plural, and two little girls looked up from the furthest end of the table)— "give your brother some jam – do not keep it all to yourselves."

The little girls, lanky, dark like their mother, but with rosy spots on their polished cheeks, grimaced and pushed the saucer of jam to their sulky brother. It seemed to them that he gobbled up more than his share, and the younger ventured on a pert rebuke.

"He didn't wunt it before – and now he wunts it all!"

"*'Wunt! Wunts!'*" shouted Simon, his distress released into anger – it was safe and virtuous to be angry with one's sisters. "Why can't you speak properly? There's no such word as 'Wunt'!"

"No such word!" repeated the little girl, astonished.

"Of course not. Spell it!"

"But what are you saying, Simon?" interposed Mrs. Black, for once opposed to her favourite. "Of course 'wunt' is a word – why not?"

Unfortunately Mrs. Black, like Sam Weller, spelt it with a "v". And Simon, paralysed once more, did not proceed with the lesson. He waited gloomily until the table was cleared and the usual space prepared for his books and pens. Absorbed in his homework, Simon almost forgot his trouble before he went to bed. He was as sleepy as usual when he chanted the *Kris'shma*, and did not bother to correct his sisters as they stumblingly repeated the words after their mother. In her utterance of the night prayer with the children grouped at her knees, Devora Black mellowed into a beauty which it is true her son did not perceive, but which insensibly softened the estrangement set up within his soul. A tide of harmony flowed from her reverent lips.

Blessed art Thou, O Lord our God, King of the Universe, Who makest the bands of sleep to fall upon mine eyes, and the slumber upon mine eyelids. May it be Thy will, O Lord my God and God of my fathers, to suffer me to lie down in peace, and to let me rise up again in peace. Hear, O Israel; the Lord our God, the Lord is One…

On that tide of harmony, of benison, conflicting standards met and sailed together peacefully to the shore of childish dreams. The God of Israel could be entrusted with the reins of sleep: and Lancelot ride unchallenged down to Camelot.

In the morning, as he strapped his school bag, Simon watched his father handle the picture Lady Hafod had left. Mr. Black removed the thin board at the back, took out the photograph, and with a pair of pincers, carefully withdrew the broken pieces of glass.

"When is the lady coming to fetch it, father?"

"She will not come – she will send the man. I said twelve o'clock. I make it ready before I go out." Mr. Black sighed as he thought of his weekly journey to collect small debts.

An idea flashed into Simon's head.

"Father, I will come home early – teacher will let me come if I say I have to help you today. I'll write out the bill. And I can take the picture to Hafod."

"But for what should you go, foolish one? The man will fetch it."

"Perhaps he won't come. May I go if he doesn't?"

The idea was carried to splendid fulfilment. Twelve o'clock came, but no man from Hafod: five minutes earlier, Simon, straining his eyes down the road, had announced there was no sign of him, and set off briskly with a parcel under his arm.

He knew the way, at least to the lodge gates, and calculated it would take him a quarter of an hour to reach that point; the walk through the grounds to the mansion might prove almost as long again. Even though he hurried, he would probably be late for afternoon school, as his protesting mother had declared. But Simon, obsessed by his longing to see and hear again the Lady of Hafod was prepared to risk disapproval and even punishment at the hands of authorities, whose favour he had hitherto preferred to win.

The noonday sun was hot on the long white road that slit the valley's side. Shops and houses dwindled. Here and there a cottage or the roof of a hedged-off farm only emphasised the drowsy solitude. Simon had often rambled, with and without companions, to the narrow mountain track, far beyond the bend of the road where the lodge gates stood; but he had never felt so intimidating a sense of solitariness. As he unhooked the iron bar and pushed his way beyond the encroaching heavy growth, he thrilled as if with an adventurous plunge into unknown forest. The voice of a man who appeared at the low lodge windows brought him to a halt.

"Hul-lo, boy! What arr 'u after?"

Simon went up boldly and explained his mission. The man put out a suspicious hand and felt the package.

"Well, indeed – her ladyship did forget, I s'pose. She's got a bad memory, sure. An' her going off to Lundun today, too."

"Has she gone?" cried Simon in dismay.

"Not yet, far as I do see," said the man grinning "And there's nobody can pass through them gates without I do see 'em. After lunch is the orders. 'U'd better 'urry, boy, if 'u wunt to catch her before she starts. 'U've got a good mile in front of 'u."

Simon promptly broke into a run. The gravel flew from beneath his boots. Concern at the possibility of missing Lady Hafod made him lose entirely the aspect of his first half-mile, which to his preoccupied haste seemed an endless avenue of giant trees: but a recurrent gleam caught his eye at last, and slackening speed at an opening, he saw a great sheet of water spreading to the right. In another moment the drive left the density of trees and curved through rolling parkland, where the artificial lake with its swans and moored boats presented the only flat surface in the beautiful grounds. Even the lawns with their shrubs and banks of radiant hydrangeas, undulated steeply towards the house, the grey gables of which appeared on a distant slope.

Simon walked forward more slowly, his heart abashed. Though he was familiar with lovely haunts on hill and vale, he had never seen such magnificence harnessed to the limits of a single home. As he came near, a carriage and horses already known to him, with the fat coachman on the box, ambled round from the side and stopped before the pillared porch. A footman looked out and grinned, then turned to stare severely at the approaching boy. Simon returned the stare with trepidation as he mounted the steps.

"Wrong entrance, boy," snapped the footman, waving him off. "Go round the other way."

"But shall I see Lady Hafod?" said Simon desperately.

"Certainly not. Her ladyship is just leavin' to catch a train. Have you a message?"

"No, but—"

"You can take your parcel to the side door."

"Morris – Morris!" – called a high childish voice.

"Let the boy come in – I believe he's got my picture—"

"Yes, I have—" shouted Simon eagerly. Almost in the vestibule, he peered past the servant into the great dim hall.

"Then come in at once," commanded the voice. "Bring him in, Morris."

The footman grudgingly led the way. A little figure darted down the wide staircase and pointed at Simon's parcel.

"Please open it, Morris, and let me see—" She was quivering with excitement, and could hardly wait until the footman's blunt penknife severed the string. Unfolding the brown paper, Morris held the little picture before the child's delighted eyes.

"Yes, yes – it's grandpapa! Look, Nanny!" She turned to appeal to a woman who had followed her down the stairs, carrying some wraps. " It's been *splendidly* mended – do you see?"

"Yes, Miss Edith. But do come and get your things on now, or her ladyship will be kept waiting."

"Oh no, Nanny – grandmama isn't nearly ready. John hasn't fetched her boxes down yet."

The boxes, however, at that moment appeared on their way to the carriage, and Lady Hafod came into the hall with her maid. She received her grandchild's excited greeting with an indulgent smile.

"Yes, darling – it is *quite* perfect – and Morris shall hang it in your room, so you'll see it directly you come back."

She watched the child kiss the glass over the pictured face, before handing it over to the footman – what a strange passion the little one had for a grandfather she had never seen! It moved Lady Hafod more deeply than she cared to show. She seldom allowed herself to become sentimental nowadays: all that, she had often assured herself since her practical, and by no means unhappy second marriage, belonged to the dead past – not only dead, but definitely discarded. Only this grandchild could evoke a temporary phase of the old obsession, though for her little self there was a permanent tenderness from which, however, Lady Hafod had determined to eradicate every vestige of folly. It was in accordance with this resolve that she was going to London now. An impulse of reacting alarm, following an emotional scene at the fall of the picture, had become a matured plan. She was going up to town to make certain arrangements with her lawyers – and with those dangerous London relatives whom the child was to visit – for the last time. The little one did not – need not know, for a long time to come. She would accomplish her object, and bring her safely home, before the return of her son from abroad and the arrival of guests could distract and delay her intentions. Wise and irrevocable, it seemed to her already, this hastily-formed and far-reaching plan. Yet a curious pang, a sense of pain and guilt, ran through Lady Hafod's frame as she watched the passionate kiss, the clinging of the warm young lips to the cold still glass.

"Now come, my darling – or we shall be late."

"Yes, grandmama." She turned obediently. "Oh – but mayn't I thank the kind boy for bringing the picture? He looks so hot and tired – perhaps he would like to rest and have a drink? Morris shall bring you some lemonade if you wish." She came close beside him and solemnly held out her hand. "Goodbye, and thank you so much."

Lady Hafod, shedding her gracious smile on the group, thought the boy's clumsy response mere village gaucherie. But another reflection made her frown suddenly and dismiss the scene. With a few brief instructions to the servants she hurried her charge to the carriage, and disappeared once more from Simon's rapt eyes.

It was altogether a bewildering experience to the boy. He drank his lemonade with the encouragement of the now friendly footman, then set out schoolwards, giddy with a draught more potent than the contents of the tall cut glass. His entry into

Hafod had thrust him into a circle of fascinations, in which it was difficult to concentrate on any single object.

The hall itself had instantly claimed attention, with its rich equipment of weapons and stuffed "kills", and other strange decorations strangely disposed: but the little girl with her odd resemblance to Lady Hafod had been even more distracting. The lady herself came second to such a miracle of Saxon charm. Great sapphire eyes in a rose and white face, flowering in a bush of honey locks – a sweet imperious voice, a flow of liquid speech – a witching grace of manner that changed with ease from childish animation to almost adult dignity – the moment when she turned to Simon, with that air of self-possession, of grave and friendly courtesy, might have thralled a grown man. It was all too much for one small boy's head. He raced down the winding path in the wildest spirits, until the heat of the sun on the open lawns brought him to a stop. His head was scorched, and he squirmed uncomfortably in his sticky clothes. It was still some distance to the avenue of trees. He looked for a shady clump nearer at hand, that might provide some moments of relief. The glint of the water invited him that way, and skirting a low border of box, he came to a seat beneath an elm. It was delightful to rest there, and watch the rippling water and the graceful passage of the swans – he longed to take his boots off and dabble in. But he must get back to school. Reluctantly he rose, with a sideway glance to the left of the elm. What was that dark object flat on the grass near the further hedge? He moved cautiously up from the path, then gave a slight whistle of surprise. The boy who was dozing there stirred, then lifted his head and gave a sheepish grin.

"Hallo, Si! Arr 'u mitching, too?"

"Mitching?" cried Simon, scandalised. He had never played truant in his life. "I've been up to the house on an errand. I'm off back now to school. Aren't you coming, Ieuan?"

"Not me," said Ieuan, lying down flat again. "You'll be late, whatever. I don't suppose you'll *clek* on me, will you?"

"Don't be a fool," said Simon. "I'm off—" he paused, curiosity uppermost, "but how the deuce did you get here? What did you tell the keeper—?"

"Keeper be blowed," said Ieuan contemptuously. "I knows a better way than that. Ay—" He raised himself on his elbow and pointed vaguely behind— "It's a short cut, too. You 'udent be so late if you went by there – if you're so fullish as to go—"

A little persuasion induced him to describe "the short cut" on condition that it was kept secret. "No cleks" he insisted. "We don' wunt a crowd comin" – and then he made another effort to induce Simon to stay.

"It's champion here, mun," he said. "I don' always come so close to the water, 'less it's quiet – there's better places to hide over by the bushes. I found it when I was pickin' blackberries las' yer. An' down by the trees there's luvly rabbits an' squirrels. Course 'u got to know when the keeper's about."

"But do you mitch often, Ieuan?"

"When it's hot," said Ieuan evasively. "School's a dam' nuisance, whatever."

"Yes," said Simon. "But we've got to go."

"Whaffor?"

" Oh, well – to learn—"

"I don' wunt to."

" – or to pass exams – if you want to be a pupil teacher – or – or—"

"Not me," said Ieuan Richards, spitting, like his collier parent did. "I ann't going to be any of those dam' things. I'll pass the labour exam all right next time, and then I'm going down the pit."

Simon was disconcerted. The short, sturdy boy, with the tousled black hair and coaly eyes, and a rough tongue ready in assurance, represented the antithesis of all his standards. He sensed a challenge in the adjuration flung at his departing back—

"Go and learn 'u an' welcome – but don' 'u talk big to me, Si!"

"I'll talk English properly, anyhow" he retorted. "And so should you."

"Whaffor?" called out Ieuan perversely. "My dad don't care tuppence about English – I can talk proper Welsh. I'm a Welshman".

"Well, I'm not," returned Simon, loftily.

"No-o-" drawled Ieuan "'U arr a Jew"—

Simon jerked round as if stung. His eyes glared out of a face red with mortification. But before he could speak Ieuan continued smoothly,

"But never mind about that, mun. You're as good as me, ann't you?"

It was obvious there was no malice in him unless it was of the kind solely meant to detain a companion. Simon mumbled something and sped away. With some difficulty he found the track indicated by the "mitcher", and after a short struggle, climbed through a gap in a thick hedge, and found himself on the high road, some hundred yards beyond the "gates". With good luck he could reach school not more than a few minutes after time, and possibly ahead of the habitual last stragglers.

II

THE FORMULATION in Simon's mind of a definite grievance against his mother, was only a clarifying development of a general sense of wrong – all the more exasperating because it was nebulous in shape and void of direction. Against whom, indeed, could one direct blame for a fact of race, which cut across all the more adjustable matters of place and circumstance? – against God, perhaps, or one's parents – the first very far from being a concrete target, and the second too immediately concrete to be perceived as anything but props against a censorious world. Yet it was bound to happen, that as he emerged from childhood with its obscuring material needs, Simon would begin to feel resentment against these beanstalk props, to suspect that they swayed on insecure foundations and that an inherent state of blemish was responsible for the blight that had infected him at birth.

For many weeks Simon fought an impulse to put his fingers in his ears when he heard his mother speaking "English". The influence of Hafod was reinforced by the visit of a London inspector to the Blaemawe schools: and though there was a curious twang about his utterance, with a disturbing trick of converting a's into e's and i's, the general effect of uncymricised Saxon was indubitably agreeable. Simon practised his accents in secret, much to his mother's alarm, as she thought he had acquired a habit of talking in his sleep. She noticed nothing strange in his manner to herself, and in any case would have found the cause of his preoccupation

ridiculous. To her the slow plain speech of the villagers was
clear and satisfactory, while the language of the great lady,
whose visit to her shop had not otherwise perturbed her, was
practically unintelligible in its rapidity and use of unfamiliar
words. It had been a relief that her husband was at hand, more
able, apparently, to cope with the needs of the unusual
customer: her own prompt reply to the query about her son,
had been dictated by instinct, aided by glance and gesture,
rather than direct understanding of words.

Least of all could she have connected the incident with any
larger process of revolt in her son's mind. It was true she had
learnt, despite her isolation from groups of her own people
settled elsewhere, that friction arose often between parents
and children born in exile. She had heard that "Englisher
kinder" were lax and heedless of tradition, that they sought
the ungodly ways of *Goyim* rather than the path of ancient
law. This seemed a strange perversity, for obedience to the
Torah, even at its hardest, in her view was pleasant and
satisfying; promoting peace at heart, health of soul and body,
domestic and social concord – all the fruits of the service of
God abloom in the garden of mankind. And, perhaps, the
habits of life in "D'r'heim", the old Ghetto home of
generations, were only a little less sacrosanct, and infinitely
clearer than the harsh confusing customs of the strange new
land. Not so strange and new after eighteen years, of course;
and Devora Black had too much native sense, too much
kindness and gratitude, not to appreciate the freer aspects of
the civilisation around her, and the neighbourly amenities that
had greeted and comforted her entry into it. Still, life in the old
Lithuanian town, in the intervals of moujik raids and other
sporadic forms of Gentile persecution, had been easier and

sweeter than life in Blaemawe, where habituation to an uncouth tongue, and many harder demands of adaptation, could not mitigate the loss of community ties. She knew it was impossible to implant in her children any strong sense of familiarity with such things, however subject to reminiscence in their hearing: but she did not expect in them any serious divergence from the holier matters of tradition, in which she took care to train them to the utmost of her capacity. Other sons might flout their parents: but not hers. Was he not a special product of her love and piety? Seven years she had waited for her beloved – more ardently than Jacob had waited for Rachel. Seven years of hope and prayer, of anguish and sacrifice. In strict devotion she fulfilled the minutiae of ritual incumbent on a Jewish wife, and one who would be a mother in Israel: she had scrupulously observed the laws of separation, she had consecrated the dough, she had blessed the Sabbath lights. But for long to no avail. At the New Year service she wept with Hannah, a woman of a sorrowful spirit, and of abounding faith. She might well have fallen into despair, in times when there was no Shiloh and no Eli, and even the potent Rabbis in "D'r'heim" were beyond all possible reach. But it was in this direction that at last there came a gleam of light. News filtered through of the arrival in London of one of these magical men. A great inspiration moved her to plan, to save the small sum necessary in those days of cheap excursions from provincial towns to the metropolis. Excitement more than food sustained her in the long tramps over the valley roads. For some time past she had begun to share the burden her weaklier husband could not bear alone – the conveyance from door to door in scattered villages of a pack of pictures, cheap prints for sale, texts and photographs framed to the order of far-off owners. The little shop in Blaemawe could not of itself gain sufficient custom to ensure a livelihood: it was chiefly a workshop in which Gedaliah Black carried out commissions, solicited and completed by "travelling". For two years Gedaliah staggered along the highways and byways of the mountainous district, until the pain of swollen feet and more serious symptoms of trouble, forced him to give up all but the nearest journeys. His wife saved part of the "connection" already established, by herself undertaking the regular calls, and so for several more years they worked the round together. It was a hard, exacting life, and took toll even of her superior strength and endurance: but for at least six weeks of a certain spring, Devora Black felt no hurt of mind or body, no pang of humiliation or ache of limb: she was buoyed up divinely with her newly-roused hope. One Saturday midnight she hurried into the station of the valley town, and struggled with a boisterous crowd for a place on the excursion train. Squeezed for over six hours in a stuffy compartment, with a mob of strangers in various stages of hilarity and discomfort, she arrived at Paddington dazed, but still determined. When, after much more buffeting, she stood outside the door of a dingy room in the East End, her face was pale with exhaustion and dread, her hands trembled pitifully, her knees felt weak. But calm fell upon her at sight of the "Rebbe". He whom superior persons scorned as a charlatan, whom numberless poor reverenced as a saint, was a weary old man with sad wise eyes, and a voice infinitely gentle and kind. Humbly she laid her plea before him, and with bent head answered the questions he asked – some of them questions a physician might have put. Much earthly knowledge, much experience of human nature, was woven into the learning of the holy man. The interview ended with a note for her husband, a blessing for herself – the old incomparable blessing:

The Lord bless thee, and keep thee:
The Lord make his face to shine upon thee,
And be gracious unto thee:
The Lord turn his face unto thee,
And give thee peace.

She went out, soothed, quieted, uplifted.

Friendly hands took her away for a brief rest and refreshment: but thankful though she was, she shuddered at the close congested quarters, the density and noise, the clamorous, airless streets. Often and often she had longed to be among her fellows in the great city – but now she felt that to live under such conditions would be the hardest penance. Back to the far Welsh valleys in relief and gratitude!

Ten months later her first-born came, a gift bespoke of God. Toil, struggle, privation – what were these beside the rich joy of motherhood in Israel? A spate of love nourished the years that followed; the years that brought some ease and relaxation – and other children – but could not sap her glory in the precious son. Such genesis might well safeguard him from the traps of exile, the traps that lay in wait for common clay. So, strong in confidence, Simon's mother helped him over the barrier she had been zealous to maintain, and, with her own hands, set him free for ever from her hold.

"That" – the inspector had said to the schoolmaster— "is an intelligent boy – he ought to go far. Speaks better than the average. You sh'd put him in for a scholarship. What's his father—a miner?"

"No," said the schoolmaster— "a Jew."

The inspector's frown did not arise from any sense of irrelevance.

"Well, well," he said pettishly. "Fancy that—didn't know you had 'em here. Amazing how the breed gets about." His fingers drummed on the desk. "Shouldn't encourage 'em too much, anyhow. They'll swamp us."

The schoolmaster agreed, not only in words but in his heart. Still, he was an easy-going man, and kindly disposed towards Simon. The soundest of generalities can be discounted by an individual experience. Besides, he could not afford to dispense with reflected credit. So a few days later he called the boy to his desk, and asked him if he intended entering the County School.

"Ye-es, sir," said Simon, flushing. "That is – I don't think my father can afford the fees just now. But I hope to try for the scholarship next year."

"Next year!" said the schoolmaster sharply. "Why not *this* year?"

Simon was staggered.

"There's not much time left, sir!" he ventured— "And there are the others—"

"*They* don't stand much chance!" said the schoolmaster, raising his hands in despair. "A poor lot this term. If the schools all over the county don't make a better showing, the Intermediate won't get even its percentage. Why, you're sure to get in – that is," he added sternly, " if you work hard."

"Yes, sir," said Simon humbly.

"You've only got a few months, it's true, but I'd like you to try. Let me see" – he stroked his chin in reflection. A lazy man himself, he loved prodding others into energy. "There's Miss Hopkins' brother – he could help you. I'll talk to her about it, and she'll let you know tomorrow." Simon went home in excitement so obvious that his parents asked the cause. His father was totally unsympathetic. He had been unwell that day, and was inclined to be irritable.

"And what's the good of it – ?" he muttered. "Another year away from the business—"

"But, father, I don't want to be in the business."

"No? and what then?"

Simon hung his head.

"Oh – other things – perhaps I can teach – or – or go in for the Civil Service—"

His voice was scarcely audible as he gave utterance, for the first time, to his great secret ambition: his mother did not fully hear or understand, but she interposed,

"Well, and why not? – let him go on learning for another year!"

"Learning?" said his father, in tones of profound contempt. "Ha! English learning! and what good is that? The English are all ignorant – they have no learning, and no scholars!"

Rage burned in Simon's soul, and mounted fierily into his cheeks: but he dared not speak, and provoke his father into prohibition of his plans. Gedaliah Black was often irritable, but seldom roused to anger. When that happened, his decrees were to be feared.

The next day Miss Credwen Hopkins detained Simon after school hours and gave him heartening news. Her brother, who was on the Intermediate teaching staff, had agreed to give the boy free coaching lessons on Saturdays for the next two months.

The Hopkins lived in another village Dawport-wards, and it would mean a walk of several miles to their home. But that was the least disturbing feature of the arrangement to Simon. When he raced home and told his mother of his good fortune, he took care to be out of his father's hearing for quite another reason. His father gave him a Hebrew lesson on Saturdays: it was true it lasted less than an hour, but Simon was expected to do no other work on the Sabbath, nor to leave the range of home for any purpose: Devora Black diplomatically told her husband that it would be well to let the boy go, and receive instruction that would facilitate his entry into the great County School, not only because of any educational advantages that might accrue, but because opportunity would thus be provided for more important tuition. As a County Scholar, his daily journeys within tram distance of Dawport would enable him to attend at the Jewish minister's house, and be duly prepared for his Barmitzvah, his religious majority, which fell due early in the following year. This would relieve the father of a duty which ill-health and business preoccupations might hinder him from adequately fulfilling. They need not even incur expense in the matter. Her old uncle had always wished to take responsibility for Simon's Barmitzvah. If necessary Simon could remain there for part, if not the whole, of each week. Devora was reluctant to visualise any separation from her son; yet it was she who could suggest the sacrifice.

The father eventually gave a grudging consent, conditional upon no Sabbath-breaking practices, such as writing or tearing of paper, being involved in the English lessons. Simon had no qualms in giving assurance on the point. He was unaware of what might be required of him by Mr. Hopkins, and entirely unconcerned.

Once having set his feet in the direction of the "Great Exam", he took care to make no further confidences on the manner of his expedition. Simon did not feel guilty of wrongdoing or concealment: he was absolutely sure he was right. The difficulty was that he could not rely on his parents' ability to understand.

It was all due, he felt bitterly, to their not having been born in England. If only they had settled in an English town, it might have been easier for them to adopt the English tongue and approve English ways. And at this thought, a new idea flashed into his head. Supposing it were not yet too late? When he had completed his education and obtained a professional post, he would transplant them all to London. There his mother would learn to speak English well – almost as well, perhaps, as the Lady of Hafod. And his sisters – perhaps they might grow to look and behave like that wonderful little English girl! – He was sitting at home with his books when this exciting thought came to him. The darklings were playing quietly in the corner of the room, their smooth black heads together. Simon gazed at them, and sighed. It was a sigh caused less by hopelessness on their account, than by the improbability of his lighting again upon that exquisite vision.

III

ON HIS way back from the Hopkins', Simon's brisk walk slackened invariably at the first habitation that marked the approach of Blaemawe. He, no more than any other boy within miles of the spot, could pass the white privet-enclosed villa among its menagerie shapes, without sidling along the hedge to the orchard behind. One could see the fruit-laden trees rising thick towards the river: and often one was not content with seeing merely. It was not always easy to elude the vigilance of old Mrs. Bowen and her daughter, not to mention the dog who helped, with a fortunately deaf man-of-all-work, to protect their treasures. But of late there had been a relaxation of guard, and an air of desertion hung over the whole place. The old woman was dead, the daughter absent, (gossip had long said she was "courtin" a busy draper in Dawport) and the dog usually accompanied the man, who attended to the cows in neighbouring fields. Peeping over the hedge one day, Simon was not surprised to see a skulking form or two among the Blenheims: but before deciding to join them, he glanced more closely at the windows of the villa, and observed an unusual freshness of paint, blind, and curtain. The paved yard, too, looked newly "tidied", the bushes clipped, the paths more trim than they had appeared for some time. As he noted the signs of care, the kitchen door opened, and a woman stood on the step, shaking a duster. She clattered away, leaving the door open. Simon hissed a warning to the marauders who replied by aiming an apple at his head. He ducked in time, and carried it off, split ready for use, in triumph. As he came into the village, he heard the clang of a familiar bell, succeeded by a loud proclamation in equally familiar Welsh.

"Cymrwch sylw, bawb ohonoch chwi!"

The crier, a short stout figure in official cap and coat, had attracted his usual audience on doorstep and roadway. A flock of youngsters circled round him, open-mouthed at the powerful tones: shopkeepers and their customers came out together to listen: houses, big and small, emptied their occupants on to the flags without.

Simon took no interest in the details of an auction of property, announced to be held in the district the following week. He paused, however, to hear the only English phrase that came at the end.

"God saave the Queen!" bellowed the crier. Immediately a shrill cry rose from a woman standing at her door, her skirt folded up over a red petticoat.

"Oe's rwpeth arall, Dai?"

The old man cocked his eye drolly, and gave a brisk nod. With an unintentional shake of his bell, which emitted a faint clang as of protest, he called out conversationally,

"Oe's, Marged – mae Lloyd Patagonia doe'd mewn ddydd Sadwrn—"

"Clywch!" exclaimed the woman. She turned eagerly to her neighbour, who was nursing a baby on the next step. The crier grinned as the two heads bobbed in gossip. He grasped his bell firmly in a gnarled brown hand, and walked away with heavy lumbering gait. As Simon came along the old man drew up to him and said,

"Hey, bachgen, that was a proper bit of news! Nobody did know before *me*! I s'pose you do remember Lloyd Patagonia?"

"No," said Simon uneasily. He did not like walking beside the rough old man, who, for all his official garb, and spruced appearance, was present to his consciousness as a drunken, evil-smelling reprobate. That was, perhaps, rather a strong picture of the Council's odd-job man, who was overfond of his glass and quarrelsome at home, but genial enough in the course of even the most unpleasant of his occupations. Simon had seen him, horridly, unforgettably engaged, knee-deep in the filth of cesspools... The primitive lack of sanitation in the valley had no terrors for old Dai, who conducted his disgusting cleansing operations in the public view, to the accompaniment of songs, curses, ribaldry and hymns. Simon had been sick the whole day, after seeing the old man drink his beer with relish in a ditch of excreta, his hands fouled on the mug as he tilted it to his lips. The recollection was still powerful and nauseating.

" D'iawl, bachgen – don' remember Lloyd Patagonia, what used to travel round the valley? But there! You wasn't born. Your father will be sure to remember him, Lloyd was cracked on the Jews. 'U tell your father, bachgen – old Dai have got the news – Lloyd Patagonia will be moving in to Ty Gwyn next Saturday."

To Simon's relief, old Dai stumped across the road into the "Red Cow". The private event so gratuitously "cried" seemed unimportant to the boy. But he grew astonished at the response made by his parents to a claim of intimacy with *Goyim*. The new tenants of the orchard villa received their warmest welcome from the Blacks. And the bond that existed between the men of the families, if not between the women, was strengthened by a link forged on the playgrounds of Blaemawe.

The feature of his village school life that Simon most disliked was the religious hour. It was not the instruction that he objected to: nor, it must be admitted, the liberty to kick his heels alone in the playground: what discomposed him was the notoriety of withdrawal.

An interview between his father and the schoolmaster on his first introduction into school had ensured the observance of this rite. But he would never have moved to leave on the signal for prayers, if his teacher had not been a conscientious nonconformist, whose principles approved the freedom of another faith. It was hateful to creep out, with scores of gimlet eyes boring through his back, scores of mocking voices inaudibly rending his retreat. "There's Simon the Jew, going out because he don' believe in Jesus Christ,"—"Ay, his father killed Christ, so he can't abear to yer His name"—

Much, much rather would he have stayed behind, to avoid the awful conspicuousness, and to join in chanting the lovely psalms. For once he had remained, his own teacher being absent through illness: the substitute either not knowing of or ignoring the unwritten rule. He had remained, listening with beating heart to the flowing, limpid words—

The Lord is my shepherd
I shall not want,
He maketh me to lie down in green pastures—

Not for a moment did he realise that it was a Hebrew poem: that it was woven of the stuff of his own ancestry; that it belonged to him more deeply than to his Christian school-fellows. It seemed to him all theirs, a strange treasure to be stolen greedily and in fear of detection – a fear soon to be justified, for while his voice blended in unison with the rest, and his posture remained in accord, nothing unusual was apparent. But when, in the singing of "Jesu, lover of my soul", he alone was stricken suddenly dumb, and when all the rest knelt, he alone stood upright, the teacher became aware of a discordant element, emphasised by the peculiar grins and glances of the other children.

Learning, in some confusion, that religious differences demanded segregation, she rectified her error with exaggerated zeal. The next day Simon was peremptorily ordered out. He slunk off to a buzz of comment, louder than thunder peals in his scarlet ears. For some moments he stalked morosely about the empty grounds, then a gurgling laugh attracted his attention. He looked round, but saw nobody. A red glass "marble" suddenly struck his head. He looked up, and saw a bright-pinafored figure on the wall above. Her hands were full of the little coloured stones.

"Catch 'em, Simon," she called, in a soft, plaintive voice, and began to drop the playthings down one by one.

He caught, and then began spinning them up. She cupped her hands to receive them just as deftly. But suddenly she flung the whole lot down, gripped the wall with her arms, and dangled a leg.

"Now come close and catch *me*," she said: "I'm going to drop"—

"Don't, Jani" – he warned— "It's too steep."

"Are you ready?" she said. "I'm coming." And she dropped, plump into his outstretched arms. He staggered, though she was only a little thing, and in a moment she had wriggled to the ground. There she sat and laughed joyously at his rueful face.

"But how are you going to get back?" he grumbled. "You can't possibly climb up—"

"Well, I can walk round, can't I? "she retorted. "The gates are open." She jumped up, and began to pick up the marbles. "But let's have a game first – we might as well, since they've chucked us both out—"

"But why on earth should you be out?" he asked, puzzled.

"Don't know," she said carelessly. "Anyhow, it's fun, isn't it?"

"No, it isn't," he said. She squatted down again with the recovered marbles, and began to arrange them carefully, motioning Simon to a place. He sank down, accepted the offered "alley", and made a poor shot. His mind was preoccupied.

"Look here," he said. "If they sent you out, there must be a reason. Or did you just sneak out?"

" No indeed" she said indignantly, "Whatever do you mean, Simon Black? I tell you they *did* send me out – it was your Miss Griffiths came in to our classroom, and spoke to my teacher about it – and then they told me to go out at prayers. I didn't like it, neither, at first – it's rotten to go out by yourself. But I got up on the wall – it's not so high on our side – and I had the marbles – and then I saw you, and I thought we could have a game. But if you're going to be nasty, you can stick by yourself – so there!" She sprang up, tossing her red curls and began to march rapidly to the exit. Simon caught her hand with the marbles in it, and they scattered once more.

"No, I say – Jani—wait a minute, I'll pick the marbles up. I didn't mean anything – only you know there must be a reason – or else it's a mistake—"

"It isn't," said Jani. She stood still, and stamped her foot. "Miss

Griffiths told my teacher I ought to go out, because my father doesn't go to chapel, and he's a Seventh Day Adventist—"

"What's that?" asked Simon. "Does it mean he isn't a Christian?"

"Don't be fullish – of course he is."

"Well, it looks as if Miss Griffiths thinks he isn't," Simon pointed out gravely. "But, of course," he added, seeing that the little spitfire had turned tearful— "Miss Griffiths doesn't know much."

"No, she's awful iggerant," said Jani, and flopping down on the ground, she began to sob. " She – she made me look a f-fool in front of the c-class – and they always t-teasing me before—"

Simon's perplexity deepened. He was used to feeling something of an outcast himself: but it confounded him that a Welsh girl among her fellows should complain of being baited by them. The ambiguous injustice created a new interest in Jani Lloyd, with her curious quality of provocative appeal. Small as she was, almost fairylike in dimensions, there was something at once vital and melting about her. Perhaps her unusual colouring contributed to the effect of piquancy. Her red hair had reflected lights in deep amber eyes, her fair skin was burnt dark by Patagonia suns. She had a way of speaking in prim precise English, as if learned laboriously from books, and then lapsing into Welsh idiom, mixed with something else that was present in intonation more than in words – a suggestion of Spanish in the gliding o's and l's. Quite apart from accent, her voice, purely Welsh, had a rich haunting timbre that searched the heart.

"Don't worry, Jani," said Simon, soothingly. "There's nothing in it. I can't see why they should tease you."

Jani shook her vivid locks out of humid eyes.

"They call after me, Red Indian" – she mourned— "and they do laugh when I speak Welsh, and mock me—"

"But don't you speak it as well as they?"

"Better!" Jani's tone had gathered scorn. "But it is not ezactly the same. They do mock my father, too."

"Oh, well," said Simon, hunting for a consolatory phrase. "You shouldn't take any notice of them." He thrust his hands in his pockets and added, flushing, "They mock *me*, you know—"

"Yes, yes, I know. They call after you – 'Jew'," Jani said it softly and sweetly, making the dreaded term innocuous. "But my father says the Jews are the best people in the world!"

The tribute did not, in its turn, console Simon: yet he could not but feel more kindly disposed towards the comforter who proffered it. They parted on the most amicable terms. Miss Griffiths was made to realise her mistake with regard to Jani, so the two did not meet again in exile on the playground. But there were more agreeable opportunites of improving the friendship. Jani had occasionally accompanied her father on his calls on Mr. Black; she now began to drop in on her own account. Games with the little girls became more joyous and exciting when Simon left his books to join in. Mrs. Lloyd had to come round often to fetch her daughter home.

"Well, there, now," she would mutter peevishly. "Whenever I do want Jani she's sure to be at the Jew's house."

"She could be at worse places," observed Mr. Lloyd.

" Oh, ay, indeed, that's what you *would* say – But I say –" she paused. Meeting her husband's steady mild eyes, her own wavered. A confusion came into her mind. Always she wished to oppose the rock-like thoughts behind that gentle gaze: always she floundered hopelessly for lack of definite idea. "Oh well, then, why don't she play with bigger gells?"

Jani, to do her justice, would have played with anybody, of any size. But she could not often find a reciprocal disposition. The "Jew's house" attracted her as it did her father, if not for the same reasons: all equally puzzling to her mother, whose settled habit it had become to nag or storm at what was incomprehensible to her in husband and child. But Mrs. Lloyd was too indolent to take severe measures. Jani could flout her with impunity. When the mistress of Ty-Gwyn was engaged in field or dairy, Jani's friends would be swarming the orchard. It was the eager little thing's way of courting favour in shy quarters, though she had to learn that orchard love rarely exceeded its fruity bounds. Simon alone did not disappoint her. He would even stroll boldly into the house, his pocket full of pears and apples, and sit there munching for an hour. Mrs. Lloyd never shrilled at him as she did at the flying figures of the others; she accepted him wholly, if without enthusiasm. Her wrath retired even from his shadow, as Jani found on the day she escaped from indoor tasks to the joys of the Wimberry Mountain. How could Mrs. Lloyd guess the "little slut's" excuse to be a reversal of the truth – that it was she who had persuaded Simon into the unlucky jaunt?

Not that Simon needed much persuasion. He left his books readily enough, even before his mother agreed that she would like some berries— "to make sock", she added to Jani's mystification. Simon seized a jug from the dresser, heedless of Mrs. Black's cry from the scullery,— "Wait – wait – not that one! I'll wash the milk-jug."

"Bother!" said Simon, impatient to be off. "I'll take care of this one, mother—"

He knew she prized the piece of rainbow ware, brought home with other trophies from his father's last "sale". Simon thought its crude glitter ugly, and despised its conservation as ornament. Of course, his mother's regard for it was half fear of pollution,—might not the jug have held impure fats – lard, or soap, or trifa gravy?

Jani laughed with impish glee as he bore it away. The two rushed along the village street, turned up a lane and began more slowly to climb the steep mountain side. Jani argued the merits of a short cut from the rear of the Black's house. "This is the quickest way to the Wimberries," declared Simon. "Oh, ay, if your mother would be stopping you the back way!" Jani laughed heartily. Simon laughed too, but assured her there was a geographical reason.

"It *looks* shorter from the back," he said, "but you'd have to go a longer way round after reaching the Bryncelog Farm. This road goes straight up to the best wimberry patch."

"There's a funny word – wimberry—" said Jani, in her inconsequential manner.

"Perhaps it's really 'wind-berry'," suggested Simon.

"But everybody in Blaemawe says *wimberry*."

"Oh, in Blaemawe!" said Simon contemptuously. As a matter of fact, he had no knowledge of the etymology of the delicious fruit that grew in profusion on these high, sunny slopes: he did not even know that it was equally prolific in England and Scotland, and variously called "whortleberry", "bilberry", or "blaeberry". It was only his deep suspicion of Anglo-Welsh that could not accept the local form. His own emendation seemed to him more likely to be correct.

"At any rate," he argued, "it ought to be windberry. It's the wind sweeping so close over the leaves that makes the berries grow—"

Jani's merry trill affected a mocking note.

"Oh, my, an'nt we clever!" she cried, and secretly believed the fact. He was clever, and knew simply everything – as much as the schoolmaster himself, she thought. As for that Ieuan Richards, who made fun of a "scholarr" wasting time on exams, she was glad she hadn't gone berrying with *him*. He had had the cheek to ask her, just after being caught in the orchard. Why, her mother would have believed she had really let him in, as he had tried to pretend!

This was somewhat unjust to Ieuan, who had been involved with another lad in the apple-stealing escapade. He was not responsible for his companion's scandalous excuse: but on the other hand, he had not disavowed it, and there had been much bickering between mother and daughter on the subject. Jani thought Ieuan a terrible "mocker", though he did not jeer at her in the same way as the other boys. But Ieuan was "ugly" and "iggerant" and "cheeky" – obviously, compared with Simon, of no consequence whatever. She made the comparison because she suddenly caught a glimpse of Ieuan's head above a ridge, visible for a moment as they mounted higher in the bracken. Other heads appeared and disappeared in the spreading folds. But no sign of life greeted them at the top, where they rested for a while on soft warm grass, a velvet carpet mottled with a design of low growing bush. In these luxuriant clumps grew the purplish black berries, round as currants but flat-topped, hazed over with a peachy bloom, clustering on their little stalks under red-green leaves. Jani soon began to pick them rapidly, a proportion of every handful raised to her mouth before her jug received deposit.

Simon stood up to gaze with absorbing eyes at the range of hills around. Often, in the village below, invisible now, he would look up resentfully at the serried crests, hemming him in as between narrow prison walls; but once above, a sense of space and freedom and roaming vision prevailed over confining outlines: wave after wave, they spanned the sky in an almost complete circle. Just there to the right, a dip between the points proclaimed the distant sea. Simon knew it to be there, unseen behind the heights, but wafting certain promise of escape. That narrow ribbon threading the valley, the gleaming stony Dawy, wound ceaselessly towards an open pouring mouth, widening into tidal surge. He, too, was working steadily towards it, sure of its power to bear him onwards to his goal, the great broad highway of life, far beyond these pent, constraining hills.

For the moment, however, their summits were pleasant enough. He stretched his arms and inhaled the sweet, strong breeze; a clean fresh wind untainted by the coal-trucks and slag-heaps piled below; the caressing wind that brought to birth these luscious little fruits, his "wind berries". He stooped and began to pluck them busily; and like Jani, was soon eating as many as he dropped into his jug. They wandered, and other figures wandered around them, some women with baskets, but mostly boys and girls with jugs and cans. All appeared only for a few moments, then vanished to subside in prone activity on the concealing slopes. The long summer evening began to draw in its beams, and Jani announced it time to retreat.

"But I haven't filled my jug," – objected Simon.

"Well, you greedy thing – don't eat so many." Jani virtuously sucked her lips. "And it's only a pint jug! Your mother won't be able to make much sock – whatever that is—"

"It's a sort of wine," said Simon dreamily.

"Wine! – but you don't bathe your feet in it, do you?"

"Why, you silly!"

"I'm not silly—" Jani's protest was mild, for she took no exception to Simon's indulgent raillery, and was too puzzled to explain the association of ideas. "Let's hurry – it will be dark soon. Everybody's gone but us. I'll help you for a minute."

She attacked a fresh clump with energy, and very soon the berries reached the curved edges of the rainbow jug. Simon held it carefully in both hands as they began the slippery descent. Both were nimble and sure-footed, and reached the lower ridge where the track commenced just as the light faded into shadow. At the same moment a party of boys came suddenly round a bend, from the fork leading past Bryncelog Farm, and almost stumbled into them.

"Hi! Look where you're going," cried Simon, guarding his precious jug. A burst of rough laughter answered him. The foremost boy, a big fellow of fifteen, who carried nothing but a thick branch, continued to push against them, with what now seemed deliberate intent.

"Ay, it's them" – he said, peering into their faces, and waving an arm to his friends. "Now then, Jew – come on quick, 'and over the wimberries—"

"I won't," said Simon, putting the jug behind him, and backing slightly up the slope.

"D'jawl, won't you, indeed?" said the other, pressing up. "Iesu Grist, who d'you think cares for a dirty Jew—"

Jani set her jug down smartly behind a boulder and flew between them.

"Clear off, you bully," she shrieked. But the fellow poked her aside with his branch.

"Clear off yourself, Red Indian, 'less 'u wants to get hurt. Now, d'u yer, 'u Jew bugger – 'and over—"

The gang closed round grinning and chuckling. Simon stared

at them in desperation. They were not Blaemawe boys, but strangers from another village, all evidently at the heel of the big ruffian who was out as much to bait as to thieve, judging by the language that continued to pour from his lips. Simon's defiance was useless. The bully flung himself at him and seized the jug. Simon's efforts to retain it and to pummel at the other were equally vain. Jani was screaming wildly, her fiery hair flying in the wind— "You devils, worse than Spaniards—" But it was not her curses in a strange tongue that made the gang suddenly turn tail and rush down the path – though probably the noise she made had attracted the new party now speeding towards them. She recognised Ieuan Richards among the rescuers, but in a flash all had disappeared from sight, and she turned sobbingly to her companion. The jug lay in splinters at his feet, the berries scattered in the gathering dark. Simon sank down and himself began to sob, overcome by shame and anger.

"Oh, don't – don't, bachgen," said Jani, stricken. She flopped beside him, and put her arms comfortingly round his neck "Never you mind Simon – never you mind those nasty blaggards. They didn't get the wimberries, whatever!"

"The – the jug!" gasped Simon, trying to check his tears. Jani sighed, then sprang to the boulder where her own jug stood intact.

"You shall have all my wimberries—" she said soothingly. "Mam don't want these – we've got too much fruit a'ready, she says. And your mother can have it for her sock." A confused image of hose floating in wine persisted in her mind. "And you can buy her a jug ezackly the same in Dawport market. I seen a lot there. I go with my mother on Saturdays – and I seen them jus' like that one – indeed, indeed—"

Hand in hand they groped their way down to the village,

Simon concerned to set himself right with his mother, Jani resolving to forgive Ieuan Richards his "cheek" for the timely rally in defence. But when they next met, the unfortunate fellow must needs spoil her mood by provocative words.

"Huh!" said he. "You wouldn't come up the mountain with me – not good enough, I s'pose!"— "you'd rather go with that smart scholarr, and get kicked down!"

"I wasn't kicked," said Jani, indignantly.

"No, lucky for you us fellows come along. And I can tell you, we give them Cwm chaps something to go on with—"

"Don't brag, Ieuan Richards—" said Jani with asperity.

"Indeed, then, 'tisn't me do brag or tell lies – criss-cross if we didn't chase 'em right to the farm. 'U should see me catch that big Samson in the jib—"

"Oh, ay, you did wonders!" mocked Jani. "That's all you can do, is fight, fight—"

She flounced off in vexation. Ieuan Richards never called her a Red Indian or any offensive names, but somehow he always managed to rub her the wrong way – and just when her intentions towards him had been so gracious, too!

Ieuan put his hands in his pockets and kicked moodily at a stone. What was the use of his defending her, and in fact always sticking up for the Patagonians against the other chaps, when all he got for it was to be sneered at and flouted? It was a hard world: and them gells was full of tricks, as his mother always said.

Jani Lloyd, fresh from the pampas stretch of Patagonia, with its miles of lonely trek from one homestead to another, thought the closely-populated Dawy Vale a more delightful place, and Blaemawe itself a hive of human pleasure. She did not pine for the wild freedom of her childhood, with its half-savage ease and uncurbed energy; its nude riverbathing and riotous horsemanship; its contacts with Indians and Spaniards, gauchos and picturesque barbarians of various types. Instead she rejoiced in the mild and restrictive amenities of her native civilisation. Native, at least, so far as tradition taught her, and the practical example of her parents had upheld. In essentials, family life on the Chubut differed little from family life on the Dawy. But the communal institutions of "Hen Wlad Fy Nhadau" were thickly grown with the tamed fruits of age, novel and delicious to the starveling desert child. The village street alone was full of fascination: so many shops – so many houses – so many people standing at their doors! Avid of sight and sound, Jani pranced about ready to respond to smile or greeting. She would have been very happy if it were not for the family unpopularity. Like her mother, she ascribed what she perceived of mocking hostility to the "oddness" of her father: they had always accepted it as something to be put up with. "But there!" Jani remembered her mother saying from earliest childhood, in a tone of resigned exasperation— "Your father is so odd, of course" – As a colloquialism on Welsh lips the word had a signification beyond that of the English "unusual" or "not even" (as a school-fellow of Jani's ingenuously explained it); it meant also perverse, unreasonable, and ridiculous. In Mrs. Lloyd's sense, it covered all the inexplicable notions and foolish practices of her husband. She had not known him in the days when his zeal for Wales first sent him into exile. The young Meurig Lloyd, dreamer and patriot, throwing up a commercial post to sail in a second *Mayflower*, on a second pilgrimage to plant the flag of freedom on unknown wastes across the seas, would have made no appeal to her. Land taxes, persecution of the Welsh tongue and religion, – why should these things matter enough to drive Welshmen from their native hearths? The question hardly arose twelve years later, when a well-dressed traveller appeared in Blaemawe, needing a wife to take back to a thriving farm abroad. The orphan drudge of Ty-Gwyn seized her chance and ran away with him. Mrs. Taliesin, the sister who was anxious to keep him home, and had sent him to visit her husband's relatives, hoping to engage the charms – and prospects – of the Widow Bowen's heiress, was left lamenting her thwarted plans. The widow herself, who would never have let her daughter marry, was furious with "the lazy bitch", whom the late Ifor Bowen (not too accurately, she suspected), had called niece and insisted on adopting. The daughter, who had already yielded to an amorous but thrifty draper, was loudest in abuse. These enmities abated. It was actually Meurig's sister who arranged the purchase of Ty-Gwyn, with its desirable orchards and dairy, when the death of Mrs. Bowen left the daughter free to claim her draper, and "sell the old pla-ace".

Marged Ann Lloyd did not regret her flight, but she had soon tired of the Patagonian settlement, and waged a ceaseless campaign against it. Bad seasons and domestic mishaps over a long period prevented any hope of change, even if Meurig Lloyd's "odd" interest in building up a new Welsh world had not remained strong. But gradually his resistance wore down. It crumbled with his dream of an independent stronghold of the Cymric race. He had hoped for sons to plant in the virgin soil. But even if Mrs. Lloyd's epileptic endeavours to produce them had not failed, he would have had to acknowledge defeat. For the generation on whom depended the new edifice of pure Welsh nationalism, was being drawn away to prop up other states. Spanish in the schools – Spanish in the service of Civil and military masters – Italian, and even English again, in the lure of commerce! Once more the fields would be abandoned with the conventicles for dominating foreign spheres.

When Jani came, her father had decided. Better return to fight the laxer tyrannies of home, strengthen the old stock at its root.

Mrs. Lloyd became mistress of Ty-Gwyn with a sense of triumph and satisfaction, greater than any she had experienced since she had cheated it of her toil. Only her husband's "oddness" continued to provoke her. The minister, the bard, the politician, shook dubious heads over him. The ordinary villagers found in his perverted nationalism, his equally perverted Sabbatarianism, his amorphous humanism (which took in the beast as well as strange man) and above all, in his pedantic North Welsh phraseology, nothing but food for derision.

But it was Jani who smarted most under reflected ridicule. Hers was a hardy temperament. She cared little for sneers or laughter directed at a parent already accepted as a target for contempt. When her eager rush of friendliness towards the teeming juvenility of Blaemawe was met by taunts at her red hair and tanned skin, her queer speech and mannerisms, she was less hurt than angered; her very fury of protest stirred her tormentors to fresh jibes. But she was an affectionate creature. Bursts of temper over, she fretted at the isolation in which she was left. In responding to Simon Black's sympathy, it was his friendliness rather than any conception of joint outlawry that was clear to her mind. Patagonianism was a misfortune: Judaism could not compare with it as a cause of offence. Simon was kind, handsome, clever, and the others were jealous of him. They slighted him for his superiority, dazzling as well as comforting to her soul.

IV

SIMON passed his great Exam, and became a scholar of the County Intermediate, with all sails set for an Exhibition to the University and a post in the Civil Service: he managed to spend a considerable amount of time in Dawport, the tram journey of half an hour from the school environs to the town seeming a slight thing, though an effectual barrier to his returning too often to Blaemawe: and evenings and weekends at Great Uncle Elman's meant an occasional visit to the theatre, burrowings in the town library, walks on the sands and trips round the coast, as an off-set to Hebrew studies and synagogal attendance.

Simon's thirteenth birthday dawned in the midst of these events, all of which appeared to him of greater moment than his Barmitzvah, which was celebrated under the Elman's wing. The occasion itself certainly made the hero of it feel important, but that was because of the unusual commotion and shower of presents. The younger Elmans, having only daughters of their own, had good-naturedly acceded to the old man's wish to do the social honours in fitting style, and had invited Dawport Jewry to partake of wine and cake at their house. The Barmitzvah's parents contributed little to the glory of the party, at least in the eyes of the real hosts, who included the young ladies of the family. Simon was disconcerted to see these superior persons cast glances of disdain at his mother's finery, which he had welcomed as a sign of incipient ladyhood to be more fully developed when he became the man of the house, materially as well as spiritually! The chocolate silk had been well chosen by Mrs. Black – her first new dress for many years; its warm shade joined with the glow in her heart to soften her sallow cheeks, and the full stiff folds gave her thin frame dignity and poise. But the village dressmaker's notion of fashion was ridiculed by the Misses Elman. Simon himself had suffered from their taunts in earlier years – "Oh, dear me, fancy coming to town in hobnailed boots!" – "What a funny suit – like the colliers buy in the shops. Why don't you have a tailor-made – a big boy like you?" He had always been made to feel that his parents' standards even in the things with which he himself was least concerned, were contemptible and crude. Partly he was swayed by these elegant little town misses, who had an air that dazzled the country eye, and partly he resented their uncertain blandishments.

To-day they graced the festivity in his honour with all the shining little arts of social ease, and he knew it was because they approved his rise in the Gentile rather than the Jewish educational scale.

They could not have been more indifferent than he to the Hebrew ceremonial. The "parsha" – the portion of the Law which he intoned at the Synagogue desk – was almost meaningless to him. He might have been chattering gibberish, with the element of tedium more marked than that of fun, but for the exciting sense that he was the centre of observation – and even that was less exciting than embarrassing. The minister's address moved him very little, delivered as it was in an accent jarred with alien notes. Admonition in such strains to "be a good Jew – always take a pride in the old faith – follow in the steps of your worthy father and mother" – echoed without reality.

At least the party was a jolly affair, even though most of the people who came were old fogies, who added stupidly jocular remarks to their congratulations— "Vell, now you are a man, you must behave yourself" – and " Now I s'pose you'll come to school every Shabbos, and run away mit all the mitzvahs?" – humour which was applauded by all, with the exception of his cousins, who tried to turn up obstinately downcast noses at the vulgar guests. What particularly exasperated these fine exemplars of the social code, was the manner in which most of those who came remained on hour after hour comfortably ensconced in the easy chairs and settees of sitting-room and dining-room, or wandered clumsily about the rather narrow passages, making no effort to conform to the obvious etiquette of a "reception". The two or three members of the elite (self-considered – for the rest of the small community would acknowledge no superiority of Jew over Jew, based on mere priority of settlement and financial luck) who took leave after a brief interval, were regarded as snobs rather than as patterns.

"What – once in a jubilee we all come together at a *simcha* – why should we go away so soon? Let us enjoy ourselves at leisure – chat over old times – it matters not if we're a little crowded – some of us can go into the yard or even into the kitchen – why not?"

Such an attitude was too much for Nettie Elman, who saw all her elegant arrangements of furniture and service, with a rigorous division of reception rooms and kitchen, pell-mell'd into confusion and disarray.

"But there, indeed!" she said in a loud whisper to her sister, forgetting to avoid being "Welshy" in her indignation. "What can you expect of *foreigners*? No idea how to behave, only anxious to pry into everything. I *told* Ma not to ask that Besamedrash set. Look at old Mrs. Jacobs – she's roaming about again – l'm certain she's going into the pantry to see if the milk's mixed up with the meat. She's been asking all the afternoon if Lizzie has learnt to keep the dishes separate. And she's dying to see if they're washing up properly!" She made a grimace of vexation, and hurried off to prevent the gratification of the old lady's curiosity – not without a qualm about the habits of "Lizzie" and the strange "washer-up" engaged for the occasion. Neither she or her mother were overscrupulous on such points, but Mrs. Jacobs certainly was, and there was a precarious reputation to be maintained among the "foreigners" – more on account of her grandfather than for any other reason. Privately she had decided not to pander to him or to them when she was married – and her dowry, for which she depended on the old man, safely secured.

The younger sister, more flippant and more openly defiant, laughed maliciously and said to Simon, who was standing near, "Nettie'll have a job to coax the old girl away! It's her own fault, as much as Ma's – she won't really stand up to any of them. Now *I* never talk to these foreigners at all – I have nothing to do with them – they'll never see the inside of *my* house!"

Simon was silent. Noticing in his glum look she tried to placate him by saying brightly,

"Well, it's a mercy Auntie isn't roaming. She is really very good to-day, hasn't stirred from her corner!"

"Mother's all right," he muttered evasively, and moved towards her, partly to escape further double-edged patronage, and partly to rejoice for once whole-heartedly in his mother's public demeanour. In such an atmosphere, somehow, everything that Devora Black did and said seemed right, and his nerves were not constrained to suffer the slightest jar. It was true that the company did not in his view, any more than Nettie's or Sylvie's, offer a criterion of fine behaviour, but he could not join conscientiously in his cousin's strictures on the guests. If they did not amuse him, neither did he find them, to-day, so infuriating. When not in juxtaposition with their Gentile neighbours, they could more easily pass muster; besides, they had all brought him acceptable gifts: several books accompanied the watch and chain, the gold-tipped pen, and similar articles – the least attractive, perhaps, being the set of *Tephilim* (phylacteries) and the striped praying-scarf, which his parents had provided. They were the symbol of a burden he was now expected to assume with pride; the precious yoke of the covenant between God and Israel.

"These words which I command thee this day shall be engraven in thy heart. And thou shalt bind them for a token upon thy hand, and they shall be as frontlets between thine eyes."

Simon was to arrive much later at the idea that tokens upon the hand were impotent to revive the spirit of words no longer engraven upon the heart. At this stage he only associated the binding of straps upon the arm during prayer with an incident that drew a galling trail of ridicule over years of his young life. During a school holiday he had once accompanied his father on an early train journey in the valley. Gedaliah Black had set out not only without his breakfast, but without having said the preliminary prayers, a much more complicated and lengthy affair. He saw no reason why the slow train journey should not be utilised for the purpose. Accordingly he opened his little black bag, drew out the phylacteries, and stood up to wind them round his arm and forehead in the prescribed manner, chanting Hebrew aloud the while – much to the diversion of workmen in the compartment, and the profound discomfort of his son. The echoes of rude Gentile comment rang about the boy's unhappy head for as long as his schoolfellows retained the garbled memory of what their fathers had witnessed. They still had power to sting afresh as he handled the handsome, blue velvet bag, with its gold-embroidered "Magen David", in which his own "reins" (as his mockers had called them) lay coiled. He put them aside, and turned gratefully to the books lying near on the table. By marvellous luck, or the advice of anglicised donors, a welcome choice of literature had been made – a morocco-bound Shakespeare, an illustrated *Treasure Island*, a set of Dickens, and two volumes of Macaulay… "Often I have heard the house shaking with 'Yo-ho-ho and a bottle of rum' … there was the sort of man that made England terrible at sea."

How much more agreeable to the palate were those words than any he had read that day! He stood beside the table, the enjoyment visible in his absorbed face, open to the hungry look of his mother, as she sat enfolded in her stiff new silk. Near her were the two little girls in duplicate frocks of blue, which deepened the olive of their skins and the purplish black of their smooth straight hair. How fair their brother seemed in comparison, how manly and prepossessing in the mother's eyes!

The first shade of anxiety she had felt that day came suddenly across her proud heart. She had caught a murmur in the conversation between Mr. Jacobs and another, sitting not far behind her. Mr. Jacobs, the most pious, the "froomest" member of the congregation, was a poor man, despised by the *élite*, but held in great esteem by the " foreigners".

"Yes, yes, yes, yes" – that was certainly his whisper – it was his habit to utter the word no less than four times— "a real gentleman he may be, as you say – *také* – but a real *Jew*? – Ah! That is another question!"

Of course it was her son who was being discussed – her hands, crossed on her lap, clung tightly together. A gentleman? Yes, that he was already. She knew him, his fastidiousness, his outward decorum and inner reserves, his exacting, bewildering standards, manifest in numberless physical and mental needs. To her and to Mr. Jacobs alike, such needs alone connoted the status of "gentleman", easily attainable by the English-born, implying at best no more than the perfect relationship of man to man: but as to the greater qualification essential to the Jew, the perfect relationship of man to God – *that* could not so lightly be taken for granted. No, not even in the case of a boy like hers.

She felt the atmosphere of the New Year creep over her, and a Hannah-like solemnity envelop her soul. Invisibly she stood before the shrine of Shiloh, and renewed her sacred vow.

"For this child I prayed: and the Lord hath given me my petition which I asked of Him. Therefore I also have lent him to the Lord; as long as he liveth he is lent to the Lord."

If the idea in her heart was not a new one, but had long ago rooted itself within, at least the form and outline of a plan only now flowered into sight. Knowledge – learning – education – these were indispensable, but they must be acquired in the sanctioned Jewish way. In this country there was a specific official medium; she had heard of it lately in connection with another lad, who had been sent to London by his parents from a neighbouring town. Sacrifice, perhaps conflict, would be demanded of her; Gedaliah might not believe in it, he scorned all anglicised forms of Judaism. Besides, he still expected his son to take up commerce – vain demand, as she had long foreseen. As long as *she* lived, there would be no necessity for it, for already she was in command of the business, and did more than Gedaliah himself in the conduct of it. With the purchase of a horse and trap, there would be still greater ease in negotiating orders and delivery of goods. And as for the writing part, the keeping of accounts and correspondence, it was simple enough now that the girls were growing older. Dinah had for some time taken over her brother's share. Mrs. Black's practical mind swept the whole routine of livelihood with the orderly housewife broom. No, the hardest part was not the provision of funds, it was the sacrifice involved in separation. But did she not acknowledge that she owed her son to God – as Hannah did – and was such a consecration *sacrifice*? With shining eyes, she leaned over the table, and touched the absorbed boy on the shoulder.

"Shimkele, come here," she whispered, and reluctantly he closed his book.

"I have made up my mind," she said, "you shall go to Jews' College, and be a Jewish minister."

"But – but – mother—" he stammered, and sat down weakly, utterly shaken by the most startling gift he had received that day.

"Sh – we'll talk about it when we get home. I haven't spoken to your father yet—"

"Well, don't mother – don't – I – I couldn't – I've got lots of other exams and things to work for here—"

"Well, well – not yet – perhaps in another year or so – I do not know exactly the time to start in London—"

"London!" He lapsed into silence. To study in London was

part of his ambition – a glorious vision, full of possibilities intoxicating to the mind – but – Jews' College! – to become a Jewish minister!

That was simply unthinkable.

The question did not come up for serious consideration until Simon had spent some years at the County School; where he was made aware, beyond all previous experience, of the acuteness of "Christian" hostility. The children of Blaemawe had, on the whole, accepted him as one of themselves; the constant sense of familiarity prevailing over the occasional sense of difference. But the County scholars came to judgment from strange and less charitable courts. Mostly the offspring of prosperous shopkeepers, they thought it an offence to their gentility to have a "dirty Jew" among them. The phrase was oftenest on the lips of the captain of the cricket team, the anglicised son of a country vicar, who was doubly scandalised by the Semitic intrusion on his field of "sport". It was at this hero's suggestion that another hardy youth strolled up to Simon one day and asked,

"Is it true, Black, that Jews can't spit?" It is regrettable, perhaps, that Simon for once belied his cleanly habits, and demonstrated more emphatically than might have been necessary, the only possible answer – full into the other's eyes. His prowess in the ring that was formed as a consequence did not increase his popularity, either with his opponent or the onlookers. Even the girls were not conciliated. Possibly he had been indifferent too long to their pouts and flutterings. If they had only known it, his nerves responded thrillingly enough to these new allurements, but some queer stiffness of fibre prevented outward sign. Shyness – pride – perversity –

he hardly knew himself what it was that obtruded itself, rigid and impenetrable, like a wall against encroaching tides, at the softest lap of the advancing feminine. But the wall could be broken down. In his third term an enchanting creature joined the pigtailed ranks – a thing of straw shiningly brushed, with a deeper glint in the lashes that curled over bright blue eyes. Her dress and manners had polish, too; a style and smartness outside the powers of the cruder valley girls. Boys revolved in her shadow, buzzing bees round a honeypot. They vied in attendance at the gate of the girls' building, and bobbed in salute at every meeting place. Lucky the youth allowed to escort her to tram or train, sit beside her in a full compartment, or win more secret favours away from rival eyes. And it was not the scholars alone whose heads were turned. Some of the masters had singled out the beauty for attention, and spiteful whisperings went round in circles always humming with such sounds. Simon heard the least, having learnt in earlier days what listening involved. Ignorance and curiosity had drawn him into the murk of talk: shame and sneering jealousies had propelled him out. It was difficult to keep entirely beyond earshot, and warring instincts swayed him this way and that. But he was loved none the better for abstentions.

Now he was surging in the same direction as his mates, caught by the smile of the dazzling belle. His wall of defence soon crumbled. Where was the weak spot the stranger had touched? – A common impulse, joined to something finer – the memory of a haunting image: blue eyes in a fair face, honey-gold curls and a graceful form. That had been a tiny young creature – this was a tall-grown girl. But the colouring was strikingly the same, the grace, too; only that childish face had been grave and dignified, this maidenly one was roguishly bright. He was bewildered and charmed, dazzled and excited. Was the mutual attraction based on something rooted in the past?

For the favourite began to look round as he passed, to drop her lashes and raise them suddenly, to smile as he bowed, and soon to stop and exchange shy greeting. Then one day he carried her books to the station, and they discussed the field sports, the staff, and the advantage of living in Dawport. She said she was a Devonshire girl, but had come to live with a relative in the valley. Her name – he bent to listen – was Enid.

"Enid?" he burst out quickly. "Oh – I thought it was Edith—"

Her fluttering gaze set in surprise. Then she pouted, and laughed – not too musically. He had a slight pang of disappointment. He had never heard that child laugh. But he had imagined it sweeter. Suddenly he remembered Jani's pretty trill. Jani Lloyd – he hardly ever saw her these days.

On the platform a crowd surrounded the belle, and she was hustled into a carriage full of girls. Simon saw her get out at the next station, and stood up boldly to wave. She waved back. Immediately the boys in his compartment broke out into guffaws.

"So *you're* after her, are you?" they jeered. "Why, she won't look at *you*, Black!"

"Won't she?" he said, glowering stubbornly. "But you see she did – now."

"Oh, that's nothing. Perhaps she thought it was Jack here" – they prodded a sulky fellow in the window seat.

"I wouldn't look at *her* – little cat" – he muttered.

The others guffawed still louder.

"Chucked you, Jack, I bet," cackled one— "and no wonder, with Jones the French parley-vooing her—"

"Oh, *he's* had the kick-out too – didn't you hear – ?"

There was a murmur in an undertone, and a hail of books flew from one corner to another.

"She's a corker, is Enid," shouted a voice above the laughter. The train slowed down at another station, and the crowd got out. Simon went on alone to Blaemawe, his mind distracted. Ought he to have defended her? It would have been none too easy in that flippant hubbub – but why had he not *tried*? When he thought of that little girl with the serious face and birdlike voice, it seemed as if any slur on her would have got him up at once, ready to bang into the whole lot; but somehow the grown-up Enid, with all her fascination (well, but her laugh *was* tinny) didn't invoke such instant championship. He couldn't help feeling that she was a little bit common – even though he wouldn't listen to gossip. But for all that, she was lovely – smart – a queen! and she had singled him out! His face grew hot. He was flattered and stirred. It was difficult to lose himself in study that evening. An arch face gleamed on every page of his books, a flickering glance brushed off the words. Between the lines came that curious smile, the tip of the tongue slightly forcing the lips apart. He went to bed and dreamed he was climbing the Wimberry Mountain with Enid, his books under his arm. When they reached the top, she pushed the pile and laughed shrilly as they scattered and tumbled down the slope. He turned to retrieve them, but she put her foot in front of his, and tripped him up. Suddenly it seemed it was not she, but Jani, who stood towering above, cursing volubly in Spanish, trying to drown a searing insult shouted in a bully's voice. He woke in a fume of anger and discomfort, dissipated by the remembrance that he would see Enid soon, and carry her bag from train to school.

But for a day or two he could not get through the throng of
Enid's admirers, and her arch looks did not help him to realise
that she did not desire his public escort. A note slipped into
his hands checked his further attempts without diverting his
attention. "Shall miss the 4.30," she wrote. "If you walk on to
the tram, we can ride to town station and catch the next train
back." It seemed an unnecessarily elaborate plan. The next
train left Dawport an hour later, and it would take nearly the
whole of the time getting to the town station. But though
Simon would have preferred spending the hour near the river,
he hurried joyfully to the tram, waiting some time at the
terminus before Enid appeared. She had got rid of her
followers on the pretext of something left behind, and her
cheeks flushed with elation as she described the success of
her scheme. On the journey she chattered and giggled, while
Simon's heart beat wildly; he tried to cover his excitement by
grumbling at the noise and discomfort of the tram. It was the
first time he had taken a girl about, and the inadequacy of the
arrangement could not dwarf the magnitude of the event.

Yet the walk through the streets was not only brief, but
wasted, for him, by his companion's attraction to shop
windows. They gazed at beads and purses and trinkets of
various kinds, pointed out as "ducky things – so sweet, don't
you think?" Chocolate-stacked panes drew comment more
direct. "Those," she said, nodding at great gay boxes tied with
ribbon— "those are my favourites." She smiled coaxingly,
and Simon walked into the shop. When he emerged, with a
packet considerably smaller than those indicated, she took it
with a pout.

It was pleasant, however, to hurry arm-in-arm over the old
harbour bridge, and up the flight of stone steps to the station.

The train was filled, and only for the last few minutes were they alone in the compartment together. Enid had finished her chocolates, and with a pensive air, rebutted his suggestion of an evening walk in the valley.

"Oh no," she said, "I'd much rather meet you in town. You come in on Saturdays, I suppose? My aunt has heaps of shopping to do, and I could easily slip away for an hour or two."

" Yes, that's fine – we'll go down the sands—"

Enid thrust out her lower lip – not too prettily.

"I'd rather go to the *Empire*," she said. "There's an awfully good show on, they say. We could go to first first house."

"Of course," stammered Simon, trying to match her airy manner. She smiled and sidled up to him.

"You are a dear. My aunt's awfully strict, you know, and it's so dull in the valley. Worse than Pembroke – and I used to think that was the last hole on earth—"

"I thought you were Devonshire," said Simon.

"Oh, I have relations there – lived with them for years. But my mother was Pembroke. It's not real Welsh, you know – thank goodness! I hate everything Welsh. It's so frightfully common."

"You don't sound in the least Welsh," said Simon.

"No – nor do you – not much, anyway. What a relief! A mean, snivelling lot, aren't they? I'd much sooner live with my Devonshire people, but – well, my aunt here is tremendously rich. She hasn't any children and I think—" she simpered archly— "I think she's rather fond of me—"

" Shouldn't be surprised," said Simon, pleased with his own fatuousness as he earned her responsive laugh; "lots of people are, I'm sure."

"Are what?" she said slyly.

"Fond of you, of course," he said, and audaciously put his arm round her waist. She giggled, then jumped up at the sound of the whistle.

"Be careful – we're nearly in the station—" she put her head out of the window as the train slowed down. They parted on the understanding that the Saturday engagement held.

Simon contrived it with the utmost difficulty. His most serious obstacle was that of funds. Gedaliah Black resented the expenses incurred under the Scholarship system. It was his wife who scraped the means to provide for the books, subscriptions, outfits, represented as indispensable to a County student. There was no margin for a spending allowance. Simon had to be content with the shilling or two that came his way occasionally. It was lucky he had kept the half-crown given by old Uncle Elman on his last visit – it had just sufficed for the fares and the small box of chocolates. But what was to happen on Saturday?

He met Enid at the music-hall with five shillings in his pocket. This magnificent total was the result of a few days' herculean effort at acquisition, on the familiar lines of beg, borrow or steal. The last comprised the discovery of a sixpence under the shop counter, and Simon's decision that to postpone announcing the fact was not actual theft! But he felt, most acutely, the sale of his books to a second-hand dealer, who gave him a shilling for a dozen precious, if battered, volumes. He ought to have made a better bargain, but he had little business instinct, and he was too overcome by a sense of treachery to his books to haggle over the deal. Another sixpence he borrowed from his sister Ruth. Two shillings came from his mother, and was meant to include fares, which he saved by walking beyond the radius of his "season". Unfortunately old Uncle Elman was still in "Shool" when Simon was obliged to leave the house, – and it had not been fitting to anticipate the usual gift by a request, or even a hint, during the Sabbath. He was reduced instead, to asking the younger Elman, Uncle Mark, whom he did not like, and who fished out a shilling with a patronising air that made the "loan" a horrid humiliation. But all his pangs were made worth while when he saw Enid, an exciting vision in a blue coat over a white muslin frock, her flaxen hair brimming under a fine straw hat. All this Saxon beauty and smartness ready for him, after a day of thralldom in synagogue and house! He could hardly respond intelligently to her greeting.

"Auntie thinks I've gone to the dentist," she laughed. "I said he might keep me waiting, so she wasn't to expect me at the station till nine."

"But must you go home with her?" asked Simon.

"Oh – well – I shouldn't be surprised if she catches the nine without me!" giggled Enid. "She won't wait later, I know."

She moved up confidently towards the circle entrance, but Simon led her to less fashionable quarters. Her gay manner chilled into sulky surprise.

"What horrid seats," she grumbled, as they sat down. "I'm sure we won't be able to see."

Nor was she placated by a small carton of chocolate. Disconcerted, Simon exerted himself to soothe her. Of course she was entitled to the best of everything, and it was hard that he could not pour luxurious gifts into her delicate lap. He was relieved that the "show" diverted her – even more than his attentions.

But the performance over, she declared a sudden anxiety to

join her aunt on the "nine". It was not easy to hurry out of the crowded exits, and they failed to board a suitable tram. They arrived at the station to see the train steam out.

Enid stamped her foot with annoyance.

"But it doesn't matter, Enid," urged Simon. "We can both go on the next – I'll see you right home. Only half an-hour – we can take a little walk in town first—"

"Much good *that*'ll be," said Enid crossly. "Auntie's sure to be in a rage. She doesn't like me to travel late on Saturday nights, the crowds are so rough. Besides, I'm rather hungry—"

"Well, let's have a coffee at the Cosy Corner," suggested Simon, naming a resort of students within easy reach, where he might be allowed refreshments "on tick".

Enid tossed her head scornfully.

"*That* place! Can't we go to Melor's?"

"If – if you like," said Simon, nervously fingering the coins in his pocket, and visualising the glittering tea palace at the other end of the town, "but it's a long way – don't you think it's too far – that is, if you really want to catch the next train—"

"Oh, very well," said Enid pettishly. She suffered herself to be taken to the despised café, and managed to consume what seemed to Simon an enormous number of cream pastries.

They got back to the station amid an unruly crowd, and sat in a packed compartment all the way. The village air was deliciously cool and refreshing in the dark lane that wound towards Enid's house. Simon's spirits had risen, and his blood began to stir anew. At last he had the wonderful prize entirely to himself – now surely he could taste those still untried delights of the flirtation chase – secret joys giggled and chuckled over by every other boy and girl. He gave his companion's hand a vigorous squeeze, but the pressure was not returned.

"Let's go down the bank," he whispered, as they came to a break in the thick high hedge. "The moon's shining on the river. Just for a few minutes hefore you go in—"

She drew away.

"No," said she, "I'm going in at once. Good-night."

"Oh, I say, Enid – come along" – he put his arm round her waist, and moved into the turning. It was darker still here, though the moon's edge showed behind a cloud. Her cheek was close to his – he could smell the scented cream she rubbed lavishly into her skin – but the next moment she struck his face a smart blow, and wriggled free.

"Don't you dare touch me," she said, coolly arranging her hat. "You can think yourself mighty lucky I let you take me about – but you'll never get the chance again. A mean stingy beastly Jew! – I might have known!"

Her little shrill mocking laugh rang out – and she was gone. The moon sailed grandly out and lit the empty space. The boy stood still for some moments, listening to footsteps that trod insolently on his nerves, until they ceased with the click of a gate, and then the slam of a door. He set out for the highway and tramped furiously home. It was not only anger at the abuse that worked like gall in his veins for days to follow. Still more bitter was the humiliation at the flagrant fraud – to be lured and stirred, to be drawn on and on – and then to be cheated! – as none of the other fellows, he thought, had ever been!

That, after all, was where the sting lay. It was easy to strip the veil of romance from the girl herself – to see her as she was under her flaunting airs – a tinsel creature, a vulgar, avaricious hussy – a – a – involuntarily the Yiddish term rushed to fill the gap – a common *Shiksa!* Her scorn was a tawdry thing, of no account; but she would not have flung it quite so cheaply at any of the others, as she had at him, a Jew!

The fact rankled, as it did in every case where the ready sneer came. Not all the signs of prejudice were as crude and fleeting, but all seemed based on that cruel distinction that he himself was the last to admit. He had come to regard himself the victim of a twofold difference – that which he felt as a barrier between himself and his parents, and that which others felt as a barrier between himself and them. Only, while he thought the first a real barrier – solid, immovable – the second seemed to him a flimsy illusion, conjured up wholly in the minds of those others.

For could not one see, touch, hear, with the evidence of the common sense, those things that marked his family off from him? Not so much, perhaps, in the case of his sisters; they were still young and plastic, able to keep pace with his growth into the British mould, and range themselves on *his* side of the dividing line. Certainly his aunt and uncle in Dawport could never cross it, though they thought they had already done so: even their conscious effort, so grievously lacking in his parents, could not obliterate the featured stamp of race.

But he knew himself free of all "foreign" flaws – born incontestably a native heir to English life. The years at the County School were mounting stages of development. As his knowledge of English history and literature grew, his sense of unity with their content increased. It was all the stronger and deeper for the instinctive approximation of tastes and standards. Simon was not specially brilliant or imaginative. The chafing of his mind by domestic and outside irritants gave rise to perceptions that were casual rather than comprehensive. And his response to the call of the Anglo-Saxon world was spontaneous. His delight in the heroes of romance in the *Boys' Own Paper* had been quite unreflecting. His devotion to Drake and Nelson and Wellington was as passionate and more understanding, with the greater powers of adolescence. It was the challenge to his natural rights in these dear possessions that forced him into conscious valuation, and made him cling more closely and determinedly to them. He burned in his suffering to illuminate them with a fiercer glow.

V

THE SMART of the Enid episode might have lasted longer but for the concentration on his work needed during the following weeks. The coming examinations would decide his fate. If he secured the University Scholarship this year he might avoid the two horns of his home dilemma. For his parents were ready to impale him on either. His mother had revived the bogy of his entry into the Jewish ministry, while his father, resisting the proposal with unexpected obstinacy, planned an extension of his business which would necessitate, he said, his son's help. A diversion, favourable to Simon but not welcomed by him, was created by the sudden arrival of a young cousin from Russia.

Simon was familiar with his parents' talk of relatives in "D'r'heim", but none of these vague figures of domestic reminiscence had seemed to belong to real life. Even their woes were fantastic. Money to rebuild homes, burnt down by enemies – bribes to placate officials with power to harry the innocent – dowries to save orphan nieces from the disgrace of spinsterhood – such were the ghetto's importunities of the wealthy heirs of Britain. It was lucky that a rouble went as far in Russia as a pound in England. Simon's parents never repudiated the claim. It was a simple duty to take charge of the son of a widowed sister, whose troubles compelled an emigrant solution for the eldest of her family. The unkempt youth, sprouting out of greenish, ill-cut garments, smelling of steerage and cattle-trucks, was bathed, fed, and decently clad.

It was a well-shaped fellow who emerged, with earnest eyes and deft alacrity. He moved early and late about the new work-shed built behind the shop, and in a very short time learnt the complete art of glazing and framing pictures.

Mr. and Mrs. Black frankly enjoyed the acquisition. Young Gershon's language and animation of eye and hand, richly flavoured with the antic relish of "home", moved his aunt and uncle deeply to tears and smiles; as much, perhaps, on account of long-missed sweet familiarities, as of the nature of his vivid tales.

But tales and teller were equally abhorrent to their dismayed children. The girls shared their brother's resentment at the irruption into their lives of a phenomenon discordant and embarrassing. It emphasised the element in their parents which they put up with as something that belonged to the "old-fashioned" – and which, they only now realised in comparison, had become modified by years of environing change. In Gershon it sprang upon them crude and raw. The strained, pitiful look in his eyes, as he listened dumbly to their English talk, touched them only to annoyance and disapproval. How could he take such a fellow about, fumed Simon, without exposing them both to unbearable ridicule? It was bad enough to endure slights on his own account; he was damned if he'd take a foreign-speaking cousin in tow! He agreed to teach him English in the privacy of home, and to take him down to the river in the early mornings (it was almost disconcerting to find that the lad was keen on swimming). But he flatly refused public association, such as was involved in visits to Dawport and other places. Besides, said Simon, when the arguments with his parents one night reached their bitterest notes, he had too much work to do, now that his great exams were in view.

"Exams – *weiter* exams!" said Mrs. Black at last, as if screwed to a final burst of determination before her husband. "This year, thank God, you are finished in the Goyish School, and you can now write your letter to Jews' College."

"But I don't want to go to Jews' College," burst out Simon.

His father looked at him in genuine astonishment.

"*You* don't want!" he said. "What is this for a story?" and he turned to Mrs. Black, whose expression had also changed to a more anxious concern.

"Do I know?" she ejaculated in Yiddish. "It is a new madness. Why, now that your father is willing" (she was eager to assume her husband's unspoken consent) "why should you say you are not? – But, Simon, you *are* willing – you are – of course—" She appealed to his silent back, bent stubbornly over his books on the kitchen table.

"Do you know what you want?" asked his father. "Perhaps, after all, you wish to come into the business?"

"No, father – you know you can manage very well without me – now Gershon is here—"

"So, you see, you have something to thank him for," said Mr. Black drily. "Well – and what then?"

Simon looked up at his father with a hardening mixture of defiance and apprehension. What was it about the frail little man, with his remote, inward glance and reticent air, that invariably discomfited his son?

"I have told you before. I want to go on to the University – I have a good chance of scholarships."

Simon stammered as he tried to define the exact course he had mapped out for himself – it was unlikely that his parents would understand – or sympathise. They did, however, grasp the fact that even if he "passed" he would still need to be supported for a considerable period in a strange town.

"But, of course," argued Simon, "I shall be able afterwards to get a very good post – a high one" – he tried to find words which would impress them— "under the Government – just think of me in a Government office."

"Put it out of your mind," said his father, in his quietest, most devastating tones. He was weary: he had long been ready for bed: but that alone did not account for this curt dismissal of Simon's dreams. Mrs. Black, settling down as usual to her midnight mending, sighed as she searched the faces of both. Impotently she felt the antagonism latent in their eyes.

"Why, father?"

"First of all, I can't afford it. You know very well we are only making a living. If God had granted me health it might have been different; it is true things have improved, and they may get still better. But Gershon, too, has to live – if he works on, he will have to get his share. And your sisters must be provided for. They are not going out to work, like *Shiksas*. Your mother has a plan – well, she has many plans – her plan for you is not what I would choose. But it is better than yours. A Jewish minister is half a Goy. But you would become a whole Goy. And do you expect me to pay for that? At least, if you are in London, we can arrange for you to live with Jews – there are *landsleit* – it would not cost you very much. Besides, your Uncle Elman also approves and has promised to assist. He thinks that some day you will be minister of Dawport Shool. Well – it may be. So, as your mother says, you can write about it at once."

It was the longest speech Simon had heard from his father for many months. Its decisiveness struck him with despair.

"But, father, they may not take me – it may be years, too—"

"Oh, no, I have inquired – it is not so hard to get in – there are not many English boys available. And besides" – he paused, his hand on the knob of the door— "even if you did not become a minister – well, there are other things—"

Simon's wits were momentarily baffled; then leaped to the slight breach.

"Well, then, it would be all wasted!"

"No," said his father deliberately. "It is not a waste to have a Hebrew education. Jews' College, I know, is not a Yeshibah – you will not learn there a quarter of what you would in D'r'heim – still – it is better than nothing – it is more than you will get in your English College. Remember, *that* is finished. In any case I do not wish you to sit for Sabbath-breaking examinations."

He went to bed. Simon pushed his books away and jumped up, looking angrily at his mother. She was placidly darning a grey sock with black wool.

"It is all your fault," he said violently. "Can't you see – can't you believe I don't want to be a minister? Not *any* sort – why, I'm not religious at all—"

"Religious – nu!" said Mrs. Black. "What does that matter? It means something for the *Goyim*. They go to chapel on Sunday—they listen to the preacher – that is religion, they think, and for them it is enough. But a Jew has something more to do – he has to live a Jewish life, to obey God's laws as only a Jew can do. Can I not see how hard it is for a Jew in this country to lead a Jewish life?"

"But mother, this is a *good* country – the best – you have often said so yourself—"

"Yes, my son – it is good. For *Goyim* it is *very* good – and for Jews, too. It makes life easier, there is not so much cruelty and bitter sorrow. It is good for the body. But for the Jewish soul there is much danger. And though, as your father sees, a Jewish minister is not as a Rabbi of old – how can one expect it? – still – he is able, more than any other man, to live a Jewish life – to keep himself pure – to honour the Sabbath – to study the Torah."

Simon muttered inarticulately. It was no use arguing with his mother – once started on this strain, she could go on for hours. And it meant nothing to him – nothing at all. Just as his dreams and ambitions meant nothing to her. The futility of it overcame him. Dumbly he gathered his books together and put them away. His father, divided from him by a blank wall, behind which he lived in a strange, alien past, would never change. His mother could only use her love to thwart and fetter him. There she sat, workworn and badly garbed, content in a dingy room that was filled with ugly things – odd chairs picked up at sales, a horsehair sofa ripped and bulging, tables covered with oilcloth, two cheap, varnished dressers heaped with their separate piles of "meat" and "milk" dishes. On the mantelpiece a litter of Sabbath candlesticks, discoloured metal trays, packets of tea, money-boxes in aid of Jerusalem charities. In the corner some home-made shelves, with dilapidated Hebrew books. On the walls a crowd of coloured prints garnered from "stock" – anachronistic Bible scenes, woolly children frisking with dubious lambs, flabby royalties and statesmen. Simon looked around in wrath and disgust. If he could escape from it all!

His heart swelling, he began to climb to his attic. The "statesmen's" eyes seemed to follow his. Halfway up the narrow flight of stairs, he hesitated and looked back. There they hung on either side the mantel – Gladstone and Disraeli – the latter nearest the stairs. Surely those strong, sardonic features held a kindly gleam – an encouraging spark of kindred life?—"You see, *I* escaped!" – they seemed to proclaim—" Why not you?"

A thrill lifted the nerves of Simon's head. He drew his eyes away and bounded up the stairs, forgetting the need for caution as he rattled the attic door. On a pallet bed in a corner lay his cousin, fast asleep. He flung out his arm at Simon's entry, but did not wake, only beginning a low muttering in Yiddish.

Simon's face clouded over. He hated this reminder of his secret chains. This fellow might serve to ease his immediate lot, but he was only a fresh link to bind his future. Had he not come, his father might have resisted his mother's plan. It might have been easier to break from the business bogy than from this Jewish ministry scheme. It was certain, at any rate, that there was no University for him. How could he escape into the greater English life? Disraeli had all the chances in his favour – *he* had all the handicaps! – A gush of tears blotted out the light of the candle flickering near his bed. The boot he had tugged off slipped between his fingers and clattered on the boards.

Again his room-mate moved in his sleep and gabbled unintelligibly. Suddenly he half raised himself and called out pleadingly in slow, careful English—

" Yes – please – yes – Dinah, Dinah—" then fell back and lay still.

Simon was startled out of his self-commiseration. What was the matter with the fellow? There was something in the use of his sister's name that annoyed him. Dinah herself, he felt would be annoyed. He listened, but there was no further sound or movement. He got into bed, pulling out from under his pillow a bulky little thin-leaved volume. It was a copy of "Pendennis". Thackeray's imaginary figures lived in a world more real, certainly more acceptable to him, than the one in which he actually drew breath. He read eagerly until the candle guttered out, and he fell back on the large down pillow, diverted from his own misfortunes by the woes of the young romantic Arthur.

VI

"I SAY, Black – the mater says you're to come to tea to-morrow. Will you?"

There was no reply, and the stolid, rosy-faced youth, strapping his satchel to a new bicycle, turned round. He was puzzled at Simon's flush and stare, the stammer with which he said at last:

"Of course. Thanks very much."

"You know our house," said Frank Werrington carelessly. "The last on the right up Cefn Lane—"

He pronounced it "Ceffen", which even to Simon had a singular sound.

"Yes," said Simon, though he had never seen the house, or, for the matter of that, the mis-called lane. But he was aware that "the Exciseman's" home would not be difficult to find.

A five-mile tramp did not exhaust the elation with which he presented himself there, to celebrate his first social success – and the only friendship wrested from the snubs at the County School.

Frank was the son of an English Revenue Officer recently appointed to the district. The Werringtons were of yeoman stock. Frank's grandfathers had both been "gentleman farmers" in Berkshire. He and Simon became cordial over cricket, but Frank could appreciate Simon's discreet assistance in "maths" and "that confounded Literature – who on earth reads Addison, anyway!" – as well as his skilful bowling. There seemed no concern in Frank's mind with his new chum's racial origin. All boys in Wales were queerish. If Simon's queerishness had an extra twist – well, Frank ignored it, with his habitual facility for leaving out of account anything perplexing that, not being in his way, need not be dealt with. Mrs. Werrington received the guest with bland kindness. Her husband emerged from his study, and an obvious official dignity, into hearty teatime humour. The meal was laid in the dining-room, on a lacey cloth that barely covered the polished oval table. There was a bewildering quantity of things to eat – cold meats, cakes, preserves, and cream. Frank's sister, Mabel, thin, sharp, with prominent teeth – rather like the salad-spoon – urged her mother to press the helpings round.

Simon spent two absorbing hours in this agreeable household. Family life here seemed based on an ideal harmony, that accommodated the stranger with effortless ease. It was woven into a background of old oak chests and tallboys, with brass, pewter, and china that had served generations. Even away from their Berkshire setting they had a natural, cohesive air. Simon knew of nothing in his own patchwork home that spoke of such linked domestic tradition. He was shown family Bibles that recorded births and deaths, a progress illustrated by photographs comfortably true to type. These nondescript individuals might not be known to fame, but they were bound up enviably with solid English life.

Lucky Frank, born heir to natural-rooted joys! More than ever, as he left, Simon felt himself a placeless, nameless being, floating without anchorage in a ghostly void; most keenly, the difficulty of responding to any gesture from the inhabited world. It seemed impossible to invite Frank to his ill-assorted home; impossible to ensure Frank's acceptability to his parents, or, what was worse, theirs to him. Yet he could not continue the friendship without some return of hospitality.

He plodded on, brooding darkly, until a ray of light came. Perhaps Dinah would help. She, too, had a similar problem to solve. How to entertain her friends without undue encroachment of the parental atmosphere. Not, of course, that there was any lack of hospitable instinct, but – more lamentably – of the equipment to dispense it. If only their mother could equal the gracious complacence of the Berkshire lady! If only their father had the Saxon sangfroid of the Exciseman! But neither would rise above the Yiddish rote, that adult gaucherie of Ghettoland. Even Dinah's friends, village girls, must be guarded from too close an exhibition of it – must not be furnished with a possible extension of the right to ridicule.

Once timid Dinah had evolved a plan. One day in each month their mother spent in Dawport: occasionally it coincided with their father's fortnightly journey to "collect". Such a day would provide the opportunity for a tea party. Dinah could re-arrange the living-room, and entertain *her* friends and Simon's at the same time! Little Ruth must be induced to keep the secret. There was only Gershon – something would have to be done about him. Perhaps he could be persuaded to remain in the shop and have his tea later. Dinah could generally manage him.

Simon brightened a little as the scheme grew in his mind. But his gloom could not be lifted wholly. He might not be able to see much of Frank for long. If he were going to London to continue his English studies only, it would be a different matter. But how could the acquaintance harmonise with the new arrangement? He had not found it possible to tell them of it. There had been no mention of his being a Jew throughout the visit. His belief that they had forgotten – as well, perhaps, as his belief in some other aspects of their behaviour – would have been painfully disturbed, had he heard the conversation that ensued in the drawing-room after his departure.

"Quite a gentlemanly boy," remarked Mrs. Werrington, settling herself in the easiest chair, with her feet up on a stool. She had just poured out a glass of port from a decanter within reach. "Nice manners. One wouldn't think he was a Jew."

"Except when he wouldn't have any meat," said Mabel shrewdly.

"Why, child, that's no reason. It wasn't pork!"

"But, mumsie, Jews don't eat *any* of our meat."

"What rot!" said Frank.

"It isn't rot – it's true!"

"Oh – and how do you know, Miss Clever?"

"Maggie Jane told me – see!" Mabel bared her protruding teeth to the gums. "Her sister's in service with Jews in Dawport – she says they only eat their own sort of meat, and they soak it in water for hours before its cooked."

"Good gracious!" exclaimed Mrs. Werrington, roused out of an impending doze. "For hours? Whatever for?"

"To get the blood out – Jews don't believe in blood, Maggie Jane says."

"How foolish! The blood's the goodness. I don't hold with washing meat at all – it takes the strength out. But fancy *soaking* it! I suppose they like it white and pasty."

"I don't know. But Maggie Jane says they have funny ways—"

"You shouldn't listen to her lies," growled Frank.

"S'not lies," retorted Mabel. "You only say that because

your friend's a Jew. Even if he doesn't look it, he is one. And I know why you're so keen on him. You think he'll do all your work for the exams. – Mr. Lazy *Stupid*—"

"Shut up, you little bitch!" bawled Frank, goaded into Maggie Jane's vernacular. Mabel set up a responsive howl.

"Children, children!" cried Mrs. Werrington. "Behave yourselves this minute, or I'll get dad in. Can't you let me have a minute's peace?"

She reached for the decanter and drank a second glass of port. In another moment she was asleep. The brother and sister glowered at each other, continuing their bickering by means of strange grimaces, directed partly at each other, and partly at their recumbent parent. It was Mabel's monkeylike imitation of her posture, and pretence of echoing the rising snores, that finally dissolved them both in suppressed laughter, and led to an implicit truce before they tiptoed out.

Simon dropped down from the mountain road to the valley and walked slowly along the river bank. He was not anxious to reach home. What use, he felt resentfully, to rush back to his books? Soon he would have to turn his mind to other studies. He might as well find a quiet spot between the slopes, and read the Scott novel in his pocket. The palm of one hand closed easily over Jack's threepenny edition of "Kenilworth". Spider-like lines of tiny print did not worry Simon. He made for the old bridge below the railway crossing. A train was rumbling past, on its leisurely way to Dawport. Its whistle shrilled inordinately as it rolled into the folding hills.

Silence came, broken by human clamour, almost at Simon's ears. Under a group of trees, which blocked the curving path from view, two figures were involved in argument. One stepped backward, her face for a moment flashing sideways to the water. Simon recognised Jani Lloyd's profile, and heard her vibrating voice. He stopped, watching a curious scene. The youth in front of her advanced as she retreated, and put out his hand to catch hers. She flung it from her. The youth laughed, and looked over his shoulder, seeming to wink to a hidden friend. The next moment he held Jani's arms and tried to kiss her lips. She struggled, screaming in spitfire rage, and managed to give the lad a vigorous blow on the chin. He let her go, jumped backward, cursed a little and slunk away, rubbing his face, while Jani stood laughing loudly.

But when Simon reached her she had sunk down on a boulder under the trees, and to his great surprise, was sobbing.

"Hullo, Jani!" he said. "What's the matter?"

She looked up at him with wet cheeks.

"Oh – Simon," she said, "I – did you see those fellows?"

"Yes. I saw what happened. But you had the best of it, Jani – so why should you cry?"

"Oh, not for that," she said, tossing her red curls out of her eyes. "I don't care about him trying to kiss me. But it's the way he and the other chaps – you see, it's to get the better of me – mocking me—" She began to sob again. "They don't ask me to go for a walk – and – and – be like they are with other girls. They only make fun of me – calling names – calling Patagonia merch after me – as if I was – as if – I was – some strange animal—"

"Let them!" said Simon contemptuously. "They are just animals themselves. Don't trouble your head about them, Jani." He knelt down beside her and tried to take her hands from her hidden, rocking face. Her words, and their attitude together, brought to him again the consciousness of fellow-outlawry that had been born in childish days. "Why, Jani, you don't really care about those fellows taking you for walks, do you? – Look here – stop crying – I'll tell you what. Come for a walk with me!"

He grinned as she let her hands drop, and her eyes smiled through the tears.

"All right," she said, and stood up confidently. "Where shall we go?"

"Over the other side," he answered, using the valley colloquialism for the opposite river bank.

They crossed the old bridge and mounted a shingly track, leading to the path that wound the mountainside. It was very pleasant sauntering along. Jani chattered like a happy bird. Her voice trickled in unison with the river caressing its little stones, with the drip of water from the crags, and the rustling leaves of some overhanging bush. Her eyes darted brightness at him like the eyes of stray rabbits, that flashed from hole to hole across their feet.

She had not grown much, but her figure showed its adult signs. The slim waist rose from rounded hips, little firm breasts pointed through her cotton frock. Now and again a more conscious red lit the small face, still bronze from Patagonian suns. Yet on the whole Jani was childishly at ease with her friend Simon. She told him plaintive stories of her discontent at home, her mother's growing irascibility and her father's absent-mindedness. She could no longer please them both, and neither pleased her. She was determined not to "slave" much longer at Ty Gwyn, lashed by her mother's tongue, venting perhaps on her the increasing inattention of old Lloyd. The village looked upon her still as a curiosity at least, and she was tired of its chapel-going gossip. Much more attractive was Aunt Gwyneth's drapery shop in Dawport. Already she had spent a good deal of time there, a welcome assistant in the busy baby-linen department. Aunt Gwyneth was willing to take her altogether, to help in the business and live in her beautiful house overlooking the bay. "Wouldn't it be lov-e-ly?" trilled Jani in exciting tones. The realisation of these raptures depended on her mother's formal consent to be obtained only by a campaign of coaxing and submission.

"It's awful hard," sighed Jani,—"but I'm going to try to be very, very good." Simon laughed loudly, and Jani pouted – very prettily, too, for pouting became her well. Her red arched lips showed little pearls within.

"You needn't laugh, Simon," she said, looking up into his twinkling eyes. "I suppose it's easy for you to be good. And I shouldn't think anybody would be nasty to *you!*"

Simon was in the highest spirits. Jani had managed her own affair very well, but he had an absurd feeling as if he had rescued her from pirates. The little creature at his side made him aware of height and manliness. He looked down at her from a vast protective altitude, increased by her admiring trust. Jani was the only person who gave him unreserved approval. The friendliness of others was warped by a hidden sting; even his adoring mother fretted over his aversions. To Jani alone his likes and dislikes seemed equally well based, and his Jewishness or lack of it in no way amiss. Above all, she gave him an extra fillip, a delicious sense of lordliness at once mental and physical. He could feel his brain soar and his muscles expand.

With the crossing of the lower bridge that led back to the village highway, the end of their delightful walk came into unwelcome view. Simon had a sudden inspiration. Just around the dip in that high hedge, he knew, was the little lane where he had first emerged from Hafod – the secret way revealed to him by the incorrigible "mitcher" Ieuan. He had used it since in solitary prowlings, but not during the last few years. A sudden wish to explore it again, and give Jani a novel treat, rushed over him. Jani was enchanted with the idea.

"Oh, yes – splendid – let's go—" she urged. "I've heard about it before – Ieuan has hinted and hinted, but he never would tell me right out – mean thing!" Ieuan loved teasing her, she declared, though he always said it was she who teased him. She paused to say indignantly – "Why, he says I tell lies – just because—"

"Oh, never mind Ieuan," said Simon, hurrying her into the lane. "Now just watch out where you're going – you'll have to crawl a bit – do you think you can manage it?"

"Yes, indeed," cried Jani, and followed bravely. As a matter of fact, it was easier for wiry little Jani than for Simon himself, who had grown longer and bulkier since those early days, to squirm through a couple of yards of undergrowth at the end of the narrow lane. They emerged breathlessly into a wide ditch, fairly dry at this time of year. Over this they climbed to a bank where the barbed wire had broken down and never been repaired. It was an easy descent on the other side to the shrubbery near the lake. Jani clasped her hands together in delight.

"O-o-oe!" she gurgled— "isn't it lov-e-ly?"

Simon enjoyed her awed amazement and the renewal of his own. The magnificent park rolling its wide green length, the lake shimmering in its shadows, seemed grander than he had thought. Yet even these were only background for a richer memory. The house was near, but not visible from this position: in his mind Simon could plainly see its doors and the flash of that little golden creature in the hall. Was she there still, lighting up the world? Of course she must be grown, though he could not visualise her as different – how stupid of him, he felt now intolerably, to have confounded her even in momentary illusion with the meretricious Enid! A mere trick of colouring – the gleam of paste – Surely the little figure had been real, and not the stuff of dreams? Warm, breathing Jani, moving excitedly beside him, gave him the answer almost at once.

"I wonder if you've seen Miss Edith," she said. "She stays here sometimes in her holidays from college, and sometimes she comes with Lady Hafod to see people in the village. They say she wants Lady Hafod to get a district nurse for Blaemawe. She says every place ought to have one now. They say she wants to be one herself."

"A nurse," said Simon vaguely. "Why?" – then quickly— "But what's she like? I haven't seen her for years—"

But Jani made no effort at description.

"Oh, she's nice," she said inadequately. "And she talks to everybody – to all the odd people. What do you think?" – on a note of astonishment— "she likes my father!"

"Sh!" said Simon suddenly, drawing Jani well behind the box hedge. A trill of voices had broken softly on the still evening air. The sounds deepened and grew clearer. On the slope that hid the house appeared a little crowd of figures, moving in twos and threes towards the lake. A servant was busy at the boathouse, unmooring some small boats: ladies and gentlemen in evening dress (their shapes and colours could now be seen) stepped in and began to row smoothly along. Jani's dancing eyes were round as moons. She squeezed Simon's hand very hard as he kept her back in the shrub.

"It's a party," she whispered repeatedly. "Lady Hafod's got a party—"

"Don't make a noise."

"It's a party – I heard about it. They say Lady Hafod is going away to live in her Devonshire house. And Sir Gwilym is getting married, and there'll be a new Lady Hafod here. Oh, are they coming down this way? – do you think we'll see them close?"

"Yes – but don't let them see you – or we'll be sent off." He grasped her firmly by the waist to control her straining little figure. She yielded, nestling lightly against his chest, her eyes peeping cautiously through the gap they found in the hedge. The boats came swishing softly down, the occupants' voices tinkled and burred; laughter broke between the phrases that were now distinct. "By Jove! There'll be a moon to-night. We can stay out later—" "What fun! We shan't let Harry get back to his billiards—" "You can't stop me – I'll drown you all first." "Oh, you'll do that anyhow – rottenest oar in the Eights for years—" "Got you at Hammersmith, Bill!" The laughter rang. Simon cocked his ears to catch the last echo. Jani's gaze devoured the flowing silks, the gossamer shawls that floated round burnished heads and bare arms. Gems sparkled on the white skins of the ladies, and the whiter fronts of the black-garbed men. Delicious perfumes spread in the receptive air.

"O-oo-oe! Aren't they lov-e-ly! That's Sir Gwilym with the red hair – like mine! That tall lady with him in blue – Miss Edith's as tall as her – I can't see her face, can you? – I wonder if that's the one he's going to marry? There's Lady Hafod in the last boat – she's grand – look at her cape all shining – with beads or something – oh, Simon, don't pinch—"

To Jani the sight on which she feasted was like a fairy tale: pleasurable to hear of, or to read; but the pages closed, the tale told, one returned to everyday life. Simon, however, felt in it the texture of reality, which he himself might touch and share. Here was the bodily flesh of the patterns drawn in print – patterns always living, even in the spells of Bulwer Lytton – disowned sons of peers, misunderstood Byronic heroes, queenly heroines. They mingled with the homelier figures of Thackeray, and still lesser fry of the schoolboy feuilletonists. All had the habits of a common world, brought nearer now to his attuned senses. It gave him warrant for his hope that in this world, he, too, could find acceptance. So why should he not look boldly as they passed – stare with the eyes of an equal, a fellow, ready for his ease among them? At least he could see Lady Hafod, now, in a clearer, more human, light. There she was before him, her fair face lined a little, her fading hair subdued; but still she had power to thrill him, and his appraising gaze must yield a meed of worship to her charm. How would that other little figure stand the test? Strain as he might, he could not recognise her, if indeed she were of the company.

The boats had turned. They curved away to the further reaches of the lake. One by one they vanished behind a belt of trees. Simon was aware of Jani's light, warm body held closely in his arms.

"There – they're gone!" she said with a little sigh. "I suppose they'll go right round and get off by the house again. It'll take about half an hour, I should think. *There's* a pity we can't wait! It's getting dark, but I don't s'pose it'll be really a dark night, the moon's coming up. But oh dear – mam will be in an awful temper if I'm not home soon."

She moved to free herself, but found that Simon's grip had tightened. Her surprise was vented in a giggle.

"Oh, Simon – we *must* go now—"

"Well, Jani," he said, in a slightly husky voice. "I took you for a nice walk – didn't I?"

"O – oh – lov-e-ly! I *have* enjoyed it."

"But it isn't finished yet," he said.

"Yes, it is," she rejoined quickly. "I told you about mam – I can't stop longer. It's a good job we can get back through that lane – I've got to go to Mrs. Hughes, the dressmaker – she lives in those first houses on the road – and I've got to give her a message from mam early to-night. Just suppose she's gone out! Won't I catch it! Now, Simon – let me go."

She did not attempt to struggle, but a curious gleam came into her darting eyes. Whatever Mrs. Lloyd's temper might be like, Simon knew that Jani had a fiery one of her own. Would she vent it on him as she had on others?

He said coaxingly— "You'll let *me* have a kiss, won't you, Jani?"

She did not stir or answer. But as he bent his head she turned hers aside as if involuntarily, and his lips just brushed her cheek. In a moment she had slipped free. No vigorous hand upraised, or scolding storm. Only a flag of scarlet in her face and a giggle in her voice.

"Well – I never – you *are* a silly—"

She ran fleetly up and down the bank and across the ditch, and burrowed into the lane. Here she waited until he had struggled through.

"Good-night, Simon!" she called softly. "I'm going to run like lightning now – and don't you dare come after me."

Simon stood still. There were footsteps passing on the high road a few yards away. He had no wish to risk a public chase.

"Good-night, Jani," he said airily. "I'm glad you liked the walk. We'll have another some time."

Jani surprised him completely. Instead of a disappearance up the lane, she came back, drew his face down with both hands, and offered her lips to his. The next moment she was gone.

Simon remained for a while slightly mazed. How sweet it was, that spontaneous embrace – the first ever given him by a girl! Freely given, too – unasked, unexpected – it filled his veins with delicious fire. The soaring sense of mastery that Jani inspired, she had heightened by the gift of her dewy mouth.

He strutted up the lane with his hands in his pockets and whistled like a village lad all the way home.

VII

DINAH entered with joy into her brother's proposal of a tea-party. It was the first time he had shown appreciation of her talents, and encouraged her to assert her own will. She did not realise that she was partly to blame for the lack of confidence between them. Tall and dark like her mother in appearance, Dinah was more like her father in nature. It was a spirit inherently shy and inarticulate that hid behind those large soft eyes and luminous cheeks, paler now in the stress of growth. Her thoughts drifted wistfully over the strangeness and promise of life, unable to frame their drift in words. It distressed her that Simon should flout their parents' standards, though she herself had no enthusiasm for them. Often she was troubled by a sense of guilt and disloyalty, for which, however, she could not clearly account. She knew, however, that her reluctance to give pain prevented the realisation of many a harmless wish. The tea-party was her boldest enterprise. It strung her up to match her brother's resolution in the choice of guests.

"I shan't ask Frank's sister," Simon said. He was afraid of the shrewd Mabel. He guessed that she "noticed things" far more than old Frank. " How many girls are you having?"

"Only two – Mary Ann Williams and Olwen Price—"

"What about Jani?"

"Jani?" said Dinah in surprise. "Why, she comes in any time."

"Oh, I just thought – perhaps she could help you—"

"I don't need help." Dinah's tone was final. Simon did not argue the case. On the day itself he was too full of his new plans to think of Jani. He had discovered that his English studies must continue, and he prepared to startle his school chum. It was as well he had told Frank nothing beforehand. Now he would say simply that he was going to London to attend University College. Frank might learn all later. In the meantime there need be no humiliating explanations. Half-statement of the truth alone could produce the degree of envious admiration proper to their friendship.

But Simon found it surprisingly difficult to impress Frank that day. The big English lad was not so stolid as to be indifferent to the news. It was merely that he could not harbour two major emotions at the same time. When Simon paused for effect over the tea-cups, Frank said in his calm drawl— "Really? Oh, I say, that's good—" and continued to stare hard at Dinah and fuss over handing her plates. His pink face got noticeably redder when she returned his gaze or spoke directly to him, in that sudden way Dinah shared with many shy girls. The other guests were by no means shy. Awkward, bumpy creatures they might be, but not shy: their loud giggles and voracious manners filled the room with noise and movement. They awed little chatterbox Ruth into dumb stillness. Simon wondered irritably how on earth Dinah could stand them. But she seemed pleased with their approval of her arrangements (she had miraculously transformed the living-room by a mass clearance of objects, and a table attractive with white linen, flowers and dainties). Perhaps she was pleased, also, for all her demureness, with the impression she had made on Frank Werrington. Even Simon noticed that Dinah was looking nice in her pink frock, with her smooth black hair drawn into plaits that freed the shape of her slender head. He could not think, however, that pale olive cheeks, and dark eyes wistful over a sloping nose, might fascinate an English youth like Frank. "I suppose he's never seen a girl like Dinah," was Simon's dubious reflection, as he shared his sister's consciousness of Frank's fixed gaze. She started as if with guilt when Simon whispered suddenly – "You've forgotten Gershon's tea. Didn't you promise to take it to him in the shop?"

"Oh, yes – I'll take it now." Hastily she prepared a tray for the patient cousin relegated to solitary vigil. Simon thought her confusion was all on Gershon's account, especially when Frank offered to carry the tray. He tried in vain to distract the other's purpose. "No, no – you needn't bother, Frank – I'll help Dinah—" It was useless. Frank, quick and deft for once in his life, was outside with the tray before either could prevent him. Dinah was obliged to follow. Simon did not know how she explained the two "fellows" to each other in the workshop. It was not long before she reappeared, still flustered, with Frank in tow. "Damn," muttered Simon, more uneasy about Frank's impressions of Gershon than anything that had happened that afternoon. But he need not have worried. Frank seemed entirely unconcerned, and became so genial and responsive to Simon's suggestions of their meeting – and perhaps working together – in London, that the incident might have promoted rather than disturbed the success of the party. And it was just at this juncture, when everyone's spirits were at their highest, that Mr. and Mrs. Black – by what combination of chance or design their children never learned – arrived home together.

Simon's mental picture was of chaos. There was a shock of

mutual disapproval that for some moments brought positive agony to the brother and sister. A strange relief came. Before the first stuttering sentence of explanation could be completed, a storm from another sphere of pain engulfed the group in the Black's metamorphosed living-room. It was Jani Lloyd, hatless and with hair dishevelled, her eyes like fireballs in a white stricken face, who rushed in and screamed—

"Oh, Simon – oh, Simon – *look what's in the road!* Ieuan Richards – they are bringing him home – he's been killed in the pit – oh – oh—"

Simon's chief sensation was the surprise of finding Jani in his arms. Fortunately nobody noticed that she had flung herself at him, to cling weeping and moaning on his shoulder. They had rushed into the street to see the procession bearing Ieuan home. When they returned – at least, when Mr. and Mrs. Black returned, the girl-guests having fled discreetly, and Frank taken leave of Dinah at the door – Jani was sitting in a chair, still half sobbing, while Simon stood talking soothingly to her. Mrs. Black was able to bring the greatest measure of comfort.

"Do not cry, Jani," she said,—"It is not so bad as you think. The boy is not killed. A big piece of coal fell on his arm. They say it is broken – but, please God, he will get better from it—"

Double relief spread peace in the household. Little was said about the party. The family were far too much preoccupied with the account brought by Mrs. Black of the Elman plans for their son.

A week later Simon sat in a railway carriage at Dawport Station, his eyes straining past the elegant figure of Nettie Elman, who stood on the platform, waving a kid-gloved hand.

"Bye-bye, Simon – best of luck! Bye-bye, pa. Don't forget that shop in Oxford Street."

Her father leaned from the window returning her signals until his fond eyes no longer saw the charming vision. He was struck afresh by the delight and responsibility of a lovely, grown-up daughter.

"Fine girl, Nettie," he could not help saying aloud, as he flopped down into his corner. Simon muttered a vague assent. He was not thinking of his cousin. And he wished Uncle Mark would stop twining his hands and nodding his head in that terribly Jewish way. Why hadn't Jani come? It was too bad of her after all she had said. The previous Saturday they had walked together for ten minutes on the sands – ten minutes snatched from her measured lunch time. For Jani was installed at last in the drapery shop and the house by the sea. Satisfied with her own affairs, she had been flatteringly enthusiastic over his. With her vivid little face tilted up at him, she told him she knew he was going to be lucky and successful, *a clever great man* – and how proud she was to have such a wonderful friend.

"You *will* be my friend always, won't you, Simon?" she trilled softly. "You won't forget me in London, – and you'll be sure to come and see me every time you're home, won't you?"

He had given her the required assurances, and they had parted on the understanding that she would be at the station, if only for a moment – if only to wave her handkerchief, and perhaps, if nobody were looking, blow a kiss to him for luck. The shop was quite near the station, and she could always slip out for a few minutes, she averred. Her co-assistant in the "baby-linen", an elderly Miss Meredith, was devoted to her, and *most* obliging. But she had not come. Her failure was a chagrin, lowering for a while the high emotion of the trip. He had even a faint hope of seeing her at Plasdarl, where in a few minutes they would change from the local train into the Fishguard express. But the only person on the platform, beside the porters was a fat old woman with an array of parcels, which had scattered in their compartment and had to be reassembled, to an accompaniment of shrill complaint.

"Duws caton pawb, there's fun-ny those porters arr – tellin' 'u go yer, go there, but won't stop a minnit to show someone the way. Ar fenid i! How do they expect a 'ooman to know? Go to Lundun I would too, for all they do care. Now dratto, mun, where is that old Dawport train? Down by there, of course, after me goin' back and fo like an ol' fool, whatever."

Mark Elman smiled quizzically, but not at the old woman. Settled comfortably in a fresh corner with his papers, he had thrown an illustrated journal across to Simon, who opened it and stared at the pictures. The boy did not seem to notice that the train – the real London train – had moved away, and was bearing him at last to his goal, or was it Mark Elman's goal? The father's heart was still full of Nettie, the plans teeming in his head included her as well as himself, but Simon, too, had a share in them. During a matter-of-course existence, in which dreams had no obvious place, the younger Elman had set his mind on two or three objects, now within sight of realisation. Primarily, his journey to-day concerned a scheme of business development. For years he had held in firm hands the reins slackening in his father's grip, slowly but surely directing the course from a chain of shops to a factory. The success of the enterprise hung on his interview with an agency in London. "I tell you, father," he had said over and over to the old man in the last weeks, "it's the only way. There's nothing in selling right. We've got to buy right. At last Galliers are ready to listen to us. And once we get the right terms from them, we can go ahead!"

The future looked bright for the Elmans – for Nettie, focus of their pride. A smart, beautiful girl – nobody like her in Dawport – nobody better in London! She was ambitious, but no more than her father for her. He had thought it all out. There was she, a little princess; and there were the Blaibergs – well, they called themselves Blay now, and so much the better. He knew as well as anyone the handicap of a "foreign" name in social and commercial life – the star Jewish family of the district, with branches in Tavcastle and Dawport, shining in the highest circles on account of their prestige and undoubted graces. Young Norman Blay ("Nehemiah" on his initiation into the Abrahamic Covenant) was in the fourth generation of "settlement": nobody now remembered the dim Israel Blaiberg who had "come over" from Poland – and the elimination of the "berg" guaranteed the sterilisation of immigrant blood. Apart from perfunctory attendance at Synagogue on Holy days, the Blays had little connection with Jewish life. But so far they had always married "within the faith". Why should not Nettie become part of the Blay constellation? It was a fortunate chance, the acquaintance of the young people at amateur theatricals; though not so much chance, considering the foresight that had not grudged expensive lessons in music and elocution during Nettie's childhood. She had always been able to "recite" and "play piano" with the best. No wonder the pretty and accomplished Miss Elman was popular in "English" circles and shared the activities of many non-Jewish friends. Norman was attracted, and the family had begun to notice her – though they had not deigned to show any sign of favour, as yet. Probably it needed only a hint of the dowry to clinch the matter. The Blays were not so well off as they used to be. Some of their coal enterprises had failed badly, and the Dawport branch in particular, had been hit in a recent strike. In any case, "money married money". Norman's brothers and sisters were all allied to wealth. Mark Elman smiled complacently. He felt in himself the capacity to meet the occasion. Plenty of time; Nettie was young, so was the boy: and the business must have a year to expand on its new basis. When he was ready to mention the figure, the Blays would open their eyes! Not much doubt about it. His Nettie would be the queen of Dawport!

The express gained speed and swallowed up curve after curve. The scarred wastes of the town yielded to undulating stretches of green countryside. The air was clear of the defiling smoke of furnace chimneys. Uncle Mark lowered the window, and glanced at Simon. The boy was still sitting stiffly over his journal. He made only a monosyllabic reply when addressed. Mark, never loquacious, lapsed into ironic reflection. "A real Englisher, by gum! Doesn't seem to feel excited, or anything, like you'd expect a boy to be. These Englishers – they're made of wood. Just the sort of feller we want." Here was the third goal he had in view – to be reached when Simon had finished his course, and the Elmans consolidated their position. Mark was not a son of old "Froom" Elman for nothing. He had a strong desire to "lead" communal life, in the one sphere where his father held a natural pre-eminence – the synagogue. "Froom" Elman was concerned only with ritual worship: his son's ambition lay in control of the institution. Such control would furnish him not only with scope for the exercise of authority and its complementary network of manipulation in administrative affairs, but with the power to turn Anglo-Jewish life into the way he sincerely believed it should go. The local congregation was still deplorably "foreign", both in its composition and its tastes. It had refused until recently to appoint a minister, regarding the office as superfluous "English" invention. A *shochet* – yes; Jews must have pure meat, ritually killed and supervised: a *chazan*, too, was necessary; Jews must have services conducted and intoned in the official manner; and such a man could teach the children, whose Hebrew education was a primary public charge. But what Jewish purpose would be served by the delivery of sermons in the *Goyish* style? Mark Elman and his friends had a hard task to persuade the "foreigners" that a preacher was essential to the dignity of the community. When the appointment was eventually made, he was still far from satisfied. The first occupant of the pulpit was a worthy man, combining in himself most of the qualifications required of the multiple post. But his English education had begun too late and stopped too soon. He still retained very strongly the accent and mannerisms of Galicia, and so did the wife who had accompanied him from that ill-chosen birthplace. They were not equipped to fulfil Mark Elman's aim of Anglicising the congregation, or become what he considered its ideal representatives to the social world without.

He welcomed, therefore, Devora Black's plans for her son, as far more likely to promote his own. Simon was not a favourite of Mark's, perhaps because he was, too obviously the old man's; but Mark could appreciate better the boy's promise of becoming a perfect Englishman. Here was the very type he needed. By the time Mark Elman was leader of Dawport Jewry, Simon would be ready to serve under him the flag of Anglo-Judaism – with the emphasis on the *Anglo*.

So it came about that Uncle Mark had for the time taken Simon into gracious charge, and was as anxious to win the favour of Jews' College for the boy as Mrs. Black herself could wish. If it depended on him, success would result from the interview on Simon's behalf, as assuredly as it would from the other, more momentous to himself.

The train roared over bridge and hill, then grew lamb-like on a stretching plain. Flat fields under low-lying ridges narrowed into streets of suburb houses, that became a town of shops and rattling trams. With the slide into Tavcastle station Simon's silence broke.

"It's bigger than Dawport," he said. "But not nearly so big as I used to think."

"H'm, Tavcastle's not so important, for all the fuss about the docks." Uncle Mark voiced the rivalry of the towns. "Quite as much business can be done in Dawport. Just wait till our new harbour's finished."

Simon did not reply. He was not concerned with commercial standards. It stirred him to remember how he had once looked forward to the greater world of Tavcastle, with its University amenities. There could be no regret for that lost dream. London on the near horizon dimmed every provincial glory. The sun of Gower Street dissolved even the cloud of Queen's Square.

Chagrin – apprehension – dropped from the woof of feeling, busy under Simon's phlegm. He hugged his window seat as passengers pressed in, a fussy matron, an attentive son, commercial travellers noisy with bags, and ignored them to watch the leaping scenery. The fields spread out once more in less angular contours, the hills retired. He saw marsh-land edging to the misty sea, docks and bridges, a mud-piled river chained to giant stacks and cranes. Then curving fields again, and suddenly, tall banks that shut out near and distant view. The train ran slow: it seemed to hold its breath, to plunge with a shriek into a black sulphurous gulf. Uncle Mark and the attentive son simultaneously closed the windows, and a lamp flickered sullenly above. Long tongues of fire sprang past the panes at intervals. Simon listened. He could fancy the waters of the angry Severn swirling round. But soon his eager thought raced faster than the train towards the daylit earth above. At last! England – English soil! His heart gave a bound as they emerged, into the long cutting between high green banks. This time his hands shot out before Mark Elman's, to unleash the window and admit the precious air. He stood up, breathing it in, watching the bankheads dip to the little station, and then – the fields of England, the dear, desired fields – surely they welcomed him, their true lover, whose searching eyes were turned to them, whose back was set against the slighted Monmouth hills, still peering vainly over the dividing river. On, on, over these gentler undulations, until a blue line far to the left made him blink and strain.

"Look, Uncle Mark," he said in a low voice – Uncle Mark could never realise that such a low voice held emotion— "Are those the Cotswolds?"

"Eh? Oh – yes – I suppose—" Uncle Mark glanced vaguely out, then returned to his reading. He was really engrossed in his papers at last.

Gloucester – Wiltshire – Berks – the express embraced them with a gusto that matched Simon's, avid of their close reality. The hours were fleet to him, despite a growing impatience for the journey's end and crown. A thrilling moment came in the first glimpse of the Thames. The father of English waters crept suddenly from the railway, frisky as an idle youth on sunlit lawns. He lolled in graceful curves between a fringe of willows and lush green banks, his bosom gemmed with little craft that drifted in and out of island dots. With elbows pressed on the window ledge, Simon stood and stared: his joy brimmed over, he could not keep his discoveries to himself.

"Uncle Mark," he whispered,—"just look – this must be the Thames! We are near Pangbourne, aren't we? Yes, there's the station. And those hills over there – I should think they are the Chilterns—"

The big fat man sleeping near had fallen at last into Simon's vacant corner, and the jar woke him up in time to hear the whisper. He rubbed his bald head tenderly, nodded it at Simon, and saved Uncle Mark the trouble of reply.

"Thet's right, young man. Never been here before, eiy? You seem to know the lie of the lend, though – pretty bit o' country, ain't it?"

Uncle Mark put aside the papers and brought out his watch. "We're getting on – soon be in Reading," he said. "Due in five minutes."

"Fast, ain't you?" said the fat man, drawing out his own watch from a bulging front. "I mike it nine."

Uncle Mark and the fat man were still arguing over the minutes when the red roofs and factories of the river town came into sight.

"Ow – y'right – here come the biscuits," said the fat man, to whom Simon had taken a violent dislike. He hoped he would get out with the other passengers who alighted. But the huge body still sprawled across the corner seat as the train sped on. Simon was too restless to wish to sit, but the man's monopoly of his place offended him, as much as the facetious cockney tones. Still, his dislike was mitigated the moment a great fist shot out beside his shoulder to point at a grey pile on the right horizon.

"See thet? Thet's Windsor Castle, thet is. Hev a good look, m'lad. Ain't too clear to-day. The sun's goin' – a bit red – shouldn't be surprised if we get a change soon. Fog, p'raps – or rain."

"Nonsense," said Uncle Mark. "We've left the rain in Wales."

Simon's goggling eyes remained fixed on the piled towers, to the last speck of visibility. A royal approach to London! But the common aspect of the altered nearer scene enthralled him just as much. Simon's present excitement was not a response to mere beauty. His heart bounded to the thickening suburbs that covered the last vestige of open country. A dark grey heaviness had dimmed the air. The fat commercial traveller was in the right this time. The atmospheric gloom was due as much to a change of weather as to the smoke of the imminent city. Ealing – and a run of walled-in stations. Then the crawl beside a sordid mass of dwelling-backs, into the cave of Paddington.

Instantly a whirling clash of metal and human beings. Crowds poured over platforms roaring with the noise of traffic. Simon forgot the fat man and all the life of the journey, as he followed Mark Elman blindly through the maze. A lull came as they walked up the exit to the street – the first London street to be trodden by Simon Black. He stood for a moment, looking up and down.

"Come along," said Uncle Mark. "It's no good waiting here. We'll walk up Praed Street and get a bus at the corner."

Simon moved along in deflating surprise. A miserable, dingy street – its hovels and shops no better than those in the meaner streets of Dawport. But at the corner a somewhat larger world emerged – certainly a noisier and fuller, if not less dirty, world. They crossed the Edgware Road into Chapel Street. Four streams of omnibuses linked and clove apart and linked again. A little knot of people swelled into a crowd, that suddenly split and raced towards a moving point:

"Quick now, Simon – into this bus – get on top—"

They sat and looked at the swirling waves below. Simon's eyes flashed from right to left, in front and behind. He clutched the rail of the bus as if it steadied the plunge of an incalculable monster, riding through human surf. A spring of exultation bubbled in his heart. "I'm in London – I'm *really* in London," he told himself. The panorama of the streets widened into Tottenham Court Road. And then, suddenly, as if a curtain had been drawn with silent stealth, a pall of darkness fell upon the scene. Only faint outlines loomed, where the lighted lamps shone through.

"What is it?" gasped Simon. "Is this a fog?"

"A sort of fog – not the thick kind, fortunately – just a hanging darkness, that comes and goes. Beastly nuisance – it's going to delay us. We'll stay up here, though. It's not raining, at least."

That was poor consolation for Simon. He would have preferred rain with sight of his surroundings. And there was no distraction now from the fact of Jews' College. He was being dragged by the slow-moving bus, gradually, but relentlessly, towards the only building in London which he did not want to see. The thought spoilt a sense of adventure in their groping progress. It even grew, as they alighted in a dimly visible street and walked cautiously from angle to angle of ghostly squares, into a consciousness of doom.

"Here we are," said Uncle Mark abruptly. He had turned through a little iron gate into space. Simon stumbled off the path upon soggy grass, then came back towards the shadows of a porch. In the light from within Mark Elman put his hand to the bell.

A wild spark flashed through Simon's heavy heart.

"Uncle Mark – perhaps they won't pass me, after all my Hebrew—"

"Never you fear," said Mark Elman, in tones the more convincing for a complete lack of warmth. "You know quite enough Hebrew. My father saw to that. And everything else is satisfactory."

The door opened. Simon abandoned hope and stepped inside.

VIII

"S-s-s! – COVER the bishop, you ass!"

"Clear off, Binsky! Who's playing this game, I'd like to know—?"

Crash! It seemed as if a trayful of china had been knocked over. But everything went on just the same.

"L'choh – dodi
Lik – ra – as – kal – oh"—

"Let's all – go down the Strand
Have a ba – na – na.

"I say, boys – look at Billy – he's giving the greeners ham sandwiches!"

Even Simon, busily scribbling on a pad shielded by a mug of coffee, glanced up at that. He was used to the medley of noise in the common-room. The young *chazan*, practising for Friday night, the music-hall habitue roaring his favourite comic song, disputative chess-players, clatter of crockery, mumbling and munching, were too familiar to distract his attention from his notes or even – what he was at the moment engaged upon – some hasty correspondence.

He had to smile at the startled look on Myer Billig's face. Of course all the others yelled with laughter, heightened by the confusion of the "greeners". They were two foreign students who had recently arrived, their lack of English more than balanced in the Principal's eyes by their "Yeshibah" training. But that the fruits of study in an old-fashioned Hebrew seminary should be valued beyond Latin and Greek, proclaimed in fact as the true classicism, was an offence to the heroes of the English curriculum. They resented, too, the unreasonable swotting habits of the new-comers. Not content with grinding away in official hours, shaming their fellows by their concentration and easy grasp of knotty points of Talmudic law, the two must sit studying the nights through, apparently exempt from human need of sleep, food, or recreation. Of course it was obvious that they had not the means to procure much of the latter things. There were no rich men's sons at the College: but none so poor, probably, as these shabby strangers. Their bony frames and pinched sallow faces told a tale that Billig for one, could read very well. His offer of sandwiches was tentative – he knew it was possible that the proud starvelings would refuse his calculated surplus – but he had not expected it to be remarked upon in any way by others. Little Mandel's shout disconcerted him doubly.

"What on earth – d' do you mean?" he stammered, stooping to recover his burst paper bag, which, to the delight of the watchers, he had dropped. "You are rude as well as untruthful, Mandel," he said, and turned his back with intrepid dignity on the other.

"Oh, come, Billy," said Mandel, winking at the "greeners", who had paused, open mouthed, in their bites. "The trouble with you is, you've got no sense of humour. Why, even Father Abraham could see a joke. and make one, too—"

"*Make* one!" said Binsky, incredulously. "*That's* a yarn, Mandel—"

"It is a yarn – and you ought to jolly well know it, after all

Perschman's put us through. Like to hear it over again? Well, it says" – he dropped into a sing-song chant— "it says, that Abraham's father Terach kept a shopful of idols, and he told his son that the biggest of them was the Creator of the Earth. But Abraham was no mug, and when his father went out and left him in charge of the museum, he took a hammer and smashed 'em all up – all except the big one. Oh, how wild his father was when he came home, and how *kvick* he got ready to give Abraham a whacking. But says Abraham, says he – 'For vy should you beat me, fader? It vosn't me that smashed the goods – I mean gods. It was that big buffer himself – I seen him do it.'

"'You're a liar,' says his father, 'That's only a stone image, that can't move – I made it myself, so I ought to know—'' Oh, father!' says Abraham in a shocked voice, ' You told me he created the heavens and the earth and everything in them— 'So I did', says his father, rather put out. 'But what of it?' – 'Why, as he was a Mighty One, I brought along some choice food as an offering. Then the other gods all rushed to eat it first and he got angry and took up the hammer and smashed 'em up – ' The joke was on Terach all right, wasn't it? Even Billy must see that – though he *hasn't* got a sense of humour."

"What *you* haven't got, Mandel," said Billig, still sitting stiffly, "is a sense of reverence. I'm not sure that you aren't positively blasphemous."

Mandel groaned.

"Don't talk like a Christian, Billy. I thought you wanted to make the Bible Fathers *real* to the congregation."

"The spiritual truths taught by the Bible Fathers must be treated in a sacred way—"

"Then they'll never be real. Take it from me, Billy, it's only

Christians who talk that tosh – after all, Abraham isn't *their* ancestor, so they can't afford to take liberties." Mandel winked again at the "greeners", conscious that they were on his side. It was they, as a matter of fact, who had put such ideas into his head, and given his flippancy a purposeful twist. He hadn't such a down on them as some of the other chaps, in spite of all his teasing. Reared in a Yiddish-speaking home, he could find some affinity with their style of thought and speech. But now their faces puzzled him. They were gazing in rapt admiration at the solemn-visaged Billig, whose last utterance had been delivered in his special "pulpit" tone. That particular aspect of religious dignity which the orphan wore so well, which was unassailable by jest or insult, and was reinforced by a sonorous finely-modulated English that always captured Simon's ear, had a profound effect on the foreign students. Myer Billig represented an ideal to them. Their quick wits, leaping over language difficulties into understanding of the common-room talk, might be ranged against him: their gratitude for his delicate charity did not blind them to the reason in their – and his – tormentors. None the less they recognised in him the embodiment of a standard they yearned, but could not hope wholly, to attain. All unconscious of his radiance – *because* unconscious – he shone upon them, perfect in his manner, bearing, outlook – the admired, the inimitable, English "cledgeyman".

"Well, you fellows," said Mandel. "Aren't I right?"

One of the two ventured on a note of defensive criticism.

"Billig not Christian," he said. "Perhaps" – he hesitated— "perhaps Reformer—"

Billig's eyes turned on him in grave reproach.

"Nothing of the kind," he declared. "Have you heard me

say a word against tradition? I'm opposed to changes which cannot be carried out without authority. Now if Reform—"

"Reform! – Reform!" chanted Mandel, seized with another spasm of impish glee. He jumped up on the table, and threw himself into an attitude. "My young friend, let me warn you against Reform. For what does it lead to?" He dropped his voice, drawling out the words on a soft, impressive note. "If you graft a pear tree upon an apple tree, what is the result? *Sterility!* And meanwhile – meanwhile – *what will become of the children?*"

There was a roar of laughter. The imitation of an idiosyncratic lecturer had been perfectly done. Simon, grinning half absently, saw even the orphan's features relax. But the next moment his own smile vanished. A leaf from his pad had fluttered to the floor, and was seized by a passing student.

"Hullo – Black's writing a love letter to a *shiksele*—"

Simon snatched the leaf out of the other's hand, so coolly that no mocking comments rose. His lack of agitation was not only wariness of his fellows. Jani was a *shiksele*, of course. But his screed was no love-letter. He thrust it into his pocket as soon as he felt himself unobserved, and quietly left the room. Time enough to finish the letter when he got back to his lodging.

Usually he sauntered through the streets, crossing and re-crossing the ceaseless traffic, lingering on the islands to watch the streams go by. He could not be sated with the spectacle of London's routine. But to-night he walked rapidly into the ruts of Soho, and pushed the door of a dingy house in Beagle Street. It was one of a block variegated with shop fronts, though even the private windows had signs of some trade carried on within. The lower panes of number Forty showed samples of cloth and a card, announcing " M. L. Finck" as a " First Class Repairing Tailor" – The dark little shop led into a darker fitting-room, with a secondary door into the passage. This door was open, and on Simon's entry, a round, pale-faced man with twinkling eyes peered out and exclaimed. "Hello, Shimki! Bist early eint!"

Simon nodded without speaking, and hurried upstairs.

The spicy smell of soup mingled with a reek of steamed cloth; a clatter of pots, voices, machines and banging doors rose and fell. At the top of the first landing a woman walked across from one room into another. She turned a pleased smile on Simon as he followed her in.

"Dat's right," she said. "You com early."

"Yes. I told you I had to go out again – to a – a – to a party at the College."

"Aff course – I remember. Everything is ready. Der is a clean shirt and collar on your bed mit the suit." She turned briskly to the fireplace. "Nu, mameh?"

The query was addressed to an old wrinkled woman, who was busy stirring the contents of a pot on the shining black hob. Everything in the big gaunt room was scrupulously clean; but there was no order or comeliness in it. The shabby furniture sprawled over ill-matched squares of linoleum, eked out with rough mats that caught in the feet. Half-sewn garments were piled on the sofa and overflowed the chairs. The workrooms proper were on the top floor, but the intervening part of the house (with the exception of Simon's room) was let, and it was convenient to use the living rooms for dumping articles in transit above or below. Besides, the tailor's wife still did odd jobs of needlework between snatches of domestic work. She picked up a waistcoat and examined it, while Simon, glancing at the table, pushed away canvas linings that encroached on the end laid for his meal.

The old woman, who was mumbling in an undertone, stopped stirring, replaced the lid of the saucepan, and said in a louder voice, "Bait fertig" ("Nearly ready"). Then she hobbled towards Simon.

"Geh – vash zach" ("Go – wash thyself" – *ritually*), she said, waving him away. She removed the offending clothes, and straightened the disarranged cutlery. All the time she was muttering Yiddish to herself or to her daughter, now busy stitching buttonholes in a corner.

That incessant muttering, stimulated by an occasional reply from Mrs. Finck, was to Simon the most maddening feature of this household – worse than the clatter of the machines above his room, the yells and antics of the many children swarming round, the pervading smells, and what he regarded as the impertinent familiarities of the tailor and his family. They were all torments, that could not be compensated for by obvious friendly intent, by every effort to provide him with comfort, by his clean bed, cosy with feather paddings, and an ample supply of wholesome food, skilfully if too blatantly cooked.

All his childish revulsions were revived by the Fincks. The mixture of Cockney and Yiddish was worse than the trail of village Welsh. The old woman's refusal to speak a word of English after twelve years in the capital of Britain was appalling. Such "foreignness" in the west of London seemed more incredible than that in the east, where his first sight of his people in the mass had dismayed and shaken him. His old conviction, that if only his parents had settled in London, their

Anglicisation would have been speedy and complete, vanished with the hope of unifying his life with theirs.

In his bare upper room, Simon completed an unusually elaborate toilet. He cleared a space on the marble top of his washstand; it was more solid, if colder, to write upon than the rickety dressing chest. From his wallet he took two letters, both addressed to him in the same spindly writing. He drew one out of its envelope, only to replace it promptly with a smile. He knew that letter by heart. It was the first he had received from Jani Lloyd. He had not destroyed it after answering, as he had her subsequent epistles. The others, though equally welcome, had never had quite the same element of surprise and pleasure. He remembered every time he looked at it how it had charmed away the misery of a certain night. He had not been thinking of Jani; in fact, he had forgotten her during those first weeks of his College life in London. There had been more than enough extraneous things to occupy his mind. But all the excitement and novelty had not worn down the impression of being caught in a trap. That it was a trap, he felt more and more grimly certain; a trap from which his energies must bend, eventually, in the direction of release. It was too early, then, to devise the means. He had to resign himself to the routine of the Talmudical professors and their incongruous and uncongenial band of disciples. The escape into Gower Street had not become sure and uplifting. The transition from preparatory stage into full-fledged studentship filled him with horrible forebodings. He had come into the Finck rooms one night too depressed to eat his dinner, savoury as it was. After a torturing grind at Hebrew texts, a discourse by a German scholar who churned English into segments, a rebuke by the Principal for evasion of a religious exercise (in order to attend an "unnecessary" English lecture) the menage at Beagle Street was overwhelming.

As he lay on his bed abandoned to despair, a shrill voice travelled up towards his door,—

"Meester See-mon – Meester See-mon," (this was the only variation he could get of the detestable *Shimki*) "a lettare far yoo—"

He had moved dully to secure the letter, and lay down again, staring at it, puzzled at the fine, spindly writing in a hand unknown to him. The puzzle remained behind the pleasure which the reading of the contents brought.

"MY DEAR, DEAR SIMON,

"After great tribulation I have managed to obtain your address. So I hasten to write and explain all. Can you forgive my cruel silence and my failure to keep my promise to you at the station? I was prevented from coming by" (here the words 'Mr. Griffiths' were crossed out, and 'Uncle Trevor' written above). "He came unexpected into the baby-linen just as I was going to slip out. He made a row and forbade me to go, or I was to go altogether – although it was our quiet time, and dear Miss Meredith was willing to attend to everything. Oh, Simon dear, how my heart did ache, and how angry I felt with the cruel tyrant who prevented me from saying farewell to my greatest friend. I can assure you that I have wept into my pillow every night at thinking you believed me to be false. But indeed dear Simon, I am quite true and always will be the same. I am always thinking of you and wondering what you are doing in the great city. And how you are going about among your grand college friends, and all of them admiring you, but perhaps in their secret hearts jealous of you for being much, much more clever. Oh Simon, I don't care for anybody like I do for you, and I shall be waiting the minute when you write and tell me that you forgive me, and when we will meet again. Oh, Simon, if only I could see you now. I could write much more, but I want to know if this will reach you safely. I think your sister did not wish to give me your address, and I was so unfortunate as to lose it and had to ask her again. So you see, dear Simon, that I have had to bend my pride a little, and I hope you will understand all my sufferings and write very soon to

"Your true friend,
"JANI."

A pleasant glow had warmed Simon's veins as he read. He sat up, chuckled, then began to walk about, listening in his mind to Jani's rich, plaintive voice. The queerly composed mixture of naïvete and grandiloquence amused and astonished him. He had never seen a word of Jani's in writing, and he could not know that in spite of her years at the Blaemawe schools, she was unable to construct the simplest sentence unhelped. And why should she bother, when her friend, the elderly but romantic Miss Meredith, was only too delighted to act as secretary? Miss Meredith's was the script, the spelling, and much of the phraseology, moulded on an intemperate addiction to novelettes. Here and there Jani broke through on her own authentic note, and it was no wonder that Simon never suspected, though he was recurrently puzzled by, the dual variations. He felt profoundly touched. It was good at this moment to be assured of the devotion of a sweet, charming creature, so confident that all the world must recognise his superiority and perfection. Her ingenuousness was amusing, but it soothed ineffably. He felt lifted above his wretchedness and despair. Jani, at any rate, was outside the jargon and jumble of the Yiddish world – aware of it, yet indifferent to it – indifferent to that aspect of Simon's which chained him to it. She could now as always, accept him in spite of it, at a valuation alluringly higher than his own. Simon was grateful to Jani, more consciously than ever before. He began to write to her frequently, describing the sights of London, delighting her by the suggestion that she should come up for a day – or longer – perhaps spend a holiday: when he would share with her his growing knowledge of the streets, the parks, the shops, the theatres, the great buildings, and the river – all the haunts and shows of the city of which he had become a proud part. He wrote to her only of what he saw and enjoyed, never of what he thought and felt about his work. She found nothing lacking; and her letters both eased and stimulated him.

To-night he finished his epistle to her in the usual indulgent strain, and folded it, smiling, into the envelope. He patted it tenderly, then stood up, walked across to the spotted wardrobe-mirror, and surveyed himself.

"Jani would like to see me now," he thought, and straightened his tie self-consciously. It was the first time he had seen himself in a dress-suit. The fact that it was borrowed from the Finck workshop, was a little tight under the arms and scanty at the wrists, detracted nothing from the occasion, and scarcely anything from his appearance. He looked what he most ardently wished himself to be – a well-set up young Englishman, rather stiff and not too polished, correct but unobtrusive, just comfortably *under* the dandical height of fashion.

He did not look at himself too long. Hastily pushing gloves and letter into his overcoat pocket, he put on his hat and descended the stairs, as quietly as possible. He was in terror of being observed by the Fincks and exposed to their familiar comments. Fortunately it was their busy time, domestically and commercially. Mr. Finck was placating the impatient customers who had waited till the last moment for the day's execution of orders. Mrs. Finck had routed out her children from the lairs where they nightly evaded their beds, and was engaged with the grandmother in belated lullaby tasks. There was plenty of noise; it was more difficult for Simon to avoid notice by sight than by sound. But he managed to get into the street without challenge.

It was a fine mild night. Simon walked along humming. He posted his letter, and the faint tinge of Jani's aura departed with it. An animation of his own gave buoyance to his stride. He felt pleased and slightly excited. For no reason in particular he thought he would enjoy this evening tremendously. It was not the first College soiree he had attended in London, but it was the first to which he went in a spirit of self-confidence. The dress suit had much less to do with it than the improvement in his social relationships. Since his matriculation he had got on easy terms with several of the University crowd, and things generally were different from the time when he was a raw outsider, strange to everybody but the few ministerial students. Even those had excluded him from intimacy until his "preparatory" days were over: but for them, both juniors and seniors, he had in any case an invincible contempt. They seemed to him a poor lot – either frankly wasting time, or dried by an incomprehensible zeal, – like for instance the orphan Myer Billig. Simon always thought of him as the orphan, because this fact about the fellow heightened his absurdity. Why an orphan without relatives, free to choose, able without hurt to cancel out his Jewishness and merge wholly into English life, should elect to train for the Jewish ministry, was a hopeless puzzle. Thinking of Myer, Simon smiled loftily. Obviously a ridiculous person. Yet there was an appeal about him – Simon had to admit it. What was it? Perhaps just a wistful, earnest manner? – anyway, something that made it hard to join in the constant "ragging" by the others. Myer was a bit of a sport in his way. At tennis, for instance: he couldn't play for nuts – his stiff, high-shouldered figure jerking around the court was a droll sight – but he *tried*. There was something game about the plunge and whirl of his innocuous racket. And in somewhat the same way, he rampaged harmlessly in the common room with his ideas. And what ideas! Fancy regarding Abraham and Isaac as if they were modern men! Even the profs. had more sense than that, revel as they might – if revel were the word – in the crumbled dust of the past. At least they knew and proved that it *was* the past. If one could only hide one's natural aversions, and mumble glibly in dutiful obeisance to the parade of that sanctified ash, they would be entirely satisfied. But not Myer. He had to prance angularly about and prod the mummies, declaring he saw and heard them breathe. It was not Simon who took this flight of fancy, but one of the senior students who was building a reputation in debate. Simon was fascinated by the image and frequently recalled it, always seeing Myer with his racket in his hand, and the cased figures of the Egyptian Room in the British Museum grotesquely disposed at the nets of Jews' College tennis-court! His own emendation amused if it did not illuminate him; the modifying smile almost endeared the absurd orphan. But he did not want to think of Myer now. That ridiculous zealot would certainly not be present at the affair to-night.

Simon stepped briskly along Gower Street. The picturesque red angles of the hospital came into view. As he crossed from one pavement to another, a number of young men who had run down the steps raced along and bumped him. They rushed through the gates without apology. Just like them – the roughs! – thought Simon in disdain. He shared the general low opinion of the "meds."

Everything was in full swing within. Lights, bustle, laughter, greetings, music, games. For a time Simon moved aimlessly about. He did not go into the card-room, but watched the dancing, and took a turn on the floor whenever opportunity came. He had a passing acquaintance with some of the girls, though those he preferred were either too haughty or already monopolised. At first he had been awestruck by them – these fascinating Slade girls – but could be critical now, appraising the margin of "effects" against their natural charms. They were clever at enhancement, not necessarily of beauty, but of the striking and bizarre. Their arrangement of hair, clothes, and posture had the arresting element of novelty, if not, as they probably imagined, of art. Simon, as ever attracted to the blondes, could note impartially the broad flat cheeks, long teeth and inadequate nose, that warred too often with the "aesthetic" conventions – or innovations. The lithe dark girls fulfilled them better. But then Simon did not like their "foreign" look. He drifted in and out of the refectory. There was a concert interval. He heard distant strains, and the loud clapping that punctuated them. But all the time a din of tongues went on. The groups near the doors were thickest and noisiest: a voice detained Simon as he was pushing through.

"Hul-lo, Black. You look swish to-night. Got a gurl?"

"Hullo, Rees." Simon stopped, though he did not particularly want to, beside a short, sharp-faced youth with roving black eyes. Rees was an Aberystwyth fellow, one of the many strangers from Wales who persisted in treating Simon as a raw compatriot.

"By yourself, I see. Enjoying the crush?"

"Yes – rather."

"H'm. It's dull enough. Thank God that gurl's finished screaming. These Saesneg think they can sing, don't they? – Christ! There's another! Coming? – Let's hunt for a coffee. I'm dry in the throat listening to the screechers."

He took Simon's arm, but dropped it suddenly.

"Wait a bit. It's a recitation."

Simon grinned. Everybody knew of the prizes captured by Rees for his recitations – he had once got second place at the National Eisteddfod – and the irresistible fascination such performances had for the hard-tongued youth.

A seat nearby was vacated, and Simon dropped down. He had seen a tall girl stand up at the other end of the room, the back of her head a swathe of gold. She must have long features, he reflected, with that shape of crown and neck. But now his view was obliterated. He did not greatly care.

What "the piece" was, Simon never knew. His attention wandered: one needed to concentrate to hear words in that scarcely subdued hubbub around. But all at once the voice caught his ear. It was low-pitched, clear, with a slight resonance that could not be said to reach emotional stress, yet somehow suggested it. Something vaguely familiar struck

Simon's sense. He listened. Perhaps there was a lull, or it may have been only a quickening of his nerves: but little airs of music from some dear and far-away haunt seemed to flow out in lure of him. He stood up suddenly. The girl had finished, in what was almost a silence at last. Applause broke out, and she looked round, bowing. Simon's heart gave a great leap. The glorious face! It shone full on him, then withdrew and was lost. He heard Rees saying peevishly,—

"Good delivery – but cold – cold Saesneg. I'd like to warm her up! But these devils of English gurls haven't got blood in 'em. It's milk." He touched Simon's elbow.

"Coming now?"

Simon shook his head, his eyes directed to the crowded corner into which the girl had retired. In a moment he swung round to ask— "Oh, Rees – do you know her? What's her name?" – but Rees had gone. Simon glanced round rapidly. He did not know any of his chattering neighbours, but he touched one on the shoulder and made him listen to his question.

"What – the girl who sang? – Betty – Betty Ross. Oh, the *last* one? I'm not sure – somebody said Miller, didn't they" – he appealed to a friend, who nodded and stared.

"Miss Miller, that's right."

Simon pushed his way through at last and got near the corner. She was there still, hemmed in the crowd. To his joy he found an acquaintance hovering by.

"Smith, you know Miss Miller – introduce me, will you?"

The stupid fellow hesitated.

"I don't know her awfully – and she's just going, I think." He stared at Simon's glowering face. "Oh well – come along —"

The group was breaking up. The golden girl – she wore a dress of bronze silk, which shimmered as she moved – was being escorted away by a sandy-haired giant, whom Simon loathed at once for his proprietary air. She paused, however, at Smith's timid hail.

"I say, Miss Miller – here's a friend would like to meet you."

Simon had her hand in his – a firm, cool hand, lightly withdrawn. He glowed in the ray of her vague smile.

"So sorry, Mr. – er – Black – I have to leave at once. Too bad, isn't it? But I'm on duty."

"*What* duty?" Simon asked Smith, as they watched the gold line of her figure vanish.

"Haven't an earthly – I told you I don't know her much. Nobody does, I think – except the fellow who brought her. I fancy she's left Col."

"But where—"

"Hullo, looks like a shindy over there. The meds. are at it again."

There was laughter and scuffling near the door. A student was holding up in a ridiculous attitude a small model of the Hospital mascot, and there was a general fight for its possession. Smith dashed off to see the fun. It would have attracted Simon, too, a few minutes ago. But quite curiously his boyish pleasure in the *soirée* had gone. The crowds, the noise, the dancing and singing, the games and talk, the antics of the fellows, the faces and dresses of the girls, had become unmeaning. He wandered about in search of Rees, and when he found him, plied him with questions about Miss Miller. But Rees either could not or would not give him information, and only mocked his desire for it. He left him abruptly and tried others, but the result was no more satisfactory. And suddenly he felt ashamed to ask. Why should he clamour her name to these smirking fools? Somehow he would find out who she was and see her again – she must be associated with the college or its staff. In the meantime he would think about her, alone. It was getting late, anyway. It might be as well to get his things and leave, and go for a long walk through the streets in the moonlight. As he was putting on his overcoat and moving slowly forward, one arm was seized, twisted, and jerked violently away.

"What the hell d'ye mean, Sheeny? – spreading yourself out and hitting people?"

"I – I'm sorry," stammered Simon, hardly aware of what had happened or been said. In his absorption he had not noticed three figures standing in the shadowed exit, and his extended arm had accidentally brushed the side of one. He flushed and regretted his apology as soon as he realised the nature of the adjuration. The other continued, in a high pettish voice, slightly slurred.

"Ex-exhibition of manners, I presume. Your tribe never had any – huh!"

"Shut it, Parker," whispered a companion. "How d'ye know he is?"

Simon had hesitated, but even in the shadow he could see that the first speaker was unsteady. Probably the others were, too. Their cigarettes waved rather wildly. He decided to ignore them, and passed out. The argument went on, quite audibly.

"I tell you he's a sheeny."

"Rot! Does he look it?"

"You blimy ass, he'd look it on the table—"

"M-might as well say he's a nigger," came a morose third note.

"It's not his colour, Jim – it's his—"

"Shut up – you're drunk."

"Drunk or sober, Parker's right. I'd kick the lot out – sheenies and niggers. C-can't think why they're allowed in."

"Lucky they're not allowed to do much when they *are* in. Know Polasky's applied three times for the assistantship?"

"He c'n go on applying, the ugly devil. Much chance he's got, ha! ha!"

"He's got the best qualifications, blast him!"

"B-but he won't get it?"

"No bloody fear. Hector'll see to that."

"Hector sees to a blasted sight too much," muttered the morose voice, heavily.

"Nursie! Nursie!" piped the high note.

"Don't rot. He's coming back in a minute. But you needn't worry, Jim. He's not on Edith's list – oh, I'm sure he won't be missed – tra – la – la—" The Gilbert and Sullivan strain floated out.

Simon had an extraordinary sense of baffled rage. The most extraordinary thing about it was that his anger boiled up less over the first part of the conversation, which he understood very well, than over the last words he overheard, which he could not follow at all. Obviously they did not apply to him, yet in some obscure way he felt as if he were vitally concerned.

He had moved so slowly that it seemed as if he had been standing still, and a turn would bring him back to face the speakers: but before he could decide upon that turn, he found himself in the middle of the grounds, his head still uncovered in the cool illumined air. His hands were clenched in his overcoat pockets; he took them out and gazed at the taut hard knuckles.

"I ought to have punched their heads," he told himself in contempt.

But he knew he did not feel outdone on that account. The time must come when he could settle once for all with insults of the low, familiar type. But somewhere here had been a subtler mockery, a dark attack on strange uncharted ground.

Simon hesitated on the pavement. He was aware of a man standing below the hospital steps, lighting a cigarette. The match went out, the little cigarette-end glowed, and the man came leisurely across the street. He, too, was bareheaded, and his evening suit uncovered. As he passed Simon he looked into his face, nodded as if involuntarily, and strolled on through the gates. Simon stared after him. It was the sandy giant who had been Miss Miller's escort. A flash of intuition opened Simon's mind.

"Hector'll see to that"—"Hector sees to a blasted sight too much"—"He's not on Edith's list."

Of course – *Hector*. And Edith was Miss Miller. He did not know why he should be so certain, but he was. The conviction, however, did not clear up his trouble. It muddled and deepened it. Simon drew a long, sighing breath. He had come away in a sort of a dream, a sweet, secret hurry of the mind and heart. Those fellows had pounced upon and spoiled his mood. But why should he let them quite frustrate it? There was something still that was precious to himself, something they could not reach with their mysterious scorn, – and it was something that he must brood and ponder over, to make it yield delicious meaning. He strode through Huntley Street into Tottenham Court Road, rounding the Corner without noting for once the shadows suddenly lit, the dolled-up windows in blazing show, the plunging buses that became

remote and dignified in the late hour's solitary state. London's
stridency had subsided into the low drone where one's
thoughts could rise into shape and clarity. The occasional
shriek and hoot and glare were only so many punctuation
marks to guide and define meditation. But Simon had tramped
from Circus to Circus, and twice passed the shuttered line of
books in Charing Cross Road, in a skirmish of the great pit
where Nelson and his lions dozed, without any sharpening of
the edges of his dream. The beautiful face looked out at him
still from impenetrable mists – of fancy? – memory? – sleep?
Suddenly he felt very tired. He knew he would not do the
hour's work at his books that should have preceded rest that
night. His feet dragged. It was almost good to be back in the
dingy cold room of the silent Finck house, treading the creaky
boards towards his comfortable bed. As he came in he found
a letter, addressed in the well-known spindly writing.
Impatient Jani had written again, crossing his own belated
epistle to her – how long ago it seemed already since he had
posted it! Instead of tearing open the envelope at once as he
usually did he laid it on his pillow, and undressed, intending
to read in bed by the light of the little gas-jet above his head.
But while he moved drowsily about, the letter slipped
unnoticed between the pillow and the rail. Simon did not miss
it. He got into bed, turned out the light, and dropped at once
into a profound sleep. His last thought was that he would have
to put in a couple of hours' extra study the following evening.
Perhaps it was not quite his last. At any rate, he woke up
suddenly before the dawn, his mind clear in a few moments,
and took up whole a seemingly snapped mental thread –
whether from his wakeful or sleeping brain he did not know.
"Edith Miller," he said aloud, in a rapture of discovery. "Why,

of course – it's Edith – Edith" – *his* Edith! The little girl with the heavenly grave face, the blue fire of her eyes and the gold flaming hair, shining in a dim great hall with swords and dead stuffed heads. Outside the carriage waited, green slopes dotted with hydrangea stretched to the rippling lake, and the magical Lady of Hafod called to the still more magical child. Miracle of his boyhood, hidden passion of his youth, his man's ideal. His heart remembered and cried her name. It was she who stood in exquisite supremacy before him, as she had done from the moment when he first encountered her, and would do, he knew, to his end.

IX

IT HAD happened. An encounter in the street, when her face looked at him unexpectedly from a nursing uniform; an equally chance meeting at an evening lecture – how lucky that she was interested in a public course on literature, furnishing the pretext for which he had cudgelled his brains. "I've picked up an old book on the Brontës" he wrote a day later. "If you like, I'll lend it you?" His note was an invitation to meet him for tea at the Austrian Cafe. She had not replied. Long before the appointed time, he had sat at a table in a recess, his fingers trembling as he handled a menu-card, his voice unsteady as he put off the waiter.

And here she was, sitting opposite him, just as he had imagined; exquisitely fresh in her neat grey costume. But his inner confidence did not quite, as he had hoped, match hers. Was she always as cool and consummate? Her eyes were kind, but casual, her ready speech and quiet poise seemed born of natural ease. Perhaps she was not so self-assured as he believed. There was a hint of shyness that escaped him in her response to his flurried greeting.

"Yes, – l've come. But I wasn't sure that I would!"

"No," he said humbly. "I'm afraid it was awful cheek to ask you."

"Perhaps," she said, with her little vague smile. "But, the fact is, I'm rather curious—" she paused.

"About the book?" He turned to lift his attaché case from its place beneath his chair.

"Not only about the book." His fingers stopped working at the troublesome catch. "I'm rather curious about *you*. Do you know – you puzzle me."

"That's good news." He tried to say it lightly. "It shows you must be a little interested."

"A little," she agreed. "I have a queer sort of feeling – it's come over me each time I've seen you since the *soirée* – that somewhere, a long time ago, we've met before. I wonder if there's anything in it?"

Though she was not looking at him directly, but pulling off her gloves with leisurely care, Simon was taken aback. He had anticipated such a moment, but not quite so soon. He dallied with it.

"Very likely. I felt it, too, as soon as I saw you – even before I saw you, when I heard you reciting."

"Really? Then you think we have met – before?"

"Yes," he said, and did not know whether to be glad or sorry that the waiter had become insistent again. Her voice, in spite of the questioning, had been impersonal – the same voice with which she gave her order for tea. The inflections were rapid, decisive, and the way in which the waiter bowed was a tribute to authority. Without any trace of haughtiness, the girl's bearing was full, not only of unconscious grace, but of some indefinable power equally native and rare. The waiter bowed to it. Simon adored and feared it.

While his eyes worshipped, his fingers fumbled with the catch of the case. He felt it slip suddenly, and lifting the lid, he drew out a book and placed it on the table.

"You didn't mention Reid," he said, and instantly cursed himself for having changed the subject. "T. Wemyss Reid. I think it's the first book on the Brontës after Mrs. Gaskell."

"Oh, I've heard of it," she opened the volume eagerly. "I've read most of the others, as I told you – Swinburne's Note, Birrell, Clement Shorter – and now there's May Sinclair. But this, as you say, is older—"

"It's a first edition – and a clean copy," he said with some pride.

"Yes, quite a find. It looks full of delightful detail."

"Nothing special, I'm afraid – just gossip, you know."

"Of course – they all gossip," she said smiling. "It's such a tempting subject. Genius cooped up in a gloomy parsonage on the Yorkshire moors – a fiery heart in a plain body – a domineering father, a drunken brother, dying sisters, romance, tragedy, fame – the passionate novels and the fascinating letters. It's difficult to see how the best of critics could avoid the gossip. They never do. And nobody wants them to."

"Poor Charlotte!"

"Poor! Oh no – *rich* Charlotte. She had fame, friendship, love, while she lived – and the knowledge that she had done something great. She brought a new strain into English literature. Interest in her personality can never die."

"I believe our friend Reid had a similar idea," said Simon, turning the leaves of the book as she put it down to handle the teapot. "But he doesn't throw much light on the literary or psychological values. He seems to think that if he proves Charlotte had her share of the ordinary joys of life, he has cleared her from some dark charge, and made her *more* interesting!"

"Is that why you pitied her?" They laughed together. "Anyway, if he's really her champion, even Victorian-fashion, I shall enjoy reading the book. I simply cannot bear to hear a word against Charlotte."

"You're an enthusiast." Simon said it with inward doubt. Was enthusiasm an attribute of this fair, calm girl, whose detached airs held no hint of undue fervency? The English type, he thought with satisfaction, even when it feels and thinks at an unusual level, is seldom carried away. Edith Miller confirmed his surmise.

"I'm afraid not. At least I see now that Charlotte isn't as wonderful as I used to believe – she's narrow and limited in so many ways. All the same, she's as fascinating as ever. She's terribly honest. Only it isn't that – her love of truth, her honesty – that's made her live. It's her vitality. Isn't it the same with individuals as with nations – the old nations – those that made their contributions to history long ago, and ought to have been used up – but still live on? It's their vitality—"

He listened to the rapid, soft voice, suggesting, challenging. Its modulations broke his thread of thought; he could hardly follow hers beyond a sentence, his mood of intoxication grew and swelled so large. He watched the long, slender fingers at work among the china and the crumbling cakes, and had no notion of how much or little he consumed himself. "Another cup?" He could have gone on accepting potfuls of undesired brew, for the sake of seeing those hands approach his own. But the time came when the enveloping gloves were drawn over their smooth, firm whiteness, and the enchanting voice said, formally—

"I have an appointment at six – at Bishopsgate. It won't take long from here, though, will it?"

"No, the City buses pass the corner. I'll walk with you to Holborn."

The little vague smile seemed to say, "You don't ask permission. I'll grant it, all the same." As she stood up, the frill of her white silk blouse foaming over the revers of her coat, he would have liked to touch her, to compel her to look directly at him, to see him – her eyes were so maddeningly absent. He had never known a gaze at once so open and so far.

"May I take the Reid now? I shan't keep it long."

"Of course – for ever."

His fountain pen dashed at the fly-leaf. She read her scribbled name as he handed her the book.

"Oh – but I thought it was a loan – I don't think I ought to take it from you—"

"But why not?"

"Well—" the waiter had come up in response to Simon's signal. She looked through him with an imperceptible change of mood— "nurses should not accept presents – except from grateful patients."

The waiter was smiling broadly: not at his tip, for he had not looked at it. He stared in eloquent admiration at the couple as they moved away. They were in the street, walking slowly, when Simon said,

"I can't understand your being a nurse. Have you taken it up as a career?"

"Not exactly. I threw up other studies in order to take the course thoroughly. But I may not finish – really, a couple of years are enough for my purpose. Probably I'll leave the hospital in the autumn."

"Then it's just a fad," he said boldly, hoping she would turn and flash a look at him. She did; instantly.

"Certainly not. I'm genuinely concerned about nursing. The conditions in some country districts are appalling – one doctor among thousands and thousands of working people, and no help or proper attention for the poor women. There is one place in particular for which I feel responsible."

"I know," said Simon. A saying of Jani's had suddenly come back to him – he could not quite fix it – something about 'Miss Edith wants to be a nurse' – It was an illumination. "You mean Blaemawe."

"Oh!" She stopped in surprise. "Do you know Blaemawe?"

"It's my home," he said, for the first time in his life without reluctance.

"Really? Then we are fellow-villagers? – how delightful!" At last she was looking at him, not with that casual gaze, but in awakened concentration – looking *into* his eyes, not merely at them. "I knew you were Welsh – but Blaemawe! – that accounts for it – that feeling that we've met before – why didn't you explain? Can you remember seeing me there?"

"Yes, very well," he said, smiling with delight, and willing to stand for ever on the pavement, with the hurrying crowds around, while she looked at him in such a way.

"And we *have* met – and spoken?"

"Once," he said. "As children, of course—"

"Of course," she said, "I've been there very little since. But how—" she hesitated. Her wide awake eyes could see beneath his smiling aspect. Obviously he was not going to tell her what she expected. She moved on, pondering. Who was he? A miner's son? She knew there were a few among the students, but nothing in him suggested it. Then why the reticence? She had been brought into contact with most of the "superior" village families – the ministers, the bankers, the schoolmasters – many of the shopkeepers – she could not remember all their names – he might belong to any of them! But he was not going to tell her, and she would not ask. She chatted, instead, about

Blaemawe, its "character". (He heard with astonishment of the picturesque dress it could wear) its mixture of the bleak with the beautiful— "what a view from the huddle of houses to the valley below" – the chain of hills, the disfiguring pits, the people— "crude and ignorant enough, poor things, but so droll and intelligent, full of such singular traits. If only one could do more for them – clear them out of their horrible slums."

"Yes," said Simon bitterly— "as horrible as any in London – your picturesque village is made up of disgusting hovels, all around the chapels and pubs."

"I know – there isn't half enough done – I want to help as much as I can. That's why I took up nursing."

"But you don't mean to nurse there?"

"I might, for a while – just to lead the way. But that isn't the idea. I undertook to train because I meant to know all about it from the inside – to gain practical knowledge and experience. It's useful, anyhow. But my object is to work up a local committee – my aunt wouldn't bother at first, but I'm persuading her now – to install a real nurse."

"You're real enough, I should think," said Simon, but he did not smile. He was thinking, gloomily – 'Fads. why not, – she can afford them'. "Do you always take things up so seriously?"

"Always – if I'm interested."

"And you're interested in Blaemawe." He made the statement almost incredulously.

"Yes. I hope to be there at the end of this year, and possibly all of next." She added impulsively— "You're home sometimes, of course – shall I see you there?"

Simon stared at the ground.

"No doubt," he said, "if you pay my father's house a charity visit."

There was a pause.

"Why do you use that tone?" she said.

"Well – my father is—" he hesitated— "He's a small shopkeeper – we live in rooms above the shop. Your home is Hafod. I don't suppose you'll invite me there!"

"Why not? Only, as a matter of fact, I shall be just a visitor myself – it isn't my home now."

He looked at her.

"Of course – your grandmother's settled in Devonshire – you live with her, not with Sir Gwilym."

"I don't live with either."

"Not with Lady Hafod?" he said in astonishment.

"No. I haven't lived with her for years."

"Oh!" said Simon. "That accounts – that's why I never came across you again. But I thought it was because you were away, being educated—"

"Only partly that. I have stayed now and again at Hafod, and at Millicombe. But my real home has been in London, with other relatives."

"I see," said Simon. He saw nothing, however, but the hint of something enigmatic about her explanation. She seemed to break an inner reserve with an effort, as if impelled to answer the question in his eyes.

"The fact is, my grandmother and I – we didn't get on too well."

"But she idolised you!" cried Simon. "Pardon me"– of course I was right out of your world, but everybody in Blaemawe knew that. I didn't listen to gossip – I'm afraid I never talked much to any of them – but even I heard them say she loved you more than her son."

"Perhaps – her love was too exclusive. When I grew older, I

found she had separated me entirely from – other relatives." The girl's tone had deepened, her look was very far-away. "Lady Hafod has a strong will. She intended I should devote myself entirely to her way of life. The others would not agree – neither would I. It was painful. I loved her, too – l did not wish to quarrel. There was a long estrangement. Anyway, it has all been smoothed over. We visit each other now, and are very good friends."

"But you have had your own way?" said Simon, conscious of some inexplicable force behind her words. "Then *you* have a strong will, too?"

"Yes," she said, gravely. "Where my convictions are strong, my will is strong."

He was holding her eyes now, as if with some magnetism outside their selves. She broke away suddenly with a little uneasy laugh.

"Why, there's another bus – gone! How many have I missed? I really must jump for the next!"

"No. 8 – it's coming," said Simon mechanically. "But don't jump. You're not in such a great hurry, are you?" He wanted to add, outrageously— "Why should you go to Bishopsgate anyway – it's your free evening – are you going to meet someone there?" A name flashed into his head: he actually said aloud— "Are you going to see Dr. Wyn?"

She stared back in surprise. Then her lips curved humorously.

"No. He's coming for me later, though." She held out her hand. Simon seized it desperately.

"Miss Miller – don't go on this" – the bus was slowing down beside them— "there's another 8 following in the line behind – don't go until you tell me when I can see you again. We must have another talk—"

"Of course. About Blaemawe." She laughed lightly. "Or about Charlotte Brontë." She patted the book in her hand. "I haven't thanked you for this – and for a very nice tea. I've enjoyed it all. Especially to find you are actually a Blaemaweite!"

"Yes," he said, in despair at her tone. "But it isn't only that – I thought – I thought – we should be friends."

"In spite of my Hafod background," she said— "and your – little shop?"

"They don't matter, do they? – not to you?"

"Everything matters," she said, changing back to her adorable gravity. "But such things don't mean much beside – more real things. You don't know me, at all, neither do I know you. Why, you haven't told me *anything* about – what you are doing – what you mean to do."

"I'll tell you everything you want to know," he said.

The line of buses moved along. One after another halted at the stop. Edith Miller saw the next number eight approaching.

"Come and have tea with me," she said, "next week. I'm at home most Thursdays. At my aunt's flat in Ridgmount Gardens. It's a sort of second home while I'm at hospital." She handed him a card.

"Mrs. Wyn?" he read aloud, uncertainly.

"My aunt took the flat to be near her son. Hector Wyn is my cousin, you know." Her smile, not vague now, said plainly, "of course you didn't know." It lit up the splendid contour of her face as she looked back from the step of the bus.

X

THE DAYS of the week ran on. But before his visit to the flat, Simon had taken his decision. A letter from his old chum Frank Werrington defined his goal for him. Simon's interest in Frank had languished. They met at intervals, and exchanged brief notes. But Frank had matriculated from the Welsh University, and his slow progress since, together with Simon's divergent course, did not foster the earlier phase of mutual admiration. Frank wrote now in a spurt of renewed friendliness, to say that he was coming to London. Not to study, but to sit for an examination at Burlington Gardens. His people were moving to a post in Sussex. "We shall all be jolly glad to get back to England," wrote Frank in his big schoolboy hand, "though for some reasons I like Wales well enough. Still, I don't want to live here for ever. I've chucked the idea of the Indian Service – it'll take too beastly long, and mums won't hear of it. Besides, I want to get a job and earn my living at once. I've entered for a competitive exam at the end of next month. There's another in June, with a better job. But if I get this, it'll do me." Details followed. "It's good enough to get married on, almost – what?" Simon had grinned at Frank's lumbering jocular strain. But it put a full-grown idea into his head. He saw, not only a way of escape, but a path to Paradise. He busied himself at once with preliminaries, inquiries, calculations, interviews. He welcomed the opportunity of declaring his mind, when Mark Elman arrived in town unexpectedly, looking harassed and furtive as if burdened with gnawing cares. His manner to Simon was as cordial as ever. Avoiding the attentions of the "landsleit" – he did not share his father's and Gedaliah Black's interest in Beagle Street – he took Simon to dine at Jacobson's, the little kosher restaurant in Soho which was their usual resort on these occasions.

"Chopped liver," he ordered, and consumed his favourite *hors d'oeuvres* with relish. In Dawport, he lamented, nobody could prepare such fare. Of course one could have the next best thing, "Tsibilis mit schmalz". But there was no kosher restaurant in Dawport, and even if there had been, one could not frequent it with home so near. Provincial life had many drawbacks and limitations. In London people had endless resources, could do as they liked without surveillance and interference – without the exaggeration by tittle-tattle of every personal move. Simon was puzzled by the undue bitterness that charged Uncle Mark's comments.

Dutch pickled cucumber, juicy and yellow, received equally generous attention, but the solid fare was played with. Mark Elman's appetite waned suddenly, and without lingering to look around the tables and scrutinise a possibly familiar face (one was as likely as not to meet other provincials in this Mecca of kosher palates) he suggested a theatre.

"Anything you like, my boy," he said with an obvious assumption of heartiness. "The lighter the better, though. And we mustn't make it too late. I'm catching the 11.30. Got to be in the office early in the morning, to complete a special order – that's what I came up about to-day."

Business, it seemed, was excellent. The great venture had prospered, and the wholesale firm of Elman & Son was established on a rock-bottom basis. The Dawport factory whirled with activity, a radiating centre of supply to the picture shops of South Wales. The managing director had every reason for optimism and pride.

"Is Uncle Elman better?" asked Simon. "Dinah wrote last week that he had a chill."

"Oh he's all right. Doesn't do much, of course, now – just potters about. He's full of plans, though. His latest is that your family should move into Dawport."

"What? – Take a shop there? But that's what they've always wanted to do."

"Yes, but you know it couldn't be done before. Things are different now. We are giving up the place in Gomer Street – the old shop and house. If your father takes it on, we'll make it easy for him. After all, the Blaemawe business is beginning to pay well—"

"But isn't that a reason for not giving it up?"

"No need to give it up. Gershon will look after it. He's practically doing all the work now."

Simon was silent a moment. Such a plan would have seemed heaven-sent during his boyhood. Was it less welcome now? For the first time in his life he felt uncertain whether he wanted his parents to leave Blaemawe!

"But will Gershon live there – alone?"

Mark Elman glanced at him queerly.

"Well – he can come to Dawport for week-ends. Or he can use a season ticket daily. But maybe he won't have to, for long. Don't you know that he and Dinah – they're young, of course. But it's as well to settle these things early."

His face took on a shade of gloom. But Simon did not notice it. He stared, aghast, at the image conjured up – of Dinah and Gershon!

"Do you mean it's settled? Does Dinah agree?"

"I don' t think it's come to that yet. Just family talk."

"I don't believe Dinah—"

"Why not? She's a sensible girl – quiet, and not fanciful. Besides, Gershon's a decent fellow."

"He's too foreign for Dinah."

Uncle Mark said an extraordinary thing – for him.

"A damn sight better than some of these English Yids – all airs and no backbone." He frowned and drew in his lips, pressing them heavily together. His little eyes glared under the thickening brows. What was it he saw that displeased him in his glass of Russian tea?

Simon frowned, too, perplexed. Dinah's letters were brief and infrequent, – she was as inarticulate in writing as in speech, – and Gershon had no place in them. No place, Simon could have sworn, in her thoughts and feelings. But what, after all, did he know of her? She was an unaccountable girl. For instance, she never mentioned Frank Werrington. Yet in Frank's occasional notes there were references invariably to Dinah, that showed they must have met quite often.

Simon's disturbed mood prolonged itself into the Coliseum. Mark Elman had made the choice himself, in the end – variety, he decided, would suit him best to-night, and he could leave at a convenient time for Paddington. But he did not seem to enjoy his choice. He sighed and frowned and ejaculated without relevance to the efforts of the entertainers. The great hall heaved and glittered with the mobility of its massed audience, responsive or subdued at appropriate intervals. Were they two, Simon wondered, the only ones out of harmony with its spirit? He kept looking sideways at the other's gloomy face, speculating as to its cause and the chance of breaking in upon it with his own claim. Somehow or other he must get him to listen – and agree. In any case, it was time Mark Elman realised he had grown up, and stopped treating him like a petted boy.

"Let's go," said the senior, abruptly. It was too early. There were several numbers yet to run. But Simon rose without protest. It was not only that he, too, had no mind for the tricks of the stage. He was embarrassed by the other's restlessness, the glances thrown at them by quizzical neighbours. Uncle Mark, Simon noted with more than a touch of his old dislike, had become more "Jewish-looking" than ever. His lack of restraint might be due to overmastering stress, but it emphasised his noticeable aspect, and made Simon more uncomfortable than sympathetic. Whatever it might be that worried the man, why couldn't he "Behave", as his daughters had a significant way of insisting? The recollection made Simon ask, as they sat in a little refreshment place for a final coffee.

"How's Nettie?"

Elman jerked his body up as if he had been pricked.

"Nettie?" he said. "Oh, she's all right." There was a pause. Simon remembered that the last time Uncle Mark was up, he had hinted freely of a magnificent wedding in which Nettie was to figure. Simon was not curious enough to question further, and Elman began to talk rapidly of something else. It was at this moment that Simon decided to plunge. He began with a tentative—

"Uncle Mark – I ought to tell you—" when the other cut across with—

"Well, my boy, I suppose we'll have you in Dawport soon for good? This year will see you through, won't it? Of course I know you could go on for another two or three. But your

B.A.'s good enough for us. You needn't trouble about diplomas—"

"I'm not going to," said Simon, unexpectedly. "That's what I meant to tell you – I don't intend to go any further—"

"That's right. We're ready for you. Everybody's fed up with the old josser at home – he's going in any case after the next *Yomtovim*. Young blood's just what the shool wants – *English* blood! You can let your beard grow a little to please the old school – why, you're such a big fellow, you'd look thirty easy, with a little more hair!" He laughed his dry, hard cackle of a laugh.

"But look here, Uncle Mark – I hope you won't be very disappointed if I don't come, after all. There are plenty of other fellows at the College keen on a job—"

"You think they'd cut you out? They won't get the chance. You forget I'm president – and my new committee is the right stuff." For the first time that day Mark Elman smiled with his eyes as well as his lips. A year's battle of wits unrolled to a victorious end in the images behind that smile. "I'll tell you what. When you come home for Shevuoth you can preach the second day's sermon – l'll fix it up. That will give you a good start—"

"I won't be home for Shevuoth. I've got to study hard for an exam." Simon almost rose in his seat. He rushed to check the protest on Mark Elman's tongue. "Besides, it isn't likely that I shall ever preach a sermon. Uncle Mark – you know I've never liked the idea of being a minister. And it's never been looked upon as a certainty, has it? Anyway, I've changed my mind about the whole business."

"Oh, indeed? And what are you going to do?"

The tone set Simon's teeth on edge. He had found it

desperately hard to make his announcement – none the less because of his wish to be reasonable and conciliatory. Mark Elman was not the sort of man to burst out in a rage. But the goad of his sneering coolness was equally difficult to bear.

"I intend to apply for a post in the Civil Service. There are several good clerical vacancies in London this year."

"Well, I'm damned! And what about the money the family's spent on you?"

Simon flushed deeply. He had anticipated the question, but he was sensitive to implications beyond its uttered range.

"I hope to be able to return it all – in time."

"Bosh. None of us want it back. The old man, at any rate, will be satisfied that you've had a good Hebrew education. It's mainly *his* money, of course. Most likely he'll think it well-spent. I wonder!" Mark Elman leaned forward suddenly. " Is there anything else in it? – a *shiksa*, perhaps?"

The flames leaped higher in Simon's cheeks. "You've no right to speak to me like that, Uncle Mark—"

"No right! – no right!" Elman fell back, the scorn in his voice evaporated into his usual dryness. "Nobody has any right to say anything to youngsters these days. You'll go your own way, of course. But I hope to God you've got enough sense" – he stopped, rose abruptly, and pulled out his watch. "Have you written home? I don't know what your mother will say about this—"

"Oh, she'll worry a bit, I expect, but not for long," said Simon airily. "After all, she must have known that I could never go *her* way. And I'm sure father won't mind. He doesn't believe in Jewish ministers, anyway – not of *my* type. Why, he thinks that all the Hebrew I know is worth – what's the old saying? – a dump into the earth!"

Simon was so cheerful, now that he had cleared his mind, that he could even quote Yiddish. Elman looked grimly at him, then beckoned to a waitress beyond.

"Your father's a fanatic. He doesn't understand the modern world. But don't forget – he's got feelings to be hurt."

"I haven't written, because it's so difficult to make them realise anything in letters. I thought I'd wait till I went home, though of course I shan't be down for some time yet. Besides, I don't know that I'll succeed at once." Simon hesitated.

"No – and expenses will have to be paid just the same till you do. Oh, it's all right" – he smiled coolly at the flash in Simon's eyes— "I know you're willing to make it all good – later." He made an effort to keep his tone free of sarcasm. "Look here, Simon – you'd better consider it all carefully. To break away now may mean a lot of trouble. The authorities won't like it – it has a bad look. Too many of these cases, I believe. And the family won't like it. They'll make a fuss, too. The old man may not mind about the money, but he's looking forward to having you down there. So is your mother. After all, she *is* your mother – even if she's old-fashioned. And – mind you, it's a first-rate job that's waiting for you at Dawport – just the sort of thing I'd expect an English feller like you to be pleased with."

The waitress had arrived. Simon stood silent while the bill was paid. Mark Elman had brought out his wallet though he used only loose cash to pay the small account. As they moved away, he drew a crackling note from a pocket of the case and pressed it into Simon's hand.

"No – no" said Simon, pushing it back— "I can't take any more from you, Uncle Mark."

"Don't be an ass; I can give you a little present if I want to, can't I? Come along – it's time I got off."

He led the way rapidly out of the cafe, and they crossed the square into Piccadilly. At the entrance to the Tube Station he grasped Simon's hand.

"Good-bye. Think it well over. Try to come down for *Shevuoth* – if you don't want to preach this time you needn't – but your mother'll be disappointed if you aren't down. Isn't that your 'bus just stopping?"

Simon walked all the way home. He felt light with relief and a triple sense of achievement. He had thrown off his burden, he had struck boldly into the future, and he had got off very easily. It was true that Mark Elman was not excitable or rash: but he could be hostile and difficult to oppose. The mildness of his protest might indicate merely the shallowness of his concern: yet why had he been so unusually insistent on regard for the parents' feelings? Simon was puzzled. Uncle Mark had never shown consideration for Devora and Gedaliah Black – otherwise they might long ago have been settled in Dawport. Why this newborn respect? Simon was not, however, as surprised as he ought to have been, that in pointing out the family disappointment, he had omitted mention of his own. Simon's knowledge of Mark Elman's mind had always been meagre. It could not occur to him now that he was defeating a pet scheme of Uncle Mark's, on the basis of which he had been spending years of uncongenial study. Otherwise his sense of something strange in Elman's manner would have been far more acute.

The five-pound note in Simon's pocket crackled with a stronger reality. After all, why shouldn't he use it – now that he had spoken out, and there was no question of false pretence? He could do a lot with the sum. Buy books for Edith Miller – take her to a theatre – dine with her somewhere "in style" – the prospect made his light heart beat more gaily. But suddenly a heavier thought dropped down to weigh it. Did he owe nothing to his mother? It was long since he had been able to do anything for her. She was expecting him home for the coming Holy days. He saw her face – drawn, sallow, patient, its vigour beaten into static lines – tense with waiting for her distant son. Poor mother! He would have to disappoint her in the small as in the greater things. He jerked his shoulders in a guilt-born shrug. Irredeemably "old-fashioned", impossible and unreasonable in her expectations, it was inevitable that his manhood should resist and baffle her: but she was the more entitled to the gentler dues of affection. He paused to gaze at the bulb-lit windows that seldom drew him now. Bags – trinkets – silk adornments: luxury toys that rarely came his hard-lived mother's way. Yes. He would change his note on her behalf, and send her a gorgeous gift for Pentecost.

XI

SIMON woke in the morning with sharpened eagerness and zest. The vibration of the machines above seemed set to the hurry of his blood. The disordered living-room with its odours of fish and soup, the muttering of the old woman, the strident scufflings of the children off to school, galled less than usual in the prospect of release.

"As soon as I get my job, I'm off," thought Simon. He would find a room in the quiet of "gentility" – the word struck him suddenly as a delicious declension of "gentile" – and be rid for ever of this jargon world.

A score of times that day he looked at Mrs. Wyn's card, with its pencilled inscription in a corner—"4 to 6 p.m." At five minutes to four he was in the street, gazing up at the block of flats. Deliberately he mounted the steps and reached the first floor entrance. Before he had time to raise his hand to the bell, the door was opened, a smart young maid stood back on the threshold, and a stooping, awkward figure ambled out.

Simon stood staring.

"Hull – Billig," he said, in a thin small voice.

The other stared back in milder surprise.

"Oh, Black – it's you—" He nodded vaguely, and moved on. The door closed, Simon followed the maid in bewilderment. Billig, of all unexpected persons! What on earth was he doing here? There was no time to speculate. He was being announced at the drawing-room door, and a very large lady who had risen from a seat in the window came

forward to greet him. Mrs. Wyn, he guessed at once – her son
had the same high cheeks and forehead and deep, sand-
browed eyes. There was no sign of Edith. He glanced rapidly
round the long, bric-a-brac room, and met the bright stare of
a young woman in a blue hat and coat, standing in a somewhat
mannish pose against the back of a settee.

"Do you know Miss Newell?" Mrs. Wyn was saying.
"Please sit down. Edith will be here directly – she has been
rather late to-day—"

"It must be the new case in No. 9," said Miss Newell,
nodding a friendly head at Simon. "When I looked in at the
hospital yesterday and was told about it, I knew that Edith
would never tear herself away. Perhaps you have heard – no?
It's a little Welsh servant girl. Knocked down by a bus in
Euston Road."

Simon tried to concentrate his thoughts, and wondered for
a moment what he ought to say. "Was she hurt much?" he
asked at length.

"Spine," said Miss Newell. "Hector thought they'd
operate." She began to pull off her gloves. "The child came up
from Glamorgan only a week ago, and hasn't any friends in
London. So of course Edith's taken the greatest interest—talks
Welsh to her – and writes to her home." Miss Newell laughed
as if agreeably diverted.

"I didn't know Miss Miller could speak Welsh," said
Simon.

"Oh, just a little," said Mrs. Wyn, with an indulgent air, as
if to excuse an embarrassing accomplishment in her niece. "I
expect she picked it up from the servants—"

"But they were all English," said Simon unexpectedly.
"Lady Hafod brought them over from Devonshire – all except

the keeper – I mean—" he was going to correct hastily the childish term, when Mrs. Wyn interposed,

"So you know Hafod? How nice for Edith," – but the look she gave him was by no means cordial. He did not resent it. This big, stately woman, whose voice was rich with a Scottish accent, might well regard him coldly: she could not know that he agreed with her implicit disapproval of the Welsh connections. He saw at once that she was jealous of her niece's interest in that outlandish quarter, possibly unknown to her personal experience, and that her doubts extended to every friendship derived, as she supposed, from within its bounds. He tried to think how he could reassure her, but Miss Newell said—

"So you're another of Edith's Welsh friends. I meet a new one every time I come here. It's part of my training, I expect." She laughed, her white, prominent upper teeth bare to the gum. "Edith has taken me properly in hand you know. She wants me to go down to her place next year."

"On a visit?" said Simon politely. He did not want to pursue the topic. It was all very well discussing Blaemawe with Edith. But with others – there was no glamorous bond to nullify distaste.

"Oh, no," said Miss Newell, "on a job. I daresay my present case will last till then, and if nothing better turns up, I *may* go down."

"Miss Newell's a private nurse," explained Mrs. Wyn, "but don't let us talk shop, Marjorie," she added. "Do sit down. I want to show you my latest crucifix – it's the wee-est I've ever seen. Are you interested in ivory, Mr. Black?"

Simon had noticed a collection of small, yellowish objects, some on trays on the tables, and others in cases on the walls.

Most of them, he now perceived, were in the shape of crosses, with the figure of Christ delicately carved in suspension. He examined them silently at Mrs. Wyn's invitation, while she produced from a drawer her newest acquisition – a tiny gem-like piece of Eastern art. Miss Newell exclaimed in delight as she held it between her strong large fingers.

"It's perfectly ducky!" she said. "Where *did* you get it? Why, I'd just love to wear it – you know, on a thin gold chain!"

"Then I'll give it to you," said Mrs. Wyn, smiling.

"Oh, Mrs. Wyn! – But what about Edith? Perhaps *she'd* like it—"

"No, she wouldn't," said a low voice behind them. "She'd prefer to give you the thin gold chain to wear it on."

"Edith, dear!" Miss Newell stretched out her arms and kissed her friend, and a stream of pleasant laughter flowed through the room. Simon sailed on it into his enchanted land. He had not seen Edith enter from a curtained inner door, but some warning nerve had quivered in him before she spoke. He had dropped the crucifixes with a little crash into the tray, and turned, to watch her reach the others and break upon their talk. He did not know whether she had seen him first; he waited, stilly, for the look and handclasp that she gave him with her smile.

"Aunt Helena's been entertaining you, I see. Do *you* want to carry off her collection, too?"

"If there's anything Mr. Black specially fancies—" began Mrs. Wyn, sorting out the crosses with a loving hand.

"No, no," said Simon hastily. "I really couldn't impose on Mrs. Wyn's generosity—"

"Meaning I *do*?" said Miss Newell, with a hearty laugh.

"Well, I don't care. I always take all I can get – except snubs from the doctors."

"You're too good a nurse to get those," said Edith. "It's scandalous of you, Marjorie, to waste your time playing with old ladies."

"I'm well paid, darling. And I told you – I need a rest this year. By the way, I want you to come and see my old dear – she's really sweet."

Mrs. Wyn disappeared. For some minutes Simon was content to watch and listen to the two girls, both fair and with the same rapid, controlled voices, yet so dissimilar, as they sat together on the settee and talked of their "cases". Edith mentioned briefly the little Welsh girl who had been operated on that morning and was now sleeping peacefully. Miss Newell continued to chatter of her patient, the rich old lady, whose failing faculties needed only casual attention.

He liked Marjorie Newell and had felt instantly at ease with her. She was a simple country girl, the fifth daughter of a village doctor who had nine girls and one son. Marjorie had thought it a jolly, as well as a necessary thing, to turn out and earn her living at an early age. Her blunt laugh went with her mannish movements, her ruddy face, streaked already with the pattern of the out-door Englishwoman, had a fresh, wholesome look. Simon found her altogether admirable. None the less, or perhaps all the more, it pleased him to observe how she enhanced her friend's charm. Beside Edith's delicate bloom Marjorie looked almost coarse. The elder girl wore a blue suit of shiny silk, which matched her eyes, but took a garish note from her rope of yellow stones. Edith's soft navy dress, unadorned by bead or spot of colour, intensified the rich hue of hair and skin, full of a life that ran stilly deep beneath.

In her eyes glowed the same vital force, dimming Marjorie's colder blue as sunlight pales the candle ray. But Marjorie's tongue, at least, was the more animated as their dialogue went on.

"We've moved to Hampton Court. The house – our flat's the lower part – is near the Palace, and we sit about the gardens a lot. Can't you run down over the week-end, Edith? We're not allowed visitors in the house – young Mrs. Wilkins is rather fussy – but the old dear likes talking to people in the gardens. We don't go to church often – she gets restless and troublesome indoors. Why not come down about eleven on Sunday and meet us there for an hour?"

"I might manage it," said Edith. "I haven't been to Hampton Court for ages—"

"I haven't been at all," said Simon suddenly. "I've been meaning to go. May I come, too, on Sunday?"

Edith looked at him thoughtfully but did not speak. Her friend exclaimed:

"Why, of course – that would be nice. I don't suppose you go to church regularly, either!" She laughed and proceeded into details, describing the spot where the "old dear" liked best to sit. While she chattered, Simon and Edith gazed silently at each other, until the drawing-room door opened to admit other visitors. Tea was served, and Simon joined in the general small talk. The few students who drifted in and out, a youthful professor and his wife, another man and woman who came and left early, were all strangers who shared some interest with Edith, but did not press unduly – in Simon's view – upon her notice. The subconscious watch he kept in this direction sprang to alertness when Marjorie Newell, reaching for her gloves, said reluctantly,—

"Well, dear, I must go. I suppose there's no chance of seeing Hector to-day?"

"He may come yet," said Edith, glancing at a clock on the mantel. "He always drops in for tea if he can manage it. Still, it's rather late—"

"Yes, I'm afraid I can't wait."

Miss Newell rose slowly. She nodded to the Professor and his wife, who rose, too. They left before her. Mrs. Wyn appeared, and the two drifted together into the hall.

Simon, the only visitor left, did not move. There was no sign from Edith that she expected him to go, as she sat back easily, regarding him with the absent smile which he resented more than ever. Had she forgotten how he had held her eyes?

"We haven't had our talk yet," he said as soon as they were alone.

"Really?" She seemed to parry. "Haven't we been talking all the afternoon?"

"You know *we* haven't."

"I heard you tell Professor Watts your plans."

"It was *you* I told. You did not say anything. Were you interested? Did you approve?"

" Of course – as far as I can judge – I don't know all the circumstances. But – you've left it rather late, haven't you – you don't think you could do better?"

"I'm sure I can't."

"Then if you're sure, what does it matter – what I or anyone else may say?"

"It matters to me what you think."

He knew he was being audaciously insistent – that some impulse urged him to it, though his mind said, "Don't be a fool. She's miles above you – she knows all sorts of successful men – why should she bother her head about you? She'll give you the cold shoulder for impertinence or else laugh at you."

She did neither. She sat still, looking away from him, colour deepening in her cheeks. He did not notice a figure bulk large in the doorway, but heard Mrs. Wyn's voice call from without.

"Here's Hector. I'll see about some fresh tea."

Simon swung round to see Doctor Wyn walk in and fling himself down in a chair. He nodded to Simon in the half-familiar, half-distant manner that characterised his greetings of students.

"Seen you before, haven't I, at U.C.?" he said, in response to Edith's murmur. "Edith, I'm expiring for your tea. I could have had some – but I refused – it's yours I want—"

"Aunt Helena's, you mean," she said. " She always makes it herself for you."

"But *you* pour it out."

The words were said lightly, but Simon, straining for significance, felt himself start. He watched the looks between them. Was it his fancy – did Hector Wyn gaze humbly, appealingly, at his cousin – did she return some mute petition with conscious, half-reproachful eyes? The blood rushed singing into Simon's ears.

"I'm an ass," he thought. "There isn't anything. They're just cousins, fooling."

Mrs. Wyn brought the teapot on a tray with her own hands. But she gave it to Edith to pour, and stood by with a smile on her large, placid face as Hector took the cup and drank eagerly.

"She likes it," flashed through Simon's mind. "She likes them to be domestic together."

Torment came of these heightened perceptions, that might as easily be the fruit of illusion as of heightened feelings. He tried to pull himself together as he answered some remarks of Mrs. Wyn's, and listened to the doctor's account of the little Welsh patient.

"Still sleeping well"—"You're in charge to-night, Edith"—"I'll come into the ward at twelve and stay an hour or two"—"You'd better rest well first" – A glance followed this at Simon. He could not ignore it.

It wasn't six yet – he could still stay on. But what was the use? Only more torment would come, if not of seeing, of hearing things that brought fresh images to the inner sight. Alone together in the ward for hours! ... He jumped up to take his leave. Mrs. Wyn – who seemed won in her fishlike way – detained him with a photograph of her home in Scotland. Under cover of it he heard a quick exchange of whispered words – (how extraordinarily acute his hearing had become!)

"You saw Polasky?"

"No. I refused to see him. It isn't any use."

"But I promised him you'd see him—"

"What! He came to worry you? The swine!"

"I'm afraid he is – rather. But it's no reason for – you know what they say."

"I don't care. It's nothing to do with me. I wish you'd take my word, Edith."

"I wish – I could." She turned her face. Simon saw those soft eyes gleam with a hard light. But the glance gave him as he approached to take her hand was different. Surely it was a gracious warmth they shed on him? Surely she did not approve her cousin, with his damnable air of superiority? Simon writhed beneath the doctor's patronising nods. Clear as speech the manner said— "Ah, you're only a boy—I don't take you seriously." He ought to have heard Professor Watts that afternoon. "Only twenty-one? I should have taken you for twenty-five, at least." The doctor himself could not be more than twenty-six for all his size, his cocksureness – his position and success. Simon reared his head with adult assurance. He'd show them soon how easily he could get into a man's stride. No more studentship. In a few months he would be in a job, earning his living independently of old associations, clear off the Jewish trail, making his way as an Englishman, with an unambiguous position to – to offer an English girl! God, he would do it! His brain worked high and clear as he stood holding Edith's hand, nodding back curtly to the doctor sprawled in the easy-chair, and saying quietly in his firmest, most manly tones—

"Then it will be all right about Sunday, Miss Miller. Shall I call for you – about ten?"

She hesitated, and murmured— "Oh – I'll let you know—"

Mrs. Wyn's large face smiled blandly at him, the smart maid showed him out with a frank stare of admiration. On the steps outside he remembered suddenly his encounter with Myer Billig. What had the Orphan been doing at the Wyns? Nobody had mentioned him. Nobody had appeared to have seen him. Had he actually been leaving the flat, or merely making some chance enquiry of the maid – perhaps a mistake had led him to the wrong hall door? The mystery could be solved by asking Billig himself. But when they next met, Simon, by some inexplicable reluctance, shirked putting the simple question. Billig seemed to look at him with speculation in his mild, far-away eyes. But he too, said nothing of their meeting at that door.

XII

NO MESSAGE came about the trip to Hampton Court. On
Sunday morning Simon could hardly eat his breakfast. Should
he call at the flat – the hospital – or look in again at University
College? He went to the College first and found a note –
handed in, the porter said, an hour earlier.

"DEAR MR. BLACK,
"I am sorry not to have written sooner, but we have only just
fixed up about Hampton Court. My cousin decided to come,
also, and is taking me down in his runabout direct from
hospital. I suppose you will meet us there – near the seat
facing the Long Canal, as Miss Newell suggested?
    How nice to be seeing Hampton Court for the first time!
                                            "Yours sincerely,
                                            "EDITH MILLER."

Was that last sentence a spontaneous reflection, or a carefully
calculated dose of syrup, administered to soothe the smart of
unwelcome news? She must have guessed that he would
regard Hector as a spoil-party. How on earth did the fellow
come to be included? Surely it was not Edith who had asked
him – Marjorie Newell might have done so, had she had an
opportunity; but he must have insisted on it himself— "my
cousin decided" – Why? Perhaps he was taking him – Simon
– seriously, after all! Simon's spirits rose in spite of his
vexation. He marched westwards, and jumped on a river-

bound bus with recovered zest. It was disappointing not to have this long ride, together – and it was not agreeable to think of Edith and Hector in the "runabout". But the top of a bus in breeze-tempered sunshine was a joyous place, conducive to exhilarating reinstatement of oneself as a significant person, suspected as a rival by the important Doctor Wyn. And to be near Edith in any circumstances was the most alluring prospect in the world. Besides— "– how nice to be seeing Hampton Court for the first time!"

Simon had not been able to imagine *how nice*, until he arrived and took his first wide glance at the grounds. Country-bred as he was, he had never seen a richer green, a more lavish ardour of nature expended in bloom and tree. A curbed and regulated ardour, lavish as it was, he soon perceived. Man's hand had trimmed for centuries these gifts of earth. But the sense of age did not yet take hold of Simon, even when he passed through the courts to the Broad Walk and looked at the facades of the palace. His hasty eyes turned forward to search more eagerly for one living atom on this storied soil. Not many people distracted his view of the great Basin and the canal beyond. Was that her figure, standing beside the tall man who stooped to peer at the lilies in the pool? She, it was clear, did not share her companion's interest: her head turned this way and that, as if seeking focus on the walks. Simon thrilled. She must be looking for him. He waved a hand and to his delight, she raised hers in response. He raced past the stiff patterned yews, observing that she did not move to speak to her cousin. Dr. Wyn, looking round at the sound of footsteps, stood up in greeting, unaware of smiles already exchanged.

"Morning, Black. So you found your way all right? I understand it's your first visit?"

Confound the fellow! He could not open his lips, apparently, without patronising. The manner, more than the words, rubbed Simon sorely. But he would not show it while Edith wore that air of welcome for him.

"Yes. It looks very jolly. I expect it's worth seeing more than once."

"The gardens are all right – fine place for an airing. Don't know about the Museum. We've had enough of it, haven't we, Edith?"

"Is Miss Newell here?" said Simon quickly.

"Oh, yes," said Edith, indicating a hunched group a little distant. "We got here early and spent a half-hour chatting with Marjorie and her old dear. But she's having a nap – Mrs. Wilkins, I mean – and we thought our talking would disturb her. Shall we walk round the grounds? Or perhaps you would like to see the Palace first? – The outer parts, of course – you'll see the State Rooms later—"

"My dear Edith," said her cousin, "you surely don't mean to do the round again? – I can't allow you to walk yourself off your feet to-day—"

"Really, I'm not so feeble—" said Edith, but to Simon's dismay, her tone was yielding and half-hearted. Where was her assured, independent self? She avoided Simon's imploring glance.

"You're here for an hour's rest," said Dr. Wyn decisively. "I'm sure Mr. Black won't mind." – he looked at Simon and hurried on— "Not that I wish to deprive him of a guide! It's jollier going over the show with a companion. I suggest we relieve Marjorie and look after the old girl, while she puts Black through it. A good turn to Marjorie, hey, Edith? And a good turn to you, Black. Marjorie's a first rate guide."

"Of course – if Miss Newell agrees," said Simon. His resentment choked itself in silence as they turned back to where Marjorie Newell sat, guarding a crumpled object in a large bath-chair. She grimaced at them across its hood, and got up, moving stealthily towards them on the grass. For all his gloom, Simon's mouth twitched in amusement at the queer figure she cut, her gawky limbs jerking up her hips, her long toes spread almost visibly, like her fingers, as she lifted them in wide, silent motion. She made him think of some animal he had seen at the Zoo, but his heart warmed towards her genial gaze.

"Hello," she whispered, as they paused some yards away. "So glad you've come, Mr. Black. It's a gorgeous morning. But we mustn't wake my old dear. She sleeps more soundly out of doors than in, but she's difficult if she wakes too suddenly. Says queer things – in fact, she might be rude!" – Marjorie grinned cheerily, but when Dr. Wyn proposed his plan, she gave him an odd glance, and protested.

"Oh, no, I couldn't think of it! – Can't leave my duty for a moment, even under doctor's orders! – But if you're so kind as to consider me, Hector, – why not stay with me here? I'd like you to note the symptoms when the patient wakes. Your opinion might be useful. Edith's not on night duty, is she? – Very well, it won't take her long to show Mr. Black the beauty spots. Besides, if she's tired, there are seats. So get along, Edith darling, before the crowd comes, and there'll still be time for a chat before lunch—"

It was Dr. Wyn's turn to be discomfited, and he showed it more than Simon had done. But it was awkward to argue the matter, especially in whispers – and Edith had already joined Simon as he was backing away. She walked on quickly, and

Simon, who had kept his face towards Marjorie, returning her friendly beams, had to swing round and increase his pace to match hers.

"Miss Newell's a sport," he said delightedly, but Edith did not answer. He saw she had a wavering, uncertain look, as if aware of drifting. It struck him as a mood unusual in her, but he was too happy to question it – besides, she must have found it pleasant, for she began soon to flow with careless talk. Her ease to-day had a light, childlike quality, that made her sweeter and nearer than her normal sure self. It made her younger, too. She seemed even less than her nineteen years. In – and sometimes out of – her uniform, with her aloofness of manner, she was apt to appear older. Simon lost a little of the awe imposed by that manner upon his adoration.

"By jove, this is ripping," he said. They had crossed a little bridge and stood, just inside the gates, looking down the vista of limes in the wide Home Park. A couple of deer bounded to the water's edge. "It's a shame to rush over it." They turned back reluctantly, but it was a joy to tread the lawns. "I wish we had lots more time. I wish you could stay on to explore the Rooms with me." She shook her head with gentle regret. "Well, you must come down with me another time – just we two."

She pointed a little ahead.

"We go down there," she said, "to the King's Privy Garden."

Simon looked vaguely at the William and Mary building, at the sundial where Edith paused, and followed her through the shady Bower. As they emerged upon the river he listened to her account of the houseboat taken by Lady Hafod a couple of seasons ago; then interrupted, as if nothing had broken upon his previous remark:

"Yes, – you must come down with me again, on one of your free afternoons. We can ramble around for hours. And perhaps go on the river." They looked down at its shining flow. "You *will* come – won't you?"

"But how can we find time?" she said, turning again. "Next week-end I shall spend with Lady Hafod – and my other week-ends are full for a month. I shan't have any 'afternoons' between, I fear. And in a few months I'll be finished – and at Blaemawe."

"Oh," he said in dismay. Queen Mary's Bower was full of shadows. "But I must see you, all the same. Please let me write and fix things up from time to time. You know – l'm finishing up too – at college. When I'm in my job, I'll have free week-ends. I can meet you anywhere. Even at Blaemawe," he added, daringly.

She laughed.

"A long way from Hampton Court. Now I suppose you'd like to see the Great Vine? Of course it's early for the grapes."

Afterwards he remembered that she had made no direct reply to his suggestions. He continued urging her to promise information of her whereabouts.

"I'll let you have my new address soon," he declared. "I'm looking out for decent digs. There's a place at Kensington. I'm going to see to-night."

"You're very sure – of your job," she said.

"I am. I mean to get it. Of course, it isn't anything great. But it happens to be the best possible starting point. If I go on as I expect—" he hesitated a moment, but catching her eye, went on gaily, sketching out his plan for the next five years.

"You'll be able to help your parents quite soon," she said. "Oh!" Simon started slightly, and coloured, "they don't need my help. Things are better with them – business prospects have improved. I hear they mean to settle in Dawport."

"Have you brothers?"

"No. Two sisters." They were descending the few steps to the lower path. A group of women, one very stout, advanced upwards without waiting. Edith moved aside quickly, and stumbled. Simon caught her arm, retaining it as they proceeded. For some moments she let it rest, her hand in his, then disengaged it as they paused, to peep through the carefully-gapped hedge of Henry VIII's garden.

" How do you like this?" she asked.

Simon's eyes cleared from a glaze; then widened over the private retreat. "How lovely!" he said. "It's just the sort of garden I'd like to have in my own home. Wouldn't you?"

"It's the sort of garden my grandmother has, at Millicombe," she said. "The grounds are larger than at Hafod – but mostly wild and overgrown, on a cliff sloping to the sea. The only flat bit, near to the house, is laid out in this charming, old-world way. Low grass terraces leading to a pond, crazy paving walks, quaint fountains and cupids. There's a sundial, too. And all the sweet smelling herbs and dear old flowers – tall phlox and iris and marguerite and hollyhock, Canterbury bells, snap dragon. Such a delicious spot. I love it."

Her voice held a yearning note that he had never heard before. He tried to picture the Devonshire home. And suddenly his new cheer, his confidence, melted away. Millicombe was Lady Hafod's personal estate – and undoubtedly it would belong to this loved grandchild – the only relic of her dead daughter. Edith Miller might seem a humble nurse, a girl of simple tastes and unpretentious aims. None the less, she was Lady Hafod's heiress.

"Of course," he said slowly. "It *is* your home – or will be one day – your own—"

"No, no," she said. And now her voice was changed – harder – the older-voiced Edith spoke. "Not unless I choose. And I never will."

She left the hedge and he followed her. He did not know what she meant, nor did he care. The fact of her position as compared with the most glowing of his prospects absorbed his mood. Together they inspected the Great Vine, and into Simon's dashed spirit there leaked a savour of ancient times. "Planted in 1768," he read aloud. "A respectable age, I suppose, for a slip."

"One hundred and fifty years," said Edith, gazing up at the roof of hanging grapes, small as yet and then down at the gnarled snake of trunk where it rose stockily from the rich dark earth. "Our vine at Millicombe is quite as large, and much older."

"You come of old stock," said Simon.

"Oh, yes," she said. A little smile hovered on her lips, and she moved absently through the turnstile. "Very old, – much, much older than anything here!" She waved her hand. They stood in the open, and her gesture swept the Palace range. "Wolsey began this place at the beginning of the sixteenth century. What, after all, is that compared with—" she checked herself. "You will think I am boasting."

"I think you have every right," said Simon. "It must be wonderful – to know one comes direct of an ancient line, rooted in an unbroken past – with all the old traditions of race and family honourably centred in oneself. It must give one a solid feeling."

"Thank you for the honourably," she laughed. " As you say, it *does* give one a solid feeling – and a sense of responsibility."

"Of course."

" But the heirs of tradition do not necessarily accept it. My cousin, for instance, thinks it's all bosh!"

Simon leaped at the tinge of censure.

"I should have thought he was a true-blue Tory," he said, as cautiously as he could. "Most doctors seem to be, and Dr. Wyn has the look, somehow, of the typical English – or is it Scotch? – Conservative."

"He'd be pleased to hear you say so! It's exactly what he believes himself to be – a typical English Conservative!" There was an odd sound in her laughter.

"Yet he hasn't any respect for this sort of thing," Simon went on, indicating in his turn the historic pile on their left.

"Oh yes, he has – lots. You mustn't misunderstand him there. He *does* respect it – only, perhaps, he hasn't quite the feeling for it that you have. I mean that strong sense of continuity – of belonging and sharing and carrying on—"

Simon was delighted.

"Yes, that is what I feel – you see you do know me."

"That may sound a contradiction – about Hector," she said. "But I don't mean it to be. Hector is really—"

"It doesn't matter about Hector," said Simon boldly.

"Of course – I ought not to discuss my cousin—"

"Pardon me, that isn't the point. What matters is that you understand me – you remember you said you didn't really know me; but you do—"

"I said also that you didn't know me," she murmured, turning her head. They had paused in front of the locked gate of the Pond Garden.

"I think I do," he said. "Give me the chance to know more."

"Look," she said, " there is someone in the garden." Simon

diverted his glance reluctantly, but was struck by the picture within. At the end of the path stood a lady, one hand among the stems of a high, thick plant, the other holding a basket. She seemed in her dark long bunchy dress and outmoded hat, with her dignified aloofness of bearing, a veritable figure of the past. So might one of the ladies of Henry's household have stood, gathering blooms for Anne Boleyn's chamber, or herbs for a posset – perhaps a savoury for Wolsey's trenchermen, to be prepared in the cool stone Tudor kitchens just beyond. So, too, might Edith's ancestress have picked her needs, in that other old-world garden in Devonshire, as long – no, even longer – ago. Simon drew in wafts of the fragrant English scents – thyme, honeysuckle, lavender and moved on – silently. As they wandered past the sundial down the glades, where statuary shone whitely among shrub and bush, he was intoxicated with the scents and visions, and that English rose who embodied them at his side. Near the entrance to the courts he quickened pace, avoided glancing down the central walk to the Basin, and hurried through the gateway into the dim stone corridors. Edith seemed to fall in with his whim. Or was it that she felt the potency of place so much, that she forgot the claims of friend and cousin, waiting in impatience just beyond? These ancient walls and floors beat back impassively the tide of modern life that surged upon them. Each individual, even in the motley crowds that came and went, must yield, must leave behind all fret and strain, and let this cool peace wrap and lull the spirit. Not that Edith could submit without a struggle. She might forget the urgent life outside; she could not but remember, it seemed, the ill that had once existed here, when in the shell of quiet beauty throbbed a fresh, active core.

"Yes – it's lovely" – she answered Simon's enthusiasm in

the Fountain Court. "And there are more ghosts inside than out. Unhappy ones, too. I see their wretched faces at the windows. You know the record of murder here. Every stone could tell of some cruelty or wrong. Monuments to pomp and greed and tyranny. Why, from Henry to the Georges—"

"Please!" said Simon, in mock petition. "Don't remind me of the crimes of Royalty. I'm feeling terribly 'true-blue' just now, and won't listen to treason—"

"Royalty was victim as well as criminal. But I won't harrow you. Revel in loyalties to your heart's content."

"It's not so much loyalty to the Crown," objected Simon, "as to the historic past."

"A vague sentimentality unless you're aware of the evil in it. One must accept everything – in the lump – and yet be able to discriminate."

"But when I discriminate, you drag in what I prefer to leave out!"

"Discrimination isn't just the liberty to choose and reject. Besides, your sort of choosing – the 'true-blue' sort – makes the 'red' come along and reject the lot. It would be madness to blow all this up because one got infuriated with the evil it recalls. But isn't it foolish to see nothing here but the conventional glory of kings?"

"I accept the lump," said Simon laughing. "In fact, I accept everything English, good and bad—"

"Just because it's English?" She looked at him intently, not smiling.

"Of course," said Simon. He threw back his head, with a conscious flourish. He had never felt so boastful, so triumphant. Confidence had come back with a rush established by the quick growth of harmony between them.

Her rallying tones assumed familiar rights – in each other – and in the place whereon they stood. She, of course, belonged to this atmosphere, grew of it, shed it; he, too, would belong to it, and to her. "Of course," he said. The utterance was like a proclamation.

Edith continued to look at him gravely. Then she said in her quietest notes— "Yes. There's a good deal to be proud of."

The quietude, the slight air of detachment, almost disconcerted him. But the next moment she resumed her pose of careless inspection.

"Let's go on," she said. "Let's bow to the charm of antiquity – and the continuity of the errors of man. Come and see, for instance, how Wren, for all this beauty here, could spoil an earlier perfection."

They left the fountain to its cloistered dignity, and entered the Clock Court. Simon walked round and round the hoary walls, with their great buttresses and magnificent windows, and stood, like others who wandered about, staring up at Wolsey's arms on the tower arch. Wren's colonnade might blur but could not wholly hide the lovely lines of oriel and turret in this triumph of Tudor brick. When he could tear himself away, he fell into another trance, passing the outer green to the old moat bridge. But Edith would not let him linger. She led him, more and more enchanted, through some of the private residential courtways: nooks of still, dark beauty, garbed in mullioned windows, deep red arches, and cobbled walks. It seemed ludicrous that men and women in modern dress should approach these doors, turn little keys beside neat brass plates, and slam their way within.

"You prefer the ghosts, don't you?" said Edith. "How much you've fallen in love with the past!"

"I understand it so much better. It's more real."

"But don't let it make the present unreal – that's a perversion! After all, the past serves mainly to illuminate the present. I hope you won't think that a mere platitude. Understanding the present in the light of the past has made a great difference to me." She hesitated, and finished quickly,— "Of course, all our lives are affected by what has gone before – only we are not always conscious of it—"

"No – and I've just become fully conscious. England to-day must mean more to me than ever, because the past has become more vivid. That isn't a platitude, either – but I'm afraid it sounds like ranting – at any rate, the sort of thing one may feel, but not talk about."

"That's supposed to be English, certainly." She smiled.

"But you know, I can tell you things so easily – even things I hadn't thought of in any clear way – they get clear when I'm with you." His voice was an eager burr.

They had been speaking very softly – it was impossible to raise one's tones in this haunt of silent age. "I'd like to tell you how much it means to me to enter the Civil Service. You see, I always wanted it, not as a career, but because it would identify my life completely with my country. I wanted to serve England and feel myself part of her. Things around were so – different." He stopped. After all, it was not easy to explain why his ambition had been a forced early growth, rather than a spontaneous flowering.

"You mean the Welsh life? Of course, not being Welsh, you wouldn't care to identify yourself with *that*—"

"Good Heavens, no! You couldn't expect it, surely?"

"No. It wouldn't be natural. Though I've noticed that the Welsh themselves don't care to, either—"

"*That's* natural enough."

"Oh no, it isn't. How can you say so? With all your feeling about history! It's natural that Welshmen should be conscious of their own, and wish to preserve it. I was wrong in saying that about the Welsh just now. Many of them are traitors, of course. But not all."

" Traitors!" Simon was a little put out at the diversion, but he was faintly amused. Besides, she looked so lovely, in her sudden earnestness, her energised erection of head and shoulders. "Yes – to their past. You know as well as I do that their records go further back than this—"

"To savagery," said Simon.

"That isn't fair. Their language – their traditional laws, music, literature – their fight for independence, and their courage – spiritual as well as physical – are all of the greatest civilised interest. And you forget the Tudors had Welsh blood in them."

"I hope *you* haven't any," he said.

"If I had I shouldn't disown it," she said. "I have nothing but admiration for the Welshmen who maintain their nationality."

"Do you know any?"

"Of course. There are some in Blaemawe. You must know one, at least – a fine old man – Meurig Lloyd."

"Lloyd Patagonia," said Simon. She smiled now, but this time he failed to respond. Jani came before his eyes – a winsome Jani, but incredibly shadowy, and remote. He had not heard from her since he had written to discourage her plan, announced in the "crossed" letter, of getting a post in London. Some rigmarole of a friend of Miss Meredith's, already established in a Kensington shop, where there was a vacancy. Since Miss Meredith could not leave her aged mother, Jani thought it a splendid opportunity for herself – to escape her uncle's " tyranny", and be near her friend Simon! But Simon, instead of welcoming the plan, had disparaged it, and advised her to wait while he made enquiries. He had made none. It did not even trouble him. Jani's misty outline sank in Edith's turned cheek.

"I'm afraid," she said, "I can't stay longer" – her hand brushed her forehead lightly.

"Oh, you're tired," he exclaimed, suddenly conscience-stricken. "Why, you haven't sat down at all! Let's find a seat now—"

"No, no," she said, as they hurried into the open. "I'm not tired. But I must get back."

Again they passed, more quickly, through the courts, which had filled with sightseers.

"I'll stay on for an hour or two," said Simon. "I suppose I can get some lunch on the grounds. Then I'll go through the Rooms—" He added— "It won't be the same—without you."

"You'll have more than enough company. The afternoons are crowded. But you must see it all. There are the kitchens below, the wine cellars, and Henry's Tennis Court, as well as the State Rooms – and of course, the Great Hall, where Shakespeare and his company performed. You'll see the old tapestries that Wolsey hung—"

"You will come again – and see them with me?"

"Yes – one day. I've enjoyed it as much as if it were *my* first time – perhaps because I've seen it with your eyes – in your way—"

"Different, you think, from yours?"

She did not answer. They had emerged once more upon the Broad Walk.

"Oh, they're looking for us," she said quickly.

Dr. Wyn was standing up near the Basin. He advanced to meet them.

"Time's up, Edith," he said. "We shall just manage lunch. I hope you're not too fagged."

"Not at all. We haven't been long, have we?"

"Marjorie thinks you have."

"It's not like Marjorie to be impatient."

"She knows it's him," thought Simon, in ungrammatical resentment. He was indifferent to the doctor's public lack of concern in himself.

"Surely Mrs. Wilkins isn't still asleep!" exclaimed Edith, as they neared the crumple in the chair.

"She is," said Miss Newell in her ordinary high-pitched tones. "It's very unusual. Expect I'll have to wake her now! – Did you enjoy it, Mr. Black?"

"Very much. It's jollier than I expected. And Miss Miller is a splendid guide—"

"Did she show you the Privy Garden? – Yes? – And the Orangery – and the Wilderness – and the Tilt Yard—"

"Oh no – I don't think so!"

"Really! Then I don't think much of the guide! – But of course you haven't had much time – I expect you hurried, rather. Well, we have to get home, anyway. But you'll stay on and see the rest, I suppose?"

"Yes, I intend to do the lot after lunch. Let me help you with the chair, Miss Newell."

Marjorie had risen and was manipulating the vehicle.

"Thank you. That's all right. I just meant to shake her up a little."

"I beg your pardon." Simon withdrew his hand suddenly. It

had touched the crumple under the hood and the crumple had stirred and shaken off a fold of covering. The face of a pink old lady was revealed, white-haired and wrinkled, but with small grey eyes, like those of a startled child.

"Nurse, nurse," she called, in a shrill, urgent voice.

"I'm here, Mrs. Wilkins. You've had such a nice sleep, and now we're just—"

The shrill voice cut across.

"Nurse! There are Jews here – nasty, horrid Jews! Send them away at once!"

Simon started violently. He did not look at the others – at Edith and her cousin, who had been speaking to her in undertones, now silenced by the outcry.

Miss Newell was laughing gently, after a significant interchange of nods and glances.

"Oh no, dear Mrs. Wilkins – there are only the friends here who came to see us. You remember? – Miss Miller, you know, and Dr. Wyn. And another friend, Mr. Black, who came along later. Do shake hands with him, and wish him good morning before we go."

The old lady sat up and looked doubtfully around. The cajoling, reassuring nurse patted her shoulders and invited the others to come nearer. The old lady peered into their faces.

"Good morning," she said obediently. "It's kind of you to call."

"We're in the gardens, Mrs. Wilkins," said Marjorie, and pointed to the grass and trees.

"Ah," said the old lady. She nodded, then gazed back at the faces around. The scared note came trembling in her pipe. "Did you see them?" she asked. "Did you see the Jews? I'm sure they were here—"

"Oh no," began Marjorie quickly, but Dr. Wyn's hand motioned her to silence. The frown that had gathered on his brow relaxed to a smile of professional courtesy. "They might have been," he said. "Of course there are many people in the gardens now. But they wouldn't harm you, you know."

"Yes, yes. They're wicked. I don't like them. And I won't have them near me. I should like to go home, please."

"Yes, dear, of course. We're just going. It's lunch time." Simon observed, this time, the exchange of looks, patently concerned with the old lady's mental state. The heat ran out of his face, and he ventured to shake the skinny, quivering hand outstretched from the chair. A sudden strong vibration shook Mrs. Wilkin's frame. It made Simon start again and move back guiltily. He was disconcerted to find Doctor Wyn's eyes fixed on him, with a peculiar searching expression difficult to fathom. It was a relief when the doctor turned abruptly away.

"We must get off at once, Edith," he said. "Good-bye, Marjorie. Call in whenever you're in town."

Edith released herself from the chat of the old lady, who had become mild and voluble.

"Oh yes, I love the gardens. They are really my second home. I must have flowers and leaves around me everywhere. My son's flat is very nice, but there is no garden to speak of, is there, nurse? It's awkward to get into. And my daughter-in-law dislikes plants in rooms. It is so sweet of you to come and see me, my dear. I like young, happy faces. Please come again."

The babble did not seem to end; but they had gone. Hector Wyn had taken Edith's arm and whisked her off, with scarcely another glance at Simon. The movement cut her smile of farewell at its root. Simon watched the swift departure without too keen regret. The lawns faded in light and colour when Edith's figure vanished; but he still felt bathed in the glow of their walk together. Nothing that happened could chill that warmth. And something strange had happened. This wretched old creature who had disturbed the spheres with her outburst, now apparently forgotten – what blind instinct had moved her to his hurt? It was not possible that the others could have sensed its direction. He was over-conscious, he told himself, as he pushed the chair towards the gates. Under cover of the traffic outside, where they waited for the policeman's signal, Marjorie whispered suddenly— "Did you think the old dear very odd? She never knows where she is on waking. It's usually some scare she's had that comes to her mind. I remember now – she told me once that she didn't know any Jews – hadn't met any, to her knowledge – but as a child she'd heard they had horns on their heads and crept about spitting in people's faces. The silly dear believed it – and it looks as if she still does – when she isn't quite awake!"

Simon laughed, rather wryly, with Marjorie, whose peal was safely lost in the din of a Ford engine. The signal to advance had been given, and he was not sorry there was no chance to reply. The old lady left him with polite regret that he could not join them for lunch. When the chair had disappeared he could not help cursing the "damned old fool", for having, so inopportunely, seen her bogy in him. But when he had returned through the Lion Gates, he was ashamed of his spleen, and could laugh again, more wholesomely than even Marjorie had done. What did it matter, after all? A revelation was inevitable – though he foresaw no accident that could make it so, before he had finally cast his Jewish skin. Edith was bound to learn the facts when she got to Blaemawe. But he must take care to tell her in his own way before she went. He could imagine what Doctor Wyn would say! But that made no difference. It was Edith's view that mattered: and he felt sure of her generous sympathies. If she had a kindly word for the Welsh, she would find something charitable to say of the despised Jew. At least she would understand his need of self-assertion and independence. He pictured her deep eyes turned on his, with that direct, vivid vision that almost drowned him when it came. Once or twice to-day he had met it, when the childlike ease set into gravity, and the drifting look vanished. Bewildering – variable – she could be, but with something rocklike always under the wash of her moods. He could trust her to appreciate his difficulties.

He lunched in the open cafe in the grounds, and then made his way back to the Palace. A crowd had gathered near the entrance to the State Apartments. He followed the queue up the wide stone stairs, and through the great chambers, rich with paintings, panels, tapestries, decorated ceilings and mantels, and relics of more domestic furniture. These, more than the audience rooms, turned his mind back to the dead kings and queens, who had lived with and made daily use of them. Edith was not there to comment on the styles, to illuminate the dull wood and marble: but in losing touch with Edith's personality, he could sink himself more wholly in those Persons of the past. In these rooms They had nursed their intimate selves; warmed themselves at these hearths, stood beside these windows, slept in the damask beds beneath the gorgeous canopies, still held aloft by tall, sturdy posts. The crowds shuffled and pushed as he tried to keep his place, at the foot of Caroline's couch.

"Say, Sadie! How'd you like to stretch on that moth-eaten sofa?"

"Guess I'd prefer a plank at Sing-Sing. But I'd sure like to cart it away home, and fix up a Royal Majesty guest-room!"

In the stream that carried him through the doorway of the chamber, Simon saw the faces of Americans and Continentals. He listened to their voices chattering – appraising – comparing.

"Ach!" said a German. "Aber Potsdam ist viel schöner!"

"Ver' nice – ver' nice," said a French lady to her companion, as they looked through the windows at the long view. "But vait till you see Versailles – mon dieu!"

"Foreigners," thought Simon. A heady complacency filled him as he descended the stone stairs. It could not be expressed in language – at least, it was not in his power to formulate the phrase. But the simplest words might have conveyed its meaning. Such words as— "I'm English. All this English stuff belongs to me. I understand it – I'm at home in it – I love it. These foreigners don't. It's finer than anything they have – and they can't see it! *My* country – *my* past – *my* Kings and Queens – England – mine!"

XIII

"MOTHER thanks you for the lovely present," wrote Dinah, "but she would have liked it better if you had come home. She is awfully disappointed. We were all going to Dawport shool, but now we shall spend *Shevuoth* at home. Are you preaching anywhere? Mother wants to know which shool you are going to, so don't fail to write and tell us."

Dinah's literal messages from "Mother" were always the same—direct and embarrassing. "Which shool?" Simon would be obliged to attend service somewhere, if only to answer the inevadable question. He had meant to ignore this festival, to continue his policy of shirking religious duties, especially the performance of public rites. His abstentions had already become marked. Questions were being asked at college, awkward comments made – far more awkward in effect than any his mother might aim through the post. But this fire was drawn deliberately, and he was prepared to meet it, knowing it could last for only a short if furious time. His escape was certain, and official censure must leave him totally unscathed. His mother's peace, however, he did not wish to disturb, until it was no longer possible to help it. Her eyes followed him everywhere, – as he knew they were following the postman at Blaemawe – waiting for the answer to the casual inquiry she had made, in her far from casual spirit. Simon could tell a lie if pressed to it – indeed, he alternated defiance with a good deal of prevarication – but it did not occur to him to invent a reply to his mother. It seemed easier to attend synagogue and present her with the fact.

Yet, going on the last day, he had to make a special effort. Why on earth had he put it off till then, he thought fractiously, hugging under his arm his paper-wrapped velvet bag – the old *Barmitzvah* present, badly frayed – as he strode along Portland Street. After all, he could have gone on the previous morning with less trouble – certainly with less parrying of vexatious inquiries. But the necessity of work for his exam. had kept him at his books; he needed every moment for study before Friday, when the first sitting was due. It was always important to "swot" on the eve of an exam. The present urgency was greater than any. Frank Werrington had failed to secure his job a few weeks earlier, and the news had given Simon a spur of unusual anxiety. It was true that the circumstances differed as much as their abilities. But so much depended on Friday for Simon! Frank had not seemed to worry: they had met before and after the event. But added to his natural phlegm, was Frank's reliance on his father to "fix him up in something, anyway," and his satisfaction in the return to the old Berkshire home. He had grinned at Simon's concern, and invited him down to the farm for the week-end. The only serious cause for regret in Frank's view, was that he would not get the motor-bicycle his guv'nor had promised him if successful. Still, that was sure to come, too, sooner or later. Meanwhile his old push-bike would continue to serve.

Simon, striding along, felt that the loss of a whole day might be vital to him. But he could not deny his mother the morning – and the afternoon he must keep free for Ridgmount Gardens. He was not sure that Edith would be there. She had gone to Edinburgh with Mrs. Wyn for a fortnight, and her one message, brief and pregnant, had given him no particulars. It had flung at him, however, an agitating announcement: her discovery of his position.

"I have met someone," she wrote, "who knows you rather well – better, it seems, than *I* do! He is a fellow-student of yours at Jews' College. He did not seem to know that you meant to leave soon, though. So perhaps, I know more about you than he does, after all! If you see him before I get back, he will tell you all I said. And more, no doubt! I think you will be pleased."

This communication gave Simon hours of restless excitement. He took no notes at lectures that day, and nearly came to blows with Rees of Aber, who cornered him unexpectedly with a violent tug of coat-tails.

"What the hell d'you mean, you young pup, passing every Welshman as if he was dirt? Wales isn't good enough, indeed, now you've been in London for a bit!"

"Go to the devil," said Simon, attempting to remove the other's grip.

"Don't come near us, now, do you? Never join the Sing-song, and can't stand up for the leek? Y'f'rn d 'jawl! Once you pups get the Saesneg fog into you, you forget the way even to *swear* in Welsh! What's the matter with yr hen iath, anyway?"

"Let go," said Simon. "I suppose you've been sending me those notices of meetings? – I'm not interested. Don't you know I'm not a Welshman?"

Rees let go.

"Born and bred in Wales, but not a Welshman. Ay, ay, that's it. Christ, I was forgetting!" He looked at Simon in the same ironic way that little Ieuan Richards once had done, using the same words.

"No – you're not a Welshman. You're a Jew."

Simon, released, had moved off quickly. The other called after him— "Hey, wait a bit – I've heard something you'd like to know – do you remember that gurl—"

But Simon had gone. Rees and his gossip meant nothing to him. He could see only six words – "I think you will be pleased" – standing out in a rosy line, clarifying and calming a perturbation remote from Rees's ken. Edith knew – and it was all right! That was the main thing. But how had it happened? Who was the student, and why did he not deliver her message? Most of the fellows had gone away that week, either to their homes or to take services at minor synagogues. As far as Simon knew, none of them hailed from Edinburgh. But it was not certain that she had met him there. Nothing was certain, except the fact, that learning he was a Jew, she had taken the knowledge well. Her frank, simple words – so they seemed to him, for he found no suggestion of the cryptic in her low-crossed t's and undotted i's – came naturally from her tolerant mind, and, he hoped, some warmer sympathies. Reassurance kept him steady for the days that followed. But his longing to see her grew more intense. It burned below the concentration on his work, and the reluctance with which he set out to fulfil his mother's wish.

The shool presented an unusually decorative scene. The steps of the Ark were banked with blooms, and high green foliage made a garden of the Almemar. The great blobs of pinky blossom deepened Simon's consciousness of Edith. They recalled the massed hydrangea of Hafod, associated with his first glimpse of the fairy child. Slowly he drew his fringed scarf across his shoulders, and opened the *machzar*, seeing her image on the page which praised God. As he turned the

leaves, passing from the service for the first day to that of the
second, a line of English seemed to fly at him,

"Not to intermarry with the nations of the land."

His lips curled inwards: he looked back coolly and read the
preceding paragraph, with the detailed injunctions.

To keep the Law; and observe the testimony.

To be holy as the children of God; and to proclaim peace in
war.

To abstain—from fornication, false judgments, hatred, the
killing of the dam and its young in one day, the eating of
blood, the wronging of women and servants, the removal of
gleanings for the poor, – and the rest of the six hundred and
thirteen precepts.

A curious jumble. Obsolete, chiefly, and therefore
meaningless. Of course the Ten Commandments were still
regarded as essential, if not up to date, even by the *Goyim*.
But all the rest was the paraphernalia of an Eastern
community, centuries ago. Loftily, Simon dismissed the
uneasiness that had pricked his soul. He continued to turn the
leaves, half wishing he had one of those new translations,
which at least clothed the antiquated thoughts in decent
English. It was absurd that just such a *machzar* was in the
hands of his neighbour, a short bearded man muttering
Hebrew rapidly, and obviously too foreign to appreciate his
advantage: Simon could look over the other's shoulder and
see the open page. But it was not a case of envy. He did not
feel that possession of another *machzar* would make any real
difference. This might be the last time he would use one, he
thought, as he found the place at last, and began to mumble as
usual, looking round vacantly now and again at his fellow-
congregants. The regular drone of voices, with the mellow

chant of the *chazan* rising and falling, gave way for some moments to a pause, through which the rustle of women's dresses could be heard. Simon's eyes wandered to the gallery opposite, where some late arrivals were moving shadowlike behind the grill. One, either in passing, or pressing back to let another pass, leaned forward, her face clear above the bar as she gazed below. Simon almost dropped his *machzar*. The scarf actually slid from his shoulders. He did not pick it up, but accepted it mechanically from his neighbour, who had stooped, frowning, to retrieve it. The blood singing in his ears, Simon kept his head strained upward. Was it an illusion born of his thoughts – or was it the face of Edith Miller he had seen? She was seated now, and he could not, from his distant corner, be sure of the outlines patterned in the grill. He waited almost breathlessly for the next upstanding. It came – women and men rose together. There she stood, partly screened by her neighbours, but unmistakably Edith in line and hue, holding a book with her own composed air.

Surprise and heartleaping pleasure yielded to acute discomfort. Why had she come here? Surely not moved by that prying curiosity – blandly called interest – that *Goyim* often displayed in alien customs? Simon, unnecessarily resentful, forgot that Jews sometimes visited churches. He had done so himself, drawn by the art of long-dead workers in stone and glass, if not by the living exemplars of a strange religion. But this simple building had no extraneous appeal. Its plain dignity, more visible within than without, enhanced as it might be to-day by the fruits of a symbolic harvest festival, could not distract the mind from the worshippers and their creed. Luckily the worshippers here were a disciplined lot. Supposing she had gone to one of the East End places, where

the service was conducted to an accompaniment of shuffling
feet and discordant voices – where some sat, some stood,
some strolled about, some leaned over to gossip, to point, to
gesticulate – a disharmony of sound and posture that flouted
every conventional idea of religious decorum. Simon had once
listened contemptuously to a justification advanced by a
College "greener" – a predecessor of the two favoured by
Mandel. The latter had undertaken a sympathetic translation
for the benefit of Binsky— "Oh, he says that the God of Israel
is not a Prussian officer, nor even an Englisher gentleman – in
fact, he's no snob like you, Bink! He's more like a kind father,
who expects his children to come to shool as if they were
coming home. He doesn't mind if they're free and easy, and
say their prayers as if they were talking to him – why
shouldn't they leave off and argue if they like, or even cheek
him, like a certain Rabbi did? It seems it's a relic of the times
when the poor Yids found the shool was the only place where
they could be *menschen and yidden* – that is, where the goy
couldn't spit and tread on 'em – where they could either cry
to God out of their sorrowful hearts, or talk in a comfy way
about their own affairs."

Neither Binsky nor Simon approved such reasoning. They
preferred the opinions of the West End anglicised officials,
who drilled the members of their synagogues into order. Here
people "behaved", as Nettie Elman would have put it. Simon
was not concerned with the quality of worship that went on
behind the subdued murmurs of this disciplined congregation,
the mechanical risings and sittings, the pauses to allow *chazan*
and choir uninterrupted flow. The aspect of reverence, at least,
was not too dissimilar from that of a Christian assembly. He
tried to imagine the effect of sonorous Hebrew on the

unaccustomed ear of an English girl. If the intonations were
strange – how much stranger, after all, were they than Latin?
"Ora pro nobis" – muttered Simon, trying the syllables on his
tongue, to the puzzlement of his neighbour, when he should
have been saying.

"Ain kamocho ba-elohim adonai v'ain k'maasecho"—
(There is none like unto thee among the gods.)

Instead of genuflexion and knee-prostration, the shawled
uprising and swaying; instead of elevation of the Host, the
conveyance to and from the Ark of the Holy Scrolls of the
Law, their ornate covers bound and unbound by the privileged.
As the latter mounted the Almemar, the central daïs with its
desk for the reading of the Law, Simon's uneasiness grew. His
eyes tried to pierce the rails behind which Edith sat. What did
she make of this strange procedure? The occasional glimpse
he caught showed a calm demeanour, the pose, he
acknowledged, of good manners and good sense: she stood
and sat with the rest, eyes fixed on open book – reading the
English page, of course, even though it might not be at the
right place. That hardly mattered, as much as her thoughts
when she looked down on the unfamiliar scene – on him, too,
no doubt, though he could not catch her gaze. He moved his
shoulders in embarrassment: the silk praying-scarf sliding on
his suit felt like a hairshirt on his skin. The hat on his head
pressed like a shell. If only she did not find him ridiculous! He
could hardly believe she had come here for his sake, undriven
by that "curiosity" he grudged its better name – but any
sympathy she might have had must be precariously held. God
knew if it would survive this ordeal! He was not aware of

taking the Lord's name in vain, though the prohibition was being uttered in his ears, and was blazoned on the page before him. The wind that lifted him up, the mighty rushing that he heard, had nothing in common with the vision of Ezekiel. The song of Habbakuk, too, would have passed him by but for the printed line that struck his glance, lowered in dismay as he caught a note in the gallery that seemed to come from her – surely she did not think it her duty to join in the chant? Her ear was good, no doubt – but this was a queer revenge for the hymn he had once enlivened in a Wesleyan Church!

"I heard," cried the prophet, "and my belly trembled, my lips quivered at the voice: rottenness entered my bones, and I trembled in my place."

Relief came to Simon with the prayer for the Royal Family. The first English syllable rang out in the quiet air, freed at last from the echoes of Hebrew utterance. A dim memory came to him of a small, impatient boy, waiting for the obliteration of another tongue in "God save the Queen" – The Queen was dead, though her House lived on: and the Blaemawe crier's broad Celtic "Sa-a-ve" died, too, in the polished Saxon accents of the Anglo-Judean minister. As he ended, the quietude broke up. Into these disciplined ranks came the rift of chaos. Some sat, some stood, some drew off their shawls and scarves and began to walk out, others whispered and gesticulated. It was the pause before the recital of memorial prayers, and those who had living parents hesitated whether to absent themselves, according to custom, or remain, according to a new code of etiquette. In this respect alone Simon preferred the old usage to the new. It seemed to him better to withdraw than perforce to share the mourners' invocation of their dead. Besides, he hoped that Edith would also leave her seat, and appear above the staircase, where he could join her for a time. He waited anxiously, but among the women who wandered out there was no sign of her. Evidently her immediate neighbours had remained, and she had kept her seat among them. He returned reluctantly to his place, a few seconds before the close of the prayer. Looking up, he saw her standing, grave and still, her head bent low on the book in her hands. It seemed an unnecessary exercise of her powers of adaptation. But he could not cavil: if only she reserved her charity for him, she might act any part she chose. He resumed his scarf in a slightly easier mood. The service continued, and he no longer disturbed his neighbour by eccentricities. Even the Benediction of the *Cohanim*, though it revived for a moment some discomfort, did not impose too great a strain. True, the voices of these "priests", whose claim to sanctity lay in their ancient name, were as unpleasing to the ear, as their shawled shapes, bowing with extended hands in blessing, were to the eye. Yet some basic harmony struggled through. Simon's gaze, straying over the short man's shoulder, widened in sudden illumination at familiar words.

The Lord bless thee and keep thee:
The Lord make his face to shine upon thee,
and be gracious unto thee:
The Lord incline his countenance unto thee
and give thee peace.

Beauty and tenderness eased Simon's soul. Trying to read through Edith's eyes, he had awakened to joy, to the sense of sharing something precious with the only other being who deserved it. Was she, too, reading the very words, finding them, perhaps, by instinct, – unless someone had turned the pages for her? He could not see her as she sat, but luxuriously he imaged her dear face, close to his as he bent to say those words – to her. If she would let him!—

"My beloved – The Lord bless thee, and keep thee—
The Lord make his face to shine upon thee,
And be gracious unto thee.

He roused himself with a shamefaced start, staring guiltily at his neighbour, hoping he had not been actually whispering – but what did it matter? Even the bearded man would have found nothing amiss in that whisper.

The "priests" had descended: the last verses of the service were being sung; men were folding up their *talithim*, and women were coming down the stairs. Simon thrust his bag beneath a seat, with a vague idea of recovering it some day, and pushed out into the lobby, regardless of orderly retirement. He stood beside the staircase, looking eagerly at the stream of dresses flowing down. There she was, at the top, a graceful form in grey with the gold gleam above – her face turned from him as she drew back, apparently making room for an elderly, creeping dame. The next moment she had made a quick movement: the old woman hesitated and seemed to yield herself up. Edith's arm closed round her in the nurse's practised grasp, and they came down the stone steps together. Simon pressed up closer: it was impossible for him to squeeze through the downcoming crowd. She looked over the side, searching, as if she knew he was waiting there. Their glances locked. His lost itself in the sweet blueness of hers, in the shy smile he had found for himself before. He would have liked to leap the banister and the intervening heads, to take her hands, away from the hobbling figure she supported. As she came nearer he called— "Can I help you?" – She shook her head negatively but moved one elbow, under which was crooked a longish volume. "Only with this" – she said— "if you can get it—" He stretched over and seized the edges of the book, which slipped into his hands as she loosened hold. He sprang back, then, from the pressing figures around, and stood as near to the foot of the steps as he could get. The book in his hand was a new *machzar* – had she bought it for the occasion, he wondered? It opened in his fingers where a blue ribbon dangled, and he saw the pages of Ruth. "Thy people shall be my people, and thy God my God." His hand closed tightly over the book. The next moment he was answering her quiet murmur— "We'll see the old lady outside." They passed slowly out, divided and linked by the old dame between them. Not so old either, Simon perceived – or else the smooth black wig beneath the silk hood was more deceptive than he supposed. The sallow skin was not much wrinkled, and her mouth and chin were firm. The most aged part of the face was the expression in the eyes – deep, sad Jewish eyes, like those of his mother. They moved something within him. He helped her down the last steps with exceeding care, hardly noticing that Edith had relinquished her share of the burden. For an instant the woman paused as he, too, released her, and looked from one to the other.

"Danke – beide—" she muttered. "A feine poor – soil sein mit mazel." Simon's face was scarlet. He dared not glance at Edith. Had she heard? But suddenly he realised that even so, she could not have understood the broken Yiddish. She was saying calmly as the old woman hobbled away,

"Poor creature! It's not age – she's crippled. She sat next to me and told me how it happened. There was a pogrom in her village, and it seems a friendly peasant hid her in his loft – the family were friends of her father's. But someone – whether a member of the family or another, she never knew – set fire to the place. She tried to get out through a trap-door and broke her leg. It was a wonder she wasn't killed. Somehow or other she was rescued. And that, of course, is quite an ordinary tale."

"Of course," said Simon. But he had listened without attention. The old woman's story, in fact, was so ordinary, that even Edith's reaction to it concerned him little. It was more important to know how she felt about himself. As they moved up the street, he wondered what to say. With that Ruth-marked book still in his hand, he could not ask, "Why did you come?" Nor could he announce "I did not expect this pleasure" – The pleasure was too mixed, and she must know it. But while he racked his brain, she did not seem embarrassed. She said, perhaps a little more quickly than usual.

" The service ended early to-day. Of course there was no sermon. I ought to have come yesterday. It's the most important, isn't it? – except for mourners."

"I didn't think – I mean, I didn't know you'd care to come—" he floundered. She seemed remarkably well acquainted with the festival. "When did you get back?"

"Only last night. Or of course I would have come. I always feel one gets the full significance on the first day."

"The significance?"

"Yes – the significance of the Promulgation."

"The Promulgation?" He felt like a helpless parrot.

"Of the Law."

He blinked at her. She continued, a little breathlessly, as if talking against time,—

"I suppose you think I couldn't understand. Of course I haven't studied, as you have done. But studying for religion can obscure the other things, as you have probably found. Anyway, I know that the importance of Pentecost is in the Law of Sinai. One gets the full sense of the establishment of a nation. Perhaps I'm too secular – but it's the legal code that interests me!" She gave a little uncertain laugh, and avoided his eyes. "The code that's served as a model for other nations – so much of modern law is based on it. But don't you agree? – the enactments as one reads them in the Synagogue make one realise the historical atmosphere. Of course the flowers bring it back, in a way more vividly – I mean the agricultural life. And it's lovely to hear the story of Ruth in such a setting."

She was speaking faster than ever, but he was so nervous himself that he did not grasp this as a sign of disturbance in her. The reference to Ruth confused him further.

"I – I'm glad you liked it." He tried to pull himself together. "You seem to have thought it all out – very sympathetically. Though I've studied, I don't know that I can see quite as much in it as you – why – it's extraordinary that you should be so interested—"

"Is it?" He could not see her face. Her voice sounded muffled, suddenly. "I gather that you are not."

"What?"

"Interested. And that seems extraordinary to me. Why – you don't even seem pleased that I came to shool to-day!" Simon was taken aback, especially at her use of the word.

"I'm – pleased – of course I'm pleased—" he stammered.

"But I was afraid you'd think it all so strange and difficult – ugly, even—"

"I don't know why."

"Edith." The name slipped out. He came so close, stopping, that she, too, paused, but her head was still turned aside. "It's very good of you – I can't express how good – here." He looked round at the swirl of traffic. They had reached the corner of Oxford Street. "We are going away from the flat. Did you mean to?"

"Yes."

"Of course I don't mind walking on – just where you please. But would you care to come in somewhere – for a coffee? – It's only twelve—"

"No, thank you. I prefer to go on walking. I have to get to the city." She hesitated. "You can come part of the way – if you wish."

"You are offended with me?"

"Not at all." She turned to him and smiled – it was her vague, detached smile. "But I'm disappointed – rather. You don't seem to take me very seriously. You don't believe, do you, that I came to shool because of my genuine interest in the service?"

"Of course I believe it," he said hurriedly. "Why shouldn't I, when it makes things so much easier – for me? If you hadn't a genuine interest, I suppose you'd hardly forgive me."

"You might have told me before, certainly. I wasn't likely to be hard on you, in the circumstances! But then, you couldn't guess, any more than I did – the whole thing's rather funny, I suppose." She laughed slightly. "And as it happened, the subject never came up." Her changing tones bewildered him. "But I wish you had told me yourself."

"I meant to, quite soon. I was only waiting—"

"Until I came back? Oh – but if you had seen me in shool first, without knowing—" She stopped and smiled gravely.

"Without knowing what?" He was completely puzzled.

"Why, that I had the same reason for being there as you had."

"The same reason? But then – *I'm* not so very keen, you know. I only came because – well, because I'm a Jew."

"As I am – a Jewess."

Simon thought he had not heard aright. He said stupidly— "What did you say?"

"I said I'm a Jewess. You know that, of course."

"I'm afraid – I don't see quite – it's not some sort of joke, is it?"

Her smile vanished. She said on a sudden note of indignation, "Why on earth should I joke about it?" "No – it isn't any joke – being a Jew," said Simon rather wildly. He was not at all sure what to say. "I just meant, you were not bringing up the British Israel, Lost Ten Tribes business, were you? Otherwise, I really don't see how—"

"It's a surprise to you. I thought there was something rather odd – you haven't seen Mr. Billig, then?"

"Myer Billig?" Simon clutched at a straw of reality in the blowing wind of doubts. "Do you know him? He's away – somewhere in the North – oh, is he the fellow who told you? – I saw him once leaving your aunt's flat."

"Yes, he gives me weekly lessons in Hebrew. His family were old friends of the Wyns – they used to live in Edinburgh. Somehow, we never mentioned you until he came to visit us there. He's been staying on the Border – near Carlisle – a friend motored him up last week. It all came out that day. I understood he was returning to London straight away, but I must have been mistaken."

Simon simply could not move. He stood still and stared.

"I – I – forgive me if I seem a fool. As you said – it's a surprise. A tremendous surprise. I know that you – get very interested in things – but I couldn't have imagined that you'd be so deeply interested in *Jews* as to want to become one."

"Oh, you're quite wrong." She smiled a little again. "I'm not a proselyte, if that's what you're thinking – a sort of twentieth-century female Lord George Gordon! I was born Jewish. My parents were Jews – certainly my father and grandfather were. My mother considered herself a Jewess. She was the daughter of Lady Hafod, and her first husband was Alfred Rachlin. You must know of the Rachlins? Of course they are not conforming Jews, and my grandfather wasn't, either. But my father was different. His people were orthodox stock from Russia. They settled in Bishopsgate, and my father's mother lives there still. I stay with her sometimes. In fact I'm going there now. Aunt Helena hasn't returned, anyway, and the flat's closed." She stopped. Simon was still staring hard at her, apparently listening, but his expression was peculiar.

"You don't seem – pleased – after all," she added quietly.

"It's a surprise," he repeated, "a tremendous surprise."

"Need it be an unpleasant one?" Her tone seemed to challenge, but immediately she continued without waiting for a response. "Of course, you can't fit me in all at once with Jewish things. I see the difficulty. We've always talked of – of purely English matters. In fact – haven't you played up to me a little? You were very English – at Hampton Court!" She tried to smile, but her lips quivered slightly. "Naturally I understand all that. It's in me, too. And when one doesn't know there's another side neither of us knew, then – it seems irrelevant. I suppose I haven't seemed to you the least bit Jewish?" – He shook his head. "Oh well – I assure you – I shall do you credit!" She had succeeded in smiling, and he fumbled for a reply. But a flush rose to her eyes. It struck her that her words held an implication she had not intended.

"I'm afraid I must leave you now to work it out," she said, interrupting him. "My people expect me to lunch. They think I'm at the Duke's Place shool, where I usually go when I stay with them." She did not hold out her hand, but waved it as she began to walk away. "Good-bye" – was there a mocking note in her voice, which had suddenly regained assurance?— "Good *Yomtov*."

He remained standing, hat in hand, and watched her go. The disappearance in the crowd of that individual grey-clad form, with the brimmed hat shading her golden waves, and the blue of her eyes washed in the azure wisp that floated from her neck, left him with the familiar blank. It was the first time they had parted without eager pressure on his side for another meeting. But he did not think of it, or of anything, very clearly. His mind seemed dulled. He walked almost blindly back to Beagle Street.

The Finck family were assembling for the midday meal. A fresh white cloth was spread on the board, free for once from a medley of needles, thread and suitings. A paper-frilled pot of aspidistra (borrowed from a Gentile neighbour, since the Fincks did not harbour such fancies in ordinary life) stood in the centre, flanked by dishes of fruit and twisted poppy-seeded loaves. The plump little tailor, the steamed pallor of his cheeks belied by their roundness, bustled about with his coat on, which showed it was a dress occasion: his wife, in a new white silk blouse, over which a gold chain was carefully looped, fussed around the children, tying pinafores over the younger ones, and admonishing the elder to greater care of their *Yomtov* clothes. The old grandmother hovered as usual over the saucepans, but she, too, wore a fresh-pressed black satin apron with a gay floral border. The smell of soup was more pungent than ever.

Simon accepted the glass of "schnapps" offered him, but set it down and forgot to drink it. The tailor blessed the bread and handed round the salted pieces. A hard lump of the coarse brine bit into Simon's tongue – melted, and stung his senses. Could it be that Edith, too, was eating such bread and salt, to the same Hebrew invocation of Israel's God – a "witness" with the Fincks?

"Behold us, thy witness by day and night, to declare thy unity"—

The family sat down, the meal began, and with it a babble of Yiddish that had no end. The lopsided aspidistra screened Simon's face, but was no bar to the tailor's peering eyes.

"Nah den, Shimke – vy don't you drink – and eat? Vot's de matter? Vorrying about something, hey? A young man like you should be happy, especially on Yonteff (Festival). Everybody's happy, even Bubè – nein, Bubè? Nu, gib mir a bissel mer kasha – es ot takè a Yomtovdiken tam" ("Come, give me some more soup – it has the true Festival flavour").

"You can't quite fit me in" – staggering, grotesque necessity – to fit *her* in with this! With the shool and its echoes of an outlived past – with the homes where tongue and ceremony perpetuated irksome bonds – with the College which made them fast in academic sanction. He had been leaving them behind, confident that he was escaping from their world to hers – and all the time she was inside, native as himself! Absurd, incredible: an outrage of his hopes; a keener, more humiliating disappointment than any he had known.

"Oy – and vat's dis?" The tailor had reached for something on the sofa behind him, and lifted up a longish volume. "A new *machzar*? (Festival Prayer-book) Did you get a present from somebody, Shimke? Den vy you look so sorry? – Ain't it good enough? It looks a good one – mit golden edges. It says someting here – 'From – my – dear – Bubele – mit – loving – pray-ers.' Vot's dat? But you got no Bubele – dey are both gone, Olav-Asholom (may they rest in peace) – only dis Bube here, you can have her if you want—"

"Please put that book down," said Simon, springing up in wrath. "It isn't mine – it belongs to someone else—"

"Oy – allriat – allriat" said the tailor soothingly, replacing Edith's *machzar* where Simon had let it drop. "Don' run around like someone's been poisoned! Dere's no harm done – if you took it by mistake, you can give it back to the shammas (beadle). Dank God, we got plenty *machzarim* – we could make presents to all the linkè (heterodox) people in the street – we don't want nobody else's."

As soon as he could, Simon retired to his room, taking with him Edith's book. They had both forgotten he was carrying it. He would have to return it, of course. He looked at the inscription and read it aloud, to efface the impression of the Finck accents that had first conveyed it to him. Edith's name, fortunately, was on another leaf, unturned by the inquisitive tailor. But then – could one Jew sully the name of another, even by uncouth pronunciation? Simon winced as if the devil were whispering ironies in his ear. Edith's own writing, clear, precise, stamped their truth upon him.

"From my dear Bubele, with her loving prayers"—. Edith, with a "Bubele" ("little granny" in Yiddish diminutive) – and – Lady Hafod!

He paced about, recalling her words, trying to link them with all he had known of her before. The task was hopeless. His brain not only refused the effort, – it was swamped by the surge of anger from his heart. So this was the English girl he had meant to win – a cheat, a fraud, a mere mask. The calm blue eyes looked mockingly at him, the fair cheek curved below derisive gold.

"Hell," cried Simon, stamping on the board— "Oh – hell!"

He rushed for his books, and flung himself down to study. Nothing must interfere with his scheme of emancipation. A thousand Ediths should not distract him from the path he meant to tread. Next morning would bring his feet directly into it – he'd plant them firmly down, and take his longest stride. But he must be well prepared. Every moment counted. He was free, after all, to use this afternoon. Precious, hateful, freedom, – to leave Edith behind, not to dally with her. Very well, he would use it – he would go on, in spite of her and her confounded bewildering changeling tricks – be damned if he'd waste another second thinking of them!

"A richtiger epikowros!" reported the tailor's wife, who having knocked in vain to bring him down to tea, had peeped through the door. "Er sitzt und schreibt wie der teufel treibt hem."[1]

"Wer soll wissen," lamented the Bube, "as a kind fon Gedaliah der Schwarzer wet auswaksen a reine Goy!"[2]

"Zog mir, Bube," chimed in the tailor, checking a long tirade, "Wie kommt es, as m'rift a weisser mensch a schwarzer?"[3]

"Gey shoyn mit deine witzlech," retorted the old dame, "Gedaliah ist takè a bissel weiss – ober sein futer und zeide, olav-asholom, sahnen beide geweisen schwarz wie mazikim – *nisht tsitsegleichen!* Die ost gedarft kennen die alter Gedaliah der Schwarzer – is her gewain a feiner Yid – ai, ai, ai!"[4]

---

[1] "A real sceptic, breaker of laws! He sits and writes as if the devil drives him."

[2] "Who could have thought … that a child of Gedaliah the Black would have grown up a pure heathen!"

[3] "Tell me, Granny, how comes it that a white man is called a black?"

[4] "Go along with your jokes! Gedaliah is certainly rather fair – but his father and grandfather, peace be unto them, were both dark as sprites of mischief – *not to compare*! You should have known the old Gedaliah the Black – ah, what a fine Jew was he!"

XIV

THE FINAL strain was over. It left Simon relaxed, and in a mood to deal more lightly with his problems. Those he had solved for the examiners might or might not have been opened with the key approved by them. He pushed his doubts aside and let other thoughts come back – eager, speculative, softening.

Something of glory had vanished from his world. The halo round Edith Miller's head was gone. It was no longer possible to worship in her a perfect English goddess. Yet she was still Edith Miller: her own fair, unalterable self, unique, enchanting, infinitely adorable. She was still, too, the granddaughter of Lady Hafod – the heiress of Millicombe in the sense of valid heritage of Millicombe blood. That strain in her might dominate the other, in the spirit as it had done in the body. The signs she showed of attraction to Jewish life – what, after all, did they amount to? A perverted romanticism, fed by reading of persecutions and martyrdoms. Edith was drawn to the down-trodden and the suffering. That was why she had taken up nursing. But the fact was, thought Simon cynically, she had no profound experience of the victims she meant to help. Hospital patients, in their clean beds and under strict regulation, were easier to cope with than in their native slums. Jewish troubles were more repellent in reality than in books. The idea rather than the actual condition had reached and affected her.

Simon would have liked to flatter himself that she had advanced into the Jewish fold on his account. His vanity could not afford to be excessive on the point: besides, she had taken Hebrew lessons before she knew him. And had she not lived with her Bishopsgate relatives? He recalled her reference to an estrangement with Lady Hafod, because of these other members of the family.

Only, why had she not admitted they were Jews, – until now? And why was she living with the Wyns? They were not, obviously, the troublesome relations. Had Hector Wyn stood in more – or less – favour with her on that account? Was he the reason that she had returned to the Millicombe fold? The questions were double-edged: they posed Simon more disagreeably than the general trend of his reflections. He tried to remember all he had heard of Hector Wyn – scraps of conversation which, if they meant anything, meant that the doctor was hostile to Jews. Why – why – was she living with his mother?

An impatience to learn all the facts beset Simon. He hesitated about calling at the flat. He was not sure if she had returned to it. Twice he telephoned without success. At the third attempt he heard her voice clear, but with its golden note slightly flattened and "tinned". Was it the instrument, or was there really an ironic edge to the amused response?

"Oh, it's you? Have you quite got over the shock?"

"I've had time to get used to it."

"Yes – it seems you've been missing for nearly a week. Mr. Billig knew nothing of you."

"Then he's back? I meant to look him up. But I've been sitting my exam."

"Of course. I guessed it must be that. I hope you did well?"

"Fairly, I think. But there were a few snags at the end, and I didn't quite like the look in the examiner's eye."

"He didn't know you were a Jew?"

"I – I don't suppose so," he stammered. "Do you think it would make any difference?"

"Perhaps not," she said. "But if you succeed, you'll *really* be lost – to Jews' College. I take it you'll resign as soon as you hear?" The ironic note seemed to have deepened. It stung him into sudden decision.

"I'm not waiting for that. I'm resigning to-day."

"Really?" There was a little pause, as if she had gauged instinctively the momentousness of his mood. Her voice came through more softly. "That's honest, of course. If you don't feel cut out for the ministry, you should not go on with it. Please accept my best wishes."

"Thank you." There was another pause, made of struggle with his inward pride. "May I call soon? I want to return your book."

"My *machzar*? You can bring it round to-morrow. Though it's not my usual free afternoon. I'm busy just now, finishing things up. It's quite settled about my leaving hospital at the end of the month."

"Are you going straight to Blaemawe?"

"No. I've promised Lady Hafod to go away with her first. Besides, Sir Gwilym and my aunt are travelling. They will be abroad until Christmas, and expect us to join them then."

Simon smiled. She said "Christmas" more naturally than she said "*Machzar*".

"You won't be too busy to come out somewhere tomorrow?"

"I'm afraid so. I have an appointment at four at a clinic – I'm studying some new methods of welfare work. In fact, I intend to devote all my leisure for the rest of the month to this sort of thing."

"Well, I'll come early. Perhaps you'll tell me more about it – and about some other things—"

From this conversation he went straight to Billig. The young minister – he was now the Rev. Myer Billig, fully qualified, and waiting for a post – received him with something less than his usual amiability. At first he did not prove very communicative. He reproached Simon with concealment of his origin in the tones of one rebuking a major crime.

"I have realised for some time that you had no wish to become a minister. Frankly, I find it hard to understand such an attitude in a student. But it is harder still to understand why you deliberately hide the fact that you are a Jew. Not that there is anything novel in that. One knows it has gone on from the time of the Marranos. But with you it's not a question of being burnt at the stake, or even of sacrificing your position. It seems to me—"

"Oh, dry up, Billig," said Simon, as good-humouredly as he could. "I don't hide anything, *deliberately*. It's just that I'm usually taken for an Englishman – and I prefer to let it rest at that."

Billig looked at him coldly.

"Have you no Jewish pride? And do you think it's *English* to deceive a girl" – Billig hesitated at the sudden flash in Simon's eye, and added more hurriedly— "to deceive people—"

"Nonsense. I knew Miss Miller would find out. I meant to tell her, anyway. Really, one doesn't go about shouting these things from the housetops." He spoke in a loud, hearty tone, to crush some discomfort under Billig's steady gaze. "You happened to anticipate me, that's all. Tell me – how did she take it? Did she condemn me outright, as you do?"

"Miss Miller would not be likely to do that – she is too conscious of her invidious position with the Wyns. Not out of consideration for them, of course. She doesn't hesitate to show her disapproval of their tactics. But since she feels compromised by her silence on their behalf, she thinks she has no right to condemn anyone else – especially in their hearing."

"I don't know what you mean," said Simon. "But what I want to know is, what did Miss Miller say about *me*?"

"She said very little. Of course she showed surprise. However, she grasped the situation very quickly. And then she asked me to explain her own position to you."

"Don't be so roundabout. Can't you give me her own words?"

The orphan drew himself up with patient dignity.

"But I'm giving you the sense. Her exact words were very simple. Let me see. She said – 'Please tell Mr. Black all about me. Say I quite understand, and shall be glad to meet him again on equal terms'."

"You call that simple?" exclaimed Simon, more to himself than to the minister. He had begun to search for hidden meanings in all Edith's recollected words. "I wish I knew her idea of 'equal'."

"If you are thinking that nothing could make you and Miss Miller equal, I agree," said Billig, with unexpected acerbity.

"No doubt," said Simon. "But I wasn't thinking of that – only of the fact that I'm actually a Jew – while after all, she's only half, and perhaps less than half, a Jewess," He smiled triumphantly.

"I should say it was the other way round," said Billig. "From what I know of Edith Miller, I should say she is wholly

Jewish. I understand she has told you herself of her descent, and the fact that she voluntarily gave up the Christian part of her life, in order to retain her Jewish identity."

"I only know there was some sort of family squabble. I'm anxious to learn the whole history, if possible. It sounds remarkable. Can you tell me what really happened? How did Lady Hafod come to marry a Jew, in the first place?"

"There was nothing remarkable in that. The beautiful young heiress from Devonshire met the handsome nephew of the Rachlins in society, during her first season in London. Alfred Rachlin had no parents – he had been brought up by his uncle, Sir Montague Rachlin, from childhood. The Rachlins, you know, have nothing to do with Jewish life. They don't even go to shool on Yom Kippur, though I believe in Sir Montague's time they did. I doubt if the nephew kept even that tie, after his marriage to Cynthia Lansome. When he died, the widow retired to Millicombe with their young child. A few years later she married again – a Welsh landowner whose friends lived on neighbouring estates. I believe they had sons. Lady Hafod was passionately devoted to her only daughter, Judith Rachlin. The girl used to visit her father's family in London, and at the age of seventeen she, too, fell in love with a Jew. But this was not a society affair. David Miller was a poor violinist, living in the East End. I don't know how or where they met, but Miss Rachlin was very musical, she played a good deal at charity concerts. Lady Hafod tried hard to put an end to the friendship and kept her daughter in the country. But she ran away, and there was a secret marriage. The family soon got reconciled. Then Edith was born at Millicombe – in a tragic hour. Her mother's life ended at her birth, and the half mad young father wandered all night around the cliffs. God knows whether there was an accident. His body was washed ashore next day."

There was a moment's silence.

"So Miss Miller never knew her parents," said Simon. "She was brought up entirely by Lady Hafod."

"Not entirely. Even as a child the Jewish side of the family had some share in her—"

"But you said the Rachlins were not Jewish enough to count."

"There were the others – the Millers."

"H'm," said Simon. "Of course – the other grandmother. At Bishopsgate."

"David Miller's elder brother opened business there some time after Edith was born. David was the first to come from Russia. I think he was sent away to avoid conscription. The elder brother was already in the army, though he had a wife and children. He came to London at the end of his service, and as soon as he could, sent for his family. His mother, who was a widow, came too. The old lady – she wasn't old then, of course – found it difficult to grasp the facts about David's marriage. She had taken it for granted that her youngest son had married into an average Jewish family – only rather rich, and therefore distant. She learned after some time that Rachlin's widow had married a Goy, though he, too, was dead, and that her grandchild might mix with Goyim. But it was not clear to her until much later that the little girl whom she was sometimes allowed to see in charge of her nurse, either at the Rachlins or at Lady Hafod's town house, had absolutely no knowledge of Jewish life. When Edith was about nine, Lady Hafod suddenly decided to cut the Jewish connection entirely .

– the child was not to visit or meet any of the family. The Rachlins were not much concerned. The old people were dead, and the younger ones not so nearly related. They knew that Edith would inherit her parents' settlements, and her spiritual welfare was of no importance to them. The only one who might have felt a personal interest was Alfred Rachlin's sister, but she had married long ago and left London. She had never got on with the Rachlins, and they seldom met. A few years passed before the Millers could get into touch again with the child. By this time Hyman Miller had prospered, and his mother had grown more familiar with the language and circumstances around her. They began to make determined efforts to establish contact once more with Edith. Lady Hafod was equally determined to put every obstacle in their way. Little might have come of it if Edith herself had been indifferent. But as soon as she learned, somehow, of what was going on, she began to insist on seeing her relatives and displaying what to Lady Hafod was a very inconvenient interest in their way of life. In the end Lady Hafod conceded visits to the Rachlins – she was not much afraid of them. She forbade, absolutely, however, any intercourse with the 'foreigners'. But Edith, young as she was, had begun to develop a will of her own. A regular tussle began between her and Lady Hafod. Perhaps you can imagine—" He paused.

"Yes, of course," said Simon. "I can see exactly how it was. Miss Miller is very much like Lady Hafod – she couldn't bear to give in – she simply *had* to have her own way. And her romantic imagination – pitting herself against a tyrannical grandmother, and all that sort of thing—" He laughed, somewhat wryly.

"Not altogether," said Billig. "It's true Miss Miller has

considerable character, and must always have resented any
sort of tyranny. But it was not only a question of high spirit.
She was drawn as if by an invisible power to the sources of her
Jewish soul." He locked his hands behind his back and walked
about, his pale mild eyes darkening with a mystic shade.
"Lady Hafod sent her to a convent school in France, entering
her as a Christian pupil. But she declared herself a Jewess.
Eventually she was sent home. It was impossible to find fault
with her behaviour in any other way. She was affectionate,
diligent, tractable in every respect but one. She insisted on
seeing her Bishopsgate relatives, and on spending the Jewish
Holy days with them. Lady Hafod was in despair. She idolised
the girl, but she threatened to disown her if she persisted in
what she called her perversities. Edith has no means of her
own until her twenty-first birthday – and even then, her
prospects are small on the Rachlin side alone. But she was
prepared to give up everything. Her feelings were reinforced
by the accidental discovery of some letters that had been
exchanged by her parents. In several of them Judith Rachlin
had declared her attachment to her father's faith. 'I agree that
if we have children,' she wrote, 'we will bring them up as
Jews'. Edith announced her resolve to fulfil her parents'
wishes. She told me she understood from the letters that her
father was anxious to secure his wife's promise, as an act of
homage to his mother, whom he reverenced deeply. 'And so
do I' Edith told Lady Hafod. 'Since I know little granny, I
understand how my father felt. She is wonderful. I mean to
go her way. Not all the way, because I can't – but just as far
as I can. Mind, she hasn't asked me to – and she doesn't want
to separate me from you. She tells me I should love and
respect you always. But she wishes me to know what Judaism

is, and to remember that my parents were Jews. And so I will'." Billig's voice dropped from a somewhat declamatory note. "I don't know all that happened. Lady Hafod does not appear to have taken any drastic measure. But there is no doubt that Edith has actually made considerable sacrifice, material and otherwise, in order to follow her conscience. She was not at University College long, but during that time she lived with the Millers, and conformed to Jewish practice whenever possible."

Simon's face had become moody as he listened.

"For all that," he said, "she lives with Christian relatives now."

"Oh no – only when she pays visits to Hafod or Millicombe."

"But she lives with the Wyns."

"Of course." Billig stared. "Don't you know they are Jews?"

"What – Dr. Wyn – and his mother? – I thought—" he stopped, incredulous.

"Mrs. Wyn's mother was Alfred Rachlin's sister, who married an Edinburgh Jew. I've known Hector Wyn since he was a boy. My people lived near his. Still, I'm not surprised you didn't know. Hector cannot be said to advertise the fact – he's taken more pains than you have to conceal it. It's true he has some reason, though that doesn't justify him."

"And was Edith willing – to help him conceal it?"

"Not exactly willing. She had nothing to do with the matter at first. It has been awkward for her. You see, Hector had an unfortunate experience at his first hospital. He had worked hard to qualify for a house appointment, which was definitely promised him by the doctor concerned. As a matter of fact, there was nobody else who stood the slightest chance, from the point of view of ability – and, also, it seemed, popularity. Hector was so confident, he announced the position to his friends, and began to make arrangements accordingly. But as the time drew near to take it up, he realised there was a change of atmosphere. The doctor put him off in a vague, embarrassed way. At last he told him he was sorry, but he could not confirm the appointment. Under pressure, he admitted there was no reason, except that Hector was a Jew, a fact which he himself had not taken into consideration, but which his colleagues resented. Hector had no option but to resign. It was a tremendous disappointment. Apart from his personal feelings, he had counted on the post for his mother's sake. The father had been unlucky in business, and since his death they had lived very moderately. It had been a struggle to enable Hector to qualify. He swore that in future he would hide the fact that he was a Jew. It was easy enough. The name is not Jewish – though I think it was originally Wein – and Hector's appearance is hardly what one might call typically Jewish. His mother, as you know, looks and talks like a Scotswoman. Besides, they were not known in London – they didn't mix even with the Rachlins. He got the post here without difficulty."

"And arranged for Miss Miller to train at his hospital?"

" Oh, no – she was there already. But he begged her to keep the secret. What else could she do? She could not injure his chance of a livelihood. And his mother is devoted to her. She stayed with them once or twice in Edinburgh."

"Do you mean that nobody at the hospital knows?"

"It seems so."

"Not even that they are related?"

"One can't be sure, but it isn't likely. Very few people outside know."

"So Miss Miller makes a secret of her Jewishness, too?"

"Not at all. But her friends don't seem to take it seriously. The Rachlins have intermarried so much that they hardly belong at all. And who knows the Millers? Real Jewish life here, as you know, is very narrowly centred. And the foreign elements don't mix with the English." Billig sighed. It was his ambition to bridge the gulf – an ambition Simon regarded with contempt. "I have been hoping that Miss Miller would be able to help in that respect—"

"Nonsense!" said Simon sharply. "She can't know anything about what you call real Jewish life—"

"Haven't I told you she has lived with her East End family?"

"Oh – well – she can't really understand—"

"Pardon me, it is you who fail to understand. Edith has entered deeply into her natural heritage. She has been anxious to learn. She has read, thought, observed. It is true she is very young, and perhaps not quite as concerned about some aspects of Judaism as I could wish—" He sighed again, and a thought struck Simon like a lash. Was it Billig, after all, who was responsible for Edith's persistence in "Jewishness" – with his "Hebrew lessons" his "aspects of Judaism" – his old acquaintance with the family – and? – no, nothing else could be possible! Simon trampled hastily on the bare suspicion that she could have any personal interest in the orphan. Myer Billig, indeed! He looked sarcastically at the lanky ill-clad form, the pale, angular face with the wandering grey eyes, the high forehead surmounted by reddish hair – well, – perhaps, the young minister was not so bad-looking in a solemn sort of way – hadn't somebody, Mandel or Binsky, said he looked like a picture of Christ? A Jewish type, of course. But could any girl be attracted to it? Edith wasn't 'any girl', it was true. She could be impressed by qualities behind the physical. And Billig had a good voice. He read beautifully. More important than his Hebrew was his perfect English articulation. Pompous – solemn – but perfect English. He had shed any Doric he might have acquired as a boy. Still, it was idiotic to dwell for a moment on a possibility of that sort.

"I should think she hadn't time for anything outside nursing," he said quickly, anxious to bring himself and Billig back to facts. "Did Lady Hafod agree to her leaving college for hospital?"

"It was Lady Hafod who arranged about the hospital. She encouraged Edith's nursing scheme because it distracted her from her interest in Jews. The idea of having the girl back in Wales or Devonshire – anywhere in the country where she could set some social work going under the direct auspices of the Hafods – seemed much better than any course of study in London which left her exposed to the influence of the Jewish family. The Hafods' town house was always open to her: But she would not use it except to visit them when they were there. Of course, Lady Hafod did not bargain for the Wyns turning up. But in the circumstances she preferred the Wyns' flat to the Bishopsgate home."

"And does Edith – does Miss Miller prefer it, too?"

Billig seemed to hesitate.

"It's hard to say. She doesn't use it much – most of her time has been spent inside the hospital. The flat's convenient." There was a fold in the high forehead, an evasive turn of his head. Simon felt instinctively that Billig, like himself, was thinking of Hector Wyn as a disturbing factor in Edith's world. It was a point he could not pursue, and to avoid it he drove back on the other spike of his dilemma.

"Anyhow, I can't believe she's seriously taken up with Judaism. It's just a fad. No doubt the family side appeals to her – to her affections. There's nothing else in it."

"You have to accept the fact that she's Jewish by blood – why can't you accept the fact that she's Jewish in mind? Surely if you know Miss Miller at all, you must be aware that she is an unusual girl – at least, that she is quite capable of taking a serious interest—"

" Capable, – oh, Lord, yes!" said Simon wildly. "I know she's capable of taking an interest in all sorts of things! As for *unusual* – don't I just know it! She's wonderful – extraordinary – exceptional—" he checked his rising tones. Billig was sitting now, with his hands supporting his face, wearing a peculiar, withdrawn look. His forefingers worked over his ears. He was either not listening, or deliberately holding aloof. Simon continued, more quietly, "But that's all the more reason to doubt that she can find any satisfaction in all this. Don't you think so?"

Billig did not answer. Simon would have liked to shake him into agreement.

"Come, now, honestly – don't you think it's remarkable that a girl like Edith Miller should bother about Judaism?"

"No," said Billig simply. "I think it's natural. What I consider remarkable is that she should not bother, as you call it, about the only part of Judaism that matters. I am afraid that, in spite of everything, she is no more religious than – than you seem to be."

Simon put his hands into his pockets and smiled.

"Isn't that exactly what I've been saying? – that it's only a fad on her part and means nothing."

"That is not in the least what *I've* been saying. Miss Miller is genuinely Jewish – she is genuinely concerned with Judaism; but strangely enough, she does not seem concerned with religion."

"*Strangely* – I should think so! Where's the difference? I mean, how can one be genuinely Jewish without being religious?"

"One can't, in my opinion. And yet, somehow Miss Miller doesn't seem to realise it—"

"Then she isn't really Jewish, – that's all – birth doesn't matter, especially in a case like hers."

Simon smiled again, as, if he had settled the point. Billig regarded him gravely, without changing his attitude. "I'm afraid, Black, you have somewhat confused ideas. I shouldn't be surprised if you think that religion is just ceremonial practice. As a theological student, you ought to know—"

"I'm not a theological student any longer, thank Heaven!" Simon made an impatient movement and rose to go. He had no desire to enter into abstract discussion with Billig. He had got the essential facts of Edith's history, and he preferred his own, to Billig's, interpretation of them. Nothing else the minister could say mattered in the least. At the door he turned back.

"I say, Billig – excuse my asking – but have you got fixed up yet?"

"No. I'm awaiting answers to two applications."

"London?"

"Yes. Suburbs."

"Well – look here – if nothing comes of them – how would you like to go to South Wales?"

"There's no vacancy, as far as I know."

"There will be, soon – at Dawport. It isn't likely to be advertised. As a matter of fact, I'm supposed to have it. My uncle is the President, and the committee have agreed. As I'm off the list, I should advise you to write in. Now's your chance. Nobody else knows anything about it."

"Thanks." Billig's hands had dropped: he clasped them before him, roused from his trance. "It's very good of you, Black. You are quite sure you won't – change—?"

"Quite. Dawport is just the place for you. Mostly foreigners, very few English. Oil and water, as usual. A chance for you to work your miracle!" Simon grinned. "I'll speak up for you to my uncle – it might be some good – suppose they arrange a trial 'preach' – ?"

"Thanks," said Billig, again. He seemed oblivious of the sarcasm in Simon's tone. His earnest gratitude followed Simon from the room, abashing the flippant thoughts it bore upon. Why had he made the proposition? A sudden impulse, born of mixed reactions to the queer, hunched way the orphan sat behind his hands. It would be a good thing for Billig, no doubt. But hadn't he – Simon – thought it specially good that the young minister should go away from London – away from the Jewish orbit in which Edith moved? An instantaneous dismay succeeded formulation of the thought. He had forgotten that Edith, too, would be in Wales! Not for long, of course. Even if the new light on clinics protracted village reforms, they would not keep her unduly at Blaemawe. Lady Hafod meant to capture her for Devonshire. And a fresh enterprise might develop at any time. One never knew with Edith! It was as well to think of her humorously, indulgently, as one would of an adorable but wilful child. No doubt Lady

Hafod regarded her as such. All very well for Billig to stress each point of conflict in his heavy-pawed style. The Lady of Shalott and her golden-haired darling were bound too closely to be parted by a swarth-nosed East End Bube. And Billig himself with his solemnities – surely, surely she must find him dull!

Simon strove to sail lightly over the stream of his uneasiness and suspense. A diversion was welcome, and he seized eagerly upon a letter bearing the Blaemawe postmark, addressed in a round childish writing he did not know. He was surprised to find it came from Jani.

"Dearest Simon", she wrote, "Why don't you write me about the place, as you promised? I have been waiting to hear about it this long time. I have been home for five weeks because my mother sent for me. She fell down the coalhouse and hurt her foot. But she is getting about now and I am glad to be going from Blaemawe, although I am not glad to be going back to my Uncle Trevor's house. He is getting more nasty every day, like a proper tyrant about the place, in the house and in the shop. My auntie is thankful to see the back of him, and the same with the girls in the drapery. But he is everywhere and his eyes are on everybody. Who do you think I saw in Blaemawe? Ieuan Richards. He has finished in that school where he was learning typewriting and shorthand. He can type and write beautiful with one hand, and he is looking for a place to be a clerk in Dawport. He sings very nice in chapel. He wanted me to go for walks with him. I did not want to go, but he was on to me all the time, so I went once. I hope you won't be minding that, dear Simon. I would rather be in London. Write to tell me soon about the place I told you of before. I think it is a good place, though Miss Meredith don't tell me anything now about her friend Tegwen Price. I would like to try for it if there is room, or else try for another place I have seen in the papers.

"From your loving friend,
"JANI.

"P.S. There is a fester on my finger, so Miss Jones, the Bush is writing this for me."

Artless Miss Jones the Bush – and artless Jani! Never had the plaintive voice come through more truly. Simon chuckled. Most of the words were mis-spelt, and his pencil jabbed at the places where the punctuation failed. The attempt to arouse his jealousy of Ieuan amused him most. Sweet, ingenuous, absurd little thing! It might be rather fun to see her in London, after all. At any rate, she seemed to be having a rotten time, and it would be decent to help her out of it. He decided to proceed forthwith to Kensington and make the necessary inquiries. At the same time he could have another look at that room he had seen a few weeks ago in a quiet side street off the Western end. Possibly it was not let yet – the landlady had not been in a hurry. She was a widow with a seafaring son, who occupied the second bedroom of her small flat whenever he came home. But his absences were increasing, and soon he was going away on a year-long trip. Mrs. Hedges had decided to let his room to "some nice, quiet, respectable young feller" – presumably like Simon. "I can let you have it that long," she said, "and if my Jim should turn in afore you can turn out," she cackled at her own little joke— "well, there's always a chair bed in the kitchen for one of you."

Her rooms were high up, on the third floor of the gaunt, ramshackle house. Simon was used to being as high, and here there were no rattling machines, no narrow stairways crammed with workers, no shop-doors clanging below. It was quiet and discreet, like a faded gentlewoman. The hall and landings were spacious, if dingy, and the rooms seemed clean. Mrs. Hedges was not a professional landlady, and her terms were low. It would suit Simon very well, if he got his job – if—! He promised to let her know definitely at the end of the week.

XV

SIMON mounted the steps at Ridgmount Gardens with the *machzar*, wrapped in brown paper, tight under his arm. There seemed a strange lack of response to his ring. Then suddenly – so suddenly that, stretching across to ring again, he almost fell inwards – the door was opened by a curious, squat little figure, her eyes dark and apprehensive under thick, black brows.

"There's nobody at home," she announced in agitated tones, broad with the vowels of Wales.

Simon stood looking at her in bewilderment. "Oh – but—" he said,— "this is Mrs. Wyn's, isn't it? Miss Miller expects me—"

"No, sir – Nurse – Miss Miller's gone away, sir. There's nobody at home."

"Gone away!"

"Yes, indeed, sir, she went away this morning—" The little maid looked as if she were about to cry, whether from nervousness or unhappiness it was difficult to tell. But Simon's own dismay left no margin for examination of hers.

"But where – ? I mean, can't you tell me anything about it? Can't I see—"

"No, sir, there's nobody at home."

Simon had a vindictive wish to shake the stupid little creature, with her "Welshy" parrot-cry. She retreated as if sensitive to the malign look on his face. At that moment a slight rustle behind her drew Simon's eye to the inner door, through which someone was evidently peeping. As he gazed, the door opened wider, and out stepped the smart maid he was accustomed to see. She was dressed in outdoor costume, and smiled brightly at him.

"It's all right, Lizzie," she said, waving a gloved hand at the other. "You can go back to the kitchen – I'll attend to Mr. Black."

Lizzie vanished clumsily. Her superior closed the door after her with lifted brows.

"What's all this about, Johnson?" asked Simon, putting his hat down automatically on the stand.

"Well, sir, I've got the afternoon off, and Lizzie is rather raw, I'm afraid. She makes a good kitchenmaid, as Miss Miller said she would, but when it comes to answering the door—"

Johnson made an expressive gesture and pursed her lips.

"But why did she say there's nobody at home?" Simon was beginning to look exasperated. Johnson was buttoning her gloves, and seemed to have no intention of showing him in.

"Well, sir, Mrs. Wyn's had a trying time to-day, and she's asleep at present – we've orders not to disturb her."

"But Miss Miller?"

"She's left."

There was something about the smart maid's manner that convinced Simon, more than "Lizzie's" agitation, that some untoward event had occurred.

"I don't mind telling you, sir," she whispered, "there's been a row. Miss Miller and Dr. Wyn – they had words. Miss Miller said she wouldn't stay. Mrs. Wyn was upset, somethink awful. But Miss Miller packed her things and went off this morning."

Simon took his hat up quickly.

"She didn't leave any message for me?"

The maid simpered.

"No, sir – she was that hurried, I expect she forgot."

"You don't know where she is staying?"

"I don't, sir. Perhaps they know at the hospital. If I find out I'll be glad to let you know."

Simon took a sudden dislike to the smart maid, with her knowing air and too-sympathetic look. He muttered something and went away. It was no good going to the hospital with the *machzar*. She would not be there at this hour – possibly she would not return there at all. She must have gone to Bishopsgate. No doubt Billig would know the address. But that afternoon Billig could not be found. It was late next day before Simon, avoiding the publicity of the College, tracked the young minister in a private hour.

He noticed at once that Billig was full of mysterious knowledge.

"I've got a message for you, Black," he announced— "from Miss Miller. She has left Ridgmount Gardens and is staying with her grandmother at Bishopsgate."

"I know. But I want the exact address—"

"137, Caramel Place – it's the Bevis Marks end. I've been asked to take you there to-morrow evening – that is, if you care to attend a meeting we are going on to."

"Meeting?" said Simon doubtfully.

"Yes – a meeting at Toynbee Hall. It's to be addressed by Miss Flora Canuto."

"A *Jewish* meeting?" said Simon, and added hastily— "All right, I'll come – I say, Billig – do you know why she left the Wyns so suddenly?"

"Yes," said Billig. He wore a curious expression – as if

some secret satisfaction were being suppressed by righteous sorrow.

"Well – can't you tell me?"

"It's a private affair. Still, you know the family history now – you might as well know this, too."

Simon waited.

"There have been rumours at the hospital that no Jewish medical student stood a chance of getting work under Hector. Edith – Miss Miller heard them, of course. But she took no notice until a definite case cropped up. It seems a fellow called Polasky tried several times to get an assistantship. He is convinced he would have succeeded but for Hector. Somehow he found out about the relationship, and came to Edith with a complaint. At the time Hector disclaimed responsibility, but a few days ago he refused to give Polasky a recommendation to another job. Polasky asked for an interview at the flat, and Edith insisted on Hector granting it. She says Polasky was very offensive in his manner—"

"To *her*?" said Simon, glowering.

"No – to Hector. He declared that out of respect to Miss Miller, he would not carry out his intention of exposing her cousin. Hector, of course would regard it as an exposure to be known as a Jew!" Billig made a sound that in anyone else would have been called a snort. "Polasky understood that – I suppose it's to his credit that he won't take advantage of it. He threatened, however, to pay him out in some other way. Hector practically kicked him out of the flat." Billig paused.

"And then – Miss Miller left?"

"She took strong exception to Wyn's attitude. He said he would not associate with Jewish scum. She told him in return that she would not associate with Anti-Semitic Jews. She said it was impossible to continue living at the flat. Mrs. Wyn begged and implored her to remain, but she left almost at once."

Simon's face had caught some reflection from Billig's. But it was certainly not righteous sorrow that he felt. "She must have been worked up," he muttered.

"Probably Hector was, too," said Billig. He eyed Simon silently for a moment, "you may have guessed – he hoped to marry her."

"She didn't agree, it's evident!" exclaimed Simon.

"But she might, if it wasn't for – her very strong Jewish feeling."

"I don't believe it," said Simon sharply.

The disagreeable idea spread like gall over his relief at her escape.

"As for the strong Jewish feeling – you're obsessed, Billig. It's just a natural hatred of mean behaviour. I admire her spirit. And it serves Wyn right."

"Hector is not mean by nature," said Billig. "It's just an example of how disloyalty to Judaism makes a man disloyal to his better self —"

"Fudge! – Preacher!" thought Simon. But he did not wish to offend Billig at this moment. And after all, it was only the orphan's way of hiding his own feelings. Simon could "let himself go" over Hector Wyn: for some reason Billig couldn't. And yet Simon was certain he shared his own dislike. It reconciled him to the prospect of Billig's escort to Edith's new abode. They arranged to meet on Saturday evening at Holborn. Billig's lodging was at Red Lion Court.

But the day was transformed for Simon in its earlier hours. The first post informed Simon Black, B.A., that he had become an English Civil Servant.

That day was neither long enough nor short enough to satisfy him. There was so much to be done as a result of the glorious news: there were so many hours to wait before he could impart it to Edith. When he met Billig, he did not blurt it out at once, as he might have done had they not been bound together for Edith's company. The third person of the party must not hear before the first. It was a queer scruple, and it cost him much to observe it. But Billig seemed to have news of his own to absorb and agitate him. His eyes were concrete with a kind of startled distress. Now and again they met Simon's, bulged with joy, as if in mute appeal. It was some time before Simon realised it. They were nearing Cheapside when he said lightly:

"What's up, Billig? You look worried."

"I am, rather," said Billig. "Not exactly worried, but—" He paused.

Simon said nothing. He walked on, almost forgetting his companion, when the latter burst out suddenly.

"I've been to see Mrs. Wyn. She sent for me."

"Yes?"

"Oh, it was only to tell me how she missed Edith and so on, and to suggest that I might be able to persuade her to return. I don't know why I should."

"Nor do I. Surely you needn't worry about that—"

"No." Billig seemed to struggle with a difficulty. "Perhaps I oughtn't to speak of it, but – anyhow, you'll keep it to yourself. Something happened while I was there. A phone call came through from Hector from Surrey."

"Surrey?"

"Yes, he spends an occasional week-end there with another doctor, who has a cottage near some golf links. He went down late last night. Of course, Shabbas is nothing to him. Nor to Polasky."

"Oh, did Polasky go, too?" Simon, roused from his self-absorption, stared at Billig. "You don't mean to say that Wyn invited him?"

"Of course not. He must have watched and followed him. Hector rang up to reassure his mother in case she had heard rumours of an accident or assault – he thought something had got into the papers. She hadn't seen anything, but she was alarmed at once. He said he had fallen in the dark lane leading to the cottage, and bruised himself on the rough path. He assured her it was nothing at all – only his face had bumped on a stone and was so swollen that he didn't care to return until it had gone down. He might stay on a day longer."

"Did he say anything about Polasky?"

"Certainly not."

"Then how do you know?"

Billig hesitated.

"I don't really *know*. That's why I oughtn' to speak of it – and I hope you won't. But somehow I feel absolutely sure. It flashed into my mind at once that what had happened was a fight in the dark lane."

Simon laughed – somewhat incredulously. It was chiefly at such an idea having occurred to Billig.

"Polasky threatened something of the kind," said the minister hurriedly. "He told Hector he'd show him that Jewish scum had English fists."

"But do you mean there was an actual *fight* – or that Polasky assaulted Wyn and cleared?"

"I mean they fought. If it was just an assault, and the assailant cleared off in the dark, Hector wouldn't cover it up in the way he did. I think Polasky challenged him. It would be in keeping with his threat to have it out between themselves."

Simon looked at Billig with admiration. He had not believed the minister's imagination equal to such an effort.

"Well, that's one to Polasky. A thoroughly sensible way of settling accounts."

"Sensible? I think it's shameful, disgusting, horrible!"

"Nonsense, Billig. It's better than going round sneaking on Wyn, telling everybody he's a dirty Jew and so on. And I expect it gave him ten times more satisfaction."

"I'm afraid your view is a perverted one. Isn't it better to expose a contemptible secrecy, to make a straightforward complaint – have the matter sifted properly, if necessary, before the right authorities – than go pummelling each other's bodies in a brutal, primitive way?"

"It's the English way," declared Simon. "And it's the best, believe me."

Billig turned from him with an expression of distaste. Simon laughed again, his buoyancy at his own good fortune increased by delight in the punishment meted out to Hector Wyn. He countered Billig's disapproval with conviction of superior judgment. Fancy the orphan, born a Britisher, unable to adopt a point of view which even a beastly East Ender like Polasky could exemplify! He was right, however, in not wishing to report the affair until it could be substantiated. And after all, there might not be much satisfaction in telling Edith, if she showed concern for the victim: That Dr. Wyn had been the victim, Simon felt no doubt whatever. Vicarious triumph was rounding off his day.

They walked along the deserted Leadenhall Street, its hives of commerce empty and silent: then turned into the still quieter Caramel Place. Tall buildings islanded this unexpected nook. Its warehoused offices, once retail shops, were probably used to workday bustle, and trails of traffic from the thoroughfares around. But now it seemed a peaceful retreat. Twilight shadows hid the scars of trade. The windows of living-rooms above were wide, and some were daintily curtained. It was strange, however, to stand before a warped shop front, awaiting entrance to Edith Miller's home. The door opened, and an elderly woman, in a shabby alpaca dress, peered out at them.

"Ow, it's you, Mr. Billig. Come along in."

"Good evening, Miss Smithson. How's the chest?"

"A little easier, thank you. The autumn's my bad time, though, so I dow'nt expect much. But it eynt no use complyning. Miss Edith's on at me, to try this 'n that, but I sy, what's got to be as got to be. And the Lord's will be done."

She wheezed asthmatically as she led them through the dark, ill-boarded interior. Simon's spirits dropped. The shrouded shop, the bare, uneven stairs, the gaunt landing, presaged an atmosphere he dreaded – dinginess, spiced soup, brined herrings and onions, guttural Yiddish. He braced his nostrils for the reek, as the woman opened, very quietly, a heavy door leading off a curve on the landing. Probably that curve shut off much sound. There was a pause as she waited for Billig, groping in the rear: and in that pause Simon received an impression of a long, light dignified room, airy and orderly. At a table near the large lace-hung window, sat a little old lady, reading in a low voice from a huge brown volume. Beside her on a hassock was Edith, her golden head against the reader's knee, her eyelids lowered to her cheeks. A furrow of trouble shadowed the lovely face. Was she listening or brooding? At the stir in the doorway she started up.

"Come in, please," she said softly, and put a gentle hand on the old lady's arm. "Granny, here's Mr. Billig, and another friend."

The reading sank to a whisper, but hardly ceased. The old lady's lips were still moving as she turned her head. A quiet greeting came.

"Good shabbas," she said.

"Shabbas is almost gone, I think," said Edith. "We ought to have the lights on – too bad for your eyes, granny! No, not just yet, Hannah—" to the woman moving with matches toward a gas chandelier— "if we are not reading we might as well enjoy the twilight a little longer. It's pleasant, isn't it? And we need not rush to the meeting, Mr. Billig. Won't you both sit down? I'm glad you decided to come, too, Mr. Black."

She accepted her *machzar* with a grave nod, and listened calmly to his stammered greetings. He was furious with himself for his nervous airs – why, it was he who ought to be cool and full of assurance, and she who might well display embarrassment at her queer position here. But nothing seemed further from her mind. The only thing that detracted from her ease was the furrow on her brow. Her smile lacked gaiety.

He looked at Billig, attending with solemn courtesy to the old lady, who had risen and advanced to them. She had taken off her spectacles and laid them on her book. Her little hands, worn and shrivelled, were clasped before her; her little face, pointed and sunk, its delicate, fine-drawn features taut beneath yielding skin, gazed in welcoming scrutiny at the stranger. He had never met a look more sweet and serene, yet more disturbingly full of mystic light. A touch of awe subdued his restlessness. It was an emanation strangely unexpected from so small, so fragile, so diffident a being.

"You are from the country, my granddaughter tells me – from the place where she has lived herself. It is far to travel to see your parents, is it not?"

She had began in broken English, and ended in Yiddish, but her voice hardly changed its low, rich note. It was a voice charged with echoes,— with his mother's harsher timbre, even with Edith's clear bell. Odd blend of dissonance in one harmonious chord.

"Yes," said Simon, held as in a spell.

"Ah, so it is with Jewish mothers – their children leave them and they cannot often meet. At least it is good if they remember them."

She sighed and returned to her chair. Simon sat down awkwardly on his.

"Mr. Billig, if you have time I should like to show you this passage – but first, you must have some tea. Mein kind, where is Hannah? Is she making tea?"

"I daresay. Shall I go and see?"

"Please don't," said Simon, starting up. "We don't want any – I'm sure I don't – really, we've just had—"

"It's no use," said Edith, with her glimmering smile. "Here comes Hannah – and you simply must drink it. Nothing would shock granny more than the departure of a visitor without tea. No matter at what unlikely hour anyone calls at this house, tea must be offered, and must be drunk. Please submit to the inevitable rite!"

He took the cup she offered him and smiled uneasily back. Why did she not ask about himself? Surely she had not forgotten? He could not announce his news unasked. Couldn't she read the message in his eyes? Her own were clouded. Some inner gloom obscured him from her. It vexed and disconcerted him. He had come here eager for attention, for her instant share in his delight. And she was cool, indifferent, withdrawn. He wished they were out in the street together. It was not only her abstraction that constrained him. Something in this room had an intimidating effect. Certainly it was not the room itself. Now that he could look round and observe its details, the impression of freshness and simplicity remained. Light spread from the ceiling and the panelled walls, low-relief lincrusta washed in cream. Below a polished rail was a bolder dado, stained, a rich deep brown, from which a brown carpet flowed across the floor. The solid walnut furniture was plain and dignified. Some silver and glass lit the surfaces, a bowl of roses stood on the white-decked central table. Bronzes, a clock, and a framed photograph looked down from the high mantelpiece. There was only one picture – a large print of Moses, bringing down the Tables of the Law from Sinai. A copy of this print hung in the Blacks' home at Blaemawe: it had stared at Simon, too, from the Fincks' jumbled walls. Here its solitary state lent it emphasis, beyond its crude and anachronistic worth. Moses' uncovered locks had a more golden sheen, the blue of his gown seemed deeper – as deep as Edith's eyes. Perhaps she was responsible for denuding the walls, leaving the favourite in possession. She could have taken only a negative part in the arrangement of the room. It was bare, it was airy, it was restful; but was almost like a blank countenance, devoid of character. If old Mrs. Miller owned other household goods, they were not visible here, unless they were concentrated in that huge brown volume, over which Billig was now bending with her. Simon knew its speckled varnished covers very well. That also had its duplicate in Blaemawe – his mother's chief cherished treasure, with loose yellow pages that testified to use from early girlhood in Russia. The Taich Chemosh – odd compilation of Talmudic lore and legend, rendered into Yiddish, to edify pious women who could not study Hebrew. To this farrago Edith had been listening.

"I was surprised to find you had left the flat," he said abruptly.

She did not answer at once. Her brows drew closer together.

"I'm sorry I couldn't let you know in time," she said. "I found I had to leave – rather suddenly." She paused, looked out of the window, and began again, in her light rapid manner— "Do you know this spot? It's full of interest. I'm glad granny desired to live on here. When my uncle Hyman – that's the family there" – she pointed to the photograph on the mantelpiece— "when they moved to Stamford Hill, they meant to take granny with them. But she refused to go. She felt she could not leave the place she had got so used to – the shool round the corner – all the shops she liked to buy from – and the friends around. So it was decided to reserve this floor for her and Hannah, who has been with her for fifteen years – and is a first-rate companion and housekeeper. My uncle attends to business every day, of course, and the family pay visits. She isn't lonely. And she loves to have me here." A glance flashed from the blue eyes to the little murmuring figure. "It suits me very well. I have a dear little room of my own – I've always kept my books and etchings here – and there are so many opportunities of studying the folk around. I'm anxious to understand them. But it's difficult to know what their lives are like unless one can really *help*. I wish I had known before – I wish I had thought of concentrating here, in the East End. Even if only to help the Jewish sick and poor."

"But you started out to help Blaemawe—"

"Yes. And I intend to carry out my original plan, as far as beginning the work is concerned. It will take months, no doubt. But once it's all set going – and Marjorie Newell installed—"

"Will she go?"

"I believe she will. If not, we'll get another nurse. Then I can safely leave Blaemawe and come back to London. I intend to keep in touch with a centre here."

"What will Lady Hafod think?"

"I'm afraid she'll be disappointed. But it can't be helped." Her face, which had warmed, took on a shade of regret. Then she sprang up in renewed animation,— "Oh, I think we must be going! – And it's time to light up. Yes, Hannah, please!"

Was that woman in the room all the while – or from what quiet entrance did she come uncalled? As her match sent a flame to the sizz of gas, and the light spread over each dark corner, Simon saw a curtained arch through which she moved. Wheezing slightly, she had brought in a tray, set with wine, a silver cup, and a jingling casket of fretted design. At Mrs. Miller's gesture, she placed them before the minister, now standing upright at the table.

Simon drew near reluctantly. Of course, he might have known, with Billig here, that the "Habdalah," the ceremony of speeding out the Sabbath, would be performed. Billig took the cup in his right hand, shook the spice-casket with its little silver bells and flags, and in his sonorous voice blessed "the King of the Universe, who made distinction between holy and profane, between light and darkness, between Israel and other nations, between the seventh day and the six working days"— There seemed a richer lilt than usual in his intoning voice— "The day hath declined like the palm-tree's shade."

Simon tried not to look at Edith as she stood beside him. He had just become aware that she had disappeared, when his eyes, drawn to the grandmother, were held by the worn, sweet face. She did not speak, but regarded him with a deep, mild gaze, that asked nothing, promised nothing, yet moved the soul with certitude of some poignant claim. It was such a strange thrall, the silent powerful magnetism of a simple look, that Simon hardly knew whether he was relieved or not when Edith's voice broke in, "I'm ready. Let us go."

She was dressed in a plain, dark suit, the fairness of her skin vivid against the deep material. Mrs. Miller looked wistfully into her face.

"Mein kind, you will not be late—"

"No, granny. But you must not wait up – nor Hannah. I have my key, and I'll let myself in."

Simon was glad to leave the room. The sense of inhibition, of check, was too strong, though how to associate it with the delicate old lady would have been a puzzle. When, after his own and Billig's farewells to her, she followed their descent down the stairs, he was the more disconcerted. There was no remonstrance from Edith. When she saw his look of surprise, she smiled faintly and whispered, as they waited at the foot.

"Granny is quite firm on her feet – she hates to be helped. And nothing hurts her more than to be prevented from escorting guests to the door. She does it invariably, with friend, relative, – any sort of caller – even a beggar!"

It was, indeed, a firm step that sounded on the uneven

wood. There was a habit of vigour and alertness that belied the frail form, the little trembling hands. Down she came, through the dark store, lit belatedly by Hannah; and stepped, after the others, into the quiet street. They did not linger. Her low voice and wistful gaze were not meant to detain the guests leaving her home. Before they turned into Houndsditch they looked back. The little figure was still standing at her door in the dim square, a visible benediction.

"Dear Bubele," said Edith softly to herself. Simon hardly caught it – he guessed at the word. But it did not trouble him. That whisper at the foot of the stairs, her touch on his arm to keep him from going to the old lady's help, had re-established their nearness. He could see something dawn in her face as she turned it on him. She was going to speak, when Billig said:

"I'm afraid I shall have to leave the meeting rather early. I've made an appointment for 9.30, with the father of a prospective pupil. He can't see me any other time. It's a nuisance, I know – having to dash out of a meeting before it's over—"

"We'll sit at the back," said Edith. "You can slip out easily. Mr. Black—"

"Even then, it's awkward. If I'm seen leaving, it may be thought I'm evading public discussion. An address by Miss Canuto on the spiritual values of Judaism may quite possibly conflict with traditional views, and it might be necessary for me to make some comments."

"You can make them in the *Jewish Chronicle*," said Edith, with a smile which added to Simon's exasperation. Why did she allow herself to be distracted? "I've been reading it lately. It seems full of comments made by lecturers on each other! I study the notices, and want to go to all the East End meetings advertised. Unfortunately I'm seldom free at the right times – and it isn't much use listening to Yiddish speeches – I can't follow too well. To be quite frank, I'm not particularly good at following *any* speeches. And they're usually so dull! I hope you won't be bored to-night. I really know nothing of Miss Canuto's views – only of her welfare work, which is splendid."

"You were going to ask me, Miss Miller—?" began Simon. He was determined to prevent Billig "butting in" again.

"About – your results – have you heard yet?"

Simon made an effort not to stop, but to go on walking, and keep his voice flat and steady.

"Yes," he said. "I've got the job."

To his delight, it was she who stopped, to begin pouring out congratulations. Billig joined in with less animation.

"I suppose it's for the best," he said, moving on somewhat impatiently. "But it's saddening to think of the number of students who have left the College to go in for other things—"

"Lamentations of Jeremiah," said Simon cheerfully. "You'll make up for us all, Billig. Why should fellows stick to what they aren't suited to? I don't know what reasons the others had. Anyway, it didn't suit *me*."

"Obviously," said Edith. "Why lament the defection of any student who isn't qualified *naturally*, as well as academically, to be a minister?"

"If he isn't qualified naturally, he shouldn't become a theological student at all," said Billig. "And being at the College should tighten, not loosen, his attachment to his original choice."

"It isn't always his own choice," said Simon.

"Perhaps the College hasn't the right methods – for tightening?" said Edith.

"It has its limitations, no doubt," said Billig. "But that isn't the fault of the authorities. They provide the student with all the material he needs in the way of literature and law. I don't know what more they can do."

"A great deal, I imagine, in the way they *present* their material. But do you know, Mr. Billig – you've left out religion!"

"Please don't be ironical with me, Miss Miller," Billig spoke rather sharply – to Simon's astonishment. "You know perfectly well that religion is synonymous with all I have already mentioned."

Edith looked at him as if taking up a gage.

"Then why do you separate them," she said, "whenever I claim a national as well as a religious interpretation of certain laws and dicta?"

"I don't separate them. I say that the terms 'national' and 'religious' are identical in Judaism. Or if not identical, then inextricably bound together – a double thread. Under no circumstances can there be a division."

"Yet a division has taken place," said Edith. "When the Jew lost his country, he held on by a single thread, the other having been broken off. Exile forced him to tie himself up tightly. Self-preservation of course. If he had loosened or been cut off from that thread, he would have been lost. I can see why the College must stress the importance of religion. And you are satisfied with that?"

"Yes, if they stress the fact that religion is more than empty ceremony – that there is a spiritual core that needs cultivation—"

"Can such a thing be cultivated? Surely, it has to be inborn. Of course you mean that the College gives all the instruction necessary for making the spiritual core effective. Perhaps. But it does not seem, from what I can gather, to cater for the students who need to be made Jews, as well as Jewish ministers." She turned to Simon. "I wonder if you agree with me?"

"I – I'm not sure what you mean—"

Simon had listened to the exchange in some annoyance. He saw no point or purpose in discussing Jews' College except in relation to his own departure from it. Why did Edith bother to split hairs with Billig?

"I mean the necessity of teaching that Israel was not only a religious sect, but a people – a conglomeration of tribes, if you like, that became a people – leading a complete national existence in its own country—"

"That sort of thing is done," he muttered. "You mean history – the facts—"

"But how are they treated? Like archeologists treat the facts of Egypt. Dead bones, turned over by dry-as-dust professors, too lifeless themselves to breathe out a vital spark. I've heard them – in public lectures. I don't suppose the private ones are better. In fact, I'm sure they are not – from all you tell me" – she addressed herself again to Billig— "you and that other student I've met – is it Mandel? I saw him again the other day with a Welsh student, Rees – at a Welsh club. We talked about it, and he agreed with me."

"What can you expect, Miss Miller?" said Billig. He had grown mild and patient again, equally to Simon's displeasure. What right had Billig to smile indulgently into Edith's challenging face? "The college spirit is academic, of course.

I deplore it as much as you do, if not for quite the same reason. But you are unfair to at least one of our professors. Doctor Sidach would probably please you, by his insistence on the historic continuity of Jewish life—"

"Yes – l've heard of Dr. Sidach – a younger man, isn't he? – Mr. Mandel told me, he's different. Do you think he's different, Mr. Black?"

"He's not dry-as-dust – in fact rather jolly," said Simon. "I haven't noticed any other difference. He's just as foreign as the rest."

They had crossed Aldgate into Commercial Street. Shabby waddling people jerked and parted them. The long stretch of dingy buildings had a sodden look. The sky was dark, not a star had appeared, and the lamps lit intermittent patches of smudged window, ugly wood and stone. The spring in Simon's heart was running down. Caramel Place had subdued him, but he had not expected this flatness in the streets. It was Billig's fault, of course. There was something on Edith's mind – she was troubled, vexed. The aftermath of the scene in Ridgmount Gardens. He might meet it, drive it clean away, if only he could get her whole attention. But the solemn orphan intervened, appealed to her argumentative vein, which was only tolerable when one received direct the glances of those deep blue eyes. She had looked at him only once or twice: and her words, when one lost the music of her tones, left a sharp, disagreeable edge.

And now this wretched meeting. What had he let himself in for? There was one bright spot – Billig's early withdrawal. Perhaps she could be persuaded, too, to leave soon after, – for a stroll or bus-ride, in the dark, clear air – where they could talk, unhindered, on subjects of his choice.

A door in a red brick frontage different from the business premises around, led into an open quadrangle, unexpected in its peace and classic shape. A lantern lit the shadows of foliage on high walls. Simon had heard vaguely of Toynbee Hall, its settlement work, its use as a centre for Jewish meetings. Notices of more general educational activities were posted in the entrance lobbies. He would have lingered over them, but Edith and Billig had passed quickly into the lecture hall, already full of people. They slipped quietly into rear seats, and Simon gazed at the audience in front.

A Jewish crowd, undoubtedly local in the main. A few well-dressed figures, many neat and unpretentious. Some shabby and down-at-heel. Distinctively Jewish, yet curiously unlike the pictures always drawn of characteristic types – sleek, luscious faces, coarse bodies peacocked and bejewelled. There were such creatures, Simon knew: he had seen them at great mixed gatherings, in West End streets, at cafes and theatres. The men and women here were different. Of spare demeanour, unobtrusive, unostentatious, with parched faces and wearied spines. Only their eyes were rich and clamant: dark, vital orbs, sad, haunting, probing, filled with a restlessness that seemed to gnaw at life.

The meeting had begun. The short, perky man in the chair was speaking. He made a brief introduction of the lady on his right, who stood up rather stiffly in a murmuring pause. Simon was surprised to see a large, humped frame, with a squarish, calm, phlegmatic face. She looked a solid, respectable country matron, without affiliations to any Semitic line – certainly without hint of spiritual preoccupation. Simon liked her clear, precise English. The limpid, practised flow could hold the ear in unexpected charm. But the address began to seem to him rambling and vague. Instead of listening, he looked at Edith's cheek, so delightfully near to his. The concentration of his gaze drew hers, and again he had that rare, that exquisite sensation of the kinship of feeling that transcended every conflict of mind. She looked away immediately, and he could not recapture her eyes. But still he watched the lovely curve, half listening again to the speaker's clear flow, because Edith herself so obviously wished to listen. She did not seem, however, to be greatly moved. That slight, hard pressure of the lips – was it an expression of dissent, or due to her secret preoccupation? Once she sent a quick glance at Billig, and reluctantly, Simon looked too. The orphan was intensely absorbed. He leaned forward to catch every word that fell, so easily and fitly, from the plain woman's mouth. Simon could see his high brow, the thin, sloping nose, the eager chin, jutting out on the other side of Edith. Of course, it was just the stuff to appeal to Billig – this talk about the salving of Israel's soul from the materialism of ritual – the return to the higher purposes of Judaism as revealed by the prophets. It did not interest Simon any more than the demands of the "ritualists". The whole thing was "played out" – an anachronism. He was glad Edith, with her disturbing reactions to Jewishness, did not seem to be catching fire at this. It showed she had her reserves: it. showed, too, that Billig had no serious influence upon her.

The speaker ended with quiet suddenness. She sat down, stiffly still again, while the chairman led a little burst of applause. Billig moved reluctantly to slide out of his seat. His long back crooked as he whispered to Edith— "Beautiful – beautiful – and so true! An inspiration. You felt it, I'm sure—"

"It seemed quite Christian, to me," she murmured. Simon looked quickly to see if Billig was shocked. He could just catch the answering protest— "No, no. But there's the danger, in the abolition of forms. We must preserve both – form and spirit. It can be done. I see no difficulty – no hardship—" Why did Edith smile suddenly into the lugubrious face – a very full, sweet, tender smile? No wonder Billig seemed to be tearing himself away— "We'll talk of it another time – so sorry I must rush. Good-night – good-night."

Simon nodded to him with alacrity, and watched his awkward exit through the door. A few others disappeared with him, but the movement to rise and shuffle outward was checked by the chairman, standing up and asking for questions. He did not seem to expect any, however, and sank back in his seat with the discomposed air as a man stood up almost in front of him.

"I'm sorry to disturb the harmony of this meeting," began the man in a strong foreign accent.

"Question," snapped the chairman.

"Yes – I'll put it in that form. May I ask Miss Canuto how it is possible to reconcile the national images of the prophets with the idea of an exclusively spiritual mission? I don't mean reconciled in a Christian sense, the seeking of an individual salvation – but in a distinctively *Jewish* sense, and therefore dealing with the fact that if you abolish ritual you abolish both national usage and the ideal of national restoration. The Jewish people cannot belie their history and their hopes of a future—"

"No speeches, please. Any more questions?"

"Yes. Is there not a ghetto of the soul as well as of the body, from which it is desirable to emancipate ourselves? And is not that ghetto created by our denial of Jewish national claims?"

The man sat down abruptly to the renewed protest of the chairman. Simon had noticed the latter's look of helpless indignation, his exchange of murmurs with the lady beside him, and her gesture of patient tolerance. But as she rose to reply, Simon forgot to listen: he had caught sight of Edith's flushed face and shining eyes as she bent forward, trying to see more of the man who had asked the questions. Simon was startled. Did she know the man? Who was he, anyway? The next moment she was asking him the same question.

"I suppose you don't know him? Such a pity! I'd rather like to speak to him!"

"Why?"

"Oh, – you heard what he said? He wasn't asking for information – he was *giving* it. I'm glad I came, if only to have heard him say what he did. He has given the right focus to the whole position. I see it clearly now. What a pity Mr. Billig couldn't wait to hear – but then, he wouldn't accept it. I do, absolutely. Don't you?"

"No, I don't think so. Not if it means being a Jewish nationalist."

They had risen with the rest. The man who had asked the questions was surrounded by a group, every member of which appeared to be arguing with the central figure. He was of medium height, broad-shouldered and squat, and a glimpse of his face showed through – pale, rather flat, with short features, of the Slavonic cast. His voice, strong in pitch and accent, dominated the buzz of sound. An outer ring of listeners had formed. Everybody else was moving to the door. Miss Canuto in her navy serge costume and bulky hat, an attaché case in her hand, had passed out, the little chairman ambling fussily after. Her broad back towered above him in the quadrangle. She turned awkwardly as Edith, with Simon a step behind, joined them. He waited while a brief dialogue ensued. Miss Canuto's face must surely have caught some radiance from Edith, to become so light in welcome and pleasure.

"Certainly, Miss Miller. To-morrow. I shall be delighted to show you round."

He sighed with satisfaction. After all, her welfare work came uppermost. But his relief was short-lived. As the others bowed and disappeared, the sweet voice said to him:

"You don't believe we have a future?"

We. He hated the sound of the word on her lips. It spurred him to quick retort.

"Our future is in England."

"Even if the English don't want us? And what about the Jews in other countries?"

They were in the street, jostled by people walking up and down. It was not so dark now. A few stars had appeared, and the air, even here, seemed fresh and tonic.

"I don't see why we should be concerned about them. I suppose eventually they will fall into line with everybody else. Except for the religious people – and they're mostly old. Anyway, I'm English, and that's all that matters to me."

"You're a Jew as well. You don't forget that, do you?"

Her tone was slightly higher. She was walking as fast as the straggling passers-by would let her. For some yards they were divided, and came together again in the noise and glare of Gardiner's Corner. Simon felt irritated and thwarted. Why did she persist in the argumentative vein?

"I mean to forget it as soon as possible. Won't you take my arm? People bump about so here. You are not going straight back, I hope. It's early, and such a fine night. Let's walk to the

Embankment – or take a bus, if you prefer, and walk when we get there."

She hesitated. He had taken her arm, which she had yielded rather stiffly. Looking down at her from his extra few inches, his suppressed inner excitement rising into his eyes, he felt her impulse warm towards him. Then it was checked.

"No, I promised granny – I know she'll wait up for me." Her chin was tilted resolutely as they walked on. "You are not serious, are you?"

"Serious?"

"In what you said just now – about wishing to forget you're a Jew."

"Of course. Really, I have no interest or belief in the old customs, and it would be sheer hypocrisy on my part to pretend I had. Especially now, when I'm free. Why, you congratulated me, didn't you, on being honest?"

"I understood you did not feel 'called' to be a minister. But that's not the same thing as turning your back on everything Jewish." Her voice trembled. She seemed to be trying to control it. "Perhaps I don't quite understand, even now. Please tell me. I'm not quite so familiar with all the old customs as you are. You mean Hebrew prayers, attending Synagogue, keeping the Sabbath and Holy days, dietary laws—"

"Yes, of course – all the religious practices—" He spoke more eagerly, persuasively. After all, it was true, – she wasn't so familiar with these things – she was simply curious about them. She couldn't realise how repulsive they were.

"Religious! Religious!" she repeated. "Don't you find anything in them but religion? Myer Billig doesn't, of course – but then, he is religious. And so is Miss Canuto, who says one can dispense with all the laws and yet keep the Jewish religion. Really, I don't see where you come in, at all!"

"I don't come in," he said, with an attempt at a humorous laugh. "I'm right outside—"

"Indeed? You think that because you don't feel religious, you are no longer a Jew?"

"Oh, I know there's such a thing as race," he said, his irritation returning,— "what you call nationality, I suppose. But it's all dead and done with. It doesn't count. Not with me. I don't bother about it."

Simon's air of ingenuous finality was made impressive by his appearance, if not by his tone. Edith may have thought so, from the long look she gave his stalwart figure, his face, older and more serious than it had ever been. But the impression did not win her. She disengaged her arm, and halted. They were turning once more from Aldgate into Houndsditch. Around them people streamed in all directions, dark, swarthy, ebullient faces, pallid, bony faces, red, bloated, swinish faces, petulant, silly, commonplace faces. In the High Street with its public-houses the Jewish types were outnumbered by others. Through the open doors of the bars and around them could be seen the Gentile revellers, sullen, cheerful, quarrelsome, glum. Their husky, squeaking cockney accents filled the air. Straggling past shop windows went workmen and their wives, carrying bags and baskets bulged with vegetables, margarine, strips of bacon, Sunday joints, and tinned goods. They carried babies, too, whose heads hung down their parents' arms like rabbits. Most of them had a pinched, vacuous, dingy look, their eyes were dull and shallow, a sour, beery, pipe-stale odour exuded from their clothes. Threading their way through the shoppers and the drinkers came their Semitic neighbours, more alert, less laden, neither as jocose nor as apathetic. As Edith paused, two people brushed against her and moved raptly on – an old, shabby bearded man, with a younger woman, smartly though cheaply dressed, her full aquiline features working with animation as she recited a tale in Yiddish sing-song. The old man nodded his head and squeezed his hands together as he listened, sending out an occasional vibrant, "Azoy? – Azoy?"

"Those two people," said Edith, looking after them, "were probably born in Poland, or Roumania, or Austria – but don't you feel you have more in common with them than with that crowd drinking in there?"

"No," said Simon, "Quite the reverse."

"That's not true," said Edith sharply.

"But I say, Miss Miller" – he remonstrated— "I don't want to be identified with the drunks, of course, – but what I mean is—"

"Yes, I know what you mean – you needn't tell me. I've heard it all before – only this week. From someone who isn't concerned about the 'old customs', because he's never known them, anyway – but feels just as anxious as you not to be considered a Jew. Just doesn't want to 'bother' about it, as you say. As if 'not bothering' can alter the fact! I'm tired of such stupidity."

"Dash it," thought Simon, stung by the sarcastic emphasis of the fast-flung words. "She needn't mix me up with that fellow – she ought to know I'm not in the least like him – wouldn't stoop to *his* level, anyhow. Wonder what she'd think if she knew what's happened to him. Perhaps after all she'd say – 'Serve him right'. By jove, she's furious with him!" And determined not to deserve even the backwash of her anger, to show her he had a definite and reasonable point of view, he made an effort to resume his persuasive tone.

"You really ought to understand, since you're English yourself. After all, being Jewish as well is just a sort of novelty to you – something to be interested in, like – like Persian poetry. You can take it up when you find time for it, and drop it when you like. But it's jolly hard to live with all the while – these foreigners don't feel it – they don't know how it rubs one the wrong way, and what an ass one feels with people who notice a difference. It's uncomfortable all round. One has to show respect to the old people one belongs to, of course. But isn't it due to oneself to live as one thinks right? Religion is an individual affair, as Miss Canuto said. One can believe in God without going to church or synagogue. All the other forms simply mess one up. It's ridiculous if one means to live like other Englishmen."

Like his father, Simon found it hard to explain himself at length. Besides, it was a strain to address a silent, unheeding back, that kept a little ahead of him. He was sure that she understood and must agree with him at heart: but he felt, too, that allowance must be made for her soreness over Wyn, and the pride with which she might defend even an "interest" – like "Persian poetry". Her silence worried him. He strode faster to keep alongside the flying figure, and look down on her still, averted face. They reached the quiet square, and his voice sounded loud:

"Don't let us argue about all that," he said. "I was hoping you'd be interested in what's happened to me. I feel tremendously bucked. You know, I don't have to start until the end of the month. I expect to move into my new digs on Monday – here's the address." He had got it written ready on a card, which he put into her hand. "You'll write to me, of course? I hope you'll share my holiday – we can have one or two jolly outings before you go. And by the way, you haven't told me where you're going. Is it to France – Italy—? By jove, I wish I could do a Continental trip!"

"Among the foreigners?" she said. Her voice was so low, that even in the silence of the square, he could hardly hear. "It might be a good thing for you. Or you might come back as you went, thanking God you're an Englishman." She paused. "I'm going on to Spain, to explore the tracks of my – of our ancestors. *Ours!* I wonder what they'd think of the water their blood has turned to in you!"

They had reached the Millers' door. With a rapid movement she put a key in and turned it. Then she faced Simon, with an expression he had never seen in her eyes before. The calm pools were lit by fiery sparks, that seemed to ray out gleams on her shadowed cheeks.

"Pure Jewish blood – poured out hot in the fires of the Inquisition – poured out cold over the iron racks in torture chambers. In defence of the silly old customs that it makes you uncomfortable to keep. Up there" – she pointed to the lighted window above them— "sits one of the old people you say you have to respect. *Her* blood isn't water. She'd pour it out to-day as readily as any of our ancient martyrs, and for the same reason. Modern Europe provides plenty of opportunities. If it isn't an *auto-da-fé*, it's a pogrom. And if it isn't a spectacular show, it's a miserable grinding persecution that takes everything but the blood. You know it all as well as I do. I daresay you have a mother or grandmother who has made daily sacrifices for her Judaism – just as a matter of course. But you think that sort of thing should be confined to foreigners. I despise you. I think you're a coward!"

Her whole face blazed. An extraordinary bitterness overran her voice.

"Really – Miss Miller!" stammered Simon.

She lowered her gaze from his. Her hand clutched the handle of the door behind her. The next words came with an unsteady rush.

"I mean it. It seems to me a despicable thing for a Jew to turn his back on his own people. Whether he's born in England or in Russia, his first duty is to keep faith with his race. I can't endure the Jew who's ashamed of it, who pretends he belongs entirely to another—" she choked a little— "if that's your attitude, then it is we who have absolutely nothing in common. *Nothing*. Good-night. Please don't try to see me again."

One moment she was standing there, her face gleaming, raving, the anger in her voice pouring incontrollably over its modulated note: the next, there were only shadows on the blinded window, and a dark, blank door. It had closed very quietly on its well-oiled lock. But the loudest reverberation from a cannon's mouth could not have stunned Simon more. It had a curious muffled echo, as of another distant door banging mockingly through years and years of youth. There was a moment's paralysis. Then all the stubbornness of his nature rose to throw up earthworks against that double reverberation – a wall high and solid with the hardening secretions of his pride and rage, his just assurance, his outraged and humiliated love. As he strode out of the square, a girl approached him. Her brilliant lips red-gashed her thin, powdered face. He stopped to listen to her greeting, then burst into a fit of rocking laughter.

"My Gawd!" reported the girl to a lady friend. "I met a toff in Caramel – dotty drunk!"

XVI

SIMON had written to Dinah immediately on learning of his appointment. He wished his sister to break the news to their parents and inform him of the result. Over a week passed without reply. He wrote again, to express surprise, and say he thought of coming down for a week-end. He was actually packing a bag for the journey when Dinah's letter arrived.

It was a long epistle, though Dinah's method of expression was not much less laconic than usual. She said she was pleased with his news, though nobody else was. "Father grunted a good deal, but said he always expected something of the kind. Mother took it very badly. She doesn't show us when she cries, but her eyes were red all next day. She wanted me to write and tell you lots of things, only something else happened, and I couldn't. A telegram came from Dawport and upset us. Old Uncle Elman has had a stroke. Mother and I went down to help. We found dreadful trouble. Nettie has run away with Ted Gregory." It seemed that the prospective engagement with Norman Blay had been hindered by the stipulations of the young man's family, and his subservience to them. "Uncle Mark was prepared to give a good dowry. They wanted a house and furniture as well, and made other conditions about the wedding. Nettie was furious at the haggling. She said at last she'd have nothing more to do with them. But I think she had been about with Ted Gregory for a long time. They have gone to Paris. The Gregorys are mad about it, too. Though they are only publicans, they are awful snobs. They would never let the ballroom at the Victoria Hotel for any Jewish affair. But Nettie used to go to their dances. I saw Ted Gregory once. He's not as good looking as Norman Blay, and they say he drinks. But even if he was perfect, our family would feel the same, as you know. Just because he is a Goy. Uncle Elman had a stroke as soon as he knew. He looks awful. The doctor says if he gets another it will be serious. Uncle Mark isn't ill, but he looks as if he is. He hardly speaks to anybody. Auntie cries dreadfully … Sylvie doesn't seem to care much. She told me she knew about Ted Gregory, and he was a real sport, and quite mad on Nettie. She thinks it will turn out all right. I think she's heartless…. You can imagine how miserable mother is. I came home yesterday, but mother is staying on till Friday. She expects you, of course. If you come early you can go straight to the Elmans, and bring mother home. Father's leg troubles him, and he can't get about much…" The last passage was the most abrupt…. "No, we haven't made any plans yet for living in Dawport. At first it was because Gershon decided to go back to Russia. And now this upset at Elmans will make it harder. I suppose we shall have to stop on at Blaemawe for another year. But you'll hear all about it when you are home…"

In the train Simon sat and stared at the familiar landmarks. The Paddington slums, Westbourne Grove, Ealing, the plain of Slough – the hazed air clarifying under a blue sky with the rise of greenery – the glimpse of Windsor, the meadowed Thames. Some of the spots beyond the river were better known to him, through rides on the long-distance buses. This very week-end had been reserved originally for a second visit to Eton and the Royal Castle, with perhaps a tramp or "lift" to Stoke Poges, and Gray's churchyard. He had hoped that Edith would have come … his eyelids flapped: for a mile or two he saw nothing through the open window. Then he snatched up a book, some trash he had picked off the stall at the station. Anything was better than to think of her.

He read steadily for an hour or more, oblivious of scenery, stoppages, the coming and going of passengers. It was a detective story, not a bad yarn – he hadn't read anything so crudely exciting since the days of the *Boy's Friend*, and the *Halfpenny Marvel*.

At the Severn Junction he put his book down to close the window, and found himself alone. The high bank beside him was rich with growth. He peered at the grass and leaves, remembering that the last time he had gone by this spot he had caught the flash of a scurrying rabbit. But the green soon vanished from the black, steamy earth. He felt almost like a rabbit himself who had jumped into the wrong hole. But he could never go through the tunnel without some return of the sensations of his first trip through it. Roar and flame still gave the same thrill, the true if blunted edge of expectancy. Above his head the Severn Sea still seemed to swish and growl. Yet it could never be quite the same, on the backward journey home. The climb to daylight was the climb to Wales, reluctant, grudging, dutiful. Only then, however, at the moment of emergence in the shafts of the Gloucester Hill, did the picture of home become full and real, its detail picked distinct where there was mere blur before. Instead of vague shapes with inaudible voices, far in the rear of his life in London, that life itself sank back into shadow before the actuality of these tones and figures. His mother stood before him, weeping and railing. His father looked silently but goadingly at him, with his sad, sceptical eyes. Dinah, Ruth, Gershon came boldly around, making demands in their live, if limited, way. And old Uncle Elman, stricken on his bed – he, too, gazed, piteous and aggrieved, while Mark showed a haggard face behind. So that was the reason. That was why Mark Elman had been worried and distrait, increasingly so at each brief meeting in town: he must have suspected and feared, all the time. A blow, a terrible blow, to love, pride, faith, ambition…. But damn it all, Nettie had the right! Why shouldn't she be happy in her own way – the modern, current way? He recalled Nettie as he had seen her that day of his first departure – often as he had seen her since, that picture held – gay, smart, grown-up, superior, "Welshiness" as well as "Jewishness" carefully eliminated from voice and manner. He always acknowledged her attractiveness, though somehow he had never been able to like her much. He would acknowledge, now, her right to do as she chose in the matter of matrimony – even to the choice of a Goy. Yes – even of a drinking Goy, let the others say what they might. "Don't you feel you have more in common with *them*, than with that crowd drinking in there?" The sweet, searing voice was in his ear again – he shrank and winced away from it.

Nobody met him at Dawport. The morning's sun had been lost in cloud. A drizzle was falling, the air was close and sticky. The town looked grey, shrunken and hunched. Simon surveyed it from the squat station entrance with distaste. "Filthy – as usual," he muttered; no remembrance came of the glories trailed by Dawport to his childhood. Instead, he debated whether he should dash for the tram, just preparing to leave its terminus, or – the thought grew more insistent – walk to the shop in the High Street nearby, and surprise little Jani. It would not be a total surprise, of course. Jani knew he was coming. He had written to tell her that he would call or arrange in some way to see her over the week-end. He had not felt eager for an immediate meeting. Any time would do – he would fix up something after his arrival. But now that he was here, it might be just as well to look her up at once, before he was involved in the net of trouble at the Elmans – and the necessity of rushing with his mother to Blaemawe, before the Sabbath set in.

He turned up his coat collar against the insidious wet and strode down the street. How dull and petty were the rows of little shops, their wares crushed together in undiscriminating display. Even the large establishment of "Uncle Trevor" had a mean exterior. Wait till Jani saw the great London store that held a place for her, with its huge sheets of plate glass, its spacious panelled backgrounds, its gorgeous dolled "effects". He chuckled as he passed the millinery window, the show of draped stuffs, the central doorway with its wings of "fancy goods", the piles of blanket and towelling. At a narrow slit beyond he stopped. This led to the baby-linen department, on a side angle almost detached from the rest. It was difficult to see through the lace-hung obscurities of the small door panel and window. There was nothing for it but to march boldly in. Two women were coming out, and he squeezed aside to let them pass. Over a counter within a bulgy young woman was leaning, in examination of some articles on the counter. Her hat touched the grey-streaked head of the assistant who bent across to her. A few feet away a little slim black back with red curls above was straining upward, arms extended in the act of pushing a cardboard box into an upper rack. The back swung round, and a little stifled squeak greeted Simon's advance into the shop.

"O-oh – Simon!"

"Well, Jani—"

The grey-streaked head jerked up; two sharp eyes glanced round for a moment, then returned to the customer.

"Yes, 'm, that's right. Pink for boys, an' blue for gells. I always says it's best to take the two if you're buying them beforehand – there's no knowing. An' it might be twins! Of course we'll change them if they aren't used. Shall I pack these up?"

Another quick backward look, thin lips curled inward as they were pressed together. Jani's little hand was in Simon's grip.

"Fancy you walking in like this! When did you come?"

"Just this minute from the station. I thought I'd run in before going on to see my people, and rushing off to Blaemawe. You're looking fine, Jani—"

Her appearance, in fact, astonished him. She had become extraordinarily pretty. The dark eyes danced in a face more vivid than ever, the skin a rich blend of brown and red. Jani's tan had been marvellously retained, and the flush of surprise deepened a natural glow. Her little nose with its wide nostrils tilted delightedly at him.

"And you, too, Simon – there's big you are! You are looking grand—"

She checked herself, unwilling to express all her involuntary admiration. Of course she had always known that Simon was well-favoured. But this handsome man before her was rather overwhelming. She knew Miss Meredith was shooting glances. And then – she turned her head uneasily, and stared down a lane between piled-up goods that led to the main building.

"Uncle Trevor's sure to be about," she murmured. "I'm afraid he'll catch us talking. I haven't had tea yet – so perhaps I could slip out in about ten minutes—"

"Sorry, Jani, I shan't be able to wait. I'm expected at Fynlon – you know it takes some time to get there. And I'm afraid I shan't be free again to-day." She pouted. "It's too bad, I know, but it can't be helped. I've got news for you, of course – we must have a talk. But there's no desperate hurry. I'll come into Dawport again as soon as I can – to-morrow night, perhaps—"

"I can't get off till nine on Saturdays," she grumbled. "We are supposed to close at eight, but there's always a crush, and we can't get the people out till half-past. Then there's all the tidying up and accounts – it's always nine before I'm out. And we're so busy all day, I can't get off for a minute."

"Well, there'll be lots of time afterwards – or does the last train to Blaemawe still leave at nine forty-five?"

"It's ten-fifteen on Saturdays," said Jani. "And I've got to be in the house by ten, anyway—"

"Damn!" said Simon softly. Her peeping eyes twinkled. "That isn't much good – unless you can come back with me. Can't you spend Sunday at home?"

She hesitated. She did not care to tell Simon that Ieuan Richards had asked her the same question the day before – when she had declared that she could not be in Blaemawe on Sunday. If she went, Ieuan would certainly know – and have another chance to call her a liar!

"I would like to," she said regretfully. "But I've promised Auntie Gwyneth to stay in this Sunday and get the dinner, while she goes to chapel. She hasn't been well enough to go for three Sundays. There's no servant. They never stay long, with Uncle Trevor potching about the kitchen."

"Surely that needn't keep you – make some excuse to go home—"

"But I can't, they are letting me off on Monday instead." This was the part of her reason that she had withheld from Ieuan. "You see, Simon, I begged to go for a trip to Ilfracombe. All the girls except me have been this summer. There is a special day trip on the steamer from Dawport on Monday. When I heard you were coming, I thought that you would like to go with me there—"

"Why, that would be fine – if I can manage it. I meant to go back on Monday – still, I might be able to work it in – anyway, we'll talk of it to-morrow. I'll wait for you at nine o'clock outside the shop."

Several women had come in, and one was standing near. Miss Meredith's customer had gone, and she was attending to two others. The remaining woman, who had a baby bound to her side in a shawl which wrapped them both, stared hard at Jani and Simon while she swayed and patted her infant.

"You'd better go now, then," whispered Jani nervously. "This woman's waiting to be served – and if Uncle Trevor came in – he'd have a fit—"

"All right, I'm off. Bye-bye for the present—"

She put her hand again in his outstretched one, and whispered, lower still,—

"It's *good* news, isn't it, Simon?"

"Of course, my dear."

He picked up his case from the wooden floor and strode out, conscious of his big manly figure in these narrow spaces, and in the reflection in Jani's eyes. She sent him a long radiant glance over the customer's head, while that customer was exposing the baby's smaller poll for bonnet-fitting. Jolly little thing! (Simon, it need not be said, was not apostrophising the bald infant.) She was full of life, and getting prettier than ever – it was really a damned shame to coop her up in this potty little shop, at the mercy of a bullying draper. In the tram, rattling its way to Fynlon, he considered her plan for Monday. It was attractive, undoubtedly – he hadn't done that trip for years, and it had always been the special feature of Dawport's summer. A day at Ilfracombe with Jani would be a pleasant close to his holiday. And it would give them time to talk over details of her future, which he had already taken some steps to arrange. But *could* he manage it? His new life started on Tuesday morning, and he must be back in town on Monday night. The steamer would return to Dawport probably by eight or nine: he could catch the late mail train and arrive at Paddington in the early hours. A fag, but he didn't mind that. Only he must make quite sure of the times. He would come into Dawport as early as possible on Saturday, and make the necessary enquiries at docks and station.

The tram was climbing up the hilly Morgan Road. These houses that had once seemed so opulent and fine, on either side an avenue of trees, had shrunk like everything else in the town. They were dingy, commonplace, parochial. To live in them had been the peak ambition of urban residence. An ambition stamped with the drear pettiness of a smug, narrow, old-fashioned life.

But as the street broke into gaps on its winding rise, the new suburb came into view. Groups of villas in daring styles of architecture rose behind each other on the high slope of the town. Their red roofs and light stone splashed bright patches through the trees. On the left, the great green spaces still ran down steeply to the sea.

Simon got off the tram, walked up a rough new road to a still higher level, and looked around him in grudging approval. It wasn't bad up here. The rain had stopped, and shafts of greenish light broke the drifting clouds. The sheet of dark grey water spread below, to the faint blur of coast that was Somerset and Devon. Nearer in were the headlands of the Welsh peninsula. The smoke of coaling vessels rose from the town harbour, a tug hooted sonorous in the middle distance, and small craft played between the sands and the piers. From this height the curve of the bay showed wide and perfect. Another Bay of Naples, it had more than once been called. Simon had heard the comparison from Edith's lips. Involuntarily he remembered the talk at Ridgmount Gardens, when she had described the lovely strip of coast that ran, as it were, out of the mouth of dirty inland pits. She knew its physical features, its history and legendary lore. As she spoke one saw the buried town below the Crumlands beach, from which bells tinkled when the waves rolled roughly over hidden spires – spires that guarded legendary citizens who had bartered with Phoenicians; saw Roman soldiers under Ostorius swarm the cliffs, to be driven back by the native Silures, spurred to desperate deed by Caractacus— "This day, this battle will give us liberty, or doom us to eternal slavery. Call to mind your ancestors, who drove away Julius Caesar from the shores of Britain; who by their valour banished from your sight the Roman fasces and axes; who freed you from tribute and rescued your wives and daughters from violation!"; saw, in the centuries that followed, Danish pirates filching what they could, and leaving traces of love and war before they fled; saw the triumphant Normans, called in like the Flemings to assist, and remaining to conquer, rearing their castles and imposing lordship in the streets still named after them.

The talk came back ravelled with anger and pain. Hell! He would not think of Edith! He turned his back swiftly on the vista of the sea and stared at the houses above. Which was "Glanowel"? Stupid, anyway, to have chosen a Welsh name – it was a wonder the girls had consented to it. But probably it was the builder's choice. He trudged upwards, scanning the painted names on gate and arch. There it was – that gabled brick perched on a corner bank. By jove, it looked a fine place, with its low wide bays and jutting angles of stone, its porch and lawns and gleaming gates. Too new, pretentious, perhaps – but when it had mellowed and grown and sunk, it would have a good homely look. A big jump for the Elmans from those rooms behind the shop.

He ran up the steps towards the porch, seeing a curtain move at one of the windows. The door was opened by his mother.

"My son!"

"Hallo, mother!"

He kissed her heartily.

"You look all right, mother. But why have you got your hat on? – Are you going out?"

"No, no. I am only ready to go home. It is Shabbas (Sabbath), my son, and I am anxious to be home. Here everything is prepared. But alas – there are no Shabbasdike hearts." She sighed, then waved her hand as if to put the matter aside. "Now, my son – as soon as you have had something to eat, we can go. Come!"

She had taken his bag before he was aware of her intention. He seized it back.

"Mother, mother, don't start working for me as soon as you see me! I must carry it in myself – come along. How's the old man?"

"Better, thank God. He is still in bed, and cannot move much. But he speaks a little, and can take food. He wants to see you, but he is sleeping, so you can eat first. In here, after you have washed."

She drew him through a door in the hall into a small, pleasant morning-room. An oval table was laid with a light meal: a slice of brown crisp fried fish, salad, bread and butter, tea. After a wash in the lavatory opposite, he returned to eat with relish. His mother watched and hovered, helping him, and talked, though chiefly in answer to his questions. She was preoccupied, anxious, seeming to hold back her main concerns. But now and again she relaxed into a smile, as she gazed at this fine, big son who had grown, she thought, quite suddenly into a man. She herself had changed so little. There were grey streaks in the smooth black hair, but it was abundant as ever, drawn over the long, sallow cheeks into a coil behind. The hat, which she would not remove, did not conceal the heavy roll. She was still thin and gaunt, but she moved briskly, and used strong, vigorous gestures. Too vigorous for Simon. He wished she would keep her hands more steady, hold them still – after the fashion of that old woman, Edith's grandmother, whom, somehow, in spite of all dissimilarity, she resembled. It puzzled Simon. He knew that old Mrs. Miller was beautiful – she must have been a lovely girl, with delicate little features and fair, curling hair – and that his mother was not: at least, he supposed not, with some uncertainty still. Absence might make Simon regard his mother more critically, but could not quite remove the familiar clouded vision. It was that look in her eyes that disturbed him, that recalled old Mrs Miller's. With all its deeper pain, it had that same strange serene conviction, that quality of imperturbable demand....He pushed his last cup of tea aside.

"I can't drink any more, mother. Perhaps I'd better go upstairs. It's a wonder aunt isn't down yet. And fancy Sylvie going out for the whole afternoon and leaving you here like this—"

"Ah, Sylvie – but she is always out. And she doesn't like to see her mother cry so much—"

"But can't she help?"

"Well, there is a good *shicksa* (Gentile girl) in the kitchen – two. One is a cook, though God forbid I should eat what she cooks. She knows from her hands and feet what Yiddish *essen* (food) is like! Besides, Sylvie won't let her try. Only English dishes must be cooked in this house. Hard, raw meat – just as the Goyim like it, with all the blood left in. Feh!" Mrs. Black shuddered. "And upstairs with uncle there is a nurse. She will not let Sylvie into the bedroom. Sylvie doesn't want, either. But she knew you were coming to-day, and she said she would come back early."

"I jolly well shan't wait for her. Let's go up now, mother."

She preceded him in silence up the thick-piled carpet on the stairs. A new Persian rug covered the landing, and fresh paint in a delicate scheme of colouring lit the walls. At a door near the end of the wide corridor, Mrs. Black stood and tapped. A nurse in uniform opened and stared. Her face was plain and dictatorial, but the hair under her white band was burnished yellow. Simon suffered a momentary throb of the heart. The nurse smiled suddenly.

"It is my son," said Mrs. Black with a gesture. "He wants to see Mr. Elman now."

"Certainly. You can come in, Mr. Black, but I'm afraid you had better not stay long. He's awake and rested, but it doesn't do him any good to talk much."

They followed her into the long, carpeted room, with its shining mahogany and low, silk-covered bed. Simon had time to marvel at the appointments, before he saw the incongruous head on the pillow. Good heavens! That shrunk, distorted face, that fringe of wilted hair, those claw-like fingers on the sheet – was it jolly old Uncle Elman, always round and rosy, fond of pushing coppers into one's pocket with big, fat hands – Very strict and sometimes stern, but jocular, too, in his own rough way. Simon couldn't speak. He simply stood and stared, while the nurse said something and pulled up the pillow, and the old man lifted dim, bloodshot eyes.

"Ach, Shimke," he said, in a queer, thin gurgle – astoundingly unlike his robust voice. "Vos machste?"

Simon muttered, trying to sound cheerful and matter-of-fact…. Sorry about the illness, but it was good news he was recovering. Soon he'd be perfectly well, of course. Yes, he himself was getting along fine. Hoped nobody minded very much about his chucking the ministry. But he had really done ever so much better. Got an excellent official post. Tell him all about it later on.

The nurse had retired to the distant window, where she was busy with some needlework. But now and again she glanced round and drew Simon's eyes. A glimpse of the sky could be seen through the net-covered leaded panes. Blue and white, with a struggling sun. A ray caught her yellow hair. What would Edith have thought of it all? If she had a "case" of this sort, with the details of its origin capturing her mind, wouldn't she be full of sympathy and sweetness? Hard she could be, hard and angry, passionately angry – but tender too, and gentle, where she cared. Golden head against an old woman's knee. Caressing touch on the arm. How softly her hands would minister to this shrunken form. Poor Uncle Elman, you don't know how lucky you might be, if Nurse Miller could know and come to you – why, she'd treat you as if you were her own beloved grandfather, stricken by a cruel, wanton act – not at all as a "case", an ugly, troublesome old Jew patient, with no sense to appreciate the romance of his grandchild's marriage to an eligible goy. That was what the peremptory tone of this nurse by the window said – oh, yes, she looked at Simon pleasantly enough – but how did she look, in her mind, at the poor old man? Simon felt dizzy, either from his unwonted imaginative effort, or from his reaction to the mumbling invalid. He was not sorry when his mother signalled him to leave. His hand shuddered in the feeble clasp of those cold claws. But as if his warm, strong flesh energised the old man, the white head lifted an inch from its pillow, and the farewell came in slightly louder breaths.

"Bleib nor a Yid, Shimke, et sein alles gut – bleib nor a Yid. A guten shabbos." ("Remain but a Jew, Simon, and all will be well – remain but a Jew. Good sabbath.")

Another door opened on the landing, and a short, plump figure in a carelessly-fastened silk dress emerged. Her hair was untidy, and she held a handkerchief to red, bleary eyes. Simon greeted her in some discomfiture.

"Such trouble, Simon, such trouble," she wailed, leading the way downstairs. "Everything was going on so nicely, and then this should happen! It's a Hannah Hora – it's the Evil Eye, I'm sure it is!"

"You don't mean to say, Aunt Esther, that *you* believe in the Evil Eye?"

"Well, I know it's supposed to be superstition – poor Nettie always said so. But I can't help it, I feel it must be true. That old Mrs. Jacobs and her daughter Frema – you should have seen their looks at our housewarming reception – their eyes could have eaten us up. – We had to ask them, though the girls didn't want to, for poor Grandpa's sake – and see the result!" She dabbed her eyes and moaned, rambling on inconsequentially as she crossed the hall to a large double door.

"Just have a look before you go, Simon – isn't this a beautiful room?" She pushed at the panels, and Simon saw an elaborate drawing-room with wide French windows opening on a lawn. Violet damask showed against lustrous grey walls, enriched in each corner by a stencilled design of a clustering purple vine. Thick grey carpet and black rugs, silver fringe on an ebony standard lamp, oxydised fittings and a black marble fireplace, carried out a bold yet fastidious scheme. "All Nettie's choice – such wonderful taste! She saw to everything. And then to go and run away like that, upsetting everybody! But please God, I hope she'll come back soon and be happy here, in spite of them all – those measly Blays and their pride! And as for the Gregorys – fancy that vulgar Mrs. Gregory cutting me in the street and telling people she wished she'd kept her rule more strictly, about not letting any sort of Jew into her exclusive place! The cheek of the woman! Won't Nettie just show her up when she's back! I know it'll be all right later, as Sylvie says. But it isn't any joke just now, with Grandpa ill, and everybody gossiping spitefully about us. Sylvie doesn't see it as I do – she laughs and says we should snap our fingers at them. But after all—"

Simon interrupted curtly,

"Any chance of seeing Uncle Mark to-day?"

"Oh, he goes to shool from business, and won't be home till late. I'm sure I don't know why he should go to shool at all now, considering the way he's treated. The men are as bad as the women – sniffing and criticising. The election is coming on soon, too, and I don't suppose he'll be president again. He might as well save himself the trouble of attending their meetings. Not that I see much of him when he's home, the way he shuts himself up and looks at me as if I'm to blame. He's so selfish, you know, Devora – he doesn't think how I grieve and worry—"

She sobbed, and Simon looked at Mrs. Black, standing in grim silent dignity beside her. He thought with horror that he had once wished his unfashionable mother to emulate the ways of this flaccid creature.

"We must go at once," said Mrs. Black, with decision, and Simon followed her promptly, across the hall. She drew on a coat with a rapid movement, and picked up a large fish-basket, bulging with parcels, that stood, oddly incongruous, upon a modern-antique monk's bench.

He took it from her with a struggle as they left the house: she was totally unconscious of anything ridiculous or demeaning in a fish-frail. Some dim apprehension, following on the scene indoors, that the quality of dignity in his mother was something inward, something that could not be affected by any absurdity of garb or appurtenance, silenced the grumble that rose to his lips. Instead he talked cheerily, as he helped her over the rough, wet road, round the bend of which came a girl, smartly dressed, picking her way with care. She was so intent on sparing her light, high-heeled shoes, that she did not lift her head until Simon said loudly: "Isn't that Sylvie?"

"Why, it's Simon!" She stopped and held out a slim, gloved hand. "Going already? I'm so sorry I couldn't get back earlier. Had tea with a friend at Crumlands – and you know what those trains are! Wasn't it you who called the Crumlands train the troglodyte express?" She laughed on a high, shrill note, very brief and sudden. "You can't stay, I suppose?"

"No," said Simon, curtly. He had always disliked Sylvie's affected tones and gibing laugh – even as a little girl she had minced and sneered. But she had grown into a striking young woman. Darker than Nettie, and taller, with a brilliant complexion and a thin, sloping nose, over which her grey eyes observed one slyly, superciliously.

"You look quite Londony," she said. Her glance raked him, and rested on the fish-basket. He coloured at the amused flicker of her lips. She could still, as always, make him feel intolerably gauche. "Otherwise you haven't changed much."

"Neither have you," he said.

"Really? Everybody says I've altered ever so these last six months. But I must congratulate you. You've done awfully well, it seems. I expect you'll be in quite a different set now. Might look you up one of these days. I'm planning an occasional London trip now that Nettie's likely to settle there. I'm sure she'll be ever so pleased about you, too."

"Thanks," he said, furious at her casual, condescending air, at the cool way in which she ignored his waiting mother – as, indeed, she ignored everything that was unpleasing to her. "I was glad to find the old man a little better. Seems to have been a pretty bad upset all round—"

"Quite unnecessary, of course. That's what comes of old-fashioned ways." She tossed her head. "Nettie's done awfully well, as a matter of fact. Ted Gregory's a real bright kid – worth fifty of that mother's darling, shilly-shally Norman Blay."

"Sylvie!" said Mrs. Black sternly. "It is a shame to talk so. Have you no fear of God?"

Sylvie shrugged her shoulders, and threw a mock despairing glance at Simon.

"Of course, Aunt, you don't understand. I know it isn't any good arguing with you – but, really, English people can't be expected to live as if we were in Russia. I *do* wish you'd be a little reasonable."

Simon interposed quickly before his mother could reply.

"Afraid we must get off, Sylvie—"

"Oh, I won't keep you if you've a train to catch. You're only down for the week-end, I suppose? I expect you'll come in again to see us before you leave. Why not to-morrow? – or perhaps Sunday? You could stay overnight and go on to London from here—"

"I might do that—"

"Come, Simon, it is too late to stay longer—"

"Shall expect you Sunday, then," said Sylvie airily. "Good-bye."

"Good Shabbas," said Mrs. Black severely.

The baggage seemed heavier and clumsier than ever as they trudged down the steep lane to the tram. Simon was thoroughly out of humour. He made no reply to his mother's strictures on Sylvie's "*Goyisha nishoma*" ("Gentile spirit"). He did not agree, yet he had no sympathy with the offender. Sylvie expressed the sentiments that he approved, but her manner made him writhe with shame and resentment. It was strange how he had always felt at his worst with the Elman girls. They scored and riddled him, their open contempt for his family was galling, and their airs of superiority withstood every slight that others put upon them. Undoubtedly Sylvie made his own beliefs seem vain and puerile. It must be just her manner, confound her! – a spiteful, affected little cat! All the same, there was something useful in her suggestion of spending a night at "Glanowen". He leaned over to his mother from the opposite side of the tram.

"I suppose there isn't time, now, to call on Uncle Mark?"

"No," she said. "We have only time for the train – besides – he will be gone from the office to shool—"

She spoke loudly above the rattle of the tram. Simon glanced round uneasily. The men next him were talking, far more loudly, in Welsh. But that, of course, was not noticeable here.

"Then I'll have to come on Sunday to see him, and stay the night," he said. "I must leave early on Monday morning—"

She pressed her lips together, and did not reply. He knew perfectly well that, once in Blaemawe, she wished to keep him there until his departure for London. But this arrangement, announced so casually now, could not be objected to, and would save discussion later. The next step, only half formulated in his mind, could follow easily.

In the train he countered the reproaches which he had known were bottled up in his mother's heart. She would have resigned herself less easily to his defence but for the Elman debacle.

"Of course the plan of your coming to Dawport shool could not be carried out now. The family is disgraced in the community." She sighed. "Poor Mark! His head is buried in the earth. Never again can he lift it in communal affairs. All his schemes, his ambitions, are in the grave with Nettie—"

"But she isn't dead, mother," said Simon irritably.

"As good as dead, my son. When Jewish blood goes into Gentiledom, it parts from the living spirit. Woe, woe, that in our family such a shameful thing should happen!" she began to rock herself and moan. The sound pierced Simon's nerves intolerably. He frowned at the slagheaps beyond the window, at the steep banks opposite that rose from the river, sluggish and dry on its stony bed. The train was mounting higher on the hillside, stuttering and panting as it curved over the valley. Just below that bend the stream was always broad and deep. The Blaemawe boys swam towards it, the Pontycynlais lads scrambled over boulders to reach it. Simon had been in many splashing fights among the early morning rivals. Once Gershon had given a good account of himself there. He had accepted a challenge on a bleak spring dawn, before the summer swimmers ventured to start, to plunge in nude and circle round the deep iced patch for five minutes. When he came out, blue and triumphant, the reward he got was to be mocked at for his "Jewish shape". Simon remembered with satisfaction that he had himself sent one of the Cynlais fellows home, bluer than Gershon, though from a different cause.

"Mother," he said abruptly. "What did Dinah mean by writing that Gershon was going back to Russia?"

"Ah," said Mrs. Black, sitting up straight. "That is another trouble. Not, God forbid, as bad as this one. Maybe it will pass over very soon."

It seemed that one of Gershon's sisters had been betrothed, on the understanding that a dowry equivalent to a sum of thirty pounds would set up the fiancé, a poor but worthy young man, in some occupation of his own. The sum had been acquired by the mother, very painfully, by rigorous saving, and the marriage fixed. The time, however, coincided with the date when Gershon was due to enter the conscript army. If he did not present himself, the dowry must be forfeited in fines to the authorities. The widowed mother, with other children to provide for, could not hope to raise a similar amount out of her scanty earnings, even if supplemented by loans or gifts from equally poor relations. A better-endowed rival would carry off the deserving young man, and the discarded Rachel, dowryless and with a cast in her eye, might be left a spinster. Such a calamity could be prevented only by Gershon's appearance in person on the fateful day.

"But surely," said Simon, bewildered— "The thirty pounds might be lent by someone here—"

"There are difficulties," said Mrs. Black. "The Elmans, in present circumstances, cannot be asked – the old man must not be troubled, and Mark is not sympathetic – besides, they have lately sent large amounts to other suffering relatives in Russia. Gershon refuses to ask – even to borrow. We have no ready cash to spare now that we have to raise money to buy the Dawport shop. But we would willingly strain ourselves to help him. He will accept nothing, however, from us, but a loan towards the expenses of the journey. He will travel in the cheapest way to save his money for the family."

"But you don't mean to say he is prepared to serve for three years, merely to avoid payment of such an amount!"

"Perhaps it will not be necessary for him to serve. He may be able to get exemption – or some other course may present itself. But he says he is willing to serve if necessary. He is strong and healthy – what, after all, are three years at his age?

Then he and his family will be freed of all obligations, his sister will be saved, – also a younger brother, who is delicate —he would be called up next year, but may be permitted to remain with his mother if Gershon is already serving. Other benefits, too, may come to the family, if Gershon is there, able to see for himself and arrange, as the eldest—" Mrs. Black hesitated, stammered— "anyway, nobody can be a whit the worse – and when he comes back—"

Simon saw that she was uneasy, repeating, not her own arguments, but another's, reluctantly accepted.

"It sounds mad to me," he said bluntly. "Besides, I thought he was to look after the Blaemawe business when you moved to Dawport?"

"The plan is deferred," said Mrs. Black. "There are reasons why it cannot be carried out at once. We may be able to move next year. Even if Gershon is not back, as I hope, we can manage both places in his absence. Your father and I can take turns."

"But it is time you finished carrying on the business, mother!"

She smiled and shook her head.

"Until Dinah is married," she said, and her sad eyes were busy with unspoken thoughts.

Simon found it a little easier to understand the situation from Gershon's point of view, when the cousins came again into close touch. Gershon, like everyone else, it seemed to Simon, had grown up chiefly in the last six months. Sturdy, well set-up, though his moustached face was thin and colourless, he had an independent individuality that explained much. It did not quite explain the subtle relationship, part constraint and part intimacy that had developed between him and Dinah. Simon noticed it soon after his arrival, though his father's less voluble, but equally emphatic covering of the ground of his "broken" career occupied most of the family attention. Dinah came boldly to her brother's support. She, too, had become firmer, more assured, in her demeanour, though it was obvious that she still suffered from inhibitive silences. On the subject of Sylvie Elman, however, she had no reserves.

"I think she's heartless," she repeated. "I know she encouraged Nettie to flirt with Ted Gregory last summer. And now she pretends that poor old Uncle Elman would have broken down in any case, and that Aunt Esther isn't suffering at all."

"Aunt Esther cries a lot," said Simon, "but it's true that she doesn't look at things as mother does."

"I know. She's snobbish, and what she's mostly put out about is losing the connection with the Blays. But I believe she feels pretty bad in her own way about Nettie marrying out of the faith. There's something – even if one isn't religious—" Dinah hesitated, and went on quickly. "As for Uncle Mark, it has quite stunned him. He avoids everybody as much as possible. And he doesn't seem to take any interest in anything."

"But it's all exaggerated – a stupid sort of fuss, after all. What else can be expected? Young people can't go on living like the old. And when we're mixed up with everybody else—"

"So you've got to that way of looking at it, too?"

Simon was struck, not by the words or tone, but by the queer look in Dinah's eyes as she spoke. She was not questioning him. Her gaze had fallen, but not before it revealed agitation and distress.

"Of course. I say, Di – *you* aren't really upset by this business, are you?"

"Well – it's seeing the others. And nothing could alter father and mother thinking it a crime. Do you know, father says the family must have nothing more to do with Nettie?"

"Bosh!"

"He means it. And mother's most terribly grieved. If – if anything of the sort happened to her – it would break her heart."

Simon nearly said "Bosh" again, more violently than before; but the implications of Dinah's last sentence checked him. What did she mean, exactly? Was it just a vague generality – that "anything of the sort" – or did she suspect that he – But there was nothing accusing or significant in Dinah's manner. She seemed, indeed, not to be thinking of him at all, as she sat at the end of the sofa where they had retired, whispering together, while the others read at the Sabbath table. The Friday evening had passed in the old manner. Nothing was changed in the Black household, except that the girls had grown taller – even Ruth was less childish, more subdued, though that might be from awe of this strange big brother. There was little that was new or different in the jumble of furniture and the pictures. But a few touches on the windows and table – daintier curtains and covers, flowers, more orderly arrangement – showed the effort at improvement.

"It's impossible to do more," murmured Dinah, in response to Simon's criticisms next morning. "Father says he won't buy a stick or change anything until we move. And mother says these things are good enough."

"Mother means they are good enough for *her*," said Ruth.

"You know, Di, she says that when you are married you can have new things to suit yourself. So that even if you live on here, you can change everything, and make it look ever so different, indeed—"

"Don't talk so much, Ruth," said Dinah angrily.

"Why on earth should Dinah live on here—" began Simon, and stopped suddenly.

There was a silence, Dinah holding her sister in check by a furious look. Simon stared at the rising colour in her olive cheeks. At the same moment Gershon approached them, and Ruth gave a loud giggle.

"It's terribly hot," muttered Dinah.

"Shall we go out for a walk – yes?" said Gershon, addressing himself to Simon, but with his eyes wandering to Dinah. "It *is* hot in the house – you don't want to stay all day here?"

"No, by Jove," said Simon, looking rather glumly from one to the other. "The whole morning's enough. Let's go up the mountain, Dinah—"

"Me, too," said Ruth. "Do you want to go the back way, Simon, like you used to? There's a lot of lovely wild ponies up the Wimberry—"

"We won't go that way," said Dinah.

"But I'd *like* to get to the top of the mountain," said Simon. "It's no good lounging about the village – or the riverside – that's just as bad. All the loafers will be there to-day—"

"We can get to the top of the mountain from the new road, leading off the village," said Dinah.

"Dinah's frightened—ever since we went one day and were chased by the ponies," said Ruth. "I jumped right over a hedge. Gershon picked Dinah up and ran all the way with her to the next field. They thought I was lost or hurt, and hunted about for me for hours. And when they came home – there I was!" She grinned.

"Yes, a nice fright you gave us," said Dinah crossly. Her face had become pink again, and she avoided Gershon's look and smile. "No more tomboy tricks. We'll go along the new road – it's much safer, and goes right up to the top, though it takes longer—"

"Well, then, you and Gershon can go that way," retorted Ruth. "And Simon will come with me the old quick way – it's much more fun – you like it better, don't you, Simon?"

"We'll all take the new road," said Simon, to her surprise and disappointment. "We can't go scrambling about among wild ponies – on – on Shabbos—" he said, lamely.

He scowled at the attentions of the villagers – staring, greeting, familiar.

"They only mean to be friendly," remonstrated Dinah.

"Meddlesome impudence. I don't know how you can stand them. I hate coming to the place – it's full of eyes and tongues. What a blessing it'll be when you're out of it!"

Dinah was silent. Gershon lifted his brows.

"I shall be glad to come back here," he said quietly.

"Oh – you—" said Simon, disconcerted. He did not mean to re-open the discussion on Gershon's departure. The enterprise seemed less foolhardy and unnecessary than it had first appeared. Gershon's independence of spirit and determination to work out his own and his family's salvation had something fine about it. And perhaps his leaving Blaemawe was not an unmixed hindrance to the Blacks' escape. He was galled by the curious understanding between the fellow and Dinah. Walking in front with his eldest sister did not prevent an exchange of glances that puzzled him. The recollection of Mark Elman's talk was clear enough: so were Ruth's hints, strangled as they might be by Dinah's anger. That was the strange thing – Dinah's own attitude. She seemed to repudiate and resent the suggested relationship, and at the same time to encourage it. Simon strode along irritably.

"Isn't it time we got to that confounded turning?" he said, as the line of shops and cottages began to show longer gaps.

"The new road begins further on," said Dinah. "Just before the Hafod lodge."

The blood rushed into Simon's head. He went steadily on, relieved that Dinah had not been looking at him. A great longing to see Hafod warred with his fierce disdain of it. If he had been alone, he would have made for the little lane, and tried to crawl through the old secret opening. Was it still there, he wondered. There was not time to find out, this visit: and there might never be a "next". He was resolved not to mention the name of Hafod. But Ruth's voice came singing from behind.

"Here's the new road – the Hafod gates are just around the corner. Oh – I wish we could go inside! We'll be able to next summer, won't we, Dinah? Perhaps you'll come as well, Simon? There's going to be a grand charity fête, in aid of the hospitals or nurses or something. Miss Miller will be there. Oh – I love to see her! She's just like a Princess! But she's only a nurse, too, and she's coming to Blaemawe soon – as soon as the Hafods come back. They've been away a long time. Mrs. Hughes, the shoemaker, says Miss Miller might come first, because—"

"No," said Simon, off his guard. "She's going abroad to join them—" he stopped abruptly.

"Oh, indeed, Simon, and how do you know—?"

"I – I just heard—" he muttered.

"Well, I never!" said Ruth delightedly. She felt free to chatter unrestrained, for the first time since Simon's arrival. "I thought perhaps you had seen her in London – that would be grand, whatever!"

"Good God!" said Simon violently. He had swung round, and the child stared open-mouthed at his savage look. "Don't talk in that way! It's high time you moved from this infernal place—"

"But people in Dawport don't speak so wonderfully well," said Dinah.

"It's an improvement on Blaemawe"; Simon, a little ashamed of his outburst, tried to collect himself. " Why, even Jani sounds less Welshy since she's been there—"

"So you've seen Jani?" said Dinah coldly.

"H'm – yes – just for a moment."

There was a complete silence for a while as the four walked on. Ruth's nervousness of her superior brother had returned, and when she resumed speech, it was in whispering monologue to Gershon, who was in a far from discursive mood. His efforts to gain Dinah's side were thwarted by Simon, who stuck doggedly to his sister. At the first incline of the new road, which soon became a mere rough lane, winding steeply upward, Simon took Dinah's arm and helped her along. His anger and impatience, the inchoate vexation of spirit that churned sourly within him, poured into the vigour of the climb. He dug his heels into the soil, jerked his knees in strong forward movements, lifted and swung his sister closely with him. The close, sunless air seemed to yield as if to an onslaught, and open in fresher waves. The flow of muscular energy relieved and braced him. He did not notice the difficulty with which the slight Dinah maintained the pace and prevented herself sagging upon him, until they had nearly reached the crown of the first great slope. Then the quivering and panting which she could no longer restrain broke on his attention.

"I say, Dinah – has it been too much for you?" He slowed down, placed both arms round her waist, and drew her drooping figure against the high bank beside them. For a moment she seemed about to collapse. Her cheeks were unnaturally bright, her eyelids fluttered, her lips stayed apart as the breath struggled through. With a gallant effort she straightened herself against the bank and gasped— "It has – rather—"

"Then why on earth didn't you stop me, silly?" he grumbled.

She said nothing, only smiled. He waited silently until she had recovered, then proposed a move to some boulders near by. A queer girl, this sister of his, he thought, as he helped her along. It was just like her to go on gamely without a sign until she sank. Was it pluck? – or just cussedness? – or that strange, overpowering bar to her speech? The last thing to occur to him was her dread of checking the impetus of his own free climb. As they sat at ease, waiting for the other two, far behind, to come into view, Simon felt a sudden reminiscent emotion. This was the spot, with its irregular crossroads, where years ago he had been attacked and his jug of wimberries smashed. He told Dinah the story, illustrating it with much frank gesture. But he omitted to mention that his companion had been Jani; even, in case the association with Jani might arise, that the leader of the rescuing party was

Ieuan Richards. Queer girl, Dinah, he thought again. She had never announced her dislike of Jani: but he was certain of her feeling. It made him uncomfortable and cautious.

The rest of the walk was disappointing. He had hoped to find exhilaration on the summit, to stand rejoicing at his freedom from these rolling slopes, which once had threatened to imprison him. But a thin mist mounted with their last furlong, and spread in thickening veils around. The sky became a grey obscurity, the green mounds with their bracken and jutting stems sank into ghastliness. As the party turned to scramble down in haste, a faint neighing and the pad of hooves echoed through the sodden air.

"It's the wild horses galloping away," said Ruth, in a voice of startled joy. "Oh Simon – suppose they come this way!"

"Nonsense," said Simon, but he tucked her seeking hand in his. "Come along – we'll race them, anyway!"

He took care, however, not to rush too far ahead of the other two. Their murmuring voices never left his ear as he led the way with Ruth. Dinah, it seemed, could talk enough to Gershon – or at least could let him talk enough to her. It would have been easy to make Ruth talk, too, about them both, and explain the situation. But he did not really want an explanation. To clarify the affair meant making it settled, permanent, and he preferred uncertainty. With the descent to the village his own immediate plans absorbed his mind, and he let Ruth chatter on, unrebuked because unheeded. It was brighter down below, the air still moist and heavy, but clear, and he wondered how soon he could slip off to Dawport. There would be tea, and then—

As they neared the house, Dinah suddenly hurried forward. A postman approached from the opposite direction, and stopped at the Blacks' shop door. The man's hand was suspended above the letter box as Simon, some perverse instinct making him race his sister, reached him and took the letters. He heard Dinah gasp, but she said nothing as he looked at the envelopes. Three were unsealed – business invoices or receipts for his father. The fourth made him stare and lift his brows, before he handed it to Dinah. She snatched it quickly and thrust it into the pocket of her short linen coat.

"So Frank writes to you, does he?"

"Yes," she said. A vivid flush spread over her face and neck. She slipped a key into the lock and hurried into the shop. Ruth and Gershon came up together as Simon passed through.

It was hot and stuffy in the living-room. After tea, the family sat in the small flagged yard. Most of the space had been filched for the worksheds, jutting out on one side from the lower level of the shop. On the other, a wall of packing-cases screened the yard from a neighbouring fowl-run. Beyond that rose a garden won from the stony slope on which the houses perched: its upper end reserved, however, for the Blaemawe cultivator's choicest bloom – a pigsty. It was fortunate when the mountain air blew down to mitigate the odours that floated round. To-day there was hardly any breeze, the atmosphere was hazed and still. Simon fanned himself with his hat, and wondered what Dinah was doing. She had not reappeared since washing-up after tea. Reading that letter in her bedroom, no doubt. So that was what lay behind Frank's allusions, and Dinah's reticence! For the first time Simon felt a little sorry for Gershon, who sat in restless submission to Ruth's laughing voice. She was reading aloud to him (careless of her mother's murmuring over pages of Hebrew Tillim) from *Pickwick Papers* – a copy Simon had sent for her last birthday. Obviously Ruth's enjoyment of the humours of Mr. Wardle's party was as keen as ever Simon's had been, and she had no idea that Gershon was not sharing it. The crease on Gershon's forehead may have come from some other distraction: but he certainly wanted to understand and enter into the English stories that the girls introduced to him. He had begged for easy ones: and the words, of course, were simple enough.

"'You see nothing extraordinary in the stockings, as stockings, I trust, sir?'

"'Certainly not. Oh, certainly not,' replied Mr. Tupman. He walked away; and Mr. Pickwick's countenance resumed its customary benign expression."

Ruth laughed heartily. Gershon sighed. His eyes wandered towards the open door of the living-room: he could not see within as clearly as Simon, who sat in the direct line of vision. Away in the furthest corner of the yard, under the shade of a wall, Gedaliah Black was dozing, an open book on his knees. For a time he had joined with his wife in reprimanding Simon for having left the Fincks. Nothing that Simon had to say in condemnation of the Finck ménage could impress his parents: they yielded only to his argument in favour of independence. There was no longer need to accept help from the Elmans. His salary would enable him to pay his own way and to discharge all obligations incurred on his behalf. "Of course I can't afford as yet to live in what you call 'style', mother," he said. "That's why I'm glad I've fixed up such a cheap lodging."

"But a *goyishe* lodging," reproached Mrs. Black. "Why should you stay with Goyim, even though you do not need to eat much there? Even their breakfast is treif, with all the chazerei they use in the tep. Why shouldn't you give some poor Yid a chance to earn a few shillings? There is so much poverty and hardship among our people in London. I have seen with my own eyes, and I have heard – Surely a room could be found with another Yiddish family, even if you don't like the Fincks—"

The argument had gone on until his father, to Simon's relief, had fallen asleep, and his mother, shaking her head and sighing, had resumed her repetition of the psalms. Simon felt stifled in his soul as in his body. He had been careful enough not to give any but the most innocuous excuses for his conduct, but the need for such restraint was exhausting. While his mother grieved over the Elman misfortunes as well as his own "defection", he could not increase her pain by baring his mind. Besides, there was Dinah – perhaps fresh trouble was accruing there? All the more reason, then, that he should be considerate of his parents' feelings. But it was dashed hard to endure this atmosphere of gloom and criticism, at the very time when he ought to be hailed with delight and encouragement. Any English family would be proud of a son who had achieved as much. Even the Werringtons, vulgar and ignorant as the womenfolk were, would make a hero of Frank if he—His thought broke: it might be that Dinah made too much of a hero of Frank, already. Could such a state of things honestly be welcomed? Turning his head from Gershon to the door of the living-room, he could see that Dinah was moving about. He got up suddenly and walked in. At the moment there was a scuffling noise in the neighbouring poultry-yard, and Dinah did not hear his step. She was standing near the fire, gazing at an envelope in her hand, and turning it over in a hesitating way. Simon could see it plainly, and noted with surprise that it was still unopened. With a sudden gesture she flung it into the heart of the fire.

"On Shabbos, too," said Simon ironically, and advanced towards her.

Her face flamed in the light of the blazing paper. She turned her head away.

"You needn't mind on that account," said Simon. "But why on earth did you do it? It was Frank's letter, wasn't it? And you hadn't even opened it?"

She nodded.

"Why did you do it?" he repeated.

"I – I asked him not to write to me again. I said I should burn it without opening it, if he did." She sat down at the table, and hid her chin in her hand. Her cheeks were paling again, and her eyes downcast.

"You've been a long time about it, though," thought Simon. Aloud he said, uncomfortably,

"What's the objection? Why shouldn't you write to each other if you want to? Frank's a decent fellow—"

"I know he is. But it isn't any good—"

A little sob gurgled in her throat.

"I don't see why you shouldn't be friends."

There was a long pause. Dinah hid her face completely for a moment, then looked up, as if with a great effort, and said in a low voice—

" Frank wants to be more than friends." There was another pause before she continued— "I always knew it – it would be difficult. But now – well, it's quite impossible. After all that's happened, – through Nettie—"

"But that's nothing to do with you," muttered Simon.

"Oh – how can you say that? It's impossible – I – I just couldn't – knowing how it would hurt them all—"

"Frank doesn't matter, I suppose? And yourself?"

Tears rushed into her eyes.

"Oh – surely you – you understand? He – won't mind half as much – later on. But you know quite well that mother and father – they'd never, never get over it. I *couldn't!*" Her words came a little faster. She seemed to find some relief in speaking, in spite of her shyness and reluctance. "Frank can't see that, of course. He thinks it's because of – of Gershon. You know about Gershon, I suppose?"

"Yes – I heard from Uncle Mark. Damned cheek of the fellow!"

Dinah's head went up stiffly. She looked straight at Simon for the first time.

"You needn't swear at Gershon. He's decent, too. I think he's fine!"

"But you wouldn't marry him!" Simon was aghast.

Her head drooped again.

"No, of course not. I don't feel—"

"I should jolly well think not. A foreign fellow! – Oh, he's not a bad sort, I know, in his way. But nothing will ever make *him* English – especially now that he's going back to Russia. A mad idea."

"It isn't. I think it's noble of him."

"Oh, do you?" Simon almost sneered. "I suppose you've encouraged the plan. Have you told him that you won't marry him?"

"Y-yes."

" H'm. That accounts for it. He wouldn't go if he thought that he had a chance with you."

"But he thinks he has."

"What? Do you mean to say you've let him imagine that?"

"You – you are horrid, Simon. I didn't expect you to be like this. I – I wanted to tell you, – because – but you mustn't think that. I've shown Gershon – quite plainly – that I – I don't care for him. But he doesn't know about Frank. I really couldn't tell him. So he thinks that – perhaps – in time" – Dinah twisted her hands together somewhat desperately— "anyhow, I've promised that I won't be engaged to anybody else until he comes back."

"H'm. Three years, possibly. Nothing in that – you're young enough, of course. Don't see why you should marry anybody till then, in any case. Besides—" Simon put his hands in his pockets and stared thoughtfully at his sister, who had grown up so suddenly and absurdly. She was nearly as tall as himself now, very supple and slight, her jet hair smoothly drawn down her sloping olive cheeks. The black lashes were long over her large, soft, timid eyes. Childishness and maturity struggled in the expression of her face. "You'll meet different people later on. When I'm fixed up a little better – perhaps next year – you can come and stay with me. I'll take you about."

Dinah was silent, to Simon's annoyance. Surely she, at least, might show a little appreciation.

"Frank never told me you wrote to him," he said grumblingly.

"I asked him not to. And I'd rather you didn't say anything about me to him, now."

"So you won't write to him again?"

"No, never."

"And you think – that'll finish it?" Simon knew he was torturing his sister, but he could not help pressing the questions on her.

"Yes – I'm sure. He won't go on writing, when he gets no

answer. And he isn't likely to come down – it's so far—" Her lips trembled. "It'll be – it'll be quite finished, then. Although he's so – so very – friendly – now, I expect he'll see other girls – and then – he'll forget?"

"And will you?"

This was an enquiry the girl could not meet. She started up with a sob and rushed away to her room. As she ran, she nearly tripped over a rug, a corner of which was turned up. Simon kicked it flat, and scowled at Gershon, who entered that moment from the yard. The cousins stood eyeing each other in silence.

"Is anything the matter?" said Gershon at last.

"No. Why?"

"I thought – I thought I heard Dinah – crying—"

He looked round with brows drawn together. Simon, his hands still in his pockets, leaned against the table and gazed at the fire. He could still see a black packet of ash where the thick letter had smouldered.

"Oh, she's upset about this Elman business, like everybody else here. A lot of fuss about nothing."

"To you it is nothing."

"You are shocked, hey? Everybody from Russia thinks that falling in love and marrying outside the faith is a horrible crime."

Gershon's brows relaxed. He smiled a little.

"No, not everybody in Russia thinks like that—"

"Don't they, by Jove! That's news to me. But in any case, it can't happen there, because no one gets out of the ghetto."

"You make a mistake. The young people in Russia are not all so froom as the old – it is the same there, too, with the *moderne* ways—" Gershon hesitated. Simon thought it was because he found some difficulty in expressing himself. But he felt, too, that his cousin was struggling with some unusual embarrassment.

"Things can't be the same there," he said dogmatically. "What with the persecutions and restrictions, the Jews can't mix with other people."

"Yes—sometimes," said Gershon. " The others suffer also from persecutions. So they are friends, together. But the young Jews, they do not want to be, any longer, as their parents. They feel it is – so" – Gershon brought his hands within a couple of inches of each other, pointing towards the floor— "low – narrow – what you call, humil – humiliating. They do not want to be such Jews."

"What do they want to be, then – Russians?" asked Simon contemptuously.

"Of course, yes," said Gershon. He looked so self-possessed as he said it, that Simon withheld the remark at his teeth's edge— "But there isn't so much difference – they're all foreigners." He moved restlessly, and said instead,

"Anyhow, you wouldn't care to remain in Russia, I suppose – and become a real Russian yourself?"

"No," said Gershon simply. "I shall come back, and I shall be English."

A curious exasperation seized on Simon. Instead of approving the ambition, it annoyed him by its manifest absurdity. The fellow was his own cousin, it was true – and, as he could not help seeing, had a considerable resemblance to himself. Except that he was shorter and slimmer in build, had darker eyes, and a different walk, Gershon had an actual look of Simon. But was birthplace and education to count for so little? The idea of Anglicisation at his adult stage was simply stupid. Why, the fellow wouldn't understand *Pickwick Papers* if he lived to be ninety! Tolstoy, perhaps, and Dostoiewsky – better than he, Simon, could ever do. To Simon the Russian tales were just as strange and baffling as to other English students he had met – though he had to admit to himself, rather guiltily, that the aroma floating out of those queer pages, had now and again a familiar whiff – as of memories – dreams – things heard and impressed in infancy —. What a confounded mix-up these relationships were! It would add to his relief and satisfaction in his new life, to know that he was rid of any identification with a Russian strain. In spite of what Gershon said, he might remain over there – once he got back to his family, and the army – he seemed to have friends with common interests – a good thing for Dinah, too. She also needed to be rid of cruel obligations. Poor Dinah! Damn it, every moment that he spent at home chafed him more and more. The ingenuity which he was obliged to exercise in order to go out again alone, was the last score piled up on the day's burden.

As the mountain train crawled towards the head of the valley, he wished more bitterly than ever that he need never step into it again. And at the same moment recollection flashed upon him, of Edith Miller's eager planning to return.

XVII

IT WAS a very dark night – starless, moonless. The sky and sea merged together in impalpable shadow. But the green and red lamps of the harbour cut brightly into the void: so did the points of light that dotted the slope of the town behind, the winking flash of the lighthouse standing out on Crumlands Head, and the gleams that came, faint and elfin, from the English coast in front.

The tide was far out, and the great expanse of sand was a promenade for Saturday night idlers, only dimly seen beyond the glare of the slipway. The courting couples were not visible at all; they stood or lay in the sand against the high stone wall. One stumbled against their toes sometimes, or heard their gurgles as one passed. Jani drew closer to Simon when this happened, but he was too absorbed in his explanations to notice.

They had jumped into a tram and come down very quickly, and as soon as they began to tread the soft, deep sand Simon told Jani his plan. He had made inquiries and studied railway and steamship bills before meeting her. He intended to spend the following night at the Elmans'. The family understood that he must be back in London on Monday, and that he meant to catch the early morning mail train from Dawport. It would be easy to leave the house before anyone was up, and instead of going to the station, walk to the docks, and await Jani there. Together they would make the outward trip across the Channel, and spend the whole day in Ilfracombe. At six o'clock Simon could escort Jani to the steamer; himself leaving two hours later, by train for London. Night travelling and arrival in the early hours did not worry Simon – "I don't start work until ten," he said bluffly – "and anyway I can sleep in the train."

It was at this point that Jani's face changed its delighted expression. Simon could just see the outline of the pout as he gazed down, and the blink of lids over the dancing eyes. She had no notion of criticising his arrangements – everything he did, she proclaimed without words, was perfect in her estimation – but the fact that he could not return in the boat with her was a disappointment.

"Sorry, Jani, but it can't be helped." Simon's voice was cheerful. "I must be in London on Tuesday morning – and I simply dare not take any risks by coming back here. The steamer might be late – I might miss the only possible train – the margin's very small. You won't be lonely on the boat – there'll be hundreds of people, and no doubt someone you know. We'll get on board early and look about. And you can arrange to be met – Miss Meredith, perhaps—"

"I'm not afraid – it isn't that – it's because you won't be there—"

"But just think of the lovely long day we'll have – from seven to six! – Besides, you'll be up in town soon—"

"Oh yes, indeed! Tell me now, Simon, – I'm dying to hear all about it—"

"Very well. Then it's settled about Monday?"

"Yes – yes—" eagerly.

"Let's sit down somewhere. The sand's dry I think, but I can put my mac. down for you. Perhaps you'd like to rest against the wall—?"

Jani giggled as he found some difficulty in securing a clear space.

"All the sweethearts are here," she whispered.

"Come along, then, and be my little sweetheart," said Simon lightly, as he spread his mackintosh and drew her down beside him. She giggled again and pushed away his arm, arranging her velvet coat carefully around her, to avoid creasing its delicate pile. She looked very smart in it, as she knew, and as Simon had noted when she emerged from the baby-linen doors. She had had no time to change her dark shop frock, but it suited her, too, showing off her brilliant colouring: and she had added a new cream georgette collar with a narrow frill, out of which her slender neck rose round and fresh. It gleamed in the light of the match that Simon struck for his cigarette. As he puffed and talked, he looked down at the vivid little face tilted against his shoulder. Something tight and hard within him seemed to ease and melt. It was good to be here in the soft, sea-laden dark, that washed away the fret and rage of his visit home. It was better still to let new balm sink into his deeper wound, that festered like a sore at every other touch.

He prolonged his tale, to enjoy more fully the sensation that Jani's upturned listening face produced in him. She had given him a foretaste more than once of the revivifying warmth of her admiration. It was doubly welcome now, in contrast with the doubts and sneers of the rest of the world.

"Thank you very, very much, dear Simon." She rubbed her head like a kitten against his sleeve. "You have done wonderful – I always knew you would be a good friend to me. But I wish I didn't have to wait for another month."

That, he had told her, was the period fixed by Miss

Meredith's friend. Simon's personal call on this hitherto unknown lady had resulted in his discovery that she had just become the head of her department, with power to appoint her own staff. She had agreed to give Jani the vacant place – an arrangement infinitely preferable to Jani's application on competitive terms for a similar post elsewhere.

Simon had been at some pains to persuade Miss Price, whom he described as "one of those suspicious Welsh-women, terribly efficient and practical, but not a bad sort, I daresay. She said she had always been willing to recommend any friend of Miss Meredith's, but somehow I think she wouldn't have bothered – as she said, there are plenty of suitable girls on the spot. I managed to impress her with your qualifications, Jani – that was what did the trick!"

"Qual-if-ic-ations?" said Jani, drawing out the long word as if bewildered.

"Yes, your experience here, you know – the long time you've been in your uncle's shop – and so on. I piled it on – I said you were practically the manageress, that you knew more about bibs and tuckers than Miss Meredith, who only had to be considered because of her age, etc.—"

"Oh, Simon, you never did!" said Jani, laughing. He could see her teeth glisten. "Miss Meredith would have a fit if she knew! She's always at me for mixing things up, and not knowing which binders – I mean – oh – never mind— How do you know about bibs, whatever? But indeed it's true that I can make the ribbon bows better than Miss Meredith. The women always want me to do them up. And I can make the baskets, too, myself – better than the ready made ones, they are, everybody says!"

"So I wasn't such a liar, after all," said Simon, laughing too.

"You aren't a liar, Simon. I hate liars." Jani's voice was indignant. She was sensitive on the point. Simon missed it in finding another implication.

"And you don't hate me, do you?" he said, patting the hand that rested near his knee.

" Of course not," said Jani promptly, putting her other hand on his, and squeezing it gently between her palms.

"Ergo, I cannot be a liar." Simon laughed again, rather fatuously, and Jani, who had not followed him, joined in his merriment. But suddenly, she said in an anxious tone,

"Oh tell me, please, Simon – why do you call Miss Price suspicious? For what is she suspicious about me?"

"Not about you, my dear. She was suspicious of me. I suppose she thought it strange that a handsome and fascinating young man – a Londoner – should press the claims of a little country girl – especially when he described her as a little witch."

"Oh, Simon, you are teasing! You didn't—"

"No," he said, holding both her hands fast— "but I *might* have done – it would have been true, wouldn't it?"

"Indeed, then, about yourself – oh, Simon, you *are*, you know—"

" What?"

" Handsome – and – and – fasc-fascin-ating." Her voice was low, and cooing. He released her hands abruptly. "And clever, too. That is why you have helped me so well. I'm sure nobody else could have done it – Miss Meredith has not been willing in her heart for me to go away, so I think she has not been recommending me very strong to Miss Price. And that is why she has not been saying much about it for a long time. I have been very miserable, thinking how I might have to be staying on in Dawport, or else going back to Blaemawe – and you know what it is like *there*!"

"A dull hole," said Simon. "But after all – your people are comfortably off. And you're the only child. I should have thought—"

"Oh, no, I could never live in Ty Gwyn again! You don't know how my mother is quarrelling with me. Nothing is right that I do, and she is not willing for me to go anywhere to enjoy myself. A real miser she is getting too, wanting to do all the work to save money, and then not spending a penny on pleasure. And I should never be having a new dress or anything nice – like these—" she touched her velvet coat and smart hat.

"That would never do," said Simon gravely. "Pretty girls must have pretty clothes."

"Oh, Simon – do you think I am – pretty?"

"Very pretty, you vain little creature," he said. But he drew himself up rather stiffly as she pressed closer, and looked across the dark patch where the water was.

"Doesn't your father treat you well?" he asked.

"Oh, dad – he's up in the clouds. Never can see anything that's going on, and don't understand anything except history and Seventh Day Sabbath and old things like that. My mother is right about him – it do vex her terrible. He is always going for long walks by himself, tramping for miles, taking a couple of bananas with him to eat. He do quarrel with mam because she attends to business on Saturday, and she says *she* won't follow the Jews, even if he – oh, Simon—!" she stopped suddenly, her face flushing scarlet in the dark. As he did not reply she went on hurriedly – "He thinks the world of your father, but he don't go there so often – your father is not so well always, and I think your sister—" she hesitated.

"Hasn't your father any other friends?" said Simon.

"Everybody do make fun of him except the minister – and *he* do get very cross because he never will go to chapel—"

"Listen, Jani – Don't say 'do make' – 'do get' – but 'makes' and 'gets'. When you're in London, you must be careful to use better English, – or people might make fun of *you*!"

Simon spoke very gently. Jani turned round eyes on him.

"Yes, indeed, Simon, I will try to speak better. I have been trying – but I do – but I forget. And there is nobody to help me. Perhaps now you will teach me if I am wrong?"

"If you wish me to – certainly."

"Oh, I shall wish – I shall be glad to learn from you. Everything will be lovely when I am in London." She clapped her hands. "I wish it was to-morrow! A month is a long, long time!"

"What an impatient little girl." He looked down at her indulgently. She was exactly like a child. "Is it so *terribly* hard at your uncle's?"

Jani nodded her head energetically, and began to detail the tyrannies that her uncle loved to practise.

"I wouldn't be minding at the shop so much, if it was comfortable in the house," she continued. "But the way he do go on – I mean, goes on, about the servants and everything, do – drives my auntie nearly mad. He wants to know the price of everything down to the pepper and salt, and nothing must be wasted – worse than my mother he is, for she is not stingy on food. If we have a chicken at my uncle's house – an old fowl it is, indeed – we have to be having the bones served up to the last, without any pickings. But it's not only because he is mean – it's because he likes to show he is the boss. And since he is the deacon, we have to be always going to chapel, although my auntie is not always wanting to go, either. Especially now. Oh – Simon" – she hesitated, then lowered her voice a little – "that is why it is getting worse. My Auntie Gwyneth is going to have a baby."

"What? At her age?"

"Yes – isn't it funny?" There was a slight giggle in her throat, contending with a note of petulance. "She is forty-three. Everybody is talking about it, and saying it may be dangerous. And they are saying too, that it is *I* will have to put up with all the trouble and the fuss. They think I will be there, doing all the work, and nursing the baby. But I won't, indeed – not me! Even if I wasn't going to London, I would be running away before *then*!"

Simon was amused.

"So you wouldn't like to nurse the baby, Jani?"

"Me? I hate babies! Nasty, squally, dirty things they are!"

She spoke with a hissing vehemence, picking up handfuls of sand and scattering it about. He laughed.

"What – and you making pretty bows and baskets for the little things?"

"Oh, I'm not minding that. I like making baskets. I have promised a lovely one for Auntie Gwyneth – blue silk stuffed with wadding and stitched with ribbon flowers – and perhaps an edging of real lace. She don't know that it is in London I will be making it for her!" Jani laughed out gleefully. Then another thought occurred to her. "But where will I be living, Simon?"

"Indoors at Bingley's, I expect. A certain number of the staff can live in – the unmarried ones. Miss Price told me the conditions are quite good. But if you don't like it, you may arrange to dig out later on."

"And do – does Miss Price herself live in?"

"Yes, though she hinted she was going out at the end of the month. I don't know if that has anything to do with her fixing the time for your start."

"Perhaps she is getting married," said Jani shrewdly. "Miss Meredith said she was courting a milkman. He is going to have a dairy of his own soon – a new shop, with rooms at the top; that is where they will be living, I suppose. But she won't be telling them at Bingley's, because she wants to keep her job for a bit."

"I daresay," said Simon, yawning. He was not interested in Miss Price's affairs. He pulled out his watch, and struck a match to see it by. Their hour was almost gone. He jumped to his feet and drew Jani up. She did not want to move, but held out her arms readily enough, and leaned against him. He caught her hands to steady her, but as he released them she remained clinging to him, her arms creeping round his neck, her lips seeking his. He gave a little embarrassed laugh. Figures were passing quite near on the sand, but he knew that faces were indistinguishable. He held Jani a little closer, and returned her kisses lightly, rather guiltily. She was a sweet little thing – who could help being fond of her? – and her childish abandon touched if it did not intoxicate him. He was grateful for the ease she had brought him, for the sense of benefaction she roused and fostered so delightfully. But this last kiss of hers – it was surprisingly breathtaking, passionate. He drew himself away a little unsteadily, balancing her on her feet.

"Come along, kitten," he murmured.

She put her arm through his and walked along, purring happily – a kitten, in truth.

The kittenishness rather than the passion remained in his mind over the long day that intervened before they met again.

It was early enough when she arrived at the docks. But Simon had already been waiting over an hour. For some time it had been interesting to stroll round the byways of the harbour, comparing its new bridges and walls with what he could remember of the old. The changes added stature to the wharves, dignity and importance to the busy life about. Only the slimy water looked the same. He watched it lap the thick supports, already greenish at the base as the ancient piles had been. It recalled, too, his secret shame at the fact that he had never wanted to run away to sea. Such an English thing to desire, if not to do. But he had never felt it. His instinct, he told himself, was never to leave England, only to remain and grow into it, to become part of the solid foundations of the land.

The morning was dull and gentle, promising a noon of cloudless sky and sun. After his prowl round the docks, he sat reading a Service manual. The brief study renewed his confidence and zest, somewhat shaken by his night at the Elmans. He had not been allowed to see the old man again, the doctor having forbidden further visits. Not that Simon was anxious to do more than fulfil a duty. His main wish, before he had been in the house an hour, was to get away from all the Elmans in it – from the provoking, supercilious Sylvie, her weeping mother, and surly Uncle Mark. Surly. That was how Simon characterised the behaviour of Mark Elman. Not a word of congratulation – or even of complaint, for the matter of that. Nothing but a barely sufferable recognition of his presence, a silent glowering indifference to his coming or going. The replies to tentative approach on Billig's behalf were almost savagely curt. The man looked as if he were going off his chump, thought Simon, in chagrin at this inauspicious visit. It was a relief to retire to bed in the luxurious room allotted to him – a greater relief, still, to creep out at dawn, and turn his back on the ornate, ghastly home.

He yawned, closed the pages of his book, and wished Jani would come. The little puss must have overslept. He himself had scarcely had forty winks all night, or so it seemed. But he did not feel tired. His veins ran with eagerness – for the work ahead, and also for these preliminary hours of ease on sea and coast, with a pretty, admiring companion. He got up, strolled round the timber stacks to where the *Devona* lay, and saw that a queue had formed at the ticket-office. Laughing, chattering trippers, old ladies with bursting handbags, girls with tulle scarves tied round their heads, couples in mackintoshes and tweeds, a lad already "tuning up" a concertina which was to enliven the starlit return. As Simon joined them, he saw Jani coming round the bend. He waved to attract her, and they exchanged smiles. She was looking very dainty and fresh, and not in the least like a tripper. The velvet coat was hanging on her arm. She had on a white voile frock, with tawny spots of embroidery on the borders, and a small straw hat. In one hand she carried a rather large attache case – to Simon's amusement. He found, when they were settled on the boat, that she produced at once a huge packet of sandwiches.

"I guessed you wouldn't have had breakfast so early," she said – "so I thought we would have it together – I had to hide in the pantry to make such a lot – that's what made me a bit late—"

"What a thoughtful little kitten," he said, delighted. He had forgotten food, and became aware that he was, in fact, very hungry. The timely fare was spread on a serviette in the open case above his own larger bag, which stood in front of their deck chairs.

He pushed a sandwich against her lips. She seized his hand and held it while she bit and munched. They fed each other alternately, laughing and making pretence of eating the wrong share. When they had finished the meal, Jani rolled up the serviette and tucked it into a corner of her case.

"What's left underneath?" Simon touched a soft flat parcel covered by a sheet of cardboard. Jani let him pull it up and discover a towel, folded over some bright green stuff.

"My suit," she said smiling archly. "We'll bathe at llfracombe, won't we?"

"By jove, yes! I'll have to borrow togs. Do you swim, Jani?"

"Yes, indeed. I used to be swimming in the river in Patagonia when I was five. But in Blaemawe my mother wasn't willing. Sometimes I go in at Dawport. But it is not often I get the chance."

"You will to-day, then. We'll have a ripping time, Jani, you'll see!"

As the steamer left the coast they strolled around the deck. Even on this calm, dazzling day there were people who lay back pale and apprehensive, their limbs and features stiff and taut. Simon and Jani grinned and sniggered at them. Their own hearts were stout, their bodies light as their spirits. They skimmed the length of the boat backwards and forwards like birds, Simon's only grumble being at the large number on board. One could hardly move, he said, without falling over the extended legs of the "sitters", or jostling the parading crowd. But Jani's eyes roamed happily among her fellow passengers, and it was with satisfaction that she recognised a face here and there. She named Dawport acquaintances whom Simon did not know, and whose stares he returned complacently. But later on he became uneasy. Jani had stopped and pointed to a group going below – "Oh, look! There's Myrddin Hughes – you know – Mrs. Hughes the shoemaker's son – and his friend Glyn Powell. There are two girls with them – I wonder who they are? There – they are just turning round on the steps – *well*!" Jani almost whistled in surprise. "One of them is Jessie Lloyd the Bank – and Blaemawe don't believe she'd go with Glyn!"

"Are they all from Blaemawe?" said Simon, frowning. He drew Jani back towards their sheltered nook, where he had arranged the chairs so that they could sit unobserved. Dawport people he did not mind: there were few who knew him now, and those few likely to be engaged in business on a Monday morning. But Blaemaweites, who would recognise both Jani and himself, and spread the tale of their association here – that was another matter. He determined to promenade no more.

They leaned together over the rail and watched the bubbles of white foam race gently below. From this side of the boat no land was visible. They were on the open mouth of the channel, and the green waves of the Atlantic spread away, in slow-heaving undulations towards limitless space.

"We might be going to America," said Simon absently.

"Yes, indeed – to Patagonia," said Jani, amused. "That would be a grand long trip – weeks and weeks. On the sea, and in trains, and little boats on rivers, and riding for miles on horseback!"

"You know all about it, Jani – you're a great traveller," said Simon. His voice was not amused, but surprised. It seemed as if he had just wakened to the knowledge. "Why, I've been nowhere at all – and *you've* been to the other end of the world! Tell me about your trip home. Do you remember much about it?"

Jani remembered a great deal. She told Simon stories of that famous journey, which made him wonder, not only at her retentive memory, but at the power of a child of eight to observe and store. It did not occur to him that the reminiscences might have drifted into her later years from her parents, and that she had not only absorbed but embroidered the theme. Jani was an unconscious artist whose dramatic gifts often confused herself. She could so easily believe that everything had happened as her fancy or her wish dictated. And nobody could be more offended by the exposure of her magic than Jani herself. But her Patagonian background was actually rich enough in material to provide a brilliant show. It was not often that, in such a scene, she had the opportunity of an admiring audience.

Simon, indeed, listened in a mood of re-appraisement. This pretty little playmate of whom he was fond, and who magnified him in his own esteem by her devotion, was a misunderstood fellow-outcast from the standards of her people, wiser than they, and more experienced than himself. She had been forced in her earliest years into a wild unconventional life, that may or may not have been superior to the proximate lives of her stock: its effects certainly made her different from the order of shop-girls to which she happened, accidentally, to belong. She had never really caught up with them in some respects: in others she was a winged bird, flying free and untrammelled above. She ought to be encouraged into this higher sphere. Once in London, it would not be difficult to release her from the cramping habits of speech and outlook acquired in the Dawy Valley. He must persuade her to attend classes, make her read, and if possible, keep up her music – he remembered that she had been one of Emlyn Richards' pupils until Madame Patti had lured him away. The master had pronounced her apt— "she got a quick ear, and will do fine when she do grow bigger – her fingers are too small for the piano now just." Where had he heard this story retailed? He looked at the little hand beside his on the rail, and another, more recent, recollection came to him. He lifted the fingers and began to examine them.

" Are you looking to see if I have a ring?" said Jani, pertly. "But that is my right hand, Simon!"

" I know. Which is the finger you had the fester on?"

"The fester?" Jani looked puzzled.

"Yes. You said you had to ask Miss Jones – Miss Jones the Bush – to write your letter for you. Was the finger very painful? It seems to have healed up well – there isn't a trace that I can see—"

She snatched her hand away and placed it, laughing, behind her back.

"Oh, there's a little mark by the nail – perhaps I will show it to you later on. But you'll have to look very, very close!"

"Let me look now."

"No. Wait till we are up on the hill at Ilfracombe. It won't be long now before we're there. Oh – look! There's the land!"

The Devon coast had risen out of nowhere. A pearly mist resolved into a long grey hump, which became a stereoscopic mass of green and white. The mass broke into crags and islets, and the shape of Ilfracombe began to emerge, clear under the mounting sun. Capstone and Lantern stretched silver arms in greeting, Hillsborough raised a noble head behind.

"There's lovely it will be there to-day!" trilled Jani ecstatically. "Oh – Simon – aren't you ver-y glad we came?"

He did not reply, and she looked round at him in dismay. Why was he staring down at the water instead of across at the land, with such a queer expression of resentment and gloom?

Simon was caught in a sudden revulsion of feeling. The first sight of Devonshire had startled him into recollection – that he was nearing Edith's best-loved home, just as she herself must often have neared it from Wales. Millicombe, he knew, was on this side of Lynmouth, and the Hafods made summer crossings in the useful pleasure steamers. Strange that he should have forgotten the fact until this moment. But now it took hold of his mind. If it had been Edith standing beside him, instead of Jani! The longing rushed at him the keener for its repression. He had fought down memory, he had trampled on every tender thought, and to-day, surprising as it seemed, he had not once envisaged her. His defences opened wide to an overwhelming evocation. Glorious, incomparable Edith – gripping the rail with him – smiling at the English land of her birth! His heart flew to meet and return that smile. It forced an inaudible cry between his very teeth – that he loved her, only her – adored and needed her. But instantly his brain denied it, drove out the vision, shut fast the gates. No – certainly not. He didn't love her. What he loved was the image of her he had preconceived – as he had done more crudely those long years ago with the vulgar Enid. And as he had rejected and forgotten his yearning after Enid – a yearning based on the same silly worship of the English ideal girl – so he could reject and forget his illusory image of Edith herself. Yes, silly worship, he repeated voicelessly, but contemptuously, his gaze dropping from the coast to the water: his English ideal girl didn't exist except in literature. In life she was more hard than gentle, more shrill than gracious. High-boned, broad-faced, large toothed, like Nurse Newell and students he had known; and those Slade girls, trying vainly to pose as pointed Rossettians or God knows what "artistic" types – Frauds, the lot of them. Stupid, tinny Enids – bewildering paragons who seemed English and turned out to be – foreigners! In that moment of furious review, Simon shirked the humiliating implications of the term "Jewish". The sound of Jani's voice, though he had not heard her words, bore his thoughts back to her on a wave of gratitude. Sweet, genuine little companion, utterly unlike those who had thwarted, and cheated him. He would put everything – everybody – out of his mind to-day, except his purpose of enjoying a holiday with her. He swung round to meet her appealing gaze.

Jani had been wrestling with her own guilty reflections. Simon's abstracted air, it seemed to her, had followed her refusal to let him examine her hand. Was it possible that he suspected her little deceit? She did not want to be found out even in that innocent sort of lie, since it involved discovery of her bad penmanship. What would his opinion of her be? – he, who was so marvellously clever, writing as well as talking like a book, must despise a dunce who could not spell or compose. Though they had been at school together for a short time, he had never known her deficiencies. As a child in Patagonia it had been easy to shirk learning – her father was satisfied with a curriculum of Welsh, and her mother, who could read and write in no language at all, was quite indifferent. The few years of Blaemawe education had not carried her far. If Simon found that she had never had a festered finger, he would guess that she had written that ill-spelt letter herself. It was all Miss

Meredith's fault! The jealous creature had refused to write as she wished, from the moment she learned that Simon was lukewarm about Jani's scheme. For once the confidant had taken the sensible rather than the romantic view. She had dinned warnings and objections into the unwilling ears of Jani, who wished to hurl her intolerable sufferings at Simon's head, and induce him to facilitate her immediate transference to London. Since Miss Meredith would not agree, Jani had been obliged, furious but helpless, to wait. She had not dared risk Simon's contempt by exposing simultaneously her illiteracy and the fraud she had practised on him. Naturally he could not know that Miss Meredith was the writer of her letters. The pretext of "Miss Jones the Bush" and the festered finger, had been an expedient of despair.

While Simon frowned at the waters, Jani grooved her right forefinger with the head of a pin. She thrust the dented digit before his eyes as he turned to her.

"Look, then, Simon," she urged softly. "I'll show it to you now. Can you see the little red mark?"

"Yes, yes," he said vaguely, smiling into her face instead. Then he seized the outstretched finger and kissed it in mock concern. Jani laughed radiantly, but she did not quite like the intent way in which he began to inspect her hand again – only – it did not seem that he was looking at the mark, after all. What was he doing now, smoothing out *all* her fingers? They were fine and white, the nails well cared for. She let him look and smooth.

"I expect you can stretch an octave now, Jani," he said. "Do you keep up your playing?"

"Not much. It's an old bother, whatever. And my Uncle Trevor wouldn't pay for lessons, as he promised – just because I wouldn't play the old organ in his chapel!"

"Why wouldn't you?"

"Well, indeed! – he would be wanting me to go every Sunday to classes as well – and to the Sunday school! When I'm in London, I won't go to chapel – never!"

"But I don't see why you should give up music. Didn't you practise on your piano when you were home lately?"

"A little bit. And once I played on the organ – I mean the harmonium – in Ieuan Richards' house."

It was the first time Jani had mentioned Ieuan. Her smiling lips had a provocative curl.

"Really?" said Simon. "So you visit there just as you used to?"

"No, indeed, I don't – his mother can't bear the sight of me! But he made her ask me when he had some friends to tea one Saturday – it was his birthday. So I went, and played for him to sing. He do – he sings very fine now. He takes lessons at Dawport, and is going to compete at the next Eisteddfod. His uncle Emlyn do – he wants him to go to London and study more."

"Does he mean to go?"

"No." Jani's eyes danced. "He'd rather stay in Wales because *I'm* here – I mean, there!" She peeped up at Simon and laughed at his annoyed expression. He had forgotten that every previous conjunction of Ieuan with Jani had merely amused him.

"The stupid lout!" he muttered.

Jani did not catch the words, but the mutter and the look gratified her highly. At the same time she was anxious to conciliate.

"It makes me laugh because he don't know I'm going to London! He was offered a good job at the biggest Blaemawe colliery office – but he started on something else at Dawport last week only because I was there – *There's* funny he'll look when he hears that I have gone!"

"You are cruel, Jani," said Simon. But he laughed, too.

"Well, his mother will be glad, whatever."

There was bustle on the boat. Passengers were no longer strolling, but picking up luggage and scrambling forward, while sailors were getting gangways into position. Simon kept Jani back from the crowd. There was no need to rush, he said. She enjoyed the sight of people waving from the pier, and waved back vigorously. They landed, to Simon's relief, without recognition or greeting at any point. Everybody but themselves seemed anxious to hurry away. They proceeded leisurely, depositing their cases in the cloakroom near the toll gate. At the last moment Jani agreed to leave her coat behind – it was hot under the brilliant sun – and Simon folded it carefully into his own half-empty bag. With a strap he secured the towel and bathing suit which Jani drew out.

"Lighter than carrying the case," he said. "I can sling this over my shoulder. But you've got something else in there." He stared curiously at a black roll left where the bathing outfit had been.

"Oh, that's my shop dress," said Jani, her colour deepening as she snapped the lid. "It's a new one – and my auntie told me to take it for fear I should be catching cold on the way back to-night. She said I was to mind and slip it on over the voile."

"Isn't your coat warm enough?"

"Yes, indeed – but my Auntie Gwyneth don't believe it." Jani tossed her head. "She's an awful fidget about clothes. I didn't want to take it – but she made me – and I don't like to vex her now—"

"I don't mind, so long as I haven't to carry it along—" said

Simon, laughing. He locked the bags and handed them to the clerk.

They set off, lightened in arms and hearts, on an amble through the quaint irregular streets of the rocky town. Jani would have liked to linger at the shops full of shells and pots and pictures and coloured baskets; would have liked too, to answer with friendly argument the appeals of burly men to enter their doors and partake of "tay and rale Demshire clotted crame". As soon as she realised what they were saying, she did, indeed, make courteous reply. "Later on," she promised them, "you see we've had our breakfast, and we aren't hungry yet—" "There's funny they do – they speak" – she said to Simon, who drew her along in somewhat embarrassed amusement. "I can hardly understand a word they say. Do all English people talk like that? – I mean in the country? I know it is different in London—"

"I'm afraid you won't understand some of the London talk, either," said Simon. He determined to teach her early to avoid the Cockney twang. "I'll tell you about it when we're out of the town. Let's get on to the cliffs." Climbing did not rob the wiry Jani of her breath: she chattered just as much on the steep ways of the Capstone, even on the smooth slippery turf to scramble over which they forsook the paths. Simon made for the top, to sprawl in the glorious air, above the sea which laved the rocks so far below, and away from the people promenading the winding walks. But it was not possible to achieve isolation.

Jani pranced about, gazing eagerly at landmarks and seacraft, pointing to the outlines of the coast from which they had come. "There's Wales," she said. "Come and see—" "I don't want to see it," he murmured from his pitch, as he stared up into the rolling blue of the sky. " I don't care if I never see it again—" "I don't, either," she said with unexpected force. She danced around him, and he watched her fluttering white frock in a growing restlessness, increased by other fluttering frocks that neared and passed and neared and stayed. At last he jumped up and said, "I say, Jani, what about bathing? By the time we get down below and have a few dips, it'll be just right for lunch. Then we can do the Tors."

They descended with eager anticipation. It was not, however, so easy to capture joy by programme. Hours passed, and the forenoon vanished in a growing haze of heat and restless seeking. Simon was disappointed in the crowded bathing beaches, and smuggled away his borrowed plumes, high and dry, to await a more secluded spot for a dip. "Can hardly see the water here for bodies," he grumbled. "I vote we have an early lunch, Janikins, and wander out to some really quiet place. Ilfracombe's so chockful one can hardly breathe, for fear of knocking somebody down—"

Jani, who delighted in exaggerations, and still more in the fancy names Simon had found for her, laughed heartily and agreed. The restaurants were already filling up, and when they emerged from lunch, the streams of visitors pouring over the streets of the town, the cliffwalks and bathing coves, had grown longer and thicker. Simon made straight for a bus just starting off for Worlathoe, a wild spot above a stretch of sands some six miles away, which he had once visited with Frank Werrington on a similar trip.

"It doesn't take long to get there, and we've got the whole afternoon. I remember Frank and I walked for hours on the cliff, caught the last bus back at five o'clock, and even then had a half hour to wait for the boat. So you see we can do it easily."

But Jani needed no persuasion. In spite of her delight in the bright town with its shops and crowd, she seemed even more eager than Simon to get away. Her charming little face, alight with zest, drew the eyes of all the passengers in the bus, as Simon noticed with a curious touch of pride. Really, Jani could be very attractive – she did a fellow credit! It was obvious that other men envied him his companion, a fact which meant more to him than its complement, which was equally obvious to Jani – that all the girls they met envied *her* her escort.

Their mutual satisfaction did not lessen on the sandy wastes and bleak uplands of Worlathoe, where there were no crowds and the few wanderers could be easily avoided. Simon proposed to ramble first and bathe afterwards, when a rest in the deepening heat would be most welcome. Up on the rocky cliffs a tonic breeze tempered the sun, and the two scrambled venturesomely up and down jagged reefs, or slid over the glossy smooth turf above, catching their feet in rabbit holes and laughing and singing like children. It was Jani who sang, her voice vibrant in snatches of Spanish and Welsh: her little red mouth round with o's, her throat richly trilling r's and ch's, the labial l's and p's mellifluously twined. Simon's ears were not critical of the words in such a delicious conjunction of sound and sight. Jani's glowing cheeks of red and brown, her eyes like damsons under the fiery hair, her slender limbs frisking in sure agility over rock and mound, made a picture not to be labelled by any known tongue or race. She seemed an elfin thing outside the conventionality of type. Neither Welsh, Jewish, English nor Patagonian – touched with some mannerisms of each perhaps, but essentially a spirit that had escaped them all.

The charm of it worked somewhat strangely in Simon's blood: as if opposing magnetisms wrought and failed, before some unpolarised tide that flowed between.

At least his holiday mood was made complete. He found it joy to lead so enchanting a sprite, who welcomed every whim of a lord by consent. They roamed and halted, climbed and lounged round spur after spur of headland, until he gave the order to retreat. On the sands below they found a tiny bay to themselves, screened by walls of slippery rock. Cave-like recesses made perfect dressing-rooms, and soon Jani was a green nymph sporting in the water, laughing discreetly at Simon's rueful face, as he stood at the edge clutching one shoulder. His borrowed suit was scanty and ill-fitting, and at the first lift of the arm a strap had burst. Jani ran out with flashing limbs to her cave, and returned with a safety-pin.

"There!" she said, relieving his grip with her own light fingers, wet and cool on his flesh. The little steel drove through the disjointed ends of stuff.

" Ow!" he said, grimacing down at her.

"Oh dear, oh dear, did I *pick* you?" she cried, squeezing her eyes into slits as she peered. "No, then I didn't – you are only pretending! For shame, Simon!" she snapped the point firmly into its groove. "There – now you're all right. But I hope to goodness you won't burst the other strap, because I haven't got another pin. Rotten old suits they do lend, whatever. This one isn't worth the postage you'll have to be paying on it. Come on, now."

She attempted to run off, but he held her fast and smiled gaily down.

"Do you know, Jani, I'm surprised at your white skin – I thought you were brown all over—"

"I was – in Patagonia—" she smiled in return – "but it's had time to go back white since then—"

He let her go, and they raced into the water together. For a time they played about within the baylet, but presently their strokes reached out to the wider sweep. Other heads could be seen bobbing in the curve beyond, and further back, figures lying on the sand or sitting on crags.

"I wonder why they don't come into our bay," said Jani, swimming vigorously beside Simon. He could see the sun catch her hair into flame.

"It's a piece of luck," he answered. "But I don't know why."

They were to discover later that the reason lay in blobs of tar, washed ashore in the spring from a wreck, that sprayed the rocks and caves of their retreat. But even the stains on Simon's suit and Jani's white frock did not chasten their satisfaction at being left alone.

It was Simon who tired first of the water and prolonged the intervals of sunbathing on the beach. Lack of sleep, long exposure to the air, muscular exercise, and the still heat of the sheltered cove, combined to overpower him with what seemed sudden effect. As they came out glistening for the last time, he could hardly drag himself to his nook to consult his watch. "Just four," he announced, drowsily. "We can rest for another twenty minutes, walk to the hotel for tea, and be ready for the bus. Jove, it's hot!"

"Shall we dress first?" asked Jani, squatting, and flicking her towel lightly across her knees. "We can spread our suits out to dry."

"Mine's dry already," said Simon. He stretched himself on the sand beside her. "You can dress if you like. But I refuse to move for five minutes at least."

He laughed sleepily at her. She rolled over on her side, digging her elbows in the sand as she propped her chin on her hands. Her unbound locks cascaded to her shoulders.

"You look a sort of fairy," he murmured, lifting fingers to her head. "But I never knew fairies had red hair, and – skin of many colours. Like Joseph's coat," he added involuntarily.

She leaned closer, so that his half-closed eyes rested on the milky flesh below the brown ring of her throat.

"Joseph's coat indeed! I'd rather be a fairy than Joseph – or a Red Indian. Nobody calls that after me now but there's plenty make fun of my hair." She pouted, then smiled radiantly, her dark ripe eyes full of points of light. "But I don't care what you call me, Simon, – so long – as long as you do like me—" She whispered the words, her head sinking with her voice. His hand dropped from her hair to encircle her neck.

"Of course I like you, Janikins."

"Better than anybody else?"

He could hardly hear the words, but lifted himself slightly towards her flushed, sparkling face. As her gaze fell before his she gave a little scream.

"Oh, the safety's open – don't move—" Her hands flew to the pin, but not before the coarse point had scratched and spotted his shoulder with blood. He did not notice it, for as she hung across him, he saw the small round breasts within the dark stockinette. His lips reached down to the flesh above.

"Oh – Simon" – she breathed, and abandoned herself in his arms. – "Oh, Simon – you *do* like me best of all, don't you?"

He laughed again, a little huskily.

"Of course, Janikins. You're the sweetest thing."

Her hands met tightly round his neck, as he dropped back on the sand.

Lily Tobias

"Dear Simon, you know I do love you – I do, I do!"

She lay against him and began to kiss his lips with the same passion that had surprised him before. But now he gave back her kisses without thought or reserve. The soft damp body pressed close upon his own grew part of the drowsed magic of the day, the still hot air and merge of sky and sea. It was sweet to love and be loved in this waking dream – or dreamful wakening? He did not realise which when he opened his eyes out of deep sleep, a moment? – an eternity? – later.

He stared and jumped to his feet.

"Jani! Jani!"

Her voice answered faintly from her cave. As she did not appear he went to the opening, and found her seated, fully dressed, stooping over an unfastened shoe."

"It's time to go, I think," she said, but did not look up at him. Without answering he sped to his own recess, and fumbled for the watch in his waistcoat.

"Good Lord!" he shouted. "It's nearly five. We'll have to rush like blazes." He began to fling off his suit and dress rapidly, going once outside, to shout – "I'd no idea I slept so long – why didn't you wake me?"

As she made no reply he repeated the question a few minutes later, when he joined her on the open beach.

"I did try," she said, still without meeting his eyes. "I thought it might be getting late, so I shook you and told you to hurry. Then I went to dress myself—"

He took her arm and began striding. "You should have kept on shaking and made sure I was awake," he said in vexation.

"Oh, Simon," she said, half-pouting and half appealing – "don't scold me – I couldn't help it. I thought you were really waking up – you said something. Besides – I think I must have dozed a bit myself – and I didn't know the time—"

He drew her arm closer and smiled.

"I should have left my watch out with you. Never mind, kitten." There was a queer note in his voice. The memory of their embraces rushed over him. Had it really all happened as he recalled – surely part of it must have been dream? – "I'm afraid you'll have to miss your tea. But if you can keep up a good rate, we'll just about catch the bus. It's the last, you know—"

"Yes, I know," she said, and began to stumble over the stones in the sloping outlet to the road. He swung her forward with a firm hand on her waist. But when they reached the level, she freed herself, quickening her short steps to a run. So fast did she race that Simon, for all his haste, was obliged to remonstrate.

"Don't overdo it, Jani – you're breathless already. Better take my arm and just keep up with me—" He slackened, and she leaned on him, with such a pensive glance that his uneasiness increased. The highway seemed deserted. The big isolated houses overlooking the shore had a closed, secret air.

"Funny there are no people about," said Simon. Jani did not speak. Her eyes had become as blank and secretive as the windows of the houses on the hill. He determined to encourage her and went on talking cheerily. "I suppose everybody's at tea. It isn't easy to see residents or visitors in a place like this. And there aren't many trippers. The few that came with us must be on the spot. Only round that bend, and we're there. I should think we'll have about two minutes to spare."

But his own expression changed to a hardening stare as they

came within view of the hotel. There was no vehicle standing on the space in front, and the only person visible was an old ostler, smoking on a bench. Simon darted up to him.

"Bus, sir? It be gone, ten minutes back—"

Useless to show him Simon's watch.

"You'm a quarter slow, sir—"

Was there anything that would take them into Ilfracombe? Not from the hotel, it seemed. Cars and horse-carriages were engaged for the next hour. There was a garage back along, where a cab might be hired – on in the village on the hill, a regular conveyance plied to the railway station, two miles distant.

Simon rushed Jani away, careless now of her short breath or his earlier misgivings. The garage was locked, and not a soul concerned with it was near. There was nothing for it but to sprint to the village. Half-way up the stony hill Jani tripped and fell, and she moaned as Simon helped her to her feet.

"My ankle's hurt," she complained, and limped painfully.

"Good Lord! " said Simon. " I hope it isn't much—" He encircled her waist once more and helped her along, but soon she was obliged to stop. Simon looked round. Two men had just walked past, and an old woman with a child was toiling ahead. In any case, what matter if people noticed? He lifted Jani in his arms, and told her to grip him fast. She was light, and the ascent was not so difficult for the next hundred yards: the heat was the most troublesome factor. But the last rise was very steep. Simon puffed and perspired.

"Hard luck," he said, beginning to stagger, "but I'm afraid I must go slow. Don't worry, Jani – we may do it yet."

Was Jani worrying? There was no trace of anxiety in the face against his chest. But presently she spoke in her soft, plaintive tones.

"Let me down now, Simon. I – I'm sure I'm too heavy. And my foot doesn't pain much now. I'll try to walk a bit."

She tried, most gallantly it seemed, and though she winced now and again, it was possible for her to move slowly with support. As they neared the top and the village shops appeared, she declared the pain almost gone. Luck, however, was against them at the old coach house. The carrier had already left for the station, with all the fares who meant to catch the train to Ilfracombe. There wouldn't be another for an hour and a half. But perhaps a local grocer, whose horse and trap stood outside his door—With a little trouble, Simon prevailed on the grocer to lend his equipage, with a youth as driver: without guarantee, however, that the train would be caught. Nor was it. Not even its smoke was visible when the vehicle arrived. The youth declined to drive on for another four miles, but fortunately a cab near the station was available, and the last stage to the town began.

Simon scrambled into his seat with an exclamation of relief, which concealed a vast uncertainty. He took Jani's hand in both his, squeezing it gently as an accompaniment to his consolations.

"We ought to manage it this time, Janikins. What a shame to rush and frighten a poor little girl! But the foot's really better, isn't it?"

She thrust it out, with a cautious air.

"Yes – there's a little swelling, I think – but it doesn't hurt much. It was only a bit of a twist."

" What luck it wasn't a sprain! Shall I take the shoe off?"

"No – no" – she drew it back hastily. " Perhaps I won't be able to put it on again – that's how it is sometimes with a swelling. And I mustn't be wasting more time, indeed." She nestled against him timidly, with a half-tearful, half-confiding smile. It touched him to a deeper sense of man's responsibility.

"It was I who wasted time – sleeping like a log for an hour!" He shook his head as if in incredulous self-reproach. "And then my watch – I could have sworn it was right! It's never let me down before." He pulled it out: "By jove, it's stopped altogether now. Something must be wrong." He rattled it and opened the inner case, but examination was useless. He put it back with another sigh. "I'll have to see I don't lose the London train, anyway. Once you're on the boat I'll keep walking round the station!"

Jani said nothing. Simon looked out vaguely at the cornfields stretching from either side the deep-hedged lane through which they drove. No vestige of tiredness remained. His mind grew more alert as his apprehensions increased. The approach to the town, the distant sound of sirens, found him ready to meet the situation. The assurance with which he helped Jani down, paid the driver, and slung the strapped bathing kit over his shoulder, was in no way affected by the sight of people straggling away from the harbour gates as he and Jani hurried in, by the replies of officials to his inquiries, or even by the thin fume of smoke that trailed back from a receding line, far out at sea.

"Our steamer's gone!" gasped Jani.

"Yes," he said, coolly. "That's the Devona out there. But it's all right, Jani. There are other ways of getting you home."

"I thought – I thought – the man said there were no more boats to South Wales this evening?"

"I know. That doesn't matter. Come with me, and you'll see what we can fix up."

There was nothing of the scene he dreaded. Jani looked

bewildered, but followed him quietly as he collected the bags and put them in another cab. She did not even comment on his directions or interrupt his study of a railway guide he had secured.

"This isn't much good," he said at last. "I shall have to get particulars from the office. Wait here, Jani" – he had led her, with the bags, to a quiet corner of the station platform – "I'll be back very soon."

She waited in the same state of puzzled calm. But he had no sooner reappeared with his "particulars", than a total change came over her. The expression of panic and dismay that he had expected to see earlier dilated her eyes, and some of the rich colour left her cheeks.

"No – no – Simon – I can't – I won't—"

"Why, Jani, what's the matter? It's the only way you can get home, child – and there's absolutely nothing to be frightened of! The journey's long and tiresome, of course – I'm afraid you'll be pretty fagged. But I'll arrange everything possible for your comfort. It's most fortunate that your train leaves before mine. The guard will keep an eye on you – here, I'll show you the best route. And I can send a wire to your uncle, or if you prefer, to Miss Meredith. After all, 2 o'clock isn't so terribly late to arrive—"

"Oh, it is – it is, indeed – my Uncle Trevor wouldn't let me into the house!"

"Nonsense!" Simon paused a moment, moved by her distress. " But if you'd rather not disturb them, perhaps Miss Meredith could put you up for the night—"

"No, she sleeps with her mother, – they've only got one bedroom. Besides, it wouldn't make any difference to Uncle Trevor – he wouldn't let me in, ever again! Oh, Simon, you don't know his terrible temper. And he wouldn't believe me – he'd say I missed the boat on purpose!"

"On purpose? – For what?"

Jani twisted her hands and moaned – "Oh, you don't know him, he'd say the most awful things. I'll never, never be able to go back there again!"

"Well, why not go straight home to Blaemawe?"

"But there's no train."

"In the morning. If you are sure you can't stay with friends in Dawport, to-night, you can either put up at Ilfracombe – I'll find you a room in a decent place – or leave by the late train, which gets in at about 5 or 6. It means travelling all night, but you'll arrive in daylight and be able to go straight on—"

"No – no – I won't go to Blaemawe – they won't believe me either, and everybody will talk about me – and my mother will call me nasty names – oh, I can't bear it!"

"But, Jani dear, why shouldn't they believe you?"

"Because – because when they know that you were with me here—" She stopped, and looked at him with strange, furtive eyes, while a high flush returned to her cheeks. Simon felt his own face burn.

"But why should they know?" he muttered, and felt ashamed immediately that he should expect Jani to screen him in circumstances so unpleasant for herself. "Oh – well – perhaps it won't be as bad as you think, Jani. After all, it's only for a short time – you'll be leaving for good in a few weeks. And really – there's nothing else to be done, is there?"

"There is, there is—" said Jani, with a low vehemence that startled him. The impetuous spirit that she had lost seemed to rush back to her. "I can't go back to Wales, and I *won't*! I'll come to London with you instead, and ask Miss Price to let me start at once!"

"Jani!" Simon was so taken aback that he rose and sat down again. "But it's impossible, child. You don't know what you are talking about!"

"But why not, then, Simon?" she pleaded. "It would be nice for me to travel up with you, wouldn't it? You can find a place for me to stay somewhere to-night, and in the morning I will go to Miss Price, and talk to her myself. I'm sure she will be willing to take me—" She hesitated, and gave a little toss of the head, as if to imply incontrovertible reasons – "And even if I did have to wait a bit, it won't matter. Look – l've got some money saved up—" She opened her silk handbag, and put into his hands a little purse with six pounds.

"That's all very well," he said, pushing it away. "There are other things to think of. How am I going to find you a room in town at such an hour of the night? – And what would your people say to you running off like that? It'll look much worse than turning up a few hours late."

"I don't care what they say when I'm not there" – said Jani. She spoke with complete assurance.

"Rot!" said Simon, suddenly annoyed. He rose again and remained standing, his hands in his pockets, a deep frown above his nose as he stared down the platform. A stifled sound behind made him turn, still glowering. Jani, her head on her arms, was bowed over one side of the bench, her body shaking with sobs. Simon gave a quick look around. There were few people about, and nobody seemed to notice them. He sat down and put his hands upon her shoulders.

"Come, Janikins," he said. "Don't give way. Be a sensible little girl."

Her sobs increased. He went on talking gently, arguing, explaining, coaxing. For some time she made no response. When he succeeded in lifting her face towards him she said, with the same vehemence, only broken with tears,—

"You made me lose the boat, and – and – and – now you don't care. But I don't trouble about any of those things you say. I have made up my mind. I shan't go back to Wales. I'd rather be throwing myself in the sea!"

"Jani – dear – how can you talk such nonsense?"

"Well, then, I *will* go to London. If you won't take me I'll go by myself!"

She reared her head defiantly, her dark eyes burned. Then she broke from his hands and bowed herself in a fresh burst of sobs. Simon leaned over in desperation.

"Very well, Jani," he said. "Stop crying at once. I'll take you up – I'll look after you—"

She flashed round at him with a marvellous smile.

"Oh – Simon" – she said. Her fingers found his and were held in a strong clutch. "Darling Simon – I knew you would help me – especially after—" the vibration in her voice, low as it had sunk, came from something else than tears – "after you loved me so much – to-day—" Her face was hidden now against his shoulder. He gazed over her head. Some people were strolling past and staring at them.

"Come along, little girl," he said huskily. "Dry your eyes, and put your coat on. It's getting cooler." He cleared his throat and helped her to her feet. "I'll get the bags into the cloak-room. What about going back into the town for a meal? We have heaps of time; it isn't likely we shall miss this train."

There was no hint of irony in his tone. Nothing but a brisk and somewhat mechanical precision.

XVIII

THREE months later Simon and Jani were married at a registry office.

Jani could have given a more or less veracious account of the steps that led to the consummation of her desire. Simon had no such grasp of the preliminaries to an event entirely unforeseen by him. Yet it seemed inevitable when it happened. He had at least grown to believe that he needed Jani, as much as she needed him: a state of mind which made his duty simple, when *her* need became paramount.

The plunge into his new career was the liberative act he had meant it to be. It was as if he had swum naked across the sea, leaving his Judaic habiliments on banks behind. But the opposite shore, though as attractive as he had dreamed, was not at first as hospitable. He found it cold and rather lonely. The work was all right: so, no doubt, were his colleagues. But office acquaintance was slow in developing. It was easy to avoid old haunts and establish a new routine: but fresh social contacts could not be forced, and London was a desert without the personal human tie. Jani supplied it naturally. It was not only her preference for Simon's society that drove her to it. She was more lonely than himself, and less capable of finding diversion. London, as a matter of fact, intimidated her essentially rustic soul. Her nervous shrinking from traffic, her little scared hops on escalators, her confusion at the network of streets and districts, all the affectations of panic which amused Simon and increased his protective sense, were only slightly exaggerated. She was really ill at ease in the huge, unfriendly city, where she knew nobody but Simon, the girls in the great store who snubbed or ignored her, and Miss Price, who alternated fussy taskmistress moods with probing familiarities. Tegwen Price was very much the sort of person Jani, with her instinctive rather than actual knowledge of Miss Meredith's friend, had expected to find. The response to her first appeal had been grudging and suspicious: but in the end a visit to the manager's office left her established in Miss Price's charge. Jani's beguilements as much as her mysteriously stressed plight won a calculated way to the Welshwoman's heart. It was not long before Jani found that Miss Price was really Mrs. Thomas, having for some time been married to her dairyman: that she was torn between desire to enter openly upon her married state, and reluctance to leave a post at which she had aimed for years. Her husband, in any case, had not been ready to occupy the premises where he meant to carry on his own business. "But it won't be long now, Jani fach," said Miss Price in an expansive moment. "The shop will be finished for sure in less than a month. They are making it out of a front parlour in an old corner house, not far from here. We are taking the rooms behind and on top as well, though we shan't be using them all – there's a nice kitchen behind the shop, and a room out of that – Llew says it will do as a store till we can have a shed in the back. So we'll have our bedroom and sitting-room upstairs. It's all on a lease, very cheap. Old and dirty, it is, but I'll soon have that put right." Miss Price's eyes glittered and her small hatchet head shook from side to side. "Llew won't wait no longer. He wants me to go and pick some furniture next week. I've got a lot of my own that my mother left me. It's in the old home in Wales – my sister will send it up as soon as I'm ready.

Then it'll be good-bye to Bingley's for me, merchi!" – a curious sound, half sigh, half exultant tremolo, came through her thin pressed lips. "Well, darro – I've had all I wanted here. I shall have to learn about butter and cheese now – and how to slice ham, p'r'aps – we'll keep a bit of everything – while Llew goes round with the milk. It's a big venture, mind you – but we've been saving up for it for years!"

"You didn't meet Mr. Thomas in London, then?"

"No, girl – in Liverpool, when I was in my first shop, and Llew came from his uncle's farm in Merionethshire to look for a job. Hard old screw his uncle was – like yours – and not much chance for him there. A year after that he was off to London and I after him—" Miss Price laughed a cackling little reminiscent laugh.

"That was like me, too," murmured Jani.

"Oh, ay? But I don't suppose you'll wait as long as me. Poor Llew had a lot of bad luck. An accident put him in hospital for six months. It was a twelvemonth before he could work again. I can tell you, I had to help him a bit. We did stick to each other, whatever—" She perked her head. Her pronounced Welsh accent, which she tried to modify "in business", rioted in Jani's favour – all the more because Jani herself was pruning her own. "There's no knowing in these days. Girls and chaps are off and on like gloves. But my Llew is steady. Not like the English chaps."

"They are the nicest though," said Jani provocatively, "and better-looking—"

"Oh, ay – your sweetheart's a fine-looking chap – and got a sweet tongue on him. He talked a lot about you – and not a quarter of it true! That's how they are at first. You can't be sure of *him*."

"Oh, yes, I can. He thinks the world of me—"

"Then you'll be marrying soon, I s'pose." Miss Price's tone rose like a sneer. "He can afford it, by the look of him. And you oughn't to leave it too long, the way you've been carrying on—"

"I haven't—" began Jani, but her eyes fell before the glint in Miss Price's. She had embroidered too many confidences to withdraw now.

"When a girl runs away with a chap, the sooner they get married the better. I didn't run away with mine – I only followed him, like, after. There wasn't any talk about *me!*"

It was just such talk on Miss Price's part that familiarised Jani with the idea of sudden marriage: it convinced her, too, of the solidity of reasons which had been built up chiefly from her own wordcraft. By the time Miss Price left Bingley's, and became Mrs. Thomas in the sight of a Kensington dairy clientele, Jani was sure that not only her love but her honour exacted tribute from Simon. Besides, she was growing miserable and unhappy. She made no friends among the cockney girls, and the new taskmistress was totally unsympathetic: the defects of Jani's service were becoming alarmingly topical. It would be wretched to hunt for a similar job without recommendations. Uncle Trevor, furious, had repudiated her. Her mother sent scolding messages, with oblique hints at a rumour of elopement, and complete lack of support of Mr. Lloyd's appeal to his daughter to return home. She would have seconded it only if Jani had begged for help – which Jani had no intention of doing. The "little slut" did not even write again after announcing her arrival at Bingley's. On no account would she have confessed that her wage was very small, and that she needed new clothing, especially as the summer ended and the cold "smoke" days drew down. Jani invented the term in dismay. London fogs were a horrid revelation to her. Her first experience came unusually early in October. She left Bingley's to meet Simon for their usual Saturday afternoon expedition. The dark grey pall thickened and lowered as she walked. Ahead of her was not the open line of buildings she knew, but a dim-lit bank of "smoke". It seemed to wreathe and float towards her, and suddenly, to her horror, she found herself enveloped. The road, houses, shops, buses, people walking on pavements, melted into weird shadow, motor engines and voices became disembodied noise. Eyes could not penetrate this stifling soft obscurity, hands and feet lunged helplessly about. Jani stood still at what had been a corner of a street, but was now a precipice, along which a movement might hurl her to destruction. She moved, all the same, cautiously but with increasing uneasiness. A glimpse of dim forms made her sway from right to left, and after some moments of uncertain progress she stopped again, completely bewildered. Had she turned or had she gone straight on, had she crossed or merely retraced her steps? Though her feet remained on terra-firma, she yielded to the awful sense of gulfs and ravines yawning at her heels. A little hysterical sob gurgled in her throat. But immediately she crushed her lips together and tried to reassure herself. She was lost, but there was no need to get into a panic. Other people were around; she could ask for guidance. Her hand stretched towards a passer-by.

"Lost, are you, my dear? Come along, I'll show you the way – Gimme your arm—" A few paces with a pressing hand on hers, a leering face horribly magnified to her frightened eye, and she had torn herself free, dashing recklessly along until she felt herself stepping off a kerb. There was a dull noise, a crunching of brakes, a shouting – and it seemed a miracle that she was still whole, trembling, huddled against a post, while a huge bus crawled by. There she remained, afraid to move, until a policeman flashed a lamp upon her, and her voice ran to meet his slow, familiar tones.

"Cymraeg? – ay, ay. There's plenty of Welsh round here. What arr you wanting? – The North End Road. You're *in* it, my gurl."

Jani would take no more chances. She asked to be led to Simon's address. "Right you are. Just across by here. What number did you say?"

The house was dark, silent, vaporous with the evil fumes. Jani stumbled up the stairs, knocked and rang in vain. The landlady was out. On Saturdays she went early to her sister, who kept a laundry in the North End Road. But where was Simon? Jani sank on the boards of the black, draughty landing and began to cry – quietly, spasmodically. She had never been more genuinely forlorn than when Simon found her so, a little later, on returning from his vain search of her in the streets. He half carried her into his room and placed her in a basket-chair before a small gas fire, where she recovered herself while he rummaged the kitchen for food.

"Confound the woman! I don't know where she keeps her stuff. It's all over the place – where the dickens is the milk? I'll have to ask her to leave a tray and things on bad Saturdays, so that we can have tea here instead of going out – isn't that a jolly good idea?"

Jani thought it the jolliest of good ideas, when having helped to make toast and watched the kettle boil, all on the little gas stove, they savoured the stolen meal with kisses.

Simon sat in the basket-chair and Jani grew radiant on his knees.

"All right now, Janikins?"

"Oh, Simon dear, I'm always all right with you. I wish I could stay with you always – I mean – on foggy days—"

The fog had lifted only slightly when they went out to a theatre, but on Simon's arm Jani was indifferent to the sinister streets. She chattered and laughed in a delicious warm companionship that shut out terrors for them both. Such Saturdays of delight belonged to them henceforward in sunshine as well as in gloom. Jani's dainty vivid presence filled Simon's empty hours, her hugs and kisses wove a flattering pattern of love. It did not seem that he was flaunting the design when he agreed to go one Sunday to the dairy. Llew Thomas and his wife were not the hosts he would have chosen, but he could not ignore their attentions to Jani. It was pleasant enough there, he found. The sitting-room upstairs was large and freshly painted, sparse with bare walls and a suite of new, small oaken furniture. The thick axminster carpet was comforting, and two chinese ginger pots looked well on the mantel over the blue dutch-tiled hearth. The polished cleanliness of the room was due as much to Mrs. Thomas's fingers as to newness, as could be proved in the kitchen down below. Here the brass fireware and candlesticks shone in old-fashioned array, the walls were covered with prints and plush-framed photographs – the true Blaemawe background for an ancient dresser choked with jugs, for patchwork rugs and wool antimicassars, Windsor chairs, a horsehair sofa, an old linen press and treadle sewing-machine, a grandfather clock, a small harmonium – Llew Thomas's wife could not bring herself to separate the relics of Tegwen Price's old home: so there they were, all crowded cosily and stuffily in the small square room with its large hobbed fireplace, and its draped glass-panelled door leading to the shop. Simon preferred the vacuity of the "parlour" above, where as guest he was entertained to a prodigious high tea. The liberal table was very welcome, after the scrappy indifferent fare upon which he now lived. Simon had never thought about his digestion until lately. Straight from his mother's board to the Fincks' supply of similarly wholesome if undecorated food, his stomach had become aware of inadequacies in restaurant meals. Mrs. Hedges was certainly no cook: her breakfasts were appalling. Simon tasted margarine for the first time in his life; porridge like poultice, eggs of doubtful age, and "fish" – he was more than disconcerted to learn that in Mrs. Hedges' opinion, only dried haddock was fish. But the most nauseating accompaniment was her kitchen smell. He had exchanged the odour of soup for that of bacon, and with all his newforged freedom from dietary prejudice, he found it vile. The reek was powerful in the mornings, when the flats below and the attics above reinforced Mrs. Hedges' special brand: the reek of bacon fried in black iron pans, rancid with fat that was never scoured away – (such a waste, Mrs. Hedges thought, of good rich grease, as she slapped a soapy dishcloth round the handle and sides).

If the Thomas menage was founded equally on pig, it was not as offensive and obvious. There were delicious sweets and solids scrupulously served – winter salads of endive and beetroot adorned with hard pale yellow yolks – pancakes, made of the same new eggs and freshest butter, with real cream and homemade jam. It was not easy to resist invitations to such teas on succeeding Sundays, but the pleasant dairy hospitality increased rather than mitigated the uneasiness which the Thomas couple's behaviour generated in Simon's mind. They not only took for granted his relationship with Jani, but began to broaden hints and suggestions which made the girl blush and bridle, and which he could not resent without explanations that were neither clear to himself nor feasible to them. His landlady's attitude was becoming marked, also. She stared and breathed hard and muttered disquietingly when Jani called on him. He knew that she had never regarded Jani with a favourable eye, from the time they had disturbed her slumbers on the night – or early morning – of their arrival from Ilfracombe. The difficulty of admittance to an hotel had compelled Simon to take the course of asking Mrs. Hedges to let Jani sleep in his room, while he was accommodated on the chair bed in the kitchen. He could never remember quite what story he told her: it was clear enough that with every wish to indulge her nice new lodger, she did not really believe him.

When Jani's calls became more frequent Mrs. Hedges showed a distinct hostility to the service of tea in Simon's room. She had reached the point of determining to "speak to him" about it, on the fatal Saturday when the whole combination, carefully built up by fate – and Jani – broke its leash.

Simon was late that afternoon. He had lunched with a colleague – the only one who did not rush off to a distant suburb. Ted Rendal's home was near Bournemouth, and he was a little excited at the prospect of sharing a flat in town with a London cousin.

"Dick's an architect – just setting up for himself," he told Simon, in an unusual burst of confidence. "His people live at

Hampstead, but he's been in digs at Bloomsbury for some time. Digs are the devil!" Simon concurred vigorously. "I say, Black – when we're fixed up in Chelsea you must look in—"

Simon flushed with pleasure. Rendal was just the quiet, decent sort of fellow he had hoped to "chum" with, but till now it had seemed as unlikely that he would emerge from his standoffish shell, as that Simon would attempt to storm it. The mutual attraction had grown without apparent progress. They did not shake hands outside the restaurant. A curt nod on each side, and Simon strolled down the Strand alone, a queer warmth at his ribs despite the raw damp air and the somewhat thin coat he was wearing. Near the station he paused. Should he take a bus or go by rail? A woman in nursing uniform hurried past and boarded a stationary bus, which began at once to move. As she turned in the doorway Simon saw the large fresh face of Marjorie Newell. Without a moment's reflection he jumped after her.

"Full inside!" yelled the conductor. "On top only." Simon climbed up, sat close to the side of the bus, and peered eagerly over at each stoppage. Nobody from within got out until they reached the Fulham Road. He scrambled down at the first exit of a passenger. Nurse Newell was seated at the far end, screened by a man who was standing and had probably given her his place. At last she came out. Simon sprang aside with a smile and salute to let her pass. To his amazement there was no answering smile, no sign of recognition or acknowledgement. She brushed by with averted head and walked rapidly to the left of the triangular road. Simon's jump down the step, his involuntary call – "Miss Newell!" were ignored. He remained standing on the pavement, the blood rushing to his uncovered head.

"Well – l'm damned!" he whispered.

Another bus came to a standstill, people jumped on and off, he was jostled and pushed. Slowly he crossed to the right of the triangle and began to walk.

He could hardly believe it: Marjorie Newell had cut him dead! Why? – Why? The friendly, smiling girl, eagerly simple and ingenuous in her role of approving third – H'm. Obviously her view of him had undergone a change. She was devoted to Edith. And she must have learned from Edith that he had been dismissed with contempt – that he was despicable, unworthy, unfit – even as an acquaintance!

It was absurd – humiliating. As if he cared a jot what Marjorie thought! But Edith still had power to wound him with this gesture of repulse, repeated at second hand. His fast long strides could not stamp away the flame of anger and pain – it leaped and leaped: until suddenly, at his own door, it passed, quenched in the light of Jani' s loving eyes.

Loving they were, undoubtedly, as she rose to greet him from the wicker chair in front of the gas-lit stove. He bent gratefully down as she stood close, tilting her chin.

"Been waiting long, Janikins?" he said. "I'm rather late – walked a lot to-day. But I didn't know you'd be here just yet."

"I had to come early to-day. I was so—" she hesitated. He noticed something unusual in her pose as she returned to the chair.

"Anything the matter?" he said, and at her light reply – "No – nothing," he moved behind the screen where his bed stood, and flung upon it his hat and coat. He talked, heartily and loudly, as he washed his hands and brushed his hair, but she did not answer in her usual eager way. When he reappeared he saw she was drooping and brooding in the chair.

"There *is* something the matter," he said, leaning over her. "Come, Jani, out with it—"

"Oh, not now," she said quickly. " Let's have tea. I brought some specially nice cakes – from a new shop I found. Mrs. Hedges said she wanted to go out early – she has shopping to do as well as going to her sister's – but she wouldn't leave it to me to make tea, all the same. She was quite *nasty*. So let's have the tea in now, and then perhaps she'll go out and leave us alone."

"Are you upset because Mrs. Hedges was nasty, Jani?"

"No – it isn't that – though it *is* upsetting. She don't like me, I know, but she needn't show it like she do—" " – she does –" said Simon absently. He tried to whip up a stronger note of indignation. "Impudence! I shall have to ask her what she means by it—"

"Oh well, she's only like the others," said Jani impetuously.

There was a knock, and Mrs. Hedges entered with a laden japanned tray.

"It's early for your tea, sir—" she said coldly. "But as I want to go out, and I s'pose you wants to do the same—"

"Oh yes – thank you, Mrs. Hedges." Simon stammered a little. The glare in his landlady's eye intimidated him. She set the tray down and flounced out, before he could think of another word. Jani, too, remained silent, helping him quietly to the tobacco-like tea and stodgy toast. She nibbled at one of the cakes which Simon praised, then let it drop back into her plate.

"Tell me now, Jani – what's happened?"

"I've got the sack from Bingley's."

She stooped over an unwieldy parcel that he had noticed beside the chair, and began to pull off the string that loosely bound it. A round basket, beautifully padded and frilled with blue silk and lace was revealed under folds of paper. "It's finished now" – continued Jani rapidly – "all but this bow here. Auntie Gwyneth don't deserve it, but there it is. I brought it here just to fix this ribbon and pack it properly for the post. I couldn't even do that much under the eyes of all those cats, with their lies and spyings. Just fancy! They fetched Miss Petherton round to peep at it under my bed, when I wasn't there, and then she came to catch me at it—"

"But, Jani – what's that about the sack?"

"Well, that's how I got it – because of this basket – and because of *you*!"

She looked up defiantly as she said the last words. Her eyes were glittering, and a richer tide of colour flushed her cheeks.

"Because of me!"

She jumped up and began to pour out a stream of excited words. Badgered and persecuted at Bingley's since Miss Price had left, the climax had come with a charge against her by the new head of the department. Miss Petherton, discovering her at work on the baby basket, had insinuated that she was selling privately, to customers, or friends, articles made up from shop pilferings.

"She said she had a Welsh girl under her before that did it! She said it was not – not – or-iy-ous that Welsh girls were thieves!" Jani laughed hysterically – "And then I called her an English liar—"

"Oh, come, nonsense—"

"I did, indeed! But it was only after she called me other bad names. She said perhaps if I wasn't selling the basket, then I was making it for myself!" Jani's voice broke; she clutched Simon's hands, and her dark eyes stared into his in a strange appeal. "I couldn't let her say it, could I? But they all do say it now – or they think it, I can see, even if they don't say it straight out – Tegwen does, you know – Mrs. Thomas – and Mrs. Hedges—"

"What do they think?"

"That we ran away together, and we ought to be married, and that I – oh, Simon, what shall I do?"

Her head sunk on his breast, and he held her to him, mechanically, silently. Her voice came muffled from beneath his arms.

"So I was all worked up at Miss Petherton's hints and spiteful words, and I called her names back. And she gave me the sack straight away – for my cheek, she said. Of course, she can't prove anything against me except that. I know I was cheeky – but I couldn't help it, could I? – And those girls listening and laughing behind the door. And now, I can't stay there, and I can't find another place – they won't give me references, will they? I'll never go home to be insulted, either! And you don't want me to, do you? – So what shall I do, Simon? – what shall I do?"

He soothed her and led her back into the chair but she clung to him, and he sat on the arm with her head still enclosed in his comforting grasp. He was deeply stirred by her plight, by the half-sweet, half-painful sense of responsibility she had increasingly brought home to him.

"Jani dear, it'll be all right – of course you can get another place. There are all sorts of things you can apply for. I'm sure Mrs. Thomas will help you, too – perhaps she can put you up in the meantime? We'll ask her to-morrow. Didn't she show us an empty room with just a bed in it? You'll pay her, naturally – I'll see about all that—"

Jani's arms reached to his neck. Her eyes were lifted to his, and the swimming ardour in them told him that his tenderness to her, his care, made her supremely happy.

"Oh, Simon," she murmured, "I don't mind whatever happens so long as I'm near to you. I couldn't bear to leave you now. You are all the world to me—"

They kissed. A slight cough was heard, and Simon freed himself before Mrs. Hedges' indignant gaze. Whether she had knocked or not he could not tell. She picked up the tea tray and stood with it in her hands, her mottled cheeks purpling as she coughed again and said,

"Excuse me, sir – but are you going out now? I'd like to clear and lock up before I goes myself." It was another way of saying that she did not mean to leave them alone in the flat. Before Simon could reply, her change of expression disconcerted him still more. She was staring at the pretty baby-basket at their feet. Her scandalised eyes, opening wider, darted a look at Jani and then returned severely to him.

"And I might as well tell you now, sir – I'd like you to make other arrangements. I shall want your room next week."

"This room?"

"Yes. I expect my son home."

"But Mrs. Hedges – I thought he'd gone for a year – and it was agreed that whenever he came, I should be able to keep the room—"

"No, sir, I'm sorry, sir, I can't do it" – she walked backwards to the door, the tray jingling in her short thick hands. She was a small woman, with an odd mixture of the timid and the perky in her sparrowlike air. Her lips tightened primly, with a secret reluctance, against her tall, gentlemanly lodger.

"It's no use, sir, my mind's made up. P'raps I ought to tell you straight – it's not altogether because of my son. I thought you was different. I can't have any goings on in my house. I'm a respectable woman—"

"What do you mean, Mrs. Hedges?"

"Oh, it's plain enough what I means. That young woman—"

"Please be careful what you say, Mrs. Hedges. Of course I shall leave your rooms. I should be doing so in any case very soon. You might like to know that Miss Lloyd and I are engaged to be married."

Something vivid, radiant, flashed from Jani into Simon. His heart rode high on the beam. But his fingers were trembling as he pressed her own firm little ones put suddenly into his.

"Oh, indeed, sir – I'm sure I don't mean to say nothing against—"

"Very well, Mrs. Hedges. That will do. You can clear and lock up at once. We are going out. Come, Jani – let's finish packing this parcel for your aunt."

Curiously enough, it was a meek, quiet Jani and a somewhat boastful Simon who gave the news to the Thomases on Sunday. Mrs. Thomas disappointed him by taking it coolly and quite as a matter of course.

"Well, there it is – you haven't got nothing to wait for now. What do Jani want another job for? She can stop with me for a bit, of course. But if you got to look for a new lodging, and Jani got to look for a new job I don't see why you shouldn't get married at once and done with it. What do you think, Llew?"

Llew sat smoking his pipe stolidly, though he was anything but a stolid person. The short, wiry angular little man was enjoying his rare hours of weekly rest.

"Right enough, Tegwen. No sense in waiting when you haven't got to. Married life is better than lodgings indeed."

The opinion of Mr. and Mrs. Thonras might have had less force but for their offer of rooms – the empty bedroom and the furnished sitting-room. Mrs. Thomas, with a view to contingencies, had already discussed with her husband a retirement to the lower floor. The kitchen behind the shop was more convenient for personal business attention: the storeplace next to it could become a bed-chamber. The pecuniary advantage, however small, of letting the rooms above, was also a consideration in this first year of their venture. And it seemed a better thing to let them to Jani Lloyd and her husband than to strangers.

In this way was prepared the bombshell that shattered the peace of the Black household in Blaemawe. It had not been a whole peace for some time past. The mother, at least, had sensed the way her son was drifting, though she did not anticipate the end. She grieved to find the gulf grow wide between London and Blaemawe – wider than any railway could bridge. Simon wrote seldom, and had not come home even for the great holydays – the solemn New Year and the Atonement Fast that followed. It would have meant asking for a week's leave of absence and he had no intention of committing himself by the request, even on a pretext. To ignore Yom Kippur was, he thought, the breaking of the final tie. It moved him to a deeper sense of severance from race and home, than the ceremony in the registry office. Perhaps the intoxication of the event – the intoxication, it must be confessed, not so much of a bridegroom, as of a boy leaping to the mastery of life – blurred his mind. At any rate he did not feel, or try to realise the repercussion of his act upon his parents, already dim and far from his sight. He and Jani had finished with Blaemawe, and it should not matter to their families that they could no longer influence the children they had lost. His father might contemptuously discard him. Very well. They had never meant anything to each other. His mother, no doubt, would weep. He wished that she would not: still, a man need not sacrifice his happiness because of a mother's tears. Callously – blindly – or merely vaingloriously, Simon went to his marriage-bed.

As a matter of fact it was not Devora Black, but Gedaliah, who wept at Blaemawe. Dinah was appalled at the sight. Never in her recollection had her father broken down in emotional strain. The news of the marriage had not given her anything like the same shock. She had heard the rumour about Simon and Jani, and had taken pains to prevent it reaching her mother: the confirmation angered more than it surprised her. She resented Simon's yielding to a temptation she had suffered in resisting, and she disliked and despised Jani Lloyd. But with all her apprehensions, she had not known that the effect on her parents would be so strange – Mrs. Black, silent and dry-eyed, listening to the taciturn father's outburst of violence, almost as if it were no concern of hers; until on his collapse into moans and sobs, she soothed and quieted him, with a kind of fiercely tender power of control. Dinah lay awake listening to their voices in the night: and next day witnessed a scene that further perplexed her.

"I was afraid father would go off like Uncle Elman—" she wrote to her brother. The phrase was deliberate: but with her queer inhibitions strong, she could not put even into writing the fact, which still distressed her powerfully, that their father had cried like a child. – "However, it hasn't turned out like that at all. He said at first that none of us were ever to speak or write to you again. But Mr. Lloyd came in to see us. He is the only one who is happy and pleased. He said he and father had always been like brothers and now they would be more so, since their children had married. Father did not say anything. He looked at Mr. Lloyd as if he were stunned. Afterwards he told mother that it would be easier to bear if Jani was – *megaya*. (Is that the way to spell it? Anyway, you know what I mean). After all, father said, better Jani than another shicksa. So mother and I are coming up in a few days to talk to you about it. You had better agree. It is the only way to make them stop breaking their hearts—"

"Never!" said Simon angrily. He flung the letter down on the breakfast-table, and for some time would not explain the message to Jani. When he did, she did not seem impressed. "What's the good of my turning into a Jewess when you don't want to be a Jew?" she asked.

His frown changed to a sudden smile.

"That's just it!" he said, patting her cheek. They were seated side by side at the thin gate-legged table.

"Clever little kitten – you've gone straight to the point!"

She smiled, too, and seized his hand, pretending to scratch it.

"Well, then, Simon dear, write and tell them we are happy as we are, without any religion. I don't want to go to chapel, and you don't want to go to synagogue, and we shan't persuade each other to go, either!"

"It's no use writing," said Simon. "Dinah says my mother is coming to see us—"

" What – come to London – come here?" Jani's tone was full of dismay. She dropped Simon's hand and looked at the letter. "Tell me exactly what she says, Simon – read it out—"

He picked up the sheet reluctantly, and read aloud the last sentences. Jani's bright lips pouted, her eyebrows arched.

"The only way—" she repeated slowly. "Oh, Simon – does she mean that if I learn the things you said Jewish women must do – all about prayers, and lighting candles, and putting salt on meat – that will really stop your mother and father from breaking their hearts?"

Simon nodded absently. He was wondering by what means he could check the impending visit. If he wrote at once that they were going away for a month – or that they were moving to another address, without giving it? – wild, foolish excuses flew through his mind.

"Oh, Simon, darling" Jani nestled close to him cooing – "write back to-day and say she needn't come, it will be all right without. Say I shall learn all the things she wants me to – I don't care if people in Blaemawe will know and call me a Jewess—"

"Nonsense, my pretty" – Simon caught her to him and kissed her, rather roughly. "You can put that right out of your head – I don't wish you to learn or do anything of the sort—"

"I know, darling silly – but let us pretend." Her eyes sparkled mischievously at him. "You tell them I'm willing and you are teaching me, and I'll pretend I do everything if they ask me. Then nobody will worry us, and nobody's heart will break, and everybody will be satisfied! Won't that be nice, indeed?" Her rosy smile beat against his hardening look.

"No, kitten – it's not so simple. And it wouldn't do if it were! You don't realise what you are saying. It's bad enough to be a humbug and hypocrite when one can't help oneself – but I've cut all that out. I wrote home plainly enough about our marriage. Perhaps. Dinah hasn't told them all I said – that we intended having just an ordinary English life. I shouldn't dream of letting you in for a stupid deceit. We shall go on as we are. If my people – or yours – don't like it, they can keep away."

He got up, and prepared to leave. Jani brought him his gloves and stick.

"*My* people will keep away, indeed. They don't care. But your mother is sure to come—"

" Well, then, I shall tell her she is asking for the impossible. I've never explained to her exactly what I thought, because there didn't seem any point in – in making her miserable when we were apart. But if she comes now, I shall be quite frank. It will be unpleasant, of course—"

Simon frowned again and set his chin hard. Jani looked up at him silently, and stroked his sleeve with timid fingers. He put his arm round her waist and caressed her.

"But you needn't be in it, Janikin. You can be out – really out, or sit downstairs with Mrs. Thomas. I'd meet her at the station and take her somewhere, if it were not impossible to talk privately anywhere but here. And besides, Dinah will come, too—"

"Oh, yes, I'd rather be out," said Jani quickly. The idea of entertaining Mrs. Black had secretly amused her. She would have liked to strut a little as the genuine if unwelcome daughter-in-law, but she had no desire at all to meet Dinah. Even in childhood the younger girl, quiet, tall, aloof, had disconcerted the prattling Jani and made her feel uncomfortable. You couldn't go on talking to a dumb wall – especially a wall with eyes. "Wall-eyed" – thought Jani suddenly, not in the least put out by a possible irrelevance.

She had heard the term used by a cockney without knowing what it meant. Perhaps it meant someone with eyes like Dinah's, boring into you, full of inscrutable criticism, against which your plausible prattle or innocent 'cheek' were vain, and made you feel a fool, helpless and cross. No, she didn't want to meet a wall-eyed person.

Mrs. Black came alone, after all. At the last moment Gedaliah's troublesome leg had made it difficult for him to attend to business, and Dinah was obliged to remain. Since Gershon's departure she had become indispensable. Ruth had a severe cold, and in any case Mrs. Black did not wish the child to be present at the interview with Simon. The mother meant to return the same night, in spite of possible fatigue or agitation: she could endure these better than the thought of staying with the Fincks in such circumstances.

Dinah wired on the morning of the journey. Simon found the message when he came home for lunch, as he did on most days since his marriage. He was slightly annoyed.

"Why didn't you 'phone me," he said to Jani. "I should have gone straight to Paddington and brought her home. It's too late now – she must be on her way—"

"I thought you didn't want to meet her at the station—"

Simon stared. It was too bad of Jani to affect a kind of silliness now.

"But she's alone – and she hasn't been to London for over twenty years!" Jani shrugged her shoulders and moved her chair away. "Oh, well, it can't be helped. I suppose she'll find the way. I say, Jani, – you've forgotten to salt these potatoes—"

"Well, then, you can always put some in after" – she pushed the salt towards him, still pouting. He seized her fingers and squeezed them, then pulled the nearest ear on the averted red head.

"Poor Jani! She's nervous," he thought, attributing to her the emotion he was conscious of in himself. He finished his meal rapidly, and then went out to the nearest post-office. He must send some excuse for not returning to the office that afternoon. There was no telephone on the premises; the economical Thomases were still "thinking" about the installation. He had not been gone two minutes when Mrs. Black arrived. By one of those miracles that she took for granted, a woman to whom she had spoken in the train turned out to be travelling to Kensington, and had accompanied her most of the way. She knew nothing of the separate entrance down a side street, and walked into the shop, which bore the number for which she had enquired.

Mrs. Thomas was serving a customer with ham, which she sliced carefully though not too skilfully on a marble slab. She picked up a few shreds and put them into her mouth, licking her fingers and laughing. Then she looked past her customer to see a tall, gaunt woman, dressed in a rough dark coat and large, rather shapeless country hat, with thick woollen gloves, and a strange air of mingled awkwardness and dignity, staring grimly at her. Within a few moments Jani was greeting her mother-in-law in the sitting-room above.

"Sit down, Mrs. Black, and let me take your things. Simon will be here in a minute. Indeed, we are sorry we didn't meet you, but we didn't get the telegram in time – there now, take your hat off, Mrs. Black – mother."

Devora Black caught the girl's hand in hers, fixing on her the great sad eyes that looked out beneath the shapeless hat.

"Jani, my child – I will be your mother – but you must be properly married to my son—"

"Indeed, then, I am, Mrs. Black." Jani pulled her left hand free and showed the new gold ring. "That's proper enough, I can tell you – nobody can say a word against—"

"But it is not enough, Jani – it must be a Jewish marriage. Jani, – Jani – you will become a Jewess – you are willing – yes?"

Jani was silent. Her eyes, round, saucy, twinkled into those darker orbs, sunk and straining in the haggard angular face. Funny thing, she was thinking – Simon wasn't a bit like his mother; his skin was fairer, his nose was a different shape, his eyes were not the same colour; yet she had seen in them exactly the same expression – sometimes, not when he was looking at *her* – a queer expression, hurt, sad, yet somehow eager – like asking for something that nobody knew of, or nobody wanted to give. It stirred her to reluctant speech. "You'll have to ask Simon about that," she said. "I'll do anything he likes—"

Mrs. Black drew a long breath.

"It must be," she said. She let Jani take the long pins out of her hat, and remove the rough coat. Her hair lay in flat grey coils upon her head. It jerked slowly up and down as if in resignation. "Beshert – beshert" (Fated), she muttered to herself. Her glance went round the room and rested on the table, from which Jani had not yet cleared the remains of the midday meal. On a plate at one end there were slices of meat, very much like those she had seen the woman in the shop cutting on a slab. A shiver ran through her body. She stood up.

"Jani—" she began. Jani was opening a door on the opposite side. She turned and said at once – " I'm taking your things in here – would you like to come and see this room?"

Mrs. Black followed her into the small bedroom. She

looked at the white walls, the white-painted cupboard in a corner, the chest and chair which were the sole articles of furniture beside the bed, upon which Jani was placing the hat, coat and gloves. Mrs. Black watched her intently for a moment, then said in a low voice—

"This bedroom – is it the only one?"

"Yes," said Jani. "It's nice, isn't it?" She was proud of the white paint, which she had helped Simon to apply, of the fresh curtains on the window, of the lace bed-cover which Mrs. Thomas had given her, and of the severe neatness of the room – she had taken pains that morning to hide away the garments and odds and ends which had been littered about. It was as well the white cupboard door stuck fast when it was closed.

"But – have you no other bed—or even a sofa?"

"No," said Jani. " I'm sorry we can't put you up for the night, but Simon said he would find you a room if you are staying—"

"No, no – I do not stay over night – but I mean, for yourself?"

Jani stared at her.

"Listen, Jani—" Mrs. Black came close and spoke with grave intensity – "you will learn, my child, about this – a Rabbi will teach you – you must know that with Jews, there must always be two beds for man and wife. Anything – no matter what – no matter how poor, how hard to manage, how little room—"

"Why?" muttered Jani.

"Because a Jewish husband must not sleep with his wife when she has her time – it is wrong, it is a sin. They must separate until she is again clean, and has gone into the special bath—or else the children are not pure—"

Jani, with flaming face, rushed out of the room. As she whispered later to Simon, in his arms in the dark, – "I was so ashamed, I didn't know where to look. Fancy talking to me about things like that—" It was true that other women – Mrs. Thomas, for example – talked to Jani about "things like that": but mothers didn't – shouldn't – and not in that particular way, as if it was *religion*. It was scandalous, indecent. Jani was shocked and humiliated. Besides, who ever heard such nonsense?

She rushed out now, with her fiery face, calling out loudly – "Oh, here's Simon – I can hear him coming."

She flung open the outer door and stepped to the landing. Mrs. Black returned to the stitting-room. She paused by the small flimsy settee near the window, her hand on its narrow ledge.

"Mother—"

"My son!"

Film cleared from her eyes, but she sat down blindly at his gesture. Her hearing seemed to have gone too far to come back as easily. It might have been an hour rather than a few moments that his excuses and enquiries beat remotely on her sense. She did not answer, only looked with her deep eyes at his dear, alienated face.

"Now, mother, you'll have something to eat?"

She shook her head, and pointed to a leather bag at her feet – a large travelling handbag which he had presented to her.

"No, I brought food with me – I had it on the train."

"Tea, then, or coffee—"

"I drank milk."

"She won't eat or drink at my table – it's not kosher" – He tried to think it sarcastically, amusedly – as if it were someone else's mother—or as if the whole affair were like one of those music-hall skits, that he and Jani had seen at the Palladium the other night – 'No. 10 – The Famous Hebrew Comedian, Julius Hambone, in "Abie's Kosher Kitchen"!' But he couldn't smile at the recollection; or at himself – and certainly not at her. That inner dignity of hers breathed through the clumsy country dress, the awkward pose. Strange, though, that she should be so quiet and composed. It was unlike what he expected, and made him the more nervous and uneasy. Suddenly, he saw that her fingers were trembling. In a moment the calm broke, her arms were flung apart and brought together, the hands locked and wrung wildly in his face.

"Simon, Simon – my son! What a journey this has been for me! Not so did I expect to visit London again! Was it for this that I came that first time so long ago – when I prayed for you, begged you of God? He listened to my prayer and gave you to me, and I promised you back to Him. But since I sent you from me, to learn and become more fit, you have turned away – away from your father and mother, away from Yiddishkeit! Eternal One in Heaven, how have I sinned, that my only son, my ben yacheed, should become – woe is me! – a goy?"

The blinding tears gushed from her eyes, her voice in its rapid stream of Yiddish was harsh and broken. She rocked herself, and a grey lock drooped from her head.

Simon's teeth dug into his lower lip. He gave a quick glance at Jani and motioned her to leave the room. She lifted her chin, but went at once and closed the landing door behind her.

"Listen, mother," said Simon coldly. "Don't blame yourself for anything. I have always been exactly as I am now. Perhaps you ought to have understood. At any rate, it is no use expecting that my way of life should be like yours—"

But he saw she was not listening. The released torrent flowed more quietly, but could not yet be checked.

"You might have had pity on your father, if not on me" – she mourned. "The Elmans at least brought their trouble on themselves – though God forbid I should judge them! Did I not always say that all who have children in cradles should refrain from judging others? Yet little did I believe that shame and anguish would come upon a father like yours who has done all that a Jewish parent should do, who has never encouraged laxity, who has been proud that his children kept their holy faith—"

"He has never shown any pride in me," muttered Simon. "He has never understood."

The mutter caught her ear. She paused in her lament.

"It is you who do not understand," she said. "You do not know how much your father has suffered – how his life was wrecked, his spirit crushed, in the hell of the Goyim—"

Simon stared. He had never heard this tone from his mother. She rose and stood with uplifted hand beside him.

"My son, it is for that reason that I fear to complain too much. Perhaps it is Fate – perhaps it is God who has made it so. And who are we to question His ways, however hard and bewildering? You know, of course, that when your father was young, he escaped from a pogrom in Poland. But you do not know all that he endured. The things that happened in the town where he was a student – I cannot tell you" – she shuddered – "it is not necessary. But when he came to this country he was already a broken man. He knew nobody, but he had been given the address of a landsman – my uncle Elman, who had not long before sent for me. Your father arrived one morning at Dawport, and through some misfortune lost the address. For hours he roamed about, unable to make himself understood. He wandered into the valley and came to the river, famished with hunger, exhausted, and in despair. The remembrance of his wrongs maddened him. He was angry with God, and he resolved to drown himself. But God was tender to him. As he stood on the brink, repeating the Shemang, a voice called to him in Hebrew. He thought it was an angel who came through the trees, crying 'Shalom!'"

Mrs. Black stopped. She covered her eyes.

"Who was it?" said Simon quietly.

"Meurig Lloyd – Jani's father. He was still a young man then – older than your father, but not married. For years he had been in Patagonia, and before that he had travelled for my uncle. Ah, he was a noble youth, always of a delicate mind, Uncle Elman said. A dreamer, a lover of mankind, a friend of Jewry. It was God who brought him into the valley on his holiday, and made him recognise, the sound of Hebrew words, which he had learnt from my uncle. It was his own good heart that made him comfort your father, feed him with bread and fruit, and bring him safe to the Elmans' house—"

"Why did I never hear of this before?"

"Who could have known, when neither your father nor Meurig Lloyd ever spoke of it? All we understood was that they had met on the way. I myself did not know until a few days ago how Jani's father saved your father's life." Mrs. Black's voice trembled into its most mournful strain. "And that is why I say that I dare not complain too much of what has happened to you. Perhaps it had to be. Beshert – beshert!"

She sat down again on the settee, and seized Simon's hands between her own.

"But, my son, it is not God's will that you should become

a Goy and your children Goyim. That could never be! Therefore I have come with my bitter heart, not to reproach or to torment you, but only to say, from your father and myself, that you must act at once – that you must see to it that Jani is made a Jewess—"

Simon drew his hands away and sprang up, turning to the window, where he stood looking down at the busy street. All that life down there – the daily, commonplace life of a busy English street, with its flow of traffic and people hurrying or dawdling, signs and sounds and shapes that he liked to feel around him, bearing him familiarly in their midst – how far away it was from the atmosphere Devora Black had created in the room. The anger that had stiffened his breast was melting in the old sense of defeat. It had never been possible to explain to his mother. She could be tortured but not enlightened. Useless to proclaim – "I am the master of my own life – I will not be dictated to by father or mother – I will not enslave myself to race, religion, or family tradition," – useless and cruel. The picture of his father saved from suicide stood behind her appeal – real, more real than his mother herself as she sat and sighed beside him. Yet he knew they would both fade into shadows again when she had gone. Was it cowardly to humour her now as Jani had wished – to let her go eased and pacified by a promise of formalities that could not bind?

"You can teach her yourself, my son – Jani will soon learn – she knows much already from being in our home. It is not as if she were a complete stranger to us. Listen, Simon," he looked round reluctantly at her pleading voice – "you will make Jani keep a kosher house – you will make her be a Jewish mother to your children—"

"I can't make her do anything – she will please herself."
There was both stubbornness and yielding in his tones.

"No, no, it is you who must see to everything – she will do
what you please! Can I not see for myself how it is? I know
something of Jani. She always looked at you as if you were a
prince – and why not, I used to think? I was a fool – I did not
dream that such a child – how should I? – Besides, pretty
shicksas are everywhere. But I thought that when you were in
London, you would see many fine Jewish girls, you would
choose one who was herself a princess – a true Jewish
daughter – Woe is me! – Ah, don't be angry, my son – I know
it is vain for me to cry. I will try to be content with what is. If
you show Jani the Jewish way, she will keep it, and then at
least your children—"

"Really, mother, there's no need to talk about children" –
Simon rapped the words out sharply, his face flushed with
irritation.

"But, Simon—" Mrs. Black hesitated. A delicacy Jani
would not have understood made it difficult for her to
continue. Her eyes veiled an interrogation Jani might have
found less shocking than that on marital purity. Even so,
Simon did not care to meet them. He turned his head away
again.

And suddenly his mother stood up once more, and put her
hand on his arm, forcing him to look into her face. It was tense
now – hard with an urgency that would have no denial.

"My son – there is need to talk. If not for the present, then
for the future. I beg of you – do not let me die in shame and
agony. Give me your promise – swear to me, as God is your
witness – that you will bring up your children as Jews—"

Simon felt her spirit sharp upon him as a sword. His throat

must be offered to the blade. "Very well, mother. I promise you – I swear – that if I have any children, they will be Jews."

She stood looking at him, trembling, and he smiled as he took her hand and patted the rough veins. He was light with reassurance and a flash of triumph. The reservation had freed his bond. "If I have any." He did not want children, neither did Jani. They would have none. The never-born alone could thwart the force of heritage.

XIX

"COMING round this evening? I'll be away, of course – spinning down to Bournemouth for the weekend. But Dick expects you."

Everyone was rushing away as usual on Saturdays. Ted Rendall never looked as if he were rushing, but he was ready for his lunch, and meant to clean up his motor-bike before setting out on his 'spin'. Simon was the only member of the staff who was actually in no hurry to leave, and who might, therefore, be presumed neither hungry nor eager for home.

"Yes, I'll be round," he said. His smile had that pleasant warmth reserved for Ted.

"And Mrs. B.?"

The smile disappeared.

"I don't think so. She isn't well, and—" he hesitated significantly, "doesn't care for visiting just now—"

"Oh – quite—" said Rendall, turning his head. He thought it rather odd of Black to leave his wife alone, if she was really, as he hinted – Perhaps she was not alone. But surely a husband's place – the proper thing – Rendall flicked his vague thoughts away. As a bachelor, unentangled, he had no idea what the proper thing might be. And anyhow, Black was such a decent sort, he would be sure to know and to do it. Pretty little kid, the wife. Everybody liked seeing her at the flat, though she seemed shy and never said much. He had nothing against her. Still, he had never got over the slight disappointment he had felt at Black's marriage, just when they had begun to get friendly. He had thought they might get about a good deal together – go for tramps and spins, – with Black pillion-riding on his second-hand Indian to his Dorset home. Mums would welcome such a friend on his occasional weekend visits. Dick, of course, was a fine fellow to live with – he admired his cousin even when he could not agree with him, thought him the cleverest as well as the kindest of men; but he was not much of an outdoor companion, in spite of an old college record for sport. Besides, one did not always want to be 'talked at'. Black was different, quiet, keen on similar things, took all the right things for granted. They got on so well – it was a pity the pretty girl had cut in just then. There was no other fellow on the staff he cared about half as much.

Simon was aware of his feeling, and though he had not reached the stage of reciprocating it in full, he went some way towards it. Without regretting his marriage, Simon, after the first six months, had begun to realise the handicaps of haste. He became more open to the view of a larger and harder world, more strained by a new sense of check in his reactions to it. The fact was, that in this particular year, Simon consciously grew up. The process might have occurred without his marriage, but it was developed acutely by it. Release from his early environment and attainment of his goal had fired his blood with a false flush of maturity. He suspected for the first time that he was still in the unripe chrome. There was a great deal yet to absorb from life, if he was to find that ease and satisfaction at which he had clutched – blindly, perhaps. What was it that had failed him? The more he pondered, the less certain he became. Vocation? No mistake had been made there. The routine of his work might be narrow, but he fitted into it exactly as he had hoped, and the gradual widening of chinks to higher service remained the finest and surest of prospects. Happiness? He had associated it once with Edith – with the dream and promise rather than the actuality of her – and since she herself had trampled on the feather he had thought a plume, he had raised it again with Jani – an ordinary feather, he knew now, but still birdlike and curling. So long as he could remember to hold it aloft and wave, he might still retain his earlier mood of fullbeing. If only – that emptiness did not so often fall between! Was it his fault, or Jani's, that her caresses could not always fill it? Did his discomforts affect her, or had she others of her own, in which he could feel no interest or concern? Were they questing apart, or together, for those harmonies that to him were most important, the harmonies of English life – rising, as naturally as might be, from a Jewish sounding-board? Some of the discussions at Dick's had aroused self-questionings – abstract discussions of the kind Dick loved to generate; but equally or perhaps more strongly they came from the attitude of people he met, and even from books that he read. Except for purposes of study he had done little reading during his first years in London. He was re-discovering the art, and beginning to think at the same time. It was not easy for him to relate the printed page to any personal problem: but apprehensions grew clearer even if they were not solved by the thoughts and records of other men. Clearest of all when they recurred in the acts and speech of persons he knew.

The dislike and distrust of the Jew that he had taken for granted, where provoked by distinctive habits, were as deep, he found, when these obvious agents were lacking. He ought to have learned as much before, if only from Hector Wyn. But he had not realised it fully until he observed it happen again and again from the open window of his emancipated life. Just as he had not realised how keenly his consciousness of his race would persist when he abandoned all connection with it. Surprise came with the knowledge that there were Englishmen like Dick, who appeared to be absolutely free from prejudice – who did not in the least care whether a man was a Jew or not – yet refused to admit any distinction between "foreign" and "English" Jews.

"Tommyrot! – bilge!" he declared in his languid voice, the incongruous medium of a slangy violence which was his only affectation. "A Jew's a man for a' that, whether he has a beard and an accent or uses a safety razor and an Oxford drawl. Absolute muck, this talk of the differences of mankind, whether Jews or Gentiles. Sort of thing that leads to bickerings, jealousies, misunderstandings, fostered by fellows of the Press and politicians in every country, usually for base and petty ends. Poisons our social and artistic life and progressive effort all over the world. Leads to wars, too, and their infernal miseries and stupidities, and ultimately to the smash-up of civilisation. It's a filthy idea – any sort of distinction between peoples, races, or sects. The only hope of a decent world is to abolish the idea and the fact!"

Both Ted and Simon demurred.

Said one, "You can't get away from nationality".

Said the other, "You can't get away from religion".

"Holy Moses! or Holy Mary! – the devil a difference do I see – nor does *he!* Don't be shocked, boys – no reflections on anyone's pet divinity. Every decent religion should join hands on the Fatherhood of God and the Brotherhood of Man. 'Love thy neighbour as thyself' comes from the Hebrew Bible, doesn't it, Black? – Most Christians forget it conveniently. Translated as 'Love thy neighbouring country as thine own' – it's the most practical as well as the most edifying precept of any religion. As to nationality, that's the rottenest of artificial barriers. *Nationalism – patriotism* – a fine flower rooted in dung! The first thing your patriots do when their blood's up, is to trample on the flower, grab the dung, and stink the world with it. Pocket-handkerchiefs aren't much good once they start – even if the hankies are as big as flags. There's a better way of honouring one's country, not to speak of loving it, than waving a flag in the faces of other people, all busy waving theirs. Stress the *likenesses*, not the differences, of nations – the interests of humanity are the same, and the ideal of the true patriot should be international equality. All the rest is – bilge!"

The two young men shook their heads in dissent; discounted, in Simon's case, by respect for a muscular Englishman who had been a University "blue", and in Ted's, by affection for a cousin, who was not only friend and mentor, but had, at personal sacrifice, cleared an educational path blocked by the early death of Rendall Senior.

"Dick's bark is always worse than his bite," he confided to Simon. " He's got some queer ideas, though. Chucked the Territorials because he didn't believe in militarism. Militarism – my eye! He was the finest officer in the corps, all the fellows said."

The identity of his views with Ted's was the more pleasing to Simon, from the dissipation of a fear that had haunted him. There had seemed no reason why Ted – or Dick – should ever know that he was a Jew. When he was led, somehow, into a blurting self-announcement, it was almost a shock to hear Ted say – "Of course, old chap – I knew that long ago. It doesn't bother me. You're English anyway—"

In his relief he did not ask how Ted had found out: the idea
of his "guessing" was too absurd. Dick might have – perhaps
– But the subject was not discussed, even when Dick took up
and disposed of the challenge on the difference between
English and foreign Jews. It was enough for Simon that Ted,
at least, confirmed belief in the favourable impression made
by the Anglo-Jew.

But even this purging and strengthening of the bond
between the friends did not renew Simon's confidence in
himself, or settle all his doubts. Baffled by the difficulty of
discriminating between the problems of Simon Black, and
those of Shimon ben Gedaliah ben Itzchak, the Schwartze
Rebbe of Belnitchik, he was not even certain of the necessity
for such discrimination. Doubtless he was, after all, the
average person he believed himself. Average, but – Yes, it was
the "but" that led to all his deeper speculation: did it belong to
himself, or to the fact that he was a Jew? Were the two "buts",
in short, one and indivisible, – making his sensitiveness to
certain factors in life as much a physiological inheritance as
an individual trait?

It did not seem, on the face of it, that such considerations
could bear on the inadequacy of his home. Both he and Jani
felt there was something wrong – something beyond the lack
in equipment that made them spend evenings on lists of
articles to be bought, and calculations on how soon they could
remove to better quarters. At first Jani had been as eager as
himself to cut adrift from the dairy. She was anxious to know
Simon's friends, to adapt herself to his demands: she
sympathised with his dislike of the Thomas' familiarities, and
herself resented Tegwen's criticism of her domestic ways.

"That woman is nothing but a scrubbing brush" – she

complained to Simon. " She rubs and scrubs all day long in the shop and her rooms, and comes spying up here to see if I'm doing the same. Mad on soap and polish she is, like Ieuan Richard's mother – that's the sort of daughter-in-law would suit Mrs. Richards the Band."

Jani laughed, almost harshly for her, as she uttered the village nickname, – though it was not the humour of the term that struck her. "If she thinks I'm going to spend my life on my knees cleaning her old house, she's jolly well mistaken."

Simon did not smile, even at her quaint mimicry of his own slang.

"But you get a woman in to do the cleaning, Jani."

"Yes, and she does it well enough – but Tegwen Thomas calls her a dirty slut, and says she leaves the place worse than she found it. Of course nobody can clean to suit *her* – she won't have any help, she's up a six doing all her work and going over and over the same things all day. And she gets red all over if she sees as much as a crumb out of place. Why, she makes me so nervous when she comes peeping in, that I drop kettles and saucepans boiling hot – it's a wonder I haven't scalded myself to death! But I've made up my mind not to worry any more. I'm going to let things lie about untidy just on purpose—"

"We'll get out as soon as we can, dear," said Simon uneasy at the litter that had become characteristic of their rooms.

But Jani raised all kinds of objections to the flats they inspected, and finally, when a suitable place was found, refused to move at all. A sudden change took place in the relations between the landlady and herself. Probably Jani had known all along that Mrs. Thomas had reason in her strictures, and that a genuine fondness warred with her rage for cleanliness. Besides, Mrs. Thomas was anxious to make amends to Jani as the months went by, convicting the elder woman of unjust suspicion.

"Well, well," she in turn confided to her husband, silently smoking his pipe as she sewed and chattered. "There's nothing the matter with Jani, after all. What did they want to get married for in such a hurry, I wonder? A pity it is, indeed – he is only a Jew, and a proud stuck-up fellow – Jani ought to have gone with a Welshman like herself. It's a shame and disgrace the way they do live without any religion. I been hinting to Jani about going to chapel with us, but she do only laugh and as good as tell me to mind my own business. I should be minding it well if I told them to go from the rooms. A shocking state they are in, I'm ashamed to see such dirt and neglect in my own house. But I'm willing to put up with her untidy ways for the sake of her being Welsh and only a young girl – perhaps she will come to her senses after a bit. You know what the minister did tell me Llew – 'Persuade her, Mrs. Thomas fach – she got a good example in you – and perhaps it is a good work you will be doing, saving a soul for the Lord.' She can sing yr hen iaith beautiful – when it do take her fancy she sings in the day by herself – and it do melt my heart, indeed! If only I could draw her to come with us and join in the hymns! She's not a bad girl, Llew, and, she never went wrong at all, far as I can make out – 'twas only her way of talking put it into my head – she do contradict herself a lot and say all sorts of fullish things. Her tongue is her enemy, merch fach anwyl—" And Mrs. Thomas wept, her tears induced partly by real concern, and partly by the hysteria that marked her present health. The same day she had gone upstairs to reveal to Jani that she had "missed twice, so it's sure to be!" – in a mystic, world-shaking manner that caught the ear of the younger married woman, and set up a curious state of confidence between them. Curious, because in it the previous hostilities vanished, and because Jani's interest in the subject might have been expected to dwindle rather than increase. To her own surprise, she found it fascinating to listen to accounts of symptoms that varied from day to day, and to watch the preparations being made for a new member of the Thomas household. It was not long before she was drawn into participation by a promise to exercise her special handicraft. So intense did this new preoccupation become, that, unwilling to explain it to Simon, she began to invent excuses for spending hours in the Thomas kitchen, and eventually for deciding to remain on in the upper rooms.

"Poor Mrs. Thomas is so dreadfully ill," she said – as a matter of fact, the dairywoman was now extremely well, and had never looked in such glowing health in her life – "I really haven't the heart to leave her here alone. She dreads the thought of strangers in the house, and I've promised we'll stay on until she's better."

Simon was seriously annoyed. He had made all but definite arrangements for taking a flat in a different district. But Jani's new attitude was unexpectedly firm. They quarrelled, and Simon was obliged to quench the stream of tears he evoked. The reconciliation was sweet enough, but Simon continued to resent his wife's absorption in Mrs. Thomas, and the increasing signs of neglect in their rooms. He was even more averse, however, to remonstrating with her, when only such scenes resulted. Much as he disliked the dairy atmosphere, he could put up with it a little longer. But other things in Jani puzzled him. She had always awaited his homecoming so eagerly, and been so prompt to go out with him anywhere at a moment's notice, to share his lightest doings and plans, that he missed the failing welcome and companionship. But he was more disconcerted than hurt. Always it had been Jani's demands that drew from him ardour or tenderness, and it was even a slight relief to be exempted from constant response. With his growing circle of friends and his renewed love of books he had resources that depended little on her help. Almost all he required of her was to provide coffee and biscuits, and to look prettier – he really meant *neater* – than usual in her party frock on occasional evenings when a few fellows dropped in. They seldom asked young women – Jani either disliked or feared those she met – Dick's sister, for instance, made her feel like a worm, she declared, though Simon thought Miss Partingdale particularly kind. Otherwise they drifted into separate compartments of leisure. Even the week-end jauntings together grew more rare. The year flew by, though to Tegwen Thomas – and to Jani sharing her vigil – the months dragged heavily enough until her baby was born. The event happened with celerity in the end. One morning Jani was summoned below by Llew Thomas (able now, since he employed a man and boy, to spend more time at home) to remain with Tegwen while he fetched doctor and nurse. But when the doctor came he laughed and went off again, telling them he should not be needed till night. The nurse bustled about, ordering articles which Jani ran to fetch, and departed also, promising to look in later. After some hours together, during which the patient retailed her feelings minutely to the attentive confidant, she ate a hearty lunch and fell asleep. Jani decided to clear her breakfast table, flick a duster round the room, and go out shopping. Simon seldom lunched at home nowadays. She generally shared Tegwen's meal or else went for a snack to an A.B.C., where it was fun to sit and watch less leisured typists and shopgirls. To-day she dawdled as usual in the busy High Street, gazing into windows and choosing frocks and jewels in the same spirit as she had done when a child, in the first flush of arrival at Blaemawe. These huge stores and smart little shops gave her no greater thrill than she had got from the treasures behind the fusty village panes. "That's mine – and that – and that" – she could still say, in imagination staking out claims with sticky fingers that darted before those of Ieuan, or Blod Jones, or John Polen Tew, or S'ran – S'ran – what was her other name? Jani sighed. She had been glad to cast Blaemawe behind her, but it was not much use looking smart and being leisured and having a husband, if there was nobody you had always known to admire and envy you. How they would stare and chatter in Blaemawe if they saw her now! Suppose she persuaded Simon to take her home at last for a holiday? Her bright eyes began to dance as she strolled on, seeing herself walk up the village road on Simon's arm. A man passing caught her smile and stopped. She tossed her head and grimaced at him as she went by, not hurrying, not frightened now as she might have been once.

When she returned, letting herself in quietly at the side door under the arch, her heart gave a little leap. A queer mewling sound came from the rooms behind the shop. She went in, and found all the doors except that of the bedroom wide open, as Llew Thomas had left them, when he rushed a second time in chase of the dilatory doctor. Fortunately the nurse had come first. She let Jani in with whispered caution, to look in amazement at the dumb, whitefaced, but smiling mother on the bed, and the mewling bundle beside her.

"In a hurry, that young man—" The nurse nodded at them in obvious pride. "Who'd have thought it! Never knew a first to come so quick. But that's what comes of an active life – never rested a minute, she didn't! I must say I was never so put out – but now all's well. Both of 'em right as trivets. Doctor hasn't come yet, and there's nothing for him to do when he does. Now, Mrs. Black, you'd better go – come back later, there's a dear."

The nurse was affectionate to young Mrs. Black, for reasons of her own. The privileges Jani enjoyed made her story full of detail, as she recounted it to Simon in the evening. But he was not in the least interested.

"Just as well you were out," he muttered. "Don't see why you should be mixed up in the affair—"

"Oh, but Simon, aren't you glad the poor woman is safe, and everything going on well?"

"Of course. And I hope they'll arrange that she continues to go on well without your assistance. Do you *want* to be a slave to Mrs. Thomas?"

Jani smiled.

"No fear of that. She's getting help in the kitchen every day for a month. I've only promised to sit with her a little. And oh, Simon – the baby's such a darling—"

"I hope he doesn't howl at nights – or days, for that matter—"

"Oh, he's good as gold – the best baby she's ever seen, Nurse Smith says – she's going to let me bring him up to show you soon—"

Simon was by no means enchanted. He gazed with what

Jani called his "nasty cross look" at the object in her arms: its pink hairless face with the watery eyes seemed to him a repulsive pulp of vapid flesh. He shrank back in horror as Jani placed it against his chest.

"Take it away, for heaven's sake," he said. "It's the ugliest thing I've seen – and the stupidest—"

Jani crooned over it, and retired, laughing. It was some weeks before Simon could be induced to look at the baby again, and then he was forced to admit it had improved somewhat, though the vacuity of expression that had struck him most remained. The good temper of the creature was undeniable. It hardly ever cried, and Jani shared the mother's raptures over a perfect angel. Simon's ridicule had no effect on Jani, except to make her tell him less of the time she spent nursing the infant. He began once more to talk of moving, and to pore over particulars of flats. Jani said nothing until he proposed an expedition to view a promising list. Then she said decidedly:

"You know I don't want to move, Simon. I'd rather stay here—"

"But Jani, – I thought it was on account of Mrs. Thomas. She's well now, and perfectly happy without you – why should you consider her further?"

"It's myself," said Jani. "I'm afraid I'll be lonely if I go to a strange place—"

"But, my dear, London isn't a strange place to you now, surely?"

"It is," said Jani. "I hate every other part but this – I'm used to everything here—"

"Very well, we'll stick to Kensington if you prefer it."

"But I'll be lonely without Mrs. Thomas and the baby. I'm so used to *them* now—"

"Nonsense!" said Simon. His tone was irritable. "We've got friends we'll make others, too – people you may like better. Besides, you ought to go on with your music."

"I don't want to—" said Jani. "At least, not if we move. I will, if we stop here." Her voice, though pettish, kept an even note of pleading, as if she meant to avoid sharper conflict.

"But it's uncomfortable here – you know we shall be better off in a self-contained flat – we'll have more room and more privacy. You'll be free to do just as you please, and not be hampered every moment by thinking of Mrs. Thomas and the baby—"

"Oh, Simon dear, but I like to be thinking of them – and to see them—"

He smiled at her dolorous expression.

"Very well," he said magnanimously. "You can call and see them as often as you like. There are places advertised here not so very far away."

She was silent as he turned to the papers spread before him. Then he looked up to find her near. With a sudden movement she scrambled on his knees, put her arms round his neck, and looked glowingly into his face.

"Simon – darling," she said in her softest trill – "it's the baby I can't bear to leave. But I shan't mind at all if – if – I can have one of my own."

"Silly little kitten! You want – another – to play with." He tried to laugh and pull her hands away. But the face looking into his was startlingly pretty, with its deep flush and luminous tender eyes. His own arms went round her irresistibly.

Jani made no further objection to exploring vacant flats in Kensington. They peeped about and climbed stairways like children, Jani's return of clinging sweetness surrounding them both with an aura of young adventure. To poke fun at small rooms and dark landings, at false plastered ceilings and bogus kitchenettes, at disproportionate rents and queer landlords, seemed unlike criticism, but was just as effective. Hardly anything satisfactory met their united gaze, and both agreed that nothing less than perfection need be rushed into. They could wait a little longer, and go on exploring. The hunt each Saturday afternoon had a novel interest of its own. Weeks slipped by. Then, suddenly, it seemed to Simon, without warning or forethought, Jani whispered a secret to him in the still of night. He drew himself taut from her nestling touch.

"No – no" – he said – "it can't be—"

"Oh, yes, it is," she said, and babbled triumphantly. The lightning torch of imagination that came rarely to Simon lit up for him a vision of repugnance. A sweet consolatory figure that healed and caressed – then went its way, indifferent to indifference – only to return, unsought but beguiling, to lay a sudden trap for his undoing. The vision fled at the sound of Jani's weeping.

"Oh, Simon," she sobbed. "You aren't glad – you don't want it – and you'll hate me as well – and perhaps I'll die!"

He turned deliberately to hold her close and murmur tender names into her ear.

"Poor little Janikins – you won't die, little kitten – think of Mrs. Thomas." Irony of ironies, that *he* should bid her to think of Mrs. Thomas! – "Why, you're twice as strong and healthy as that bone of a woman. I'm not so terribly glad – but if you're happy about it – well, I'll make the best of it, too—"

It was heroic, but it did not last. Though he never uttered a word of dismay or foreboding, they grew upon him with every perplexity of mind.

A triumph for Devora Black – for Judaism! It could hardly be more than an evasive one, at best. But it chagrined him to think of the busy weaving of his mother's thoughts when she heard. She would begin again to send those messages that had lapsed – for lack of news to feed them. He wrote home seldom and briefly, and no visits had been interchanged. Once Dinah had come up on a business errand. He met her for an hour at a City restaurant, and found her colder, more reserved than ever. He realised only after she had gone how little she had told him – and that she had not as much as mentioned Jani. When he spoke of his wife she was silent. The fact rankled less than her obvious disapproval of himself. Stupid girl – buried alive in her Welsh village, how could she judge his life? But he knew she was neither stupid nor narrow. A simmer of curiosity mingled with his resentment at her secret condemnation. How did she arrive at her conclusions? What made her shrink from his self-won freedom? She was actually in his thoughts, for no reason that he knew, when he reached home on the Saturday Ted Rendall went to Bournemouth. He ought to have been thinking of Jani, who had complained of feeling specially unwell when he left her that morning. But Jani, as he knew, so often exaggerated her symptons, that he could not be expected to dwell on them long. It was only the unusual stillness as he mounted the stairs that brought remembrance back uneasily, and he made a sudden leap over the last three steps.

Mrs. Thomas was standing outside the bedroom door, her eyes distended, her lips pursed tight. She held up a hand and spoke in a hissing whisper.

"There now, don't be flurried – but Jani was taken bad this morning and I had to get the doctor. Don't you go in yet, please – she's all right now, sleeping it off. The doctor gave her something, and said she better be left quiet for a bit."

She moved aside, however, as Simon, without a word, stretched his hand to the handle of the door, which he pushed as gently as his haste allowed. In a few moments he returned, and closed it even more gently again.

"What has happened? – Why didn't you phone me?" His low tones were less abrupt than the words implied.

Mrs. Thomas told him briefly in her annoying if discreet whisper. She had been too busy helping Jani to phone him uselessly, from the moment she had heard a bump and shriek, and rushed upstairs to find Jani in a serious state on the floor, a chair overturned beside her, to the exit of the doctor, which had taken place only ten minutes ago.

"He waited as long as he could, but he had to be off to another case – and there it is, poor girl, he did all he could for her. He'll be coming back again later on. It's a mercy I was here, and Llew at home and that little gell that comes in to help – not such a fool as some – she can watch the shop, though I don't trust her with the baby. He's sleeping too, thank goodness. And I got a bit of lunch for you hot downstairs. I'll send it up on the tray for you now—" She was obviously anxious to hurry away.

"Thank you. But tell me, Mrs. Thomas – did Jani actually fall from the chair?"

"No – she had some sort of fit, I think, and dragged the chair down with her."

"But what was she doing?"

"Oh, just tidying – she felt bad first thing and then said she was better – she took it in her head to turn the room out herself this morning, and clean the pictures – that slut that's been coming here never touches them!"

Simon was silent. It was true that Jani had lately developed a surprising activity in imitation of Mrs. Thomas. Though the results were agreeable, he resented the cause. "Curse the woman," he thought now, but he could hardly show Tegwen that he blamed her for the accident, especially in view of the care she had shown in attending to Jani – and to himself. Tegwen could not have conceived it possible that anyone should deem housework an agent of calamity. In her own case it had been so notoriously the reverse. She had impressed Jani with her conviction that it was an unfailing road to normal and easy childbirth. The "kind of fit" she believed Jani to have had came, in her opinion, from a very different source. But this, in her turn, she avoided telling Simon. The only comment she made to him was:

"Well, well, its hard luck on poor Jani – to lose her baby like that!"

"It doesn't matter, so long as she's safe," muttered Simon.

"But she'll feel it hard, poor girl—"

Simon did not go to Dick's that evening, nor did he go away on a longer and graver journey. When he was sufficiently reassured to calm and refresh himself, he discovered a brief letter that had arrived by an earlier post from Dinah.

"Uncle Elman has just passed away," she wrote. " I thought there was no need to send a wire, as the funeral is not till Sunday. Of course you will come down by the early train."

The news was only a momentary sorrow. The old man had ceased to be more than the shadow of a memory. But in other circumstances Simon would not have failed to attend at Dawport. He could not, however, leave Jani in her still precarious state. More than all else she needed the comfort he was bound to give her, not only in her physical but in her mental distress. As Tegwen Thomas said, she "took it hard." For some time after her recovery she moped and wept over her loss. But her resilient spirits won. The doctor's words – "Don't let this mishap worry you, Mrs. Black. There isn't any reason why you shouldn't have a great fat son next year!" stimulated a natural buoyance of mind to renewed hope: not even to be dashed, apparently, by the sinister footnote Tegwen Thomas could not, at last, resist adding— "All very well for that doctor to talk – he don't know the ins and outs of your married life. Oh – merch fachi!" She shook her head in dolorous affection and dropped her voice mysteriously – "He don't know that your husband is a Jew – and that he promised his mother that his children should be Jews—"

Jani, who had long ago imparted the secret learned by listening behind a door, laughed lightly.

"What's that got to do with it, anyway?" she said.

Tegwen Thomas's face tightened inwardly. The wail of her folktones sang through her words, still low and intimate. "Jani fach, it's Welsh you are, and there's no religion between you and your husband. Perhaps you can't be having children from a Jew like that. Perhaps the Lord is not wanting it to be."

XX

A MONTH later Dinah came to town again. She asked Simon to meet her at the same place in the City, as she had news to give him. Her black dress did not suit her, he noticed with vexation. It made her look thinner and more sallow, and with the wistful look in her eyes, carried a strong impression of their mother.

"You ought to stay longer," he urged, when she told him she must leave within an hour. "Why not let me take you to a theatre? – though I wish you had a lighter dress—"

"Thanks, I don't want to travel all night. And I'm in mourning." She stared reproachfully at his shrug and frown.

Her news was of the old man's will. He had left a thousand pounds to each of his grandchildren, and five hundred pounds to each grandniece and grandnephew – on condition that they married Jewish husbands or wives.

"Of course the will was made long ago, before anything happened," said Dinah, crumbling the bread on her plate. "But naturally Uncle Elman wouldn't have altered it—"

"Not in *my* favour," said Simon. He smiled faintly.

"Nor in Nettie's. He didn't know about you – the Elmans kept it from him. Nettie will get nothing, of course – unless she divorces her husband and marries a Jew."

"Which isn't likely."

"One never knows. Aunt Esther says she's coming home to have her second child. She's afraid to stay with her husband. He's all right when he's sober, but when he's drunk he knocks her about. In any case his mother wants him back and would like to separate them—"

Simon lit a cigarette in silence. He was surprised at Dinah's matter-of-fact air, and the lack of hesitation with which she spoke. He had forgotten the probability of the subject being a staple one in his parents' house.

"Mother thinks you can get your five hundred pounds." Dinah did not look at her brother as she continued. "She believes Jani has become a Jewess, of course. And if you prove that is so, it will conform with the terms of the will."

"I won't try to prove it, thanks."

"I know Jani isn't," said Dinah. "But it's not too late for her. And after all – five hundred pounds would be useful to you."

"Very useful. Especially just now, when I want to buy furniture – and books – and all sorts of things, but never mind. I'll make enough myself soon. I'm glad you'll get yours, though, Di. When are you twenty-one?"

"Next month! – But it doesn't depend on that. It's a dowry – if and when I marry – surely you understand?"

"Yes." Simon flicked the ash from the end of his cigarette, and examined it vaguely. "By the way, Di – I saw Frank Werrington in town the other day. He's on his father's staff now, so all's well at the farm. His sister was with him – horrible little shrew. And another girl, a fat, red-faced country girl. I don't know whether she was Frank's friend or his sister's – but I fancy she thought she was *his*." Dinah was silent now. He took a quick glance at her averted cheek, still pale, however, and composed. "He got rid of her, though, to talk about you – he asked quite a lot, and seemed disappointed that you never came to stay. But that's all off, I take it?"

"Of course."

"Quite right, Dinah." There was an unexpected note in Simon's voice – unexpected to himself. "That sort of thing's no good to *you*. You'll have to marry a Jew – I don't mean for the sake of the five hundred pounds."

"Hardly. Not even if it was the thousand. I'm not like Sylvie Elman."

"Why – do you mean that Sylvie—?"

"She's a real little beast. You know how she hates everything Jewish. Just the sort that does the things that – that Jews are jeered at for. What *do* you think? She's making up to Norman Blay now!"

Simon laughed drily. He approved his sister's somewhat confused indignation. It had brought a warm tint too, into her clear olive skin.

"I hope I shan't see much of her, whether she marries him or not. We are moving into Dawport in March. The property in Gomer Street has been left to mother. Uncle Elman's instructions were that father was to have the business on very low terms. Will you come down to Blaemawe before we move?"

"No. I may come to Dawport later."

It had never been stated, but was implicitly understood that Simon had not been pressed to visit Blaemawe since his marriage, solely because Jani's people were there. His own reluctance was still strong, too strong for Jani's recent persuasions to overcome. If she wanted to go home, he told her, she could do so. But Jani had no desire to go unaccompanied by him.

"Mother's never been so anxious as now to give up Blaemawe and live in Dawport. We should have been there long ago if Uncle Mark hadn't haggled. Out of spite, I suppose – or just cantankerousness. Like a dog over a bone he doesn't really want, but won't part with. He's got plenty of better bones. But he's never been pleasant to us – or to anybody – since Nettie's affair. He's quarrelled with the congregation, too. They've appointed a new minister just because he opposed him, I believe."

"Who is it?" said Simon idly.

"I don't know – a young man called Billig – an Englishman. Uncle Mark said he was a friend of yours, – and just about as fit, he said! He never has a good word for any of us."

"What! Old Billig?" – Simon was roused a little. "So he put in for it – and got it? Why, he's the very man, Dinah. I'd rather like to see him when I go down." He smoked on thoughtfully. But the memories evoked were too disturbing. He said abruptly, "How about the business at Blaemawe?"

"We've got an assistant – he drives the delivery trap, too. Of course most of the work will be done at Dawport. And I'll have a season ticket. We'll carry on somehow – until Gershon comes back. Father won't agree to sell it until then, even if he does afterwards. Of course Gershon might do better at Dawport, especially as father feels less and less able to stand about. His legs seem to be getting worse."

Simon had always heard so much about the legs that the reference hardly affected him. But he was struck with the hesitation – the old hesitation – of Dinah's manner.

"Gershon, eh?" he murmured. "I suppose he has another eighteen months or so to serve. Poor devil! Why doesn't he escape?"

Dinah started. Her mouth opened. She stared with dilating eyes at her brother.

"How – how did you know?" she stammered.

"Know what?" Simon removed his cigarette and stared back. "Do you mean he *has* escaped?"

"Oh, no!" She tried to cover her confusion. "I thought you knew he had tried – I mean, that he wanted to try—" she stopped.

Simon leaned forward over the table.

"Tell me about it, Di. He writes to you, of course. Did he say he had a chance of getting away?"

"Yes."

"Then why didn't he?"

"He – he asked me to – to decide," she said reluctantly. "He explained how he meant to do it. He would get across the frontier while they were at manoeuvres. There were friends ready to help. Then he'd come straight back to England."

"Of course you urged him to do it?"

"No. I begged him not to."

Simon's cigarette fell from his fingers over the edge of the table.

"Why the hell!" – he said, stooping to recover it. "Sorry, Dinah. But no doubt it is hell for the conscripts out there – especially when a fellow's been to England. What made you write like that? And why should he listen, anyway?"

"Because he said if I agreed, it meant – we should get married when he was back."

"Oh – I see. You don't mean to marry him, then?"

"I – I don't know—"

"You don't know! Then why didn't you let him try to escape?"

She threw the crumbs over the cloth in distraction.

"I don't know," she said again. "Oh yes – I do. He might have been shot at the frontier."

"Bit of a risk, perhaps. But I should think he'd have known all about that – and if he had friends to help—"

"I couldn't take the responsibility."

"It seems hard lines, somehow." He gave her a quizzical look. "You could have had your five hundred pounds quite soon."

She was vexed and disconcerted. He had dragged out of her something she would rather not have told.

"I can do without it as well as you. Don't let's talk about it any more. I had to give you the message – mother, of course – she'll be terribly upset if she finds you won't have yours. It isn't only the money, as you know. It's the *idea*—"

"She ought to be used to the idea." It was his turn to speak with annoyance.

"Oh, we're used to it." Her voice trembled a little. "Simon – isn't it – a *mess*!"

"Not at all," he said emphatically. But he had never realised more clearly than at that moment that it *was* a mess. He jumped up to avoid further comment, though Dinah had no intention of making any.

"I suppose we'd better go, if you really mean to catch that train."

They travelled to Paddington almost in silence. The tube train roared enough to cover it, the noise on the upper platforms as they mounted from the escalator was deafening; hiss of steam and shriek of whistle blent with clattering trucks and churns. A crowd came hurrying from the opposite way.

"We're much too early," said Dinah. "That must be a South Wales train just arrived." She stopped, and suddenly waved her hand to a tall young woman in a neat costume, who was carrying a suitcase in a strong, swinging grip.

"Nurse! Miss Newell!" she called. "I didn't know you were leaving Blaemawe to-day—"

"Why, it's Miss Black," said Marjorie Newell's high, pleasant tones. "And your brother, of course – how d'ye do, Mr. Black!" She shook hands in a totally unembarrassed manner, but her smile widened at Simon's uncertain stare. "Yes, I've left – I've really had the short, sharp sack – they couldn't put up with me any longer!"

"Oh, Miss Newell—" Dinah turned to Simon to explain. "Perhaps you've met before – but I don't think you know Miss Newell was our district nurse – the first one at Blaemawe—"

"Not the first – Edith Miller carried on herself for a time – just to get a hand in! Then she made me go down. And now she's sent me flying!" Marjorie laughed in evident good humour. "You know, Mr. Black, what a tyrant Edith is!"

Simon was unable to reply. He coloured and stammered, to his own disgust. Dinah looked from one to the other with a slightly puzzled air.

"I'm sure Miss Miller couldn't be unkind," she said.

"No, bless her! It's really because she's *too* kind – to her dear Welsh protegees – though she hates me to call them that! And I'm willing to oblige by calling them much harder names, though she won't have that either. The fact is, I found my Welsh patients rather a handful. Or else they found *me* one! Anyway, we couldn't get on," she laughed again. "Of course, we get the same trouble everywhere. The women think we are busybodies running them into fearful expense and upsetting their fusty households, because we open the windows and insist on hot water and make a few necessary sanitary arrangements. These Welsh folk have a few extra prejudices of their own – they simply loathe an Englishwoman bossing them! I should have conquered them in the end, of course. But Edith wouldn't have it. She thought her scheme was being endangered, and that the only thing to do was to get a Welshwoman in my place. All nonsense, believe me! The methods will have to be the same. It won't work any better—!" She shook her head, with a superior confidence that won Simon's esteem.

"You are not sorry to leave Blaemawe, I suppose—"

"Oh, I don't know," she said. "Edith's there, you see! And we had some good times. Still, I've a splendid job waiting for me in town – a friend of Lady Hafod's. So when Edith's up again I hope to see a bit of her." She asked Dinah about her journey, chatting with the sprightly good nature which did not seem in the least deflected by her experience. Another victim of Edith's ruthless principles, thought Simon – but a victim without rancour or resentment. It seemed, indeed, that she could only show such feelings on Edith's own behalf. A rare, loyal friend! In the midst of a queer surge of sensations, he was amused at the way in which she ignored her offence against him. Yet that she had not forgotten became obvious by her manner as they shook hands. She looked oddly at him, and said in a hesitating way,

"I wonder if we shall meet in town again? I'm going home for a fortnight first."

"Let me know when you're back – come and see us if you can." He handed her a card. "I'm sure my wife will be pleased to hear about Blaemawe." He did not know what made him say it – neither the two who listened, nor the one who spoke, felt any pleasure in the statement. Miss Newell did not reply, but produced a card of her own. She scribbled something on it.

"Goodbye, then, for the present." She had gone, swinging her suitcase towards the Praed Street exit. Simon and his sister walked up Platform one, where an empty train was running in. He had found a corner seat and installed her in it, before they were able to exchange further comment. Then he said, as casually as he could:

"So you've been seeing a lot of Miss Newell and – and Miss Miller at Blaemawe. Why didn't you mention them before?"

"I haven't seen such a lot of them – and I didn't think you'd be interested. I *did* mean to tell you about Miss Miller. I don't know why, somehow, I never did." She had not written more than twice since his marriage – the briefest of notes. And her visits had been short and quite as full of omissions. She did not feel compelled to dwell on the fact. "I wasn't sure that you knew Miss Newell. Of course Blaemawe's been full of the nursing scheme since last year. Some people like it and some don't. It's true the women hate the way Miss Newell orders them about. But it's all for their own good, as she says."

"And do they blame Miss Miller?" Simon wanted to bring Edith back into the talk, little as he was interested in the nursing scheme.

"I've never heard a word against Miss Miller. Everybody likes her. It isn't only because she's Lady Hafod's granddaughter – the people really don't care much about the Hafods. They are charitable, of course. But Sir Gwilym isn't very Welsh, and his wife's an Englishwoman, and they spend most of their time away. Miss Miller's different. She takes the greatest pains to understand what people want. I think she's wonderful!" Dinah clasped her hands on the window ledge. A note of excitement came into her voice. "Do you know, Simon – she's got Jewish blood in her!"

Simon nodded.

"Yes. I've heard of it."

"Oh – really? Well, nobody has in Blaemawe. The Hafods don't wish to talk about it, she says. But she told us."

"You mean she's spoken to you – and mother—?"

"Yes. She talked to us first at the Fête, in the summer. You remember, I mentioned the big Fête at Hafod, in aid of the Dawport Hospital. Everybody went, Lord Dawport and the county families were there, and speeches were made about the District Nursing. The shops in Blaemawe closed for two afternoons, and the shopkeepers were specially invited into the House. Miss Miller shook hands with everybody and when she saw mother and father, she took them aside and they had a long chat. Then one day soon after she called in, and mother made tea, and she stayed quite a time. It was then she told us she considered herself a Jewess, and that she had a Jewish grandmother in London. Of course we are keeping the secret."

"Oh, it's a secret?"

"Well – she said she didn't wish it to be, except in Blaemawe, for the present. She said she was going to live as a Jewess when she went away. She asked father's advice about it."

"*Father's* advice!" Simon choked a little. He gazed down the platform, and added slowly. "Did she say she knew me?"

"She said she had met you, but she didn't seem to know much about you – at least she didn't say much. But mother, of course, told her everything."

The guard came round inspecting tickets and locking doors, and Dinah continued to peer for a familiar face. Some women in the compartments were gossiping loudly together; and a child jumped from one seat to another. As the whistle blew, she sank into her corner. Leaning forward slightly, she thanked

her brother for the papers he had provided, and in a shy tone
said she would look forward to his visit in March. He did not
seem to hear as he bent and pecked her cheek. There was
hardly time for formal farewell; the train moved out so
quickly.

Standing back on the platform, waving his hat, Simon saw
neither his sister's wistful face at the window, nor the long
curving train itself. Edith seated at the Blaemawe tea table,
listening while his mother "told her everything," was a
sufficiently exclusive picture. As he turned and walked away,
he wondered why he had not asked Dinah a score of things.
There had not been much time, and he had had to guard
himself. But Dinah was not very observant. She lived too
much in herself – brooding and dreaming in her inward way.
Perhaps that was why she had not been too greatly impressed
with Edith's "secret" – at any rate she had conveyed no effect
of being swept away by it. Why, she might not even have
mentioned it but for the accident of meeting Marjorie Newell!
He felt unreasonably annoyed. Surely Dinah could not take
such a thing as a matter of course? Probably, however, she had
not fully grasped the situation. She saw Edith Miller as the
gracious young Lady Bountiful of the Hafods: the Jewish
touch must seem remote, fantastic. He had a flash of
conviction that to his mother, giving her marvellous guest tea,
there was a much easier, much closer, acceptance of reality.
Strange, but true: Lady Hafod might perplex and embarrass
Devora Black – her ladyship's granddaughter did no such
thing. For she was Bubele's granddaughter, too. The idea
pleased him, somehow, despite the slightly disturbing
sensation of being the subject of that significant "everything."

Only slightly disturbing. Was it that the old spell no longer worked, even to pain and anger – or that the lack of response meant a "deadness" in his soul? It stirred, at least, to the fact, that though Edith had lost interest in him, she was capable of interest in his parents.

He reached Bishop's Road, and waited for the homeward-bound Metropolitan train. As he entered, his fingers, twirling in his pocket, found and withdrew the card Marjorie Newell had given him. Why, of course – she had written something on it! He dropped upon the first empty seat and read.

"Thanks for overlooking it – my rudeness, I mean, I intended to apologise, but I can't before your sister. Edith made me promise I would – she thinks my behaviour shocking!"

A tingle of delight ran through his veins. He laughed aloud, though quietly, to himself. A pretty girl sitting opposite put her chin up, and looked away, then brought her glance slyly back to meet his. But he had not even seen her. "She thinks my behaviour shocking!" – Really? Then she no longer thought badly of him herself? How, then, did she think of him? He pulled himself up. It couldn't matter, anyhow. He was out of her world for ever. Yet knowing that, accepting it, he might let his thoughts linger on her kindness, on her more reasonable mood, on her gracious friendship with his mother.

As he stepped outside the station at Kensington, he felt a reluctance to go straight into his home. It was a still, clear evening in January. The shadows of the old gaunt houses, the bare spikiness of the trees, their thin new branches rising weirdly from black lopped knots, merged into a velvet depth of sky, that held a faint occasional twinkle. Minute beads of frost glittered up from the pavement. He walked sharply along and took a wide detour to the Park. The sense of space and freedom was unconstrained by the moving groups of people, vague shapes between the lamps. When he got in, at last, his rooms were dark and silent. He put a match to the gas fire, and saw that supper was laid for him on the table. A moment later Llewellyn Thomas knocked at his door. With a sheepish grin, the dairyman explained that he had been left to "mind" the sleeping baby. His wife and Jani had gone together to the vestry rooms of the Wesleyan chapel near by, where a monthly "social" was being held. "They won't be very late. Mrs. Black was not expecting you back for a good bit, and she thought you wouldn't mind her going out with Tegwen—"

"Oh no, of course not," said Simon, but when the other had gone, he frowned half-vexedly. A chapel "social"! How ridiculous! But he was not sorry to be alone. It was good, indeed, to draw a chair up to the fire, and plunge into a book. On the mantelpiece, sticking out on end, just as he had left it the night before, was a thick new red bound volume. Simon smiled oddly as he took it down. Edith might appreciate more than he did, the only prize he had won in a missing-word competition, set by a literary journal every week. Gaps had to be filled in quotations from novels, copies of which were given in reward. The novel sent to a successful competitor was not necessarily that from which the winning lines were drawn. Simon, for instance, had not even tried to complete the unfamiliar sentence— "A ... that persist in celebrating ... ... though they have no ... to gather, will regain ..." It was for a later and different effort that he received the handsome volume of *Tancred*.

The tale of an English aristocrat's yearning for Sinai bored and riled him. But last night, when he had begun reading, only to skip and set it aside, he had not found Edith sharing his perusal. Now the blue fire of her eye played on the page, her smile and lift of brow made intimate comment. She swept him over epigram and extravagance of thought, over false romance, redundant, obsolete, to grasp the race idea that thralled her mind – as it had thralled Tancred's creator. Was it quite the same? He saw her shake her head over the blend of Judaism and Christianity that Disraeli urged so audaciously – audacious, surely, to the protagonists of both, since by them equally his authority was denied, his sincerity impugned. To her Disraeli's harping on race must seem the answer, not only to his critics, but to himself – to his own perversions. Simon strove uneasily to catch the gleam of Edith's thought. Could he shape argument with which he had such little sympathy? – yield to a stir of longing to be on Edith's side, raising with her a defence against detractors – against not only enemies but dangerous friends?

The book slipped down on his knees, his hand across it, while he stared up at the ceiling. The passage under his palm mocked through the flesh to his brain. It told of the daughters of Laurella, back from school at Marseilles, reluctantly celebrating Succoth at Besso's house in Damascus. They were "ashamed of their race, and not fanatically devoted to their religion, which might be true, but was not fashionable." One professed despair, the other "felt persuaded that the Jews would not be so much disliked if they were better known; that all they had to do was to imitate as closely as possible the habits and customs of the nation among whom they chanced to live; and she really believed that eventually, such was the progressive spirit of the age, a difference in religion would cease to be regarded, and that a respectable Hebrew, particularly if well-dressed and well-mannered, might be able to pass through society without being discovered, or at least noticed. Consummation of the destiny of the favourite people of the Creator of the Universe!"

A mere passing sketch. A simple parenthesis. But what a microcosm of experience and penetration! Only a Jew could understand its anguished satire. Even Edith could not enter into that. She was harsh and inflexible in her judgment, because she had not known in her person the odium and obloquy of Jewry. But Disraeli, who had felt it and escaped from it – how did he come to turn on his fellow-victims, and fling that last stinging comment at their heads?

Edith's voice, it seemed to Simon, interrupted – "But Disraeli never escaped" – The illusion was so clear that he involuntarily looked around. A sigh broke from him into the silence and loneliness of the room. He knew himself confused and unhappy. If he could really talk to her again, listen and argue – it might help to resolve his mind. They had both changed, become reasonable, since that ridiculous – wretched – night. She was at least not angry with him now: her rage had calmed as had his fury of resentment. He remembered only the sweetness of her tones, the grace of her young gravity.

He started when the sound of voices burst below – voices of Jani and Mrs. Thomas, hushed from their first loud pitch by fear of "waking the baby." Then Jani's light footsteps came running up the stairs, and her head peeped in at the door – a flame-like head, slightly dishevelled, with shining eyes and brilliant cheeks. Simon looked at it coldly.

"Fancy – you came in early after all," she said, holding her velveteen cloak in a graceful pouch before her. "And you haven't had your supper." She arched her brows at the table.

"I wasn't hungry," said Simon. The book was still open

under his hand. "I had a meal with Dinah. She went off afterwards."

"You aren't grumpy because I went out?" said Jani. Her tone was gay and indifferent. She tripped about the room as if restless and excited, touching articles, peeping into the mirror, and humming a snatch of Welsh melody. She had not been as animated since her illness. The yellow tinge that had lingered round her cheeks was now the old healthy cream and tan.

"Certainly not. But why a chapel affair? I thought you meant to have nothing to do with that sort of thing—"

Jani laughed, her little birdlike trill.

"Well, there it is! I meant not to – but Tegwen kept on worrying me, and suddenly I thought I might as well. I didn't feel like staying in alone, and you said you might be late."

"And you enjoyed it?"

"Oh, yes, indeed! It was quite good fun. Such a crowd of real old-fashioned Welsh people – I didn't know there were so many of that sort in Kensington! They talked about their homes in Wales, and ever so many invited me to tea. They liked the way I sang some old hymns—"

"Oh, you sang?"

"Yes – there was a lot of singing." Jani hesitated. She seemed to check something on the tip of her tongue. Stopping in her walk, she lifted her heels in and out of her tiny court shoes – that tiny as they were, seemed too large for her feet.

"Why don't you take your cloak off and sit down?"

She let her cloak slip over the settee, against which for a moment she leaned. From her frock of favourite green, with its short sleeves and rounded neck, her brown-red tints flowed vital and glowing. With a sudden movement she came and perched herself on the ledge of Simon's chair. He looked through, rather than at, her, and made no attempt to touch her bare, quivering arms.

"Oh, Simon" – she said, "Who do you think was there?"

"Lloyd George, perhaps," he said, with a vague smile.

"Oh, don't be silly." She pushed his shoulder in petulant rebuke. "But of course you can't guess. It was Ieuan!"

"Ieuan?"

"Yes – don't you remember? – Ieuan Richards."

"H'm. What's he doing in London?"

"He's living with his uncle – at Fulham. He came up last month to study music, after all, because they think he has a good voice. He won a prize at the National Eisteddfod, and his uncle offered to help with his training for a year, though he don't believe much in it himself. That Emlyn Richards is a queer one! But Ieuan says if he can't make a living out of concerts, he can always go back to his job in Blaemawe."

"I thought he worked at Dawport."

"He gave it up – his mother made him go back to the colliery office in Blaemawe!"

Simon laughed a little drily.

"Perhaps he left because you ran away from Dawport! And now he's followed you to London, eh?"

Jani gave his shoulder a still more vigorous push, but she, too, laughed, though not at all drily.

"Oh, that old nonsense is finished, I should think! He came to the "social" with some friends of Emlyn's. They live in Kensington, and the daughter is a pupil at his school. She's a pretty girl, and I think Ieuan is sweet on her. She plays for him to sing, so they are together a lot. But it was nice to see him again. You don't mind my being friendly to him, do you? Tegwen has asked him to tea here on Sunday, and I promised to go down, too. You needn't if you don't want to, Simon—"

"Good heavens, no! Leave me out of it. With all this Welsh tea-partying and hymn singing, you'll be going to chapel next, I suppose?"

Simon's voice had a satirical note. But Jani did not seem to resent it. She nodded in literal assent.

"Well, I've half promised Tegwen I will go one day. There's no harm, is there? I don' t mind where *you* go, Simon – and you said I could do as I liked."

"Of course you can – if you *really* like. I mean, it's not just because of what Mrs. Thomas likes, is it?"

"No, indeed. I can have my own wish, whatever—".

She tossed her red locks. Simon noted her flattened vowels, the ease with which she had slipped into old forsworn words. A frown creased his forehead. ·

"Listen, Jani. I've been thinking over those rooms we saw at Baron's Court – I mean the ground floor flat. I like it better than anything we've seen – and you said you did too. It's really cheap at the price. My mind's made up definitely – first thing in the morning I mean to fix it up. I've had enough of this place, anyway, it's high time we cleared out. We shall move at the beginning of the month."

Jani opened her mouth, but said nothing. She slid slowly from the arm of the chair and stretched her hands to the gas fire.

"Of course you can visit these people if you want to – they've been decent enough, I admit. But I hope you'll pay a little more attention to our other friends. We're invited to Hampstead on Saturday night. Ted asked me to-day."

"The Partingdales?" said Jani. Her tone lacked enthusiasm.

"Yes. I wish you'd practise something. Not hymns, of

course, but another of those old airs they asked you to try one night."

"But I'm nervous with those people," said Jani. "It was different to-night – so homely, and everybody joining in. But at the Partingdales they are so-so stiff and critical—"

"Nonsense! Though they are so deep in classical stuff, they are keen on folk-songs – You're a success there, Jani – they like you, you know—"

She seemed to listen to his persuasive intonation with, in her turn, a slightly ironical air. Then she smiled as if in resignation. Her arms reached up in accompaniment of a yawn.

"I'm tired," she said. "I'm going to bed." She stooped suddenly and picked up Simon's book. "What's this you're reading? Some dull old rubbish!"

"It's not very – exciting." Simon took it back. "But I think I'll finish it to-night all the same. You can turn in, if you want to—"

When he came into the bedroom Jani was fast asleep. She was restless, however, and disturbing. Her right arm moved across the pillow, the clothes disarranged. He covered her twice before settling in himself, and then her low muttering continued. It was a long time before he sank into slumber: but it was not Jani, with her restlessness, that kept him awake.

On Saturday evening they arrived early at Hampstead, Jani in her green frock, but with the subdued and uncertain air she always wore on these occasions. Simon, on the other hand, was in easy spirits. He enjoyed visiting the home of Dick's mother and sister. The gracious white-haired lady seemed to him the most adorable mother one could have. Had he been *her* son, he would never have wished to leave the parental roof.

Dick's sister, too, reminded him a little of his own. Nan Partingdale was a slim dark-haired Englishwoman with something of Dinah's reticence, low voice and sudden smile. But her features had nothing of Dinah's sloping lines. The nose and chin were as fine, but short and tip-tilted. And unlike Dinah, her reserve had nothing shy about its social air. She sang, too, and played like a true musician. At her feet – literally, for he liked sitting on a pouffe near the piano – Simon learnt to discriminate between Bach and Brahms, to appreciate the subtleties of technique for which he had an instinctive but uninstructed ear. A little way off Jani would share a divan with Ted or Mrs. Partingdale, or some guest who admired the dainty, red-haired vivid-faced little girl, so unexpectedly prim and monosyllabic. Though unembarrassed in her pose, Jani was inwardly uncomfortable, and a little shocked at the continuous cigarette smoking of Nan and her lady friends. She wondered that the white-haired hostess could permit it. More than ever lately, Jani viewed behaviour from the Blaemawe angle. What would the village gossip say of this, that, or the other act? It was less that she had not shaken free of the "chapel" atmosphere, than that she was absorbing it anew from Tegwen Thomas and her circle.

The Partingdale evenings were chiefly musical. And Jani, too, could enjoy, at least more than the intervals of unfamiliar talk, the brilliant if not necessarily melodious performances of a professional who sometimes "dropped in." To-night there was a strange siren whom Jani watched with fascinated eyes – watched, rather than listened to. For the fingers that drew rhythmic secrets from the keyboard were obviously ruled by the sinuous graceful body, swaying in expression of the composer's soul. Jani had never seen a body clothed – or unclothed – in quite such an extraordinary fashion. The pianist's dress was of steely blue satin, high at the front, flowing in long lines from the waist, which rose bare to the shoulders at the back. A sheath of black smooth hair curved into a roll on the nape. Below it the marble skin stretched over a ripple of spine. As she moved and rocked, the skin writhed like a thing of separate life.

"Caton pawb!" thought Jani, using an old exclamation of her mother's. "She's exactly like a snake!"

Simon watched, also, from his pouffe, but he could see the pianist's face. Someone whispered behind him, that in the same dress and with the same rhythmic chords, she had spellbound a Queen's Hall audience on the previous night. But he did not know who she was. She had come in suddenly and been surrounded at the drawing-room door, and to the cries of "Lena! It's Lena! – How nice of you to come!" – he had heard her deep-toned reply – "I can't stay long – got to go on to Portico's—" . A little later she had come to the piano, sat down and spread her long fingers on the board. The dark eyes gleaming in a kind of rich pallor had given him one swift look, that thrilled him with a sense of probing magic. Dick and Nan, who had followed, fell back as she began to play.

A Jewess, of course. Anybody could see that. But could anybody see, as he did, that film of sadness behind the bold, brilliant stare, that shadow of unease behind the confidence? Successful artist, beautiful woman – mistress of your art and of your body – are you mistress of your soul? Does it rankle, does it trouble you, that it is a Jewish soul? No doubt you've cut your traces – but aren't you conscious, always, within yourself—? Simon shook himself impatiently. This was obsession. He drew his eyes reluctantly from that compelling face, closed them, and listened. The patterned notes of Liszt beat with a piercing sweetness in the air – beat through his ear into his heart. That strange lift to an intenser plane of feeling that music gave made his secret emotion more acute. Closed eyes did not shut out the dark appealing insolent glance: its meaning ravelled with the weaving threads of sound.

There was a moment of perfect silence. He got up quickly as she turned, and stood near until the first glow of talk and circling ebbed. Dick pushed through with a cup of coffee, and caught Simon's eye.

"Lena, let me introduce a new friend – Simon Black is a colleague of Ted's. Miss Rachlin's been abroad, Black, or you'd have seen her here before. Nan says this coffee's just as you like it, Lena. She says that's what you come here for. Biscuits? Harman's got them, just behind you—"

She waved the plate away, but accepted the chair that the man called Harman vacated for her. As she drew her drapery aside and sank gracefully into it, she half smiled at Simon, while she listened to what the two men, Harman and Partingdale were saying. Simon stood still, staring at her, and then blundered into speech.

"Miss Rachlin – I wonder if you – I hope you won't mind my asking – but – are you related to Miss – to Edith Miller?"

She turned those dark eyes full upon him.

"So you know my cousin Edith? – Cousin twice removed – but near enough. I'm the only one of the Rachlins she hobnobs with. Perhaps because I don't have much to do with them myself!" She laughed a little abruptly. "I haven't seen her for ages. Where is she now, the darling crank?"

"With the Hafods, in South Wales. But really – she isn't—" he hesitated.

"What? – a crank? – or a darling?" Lena Rachlin laughed again. "Perhaps you don't know her well enough to call her either."

"I know she's – sincere." He made an effort to be easy. "Don't you think her nursing scheme a sound one?"

"Oh, that!" Miss Rachlin shrugged her gleaming shoulders. Simon broke the little pause impetuously.

"As to her – Jewish ideas – it's brave of her, isn't it? I mean, to go back to that side – call herself a Jewess when she need not. Though I don't agree—"

"Ah, you don't agree?" There was soft irony in the slow rejoinder. She was looking at him curiously.

"I suppose I have a right to disagree, – since I'm a Jew myself.—"

A quick change came over the bold, mobile face. A shadow like a passing cloud veiled and ruffled it.

"Really? I shouldn't have thought it. Though now I can see *something* – it always shows, somehow, doesn't it? – except, of course, in Edith." Her laugh now had a little rasp in it. "Appearances have been most unjustly distributed in our family. Edith should have looked like me – and I like her – it would have suited us both better – and been so much truer to facts! I'm supposed to resemble Judith Rachlin, who was exactly like her father. Edith, you see, took after the wrong grandmother!"

Simon looked steadily at her.

"You both seem to me perfect as you are."

"Thanks. But I'm afraid you're not a good judge of character." He flushed at the tone.

"You mean of *blood*, perhaps?" he said coolly. "I take it you're as Jewish as myself in that respect."

Lena Rachlin raised her chin and looked down her nose at this extraordinary young man. But suddenly she laughed again.

"Really – for a Jew who disagrees with Jewish ideas, you are remarkably anxious to proclaim yourself! And why this anxiety to rope me in? No doubt you think I ought to support my charming cousin. But I'm not opposed to her. I'm just indifferent. It's my family who think she's mad. There isn't a scrap of anything Jewish about them, except their features. And they're so anxious to avoid identification that they hate my professional work – they seem to think it's a stamp, somehow!" She began to speak more rapidly, in a low tone, with a slight disconnected vehemence. "Patron of the arts – yes, that's all right – it's quite English society, and so on – but an *artist* – with a career – that's Jewish! What annoys me is that English people take the same view. Art to them isn't art – no, it's something Jewish!" She tapped her satin-shod foot impatiently. Her voice rose a little higher. "Do you read my critics? I'd welcome honest slating – if I deserved it. But what do I get? 'A touch of Semitic flamboyance' – 'The Eastern note was over-emphasised' – 'Miss Rachlin's temperament, unable to subdue itself to the cold pristine quality'—"

"Bilge!" said Dick, turning round. "I've told you what to do about it, Lena. Bleach your hair and change your name, and they'll find nothing Semitic in your art—"

"And possibly no art to speak of, either," said Harman. He had heard imperfectly, but his quick brown eyes, lighting a plain yet attractive face, met Lena Rachlin's comprehensively.

"Most of the critics are Jews, anyway" – said Dick. "Necessarily the last to care about national music or national interpretation. Of course they know that art belongs to the world—"

"And that artists may be as *a*national as *a*moral," finished Harman ironically. "Don't scowl at me, Dick. Can you deny that, primarily, the finest art is national, in conception and interpretation? First it must come poured through the mould of a people – the expression of their specific character—"

"But there's no such thing as Semitic nationality – or a Semitic artist—" broke in Lena Rachlin impatiently. "Faugh! It's dirty prejudice – bilge, as Dick says – No, Nan darling – no more coffee. It was perfect, as usual. Perhaps that's what I *do* come for – again as Dick say! Of course I knew you hadn't said it!" – She rose with a magnificent shimmer of dress and skin, and put an arm round Nan Partingdale's slight, stiff waist. "I'll just say a word to your mother, and then I must fly—" She waved the other hand at the men. As she passed Simon she inclined her head with a smile, and her glance mocked his as she murmured – "You're illogical, you know. But I'm glad Edith's found a champion."

He flushed and watched her go. He had amused her, it seemed – and riled her a little, too. What on earth had possessed him to speak out as he had done? Reluctantly he tore his gaze from her audacious back. The scaly sheen of steel-blue satin on her long, supple limbs suggested to him, also, something serpentine. As he turned his head, he met an appealing look from Jani, and moved towards her.

She was still sitting on the divan, surrounded by some women who talked across her, in that high-toned rapid manner she found disconcerting. She was tired of the strain of following their remarks.

"You haven't come to take your wife away, Mr. Black? It's

early yet – and she's going to give us one of her quaint little songs. Do sit down – there's heaps of room—"

But Simon preferred standing, and Jani got up and touched his arm.

"I'd like to walk about," she whispered. "Who's that foreign woman that played the piano? I saw you talking to her. Emlyn Richards would like to hear her play! But isn't she odd? Did you ever see a dress like that?"

The woman nearest her had caught parts of the whisper. As Simon did not speak at once, she interposed.

"Lena Rachlin isn't foreign, my dear. She's a Jewess though – and odd, as you say. But then, all these Jews have something odd about them – sinister I should call it – don't you think?" She bared her long teeth at Simon.

" Not all, surely—" he muttered. He wanted to move away, but the shimmering figure was crossing to the door, and somehow he did not wish to catch her eye again with Jani on his arm. In this corner of the room a shaded lamp screened them from view.

"Oh really, darling – not *sinister*" – said the second woman. "Vulgar, of course, and assertive, and all that. Though I must say I've met some Jews and thought they were quite ordinary English people – until I knew. Somehow, when one knows, one gets a feeling—"

Simon left her unchallenged to the feeling. Lena Rachlin had passed through the door, and he could take Jani through the crowded room. There were too many people here to-night, he thought. But he felt strangely lifted above them, lifted, too, above the easy mood in which he had arrived.

Jani sang "Ar hyd y Nos" in plaintive liquid Welsh. Everyone was charmed with the "quaintness" in which the singer's personality blended so perfectly with the song. Simon saw it through their eyes and heard it with their ears – a quality which added spice to an evening's entertainment, but had no deeper value, no claim to be taken seriously. The viewpoint was not strange. It marked the normal temperature of the party, and of similar parties that he continued to attend through the months. Only something had happened that night, in the brief encounter with Lena Rachlin, that seemed to have altered the pressure of his life, and almost the focus of his brain.

He did not meet her again for a considerable time. His visits to concert halls where she played were deliberately impersonal. He tried intently to catch the colour rather than the texture of her music, he watched her sinuous movements and dark, Hebraic face, but never attempted to see or speak to her when she left the platform. Miss Rachlin toured a great deal during that season, and was not enough in London to "drop in" again at the Partingdales: or else he missed the occasions when she did. The fact was, her "aura" was so strongly haunted by that of Edith, their dissimilarities twined by so strange and dazzling a thread, that he had an instinctive fear of perpetuating rashness in her presence.

It was another aspect of his fear that deterred him from writing home. For the first time in his life he longed for Dinah's letters. He had discouraged them too long to be surprised at their rarity. And to invite them now was not easy – harder still to comment on their omissions when they came.

He had thoughts, instead, of a note to Marjorie Newell. She had not called. Perhaps she was too busy. Her new post was at Croydon, an inconvenient distance away. He might ask her to meet him somewhere for tea. He played with the idea, but did not put it into practice – the subtle, unfaced fear kept him irresolute.

The move into the new flat absorbed less energy – and interest – than he could have supposed. Undoubtedly it was a relief to be free of the Thomas invasions, and a greater sense of comfort came with privacy and a change of furnishings. But the lack that had been conspicuous above the dairy was equally obvious here. It did not seem possible to import the true spirit of home. That spirit existed, he knew without acknowledging, in the close-packed kitchen *below* the dairy, as it did in the charming house of the Partingdales'. Why was it that he and Jani could not create it, in these pleasant rooms exclusive to themselves? Irritably he felt it must be Jani's fault. She was shiftless and a sloven. She had no gift for the intimacies of little things. Even flowers in a bowl lost their charm, when jumbled and allowed to decay. Her cooking had always been erratic, and her attempts to follow Tegwen Thomas's instructions seldom successful – even under the eye of the instructor. "Oh, bother! I haven't the patience," she would cry. "*You* finish it, Tegwen." Tinned fare replaced the strange products of emulation. But the absence of mental and spiritual food at their common table became even more marked. For this, of course, there had never been preparation – the utensils or kitchen equipment, the shrines for household gods, the gods themselves, had deliberately been omitted.

While neither of the pair had experienced appetite for such things, the vacuity, though felt, had brought no pangs. But now Jani had developed a taste for her abandoned heritage. She attended chapel regularly, not because she had grown religious – so Simon declared – but because the associations fascinated her. She enjoyed the chapel "socials," and the activities of the Welsh community with whom she grew familiar, far more than anything the Partingdale sets could provide. As Simon could not share her new enthusiasm, and she could establish no focus for it inside her home, she became absorbed in it without. Jani had the power of being attractive and enchanting, even to his own friends, as Simon had perceived: he realised that she must be doubly so to friends of her own, who encouraged and appreciated traits common to their folk. It was not hard to account for her absences and preoccupations, and the signs of hospitality which he sometimes discovered, on returning to his solitary meal. In spite of his discontent, he had not the heart – or perhaps not sufficient driving pain in that organ – to reproach or condemn her. If she had been carelessly happy, he would have tried, even, to accommodate himself to her whims. But he was puzzled by the more sombre variations in her moods – in Jani, who had never been moody! She was excitable and restless, sometimes wildly gay, singing and playing on their "instalment" piano – and at other times unaccountably depressed and almost sullen. She seldom cried, however, as she had been used to do: those facile tears that no longer moved him at all. Perhaps it was this fact that stemmed the flow, though it might have been due to a hardening of emotional arteries. Hard, at any rate, she often seemed to Simon, now.

Not only did he not attempt to interfere with her pleasures, he tacitly approved them by listening, without comment, to any account she chose to give: and at times she could be extraordinarily voluble over her visits, and the doings at the dairy, which had apparently become a centre of Welsh society. The Thomases were flourishing. They occupied their upper rooms, and entertained the more since "Baby" made it awkward for them to go out together. Ieuan Richards almost lived there, it seemed; at least, when he was not with the friends whose pretty daughter attracted him. He was able to practise music at both places, and even at Simon's flat, where he was invited with the Thomases one Sunday. Simon was obliged to agree that they must be asked occasionally, and that of course they could bring the baby. Jani's raptures over the growing infant – still amiable but no less vacuous, with its large bland face and covering of thin hair – seemed to Simon hysterical. Did she always lavish such tempestuous affection on the creature, or was she using it as a medium for venting a general excitability of mood? The more she raved, the stiffer and more silent he became.

Ieuan had grown into a fairly presentable fellow – rather short still, but not so squat. He was thin and angular, his face still pale with the miner's bleach, but his black glossy hair and beautiful large eyes gave him a distinctive look. His singing voice was pure and pleasant, if not powerful: he sang the Factotum Song from "Figaro" with great spirit. Simon congratulated him on his achievements and politely wished him further success. Ieuan received the compliments almost in silence – which might have been modesty, but seemed more like awkwardness. The fingers on his one whole hand twitched spasmodically, and he kept his gaze on the floor. In general conversation he talked with a strong Blaemawe accent and showed no trace of his boyish mockery. Yet Jani hinted that he still had it, and used it against her, though no longer to the extent of rousing her indignation. Perhaps it was she who had changed in her attitude to it. Simon had never taken seriously Jani's talk of Ieuan's taunting chase of her. The remembrance merely amused him. Ieuan, furbished up as he might be, spruce as a little gentleman, with his smattering of "commercial school" and extension education, that had fitted him for a clerical post, and the conscious airs of a platform singer – though perhaps this was the instinctive Welshman's artistry, posing unawares – was still to Simon simply a village lout. Something of this must have come through the host's superior manner, for a· spark of strange fire glinted in the guest's great eyes, when at the close of the visit, Simon echoed Jani's wish that "he would come soon again." Simon never saw him at his flat a second time.

It was about five weeks later that Simon came home unexpectedly to lunch. He had telephoned to Jani as he was leaving his office, explaining that he had left something at home which he needed for his work during the afternoon. The loan of Ted's motor-bike (Simon was contemplating a similar second-hand purchase for himself) enabled him to reach the flat under the usual time. To his surprise, Jani was hurriedly removing the traces of a meal, which had evidently been partaken of by more than one person.

"Hallo – had your lunch already? And company, too?"

Jani was wearing a new jumper and skirt, and a long necklace of turquoise beads that her husband had never seen before. She looked discomposed for a moment, then smiled.

"Yes, I had to send them off quick when your message came – l thought perhaps you wouldn't like to see visitors, as you hadn't much time to stay—"

"Sorry to push your guests off, I'm sure," said Simon. He was rather cheerful at sight of a rare dish – salmon, not tinned, but fresh. Expensive fare, as it had only just come into season, and actually trimmed with cucumber, equally new. Only the remains of a dish, it was true – but sufficient, and attractive enough on the plate into which Jani slid it.

"You did them rather well – must have been important people, eh?" He laughed as he sat down to the meal.

"Some of the sisterhood, I suppose – no, by Jove! There's a cigarette half smoked. Not by those old girls – or even the minister, I bet? Who was the lady and gentleman friend?"

"Oh well, it was only Ieuan and his girl. I saw them when I was out shopping, and they came home with me – so I had to get them something nice. Miss Jenkins hasn't been here before —"

Jani's voice was slightly muffled, coming from the kitchen stove through the half-open door. She was making fresh coffee. The voice sounded rather cross – naturally enough, he thought. Jani wasn't used to being hustled in the middle of the day.

"I hope she deserved it—" he said – "I don't know that *he* did! Still, I don't grudge it them – since they've left me a share! It's jolly good, Jani. Best meal I've had this week—"

She did not answer, and suddenly he laid down his fork. He had noticed only two used plates and sets of cutlery, on the tray which Jani had left at the table end."

I say, Jani – I hope you had *yours*!"

"Oh yes, indeed – you can finish it all up. Here's your coffee."

It had boiled over, and had a bitter burnt taste. But he did not complain. The incident completely vanished from his mind on his return again that evening, when he found Jani out, and a letter with the Blaemawe post-mark on the mantelpiece.

For several seconds he stared at the envelope. Impossible not to recognise that handwriting – but impossible – incredible – that she had written to him – He tore the flap with his fingers, took out the letter, and looked at the signature. There was no mistake. "Yours sincerely, Edith Miller."

"Dear Mr. Black," she wrote. "You will probably be surprised at hearing from me. But you are aware that I am at Blaemawe, and that I have had the pleasure of knowing your people for some time past. It is on their account that I have decided to write to you. While visiting your parents only as a friend, I have naturally been able to learn very fully their state of health. It will not be news to you that your father is suffering from a painful condition of the limbs – perhaps you do not know exactly *how* painful. I do not wish to alarm you, but I think you ought to know that he needs special treatment at once if he is to be saved from very serious trouble. Such treatment is not available here, but I can arrange for him to receive it at a London hospital, where the services of specialists can be secured. Treatment at this stage may prevent the necessity of a major operation. But should the necessity arise, it will, of course, be wisest to have it carried out in the best possible conditions. I tell you this frankly because. I think you will wish to help, and to share my responsibility in advising this course. I hope you will come to Blaemawe as soon as possible, and allow Doctor Williams to give you fuller details.

It may seem strange that such a request should come from me rather than from a member of your family but you will realise that I understand the case better than they can do, and that I have avoided discussing it too freely with them.

I take this opportunity of saying that I hope you are happy, and finding all the satisfaction you expected in your work."

XXI

THE DRAWING-ROOM at Hafod had long wide windows overlooking an aspect of the grounds that Simon had never seen: gardens, of which the prettiest feature was an avenue of almond trees, just now in full spray, and a green lawn tennis court, brought to an end somewhat abruptly by a bleak hill, rearing in contempt of the thick boundary hedge. On the far side of that hill were the coal pits owned by Sir Gwilym. Cageheads could be glimpsed from the bend, smoke curled incessantly around, and the scream of whistle and rattle of truck were familiar sounds, only faintly subdued. It was an aspect with a character of its own, in keeping with the soil and the men who lived upon – and within – it; yet likely to disconcert the visitor whose eye was filled with the beauty of the main approach, the elm-gladed vista of the park and swan-ridden lake.

The slight fall in Simon's expectancy on being shown into the drawing room was not, however, due to disappointment in the view. The long windows were open, as it was an unusually warm day for March: and the coal-streaked panorama existed for him only in the figure into which all there was of loveliness verged. To have stood alone in the room watching Edith, as she reached up to examine a branch in exquisite blossom, might have been enough. But as his glance reached out, it was blurred by the shape of Lady Hafod, turning from the window to greet him.

"How d'you do, Mr. Black?" He took her hand, soft and

delicate, without the thrill that ought to have come of contact with the Lady of Shalott – with, instead, a revulsion at her presence. But the next moment he repaid her look of interest with his own. To have found a mere old lady in the Magic Dame would not have been too strange: what was a little surprising was to see the still youthful mould of a lovely woman – hair unfaded and carefully dressed, the slightest crumple at eyes and mouth of rose leaf skin, a slim and dainty uprightness of figure. She seemed to have aged even less than he had imagined in the stolen glimpse of years ago. Impossible to believe her old. Yet this could not be youth, only a masked semblance, that pleased without the power to enchant. Her voice, however, had still its lure of music in Simon's ears.

"So you walked all the way? It's a delightful day, of course. And my granddaughter always walks to the village – unless I'm with her." Her eyes appraised him kindly as she talked and listened to his replies. Then she turned again to the open window.

"Dar-ling!"

Surely Edith had heard their voices before that soft call came? She had let the branch spring back, and was standing motionless, gazing away from the house. Now she looked round. He saw her face, sweet with welcome.

"Go and look at the trees, Mr Black, before the sun goes. Aren't they charming?"

"Very." He had stepped out immediately on the terrace, and made for the path along which Edith was approaching.

"I'll order tea at once, darling – Mr. Black must need it after his walk." Lady Hafod retired from the window.

Had Edith grown? Taller, more overpoweringly a woman,

she seemed to have raced his dominating inches. Their glances drew together on a level.

"I needn't ask how you are" – he stammered out. "You look – better – than ever—"

"But you are thin, and very pale," she said as if involuntarily. "Are you well?"

"Quite well." At that moment he felt the keenest sense of well-being, simply because she had showed concern. But as she smiled, her face composed to a frank friendliness, something lowered in him once again.

"You arrived last night?"

"Yes. I should have come here straightaway, but for your message about to-day. I hope I – didn't keep you away. From my people's house, I mean. My sister tells me you have spent every Friday evening there for the last month."

"You must have wished to be alone with them – and naturally they would want you to themselves."

"They look on you almost as one of the family." He said it with the surprise that had overwhelmed him at his parents' talk.

"It's kind of them. I'm a stranger, all the same."

"It seems impossible," he murmured.

"That I'm a stranger? Or that I'm like one of the family?" She spoke in her old tone of banter – so like Lady Hafod's – and moved forward under the trees.

"You've been more like an angel to them. What I can't believe is that – that—" He hesitated. It was terribly difficult to speak to her. She had grown, undoubtedly: not only in height, in beauty, in self-possession – in all the attributes he had known were hers – but in some new inner quality he could not gauge. It was that, more than the bright cool air of friendliness, and the superficial Lady Hafod-like tone, that held him off.

"That angels exist – or miracles come to pass?" she said lightly. "You are right. Everything turns out to be natural, once you look below the surface. And yet it is a sort of miracle that you and I are here."

"It is," he said desperately. "That's what I can't believe – that you've – forgiven me—"

"But it isn't for me to forgive – anything. Besides, wasn't I rather horrid to you? Perhaps you've forgotten; it's a long time ago, and so much has happened. I hear that everything has gone well with you – all you wanted has come your way—" She broke off in her rapid speech, tilting her head upward, though without pausing in her walk. "Have you admired the almonds? Please don't come in without a good look – grandma is so proud of their bloom. It's earlier than usual this year. I hope you won't tell her you've seen any trees as advanced, on the way from Paddington."

"I didn't notice," he said, staring up obediently at the lace of pinky-white – there seemed to him rays between of blue and gold. "All the way I was reading your letter, trying to understand – more than you had written. The things my people have told me since I came have cleared up a good deal – but not everything—"

"You realise about your father?"

"Oh, the illness – He doesn't seem much worse to me, except that he hobbles more—"

"He should not be on his feet at all." Her face grew stern. "I've told him he must rest—"

"He obeys you, I believe, almost entirely. But either he wanted me to think him better, or else he actually *is*—"

"He can't be, yet, unfortunately."

"You must be right. You'll tell me exactly what the trouble is, and what has to be done?"

"Of course. Doctor Williams has promised to look in this afternoon, if his calls allow – we'll wait, shall we? and talk it over when he comes. He never takes tea, so we needn't wait for *that*—"

They had reached the terrace. She sprang up the steps, and he followed her into the room. Lady Hafod was seated near the fire, a tray of silver and china on a table before her. A butler was closing the door.

"The sun has quite gone, I'm afraid," Lady Hafod shivered slightly, and put her hand to the lace of her tea gown. "Darling, the windows had better be shut—"

Simon moved back and drew the long glass panels together. He had a dreamlike feeling of intimate return. The high white drawing-room with its gilt decorations, the fire leaping in its stand on the marble-domed hearth, the fragile china on the glinting silver tray, offered nothing that was homelike to his sense. Yet every detail seemed to compose a familiar setting for Edith's head, as she leaned near her grandmother's elbow.

Lady Hafod approved him, it was evident. She liked the admiration in his eyes, though she was too used to young admiration to be either touched or amused by it. Other things in her guest's manner and appearance won her from an initial lack of interest to a real rather than simulated graciousness. She asked frank questions about his career, and proffered encouraging comment. Edith listened with a faint smile to their discussion of London. There was not much, it seemed, that Simon had left unexplored. But his enthusiasm found no echo in his hostess.

"I used to love London," she said with a sigh. "I don't care for it at all now. If it were not for Edith, I should never go up to town—"

"Grandma, I protest! It isn't on my account that you are going up in May."

"In May?"

"You know you promised Lena. If it isn't the wiles of London, it must be the wiles of Lena—"

"Ah, I couldn't resist *her*!" Lady Hafod sighed again. "She's so much like your mother – I was startled by it – not having seen her for years. But you'll be there too, my darling."

"Not if I'm to get on with my work at Millicombe."

"You'll be able to leave it for a month, surely, my pet?" Lady Hafod's tone was pleading. "Of course you can come back with me."

Edith shook her head decidedly.

"I'm sorry, grandma. It isn't possible to change my plans for the year. I shall go to London on Monday to arrange about Mr. Black's father, and I'm due at Millicombe at the end of April. I can't leave again until I go back finally to my London work."

"I – I hope the arrangements for my father aren't the stumbling block—" stammered Simon. He felt a little shocked at the way in which Edith over-rode Lady Hafod.

"Not at all," said Edith coolly. "Lady Hafod knows that I must be in London during April. I always spend Passover with Grannie Miller."

There was a moment's silence. Simon held his frail legged cup at a dangerous angle. Lady Hafod relieved him of it with a somewhat sharp movement.

"I ought to be in Millicombe myself during May," she said.

"As soon as Gwilym and Ann are back at Hafod, I shall go on to Devon and stay there with you. I'll write to Lena and say I can't come." She smiled. "Perhaps I'll go up in the autumn instead – she isn't going abroad this year. Have you heard Lena Rachlin play, Mr. Black?"

"Several times – at the Queen's Hall. And once – the first time – at a friend's house. She told me she was a relative of yours, Miss Miller."

Edith smiled and looked swiftly at him – an inscrutable look that he found exciting. It stirred into ferment the thought that had made him address her so abruptly. Had she seen Lena Rachlin lately – and heard of that meeting? Was it through him that Lena had taken up the thread of relationship – and had she conveyed the fact? Edith said nothing. It was Lady Hafod who answered his remark.

"Yes – a sort of cousin, She played at Tavcastle and Dawport during her recent tour, and stayed with us. My son and his wife were home, and we gave a dinner for her. It was a wonderful evening! Patti came, though she doesn't visit much nowadays, and she was delighted. She wanted to arrange a party at Craig-y-nos, but there wasn't time – Lena could not fit it in. Ah, what a musician! But you know, my darling, your mother would have been just as fine. It's simply extraordinary – the resemblance in many ways. But my Judith had a more lovable nature." She stroked the head beside her.

Simon listened, in a kind of abashment. The picture called up by Lady Hafod disposed of his absurd idea that Lena Rachlin and Edith had talked of him. But Edith still wore that baffling smile. She said suddenly:

"I don't suppose Lena would care to be called lovable. She prefers her reputation of being hard. But she can be gentle when she likes. She was very sweet to your mother, Mr. Black."

"My – mother?"

"We met your mother in the village, and I introduced them. Lena told her she had seen you."

They *had* talked of him – they *had*! That queer dance of the nerves began again. But Edith turned directly to Lady Hafod.

"Grandma, Mrs. Black recognised Lena at once."

"You mean she saw that Lena was a Jewess," said Lady Hafod calmly. "That's not very remarkable, I suppose."

"I don't mean that, grandma. What Mrs. Black saw was the likeness between Lena and grandfather Rachlin."

"But – how?" Lady Hafod's bewilderment was reflected in Simon's face. She looked at him. "I understand you know something of our family history, Mr. Black. But surely your mother did not know my husband?"

"Not to my knowledge, Lady Hafod. I never heard of it."

Edith laughed softly.

"There was no personal acquaintance. But in a way your parents have known about my grandfather, ever since his photograph came into their hands – you remember, grandma?"

"Ah – the photograph – yes, I remember – I took it there to have the glass replaced. You were a child, darling – and simply heartbroken when the picture fell from the wall!" She leaned forward and took the laughing face tenderly between her hands. "It was all I could do to pacify you by arranging to get it mended at once."

"Poor grandma! But I *was* pacified, I'm sure – the mending was done so promptly and well. I thanked Mr. Black for it only the other day. I don't suppose you knew, grandma, that in place of the thin wavy greenish glass that was broken, Mr. Black put in a piece of stout clear twenty-one ounce,

English—" her eyebrows arched at Simon – "instead of the fifteen-ounce, *foreign*, that's usually considered good enough for pictures. You see I've learned quite a lot about your father's business!"

"But, darling," said Lady Hafod, absently fingering the golden hair, "I had no idea that Mr. and Mrs. Black could tell from a photograph—"

"Why not? It's a particularly revealing one, in profile – an unmistakable Jewish head, dark, aquiline—"

"He was very handsome," said Lady Hafod dreamily. "A true Rachlin."

"Of course. If mother was so like him, and Lena – you see why Mrs. Black recognised her."

"Yes – Lena, certainly – even more than your mother. There's nothing of the Rachlin in *you*, my pet – nobody could be recognised in you but myself. Why, everyone who knew me has always said, you are just Cynthia Lansome all over again!"

Edith made no response. Simon rose abruptly and stood leaning against the mantelpiece. He did not know that even the majestic pillared marble, failed to dwarf the lines of his figure.

"I don't recall hearing my people speak of the picture," he said. "You were too young to understand," said Lady Hafod, "and probably you never saw it."

"But I did! I brought it back here!"

"*You* brought it?"

"Yes – don't you remember, Lady Hafod, a gaping little boy, who arrived just in time – or was it, perhaps, the *wrong* time? You were in a desperate hurry to catch a train for London, and hustle your granddaughter off with you – much to that gaping little boy's regret. He thought you both the most wonderful beings on this earth!" – "And thinks so still" – he added inaudibly. Whether or not his eyes spoke, Edith lowered her own, and did not utter the gay rejoinder on her tongue.

Lady Hafod too, was silent for a moment. Then she said:

"So it was you." Her tone and glance had sharpened. The blue orbs, lighter than Edith's, colder, with that sea-filmed coldness that belonged to English eyes, were raised to Simon in newly-intent regard. "How strange! Perhaps, after all, you *did* come at the wrong time—"

"Oh, no, grandma dear! Surely you meant me to see the picture before we left?"

"For all that, my love, you'll agree it was the wrong time, as Mr. Black says – since it was really that little boy who helped, at the last moment, to make up my mind – about keeping you away from everything and everybody Jewish—"

"Grandma!"

Both Edith and Simon stared incredulously at the exquisite, fair-haired old lady. A sudden warp of age had marred the rose-leaf skin. She relaxed her own gaze and smiled pensively before her.

"It's true, Edith. I was undecided about you. It was just at that time it had come to me that the wisest plan for your happiness, as well as mine, was complete separation from your Jewish relatives. I was going to London with that plan in my mind. Still, – I wasn't quite sure. Something held me back – and the photograph – it worried me – until the moment when I saw the gaping little boy – forgive me, Mr. Black, for using your words again. But I recall the fact vividly now – the way in which it struck me, as I watched the boy's eyes fixed on my little darling" – she hesitated, looked from one to the other, and finished somewhat lamely – " I mean, I was suddenly convinced that I was right—"

There was another pause. Simon looked puzzled. A deep spot of colour spread in Edith's cheek. She seemed a little startled and anxious as she met her grandmother's eyes. Lady Hafod continued with more ease.

"Ah, my dears, I know now it was all very stupid of me. As if I could alter the course of nature – and especially when nature had an Edith on her side!" Her soft, lingering laugh was like a gracious retreat. She patted the arm extended near hers. "I'm content, at least, to have my share in these days—"

Simon swam in a tide of thwarted comprehension. A spark of his old resentment flared at the smile growing on Edith's lips. Was it at him she was directing her air of restored assurance? Did she think she would conquer him as she had conquered her grandmother? (And in his inmost heart he was astounded at the feat – to have conquered Lady Hafod, that towering citadel!)

The spark was quenched in a cool, sweet wave. Such a smile, rising and enveloping him, might drown a man and welcome—.

He started to find Lady Hafod scrutinising him again. "You are married to a Blaemawe girl, I think, Mr. Black? Did your wife come down with you?"

"No – she did not – she could not come." He stammered a little, not only because of the abruptness, the sense of some underlying deliberation in Lady Hafod's query, but with the effort of recalling Jani. Since his arrival home he had scarcely thought of her. It was strange she should be so shadowy, here in Blaemawe, where she belonged. Even when he brought her firmly to mind, he was unable to account for the astonishing fact that Jani, who had pestered him months before to take her to Blaemawe, had declined to accompany him now. He had been too relieved to press her or to speculate on her reasons. Jani's whims were not worth serious attention. She – and they – seemed vaguer than ever as he answered Lady Hafod.

A few moments later Doctor Williams was announced. Simon met a stoutish young man with a shrewd square face, a genial air, and an almost unmodified accent.

"But you are not the Doctor Williams I knew—" Simon exclaimed after the first greetings.

"Ah, you mean old James," said Lady Hafod. "There isn't even a relationship, is there, doctor? – I thought not. Poor James has practically retired. He does very little now—"

"He never did much," said Edith. "The dear old man means well – but he's hopelessly behind the times. You'll find the new partner quite different, Mr. Black."

"I have a good friend in Miss Miller, you see," said the doctor, smiling at her. Simon saw – more, perhaps, than was reasonable. It set up a perverse desire to dispute her view.

"But old Doctor Williams is all right, surely. He was always decent to us – we kids liked him. When we had measles or whooping cough and so on, he was first rate. We always got well quickly under him – too quickly, he used to say."

Edith laughed. "You were a healthy brood. And really – he couldn't very well go wrong over those childish things—"

"I don't remember any other illness in the family. Except my father's rheumatism."

"Exactly – that's what Dr James calls it." Edith exchanged a significant glance with Williams. It annoyed Simon still more.

"And I suppose you've found that it isn't," he said irritably. The young doctor bent considering eyes upon him. He no longer smiled as he said in a conciliatory tone,

"Well, now, all doctors are liable to mistakes in diagnosis, especially with a disease like this. I don't blame old Williams in the least. There aren't many modern men who understand Thromboangeitis obliterans. It just happens that I saw a lot of cases in hospital. And even so I might not have spotted it in your father if Miss Miller hadn't got in first. She knows as much as I do about Polish legs."

"Polish legs!" said Lady Hafod, in a slightly scandalised voice.

"That's the popular term, grandma," said Edith. "It's easier than saying Thrombo etc., isn't it?"

"But why Polish?" Simon asked her.

"Because, as a matter of fact, it occurs mostly in Polish Jews. It's also known as Buerger's Disease – after the surgeon who made discoveries about it. He was a Jew himself. Naturally" – Edith's rapid tones deepened – "I took a special interest in the subject."

Doctor Williams nodded. They exchanged another glance. So he knew, thought Simon. Evidently the "secret" was not too rigidly kept, even at Hafod. Or had she known him in London?

"It's fortunate Miss Miller made such a study of it. The early signs are indeterminate. Rheumatic pains, as I said – various symptoms of defective circulation – troublesome corns, chilblains, and so on. The next stage is more marked. Cramp spasms, feet blanching, and skin affection. Miss Miller's observations were made at what was practically the height of this stage. The third and most acute is just setting in – septic toes, intense pain, insomnia, prostration. The inevitable result, hitherto, has been partial if not complete loss of limbs."

"Loss – of limbs?" – stammered Simon. He had listened

with increasing uneasiness. The doctor, watching him closely, had made a sudden change into abrupt precise speech. It was as if he had determined to give his hearer a shock.

"Amputation," he said curtly.

"Good God!" exclaimed Simon. He was thoroughly awakened at last from his trance. In a flash he realised how superficial had been his concern with his father's state. Had he even tried to understand it? Pre-occupation with the fact of meeting Edith had dulled his sense of urgency, struggling to react to her letter. He had merely taken for granted what he had seen and heard at home – the taciturnity of the patient, the uninformed anxiety of his mother and sisters. He had not looked for, and therefore had not found, more than a slight accentuation of familiar features.

"Surely something can be done? That was not what you meant, was it?" – he looked at Edith, his eyes dilating. "You wrote about a special treatment – a remedy, I thought—"

"Yes, yes," she said eagerly, but gave way at once to the doctor's interposition.

"I said – inevitable hitherto. There is a special treatment – a recent discovery – a preventive operation which has already been successful in a number of cases. I am cerrtain—" for once Simon delighted in the emphatic roll of r's – "it will be successful in your father's, if undertaken immediately. We have not told him about it yet. Miss Miller thought it best to leave that to you. The idea of going into a London hospital – into any hospital – may be disagreeable to your people, she thinks. Of course you'll use your influence to persuade them."

"My influence?" thought Simon. "But she has more influence with them already than I ever had—" Aloud he said – "Why not a nursing home?"

"Expensive – fees heavier, of course. But if you can manage it—"

"It could be managed," said Simon stiffly. He made a quick calculation of resources. He had saved fifty pounds towards a continental trip. In May he intended to sit for a special examination. The higher post he was confident of securing would mean a considerable increase of salary. All he could scrape together meanwhile he must add to his parents' store. But it was embarrassing to ask for figures at the moment. Lady Hafod was looking slightly bored.

"Of course it could be managed," said Edith.

It was not difficult to read those generous eyes. Only he could not let his parents accept money – even a loan – from *her*! She looked away instantly from his flush and stare.

"But really, it isn't necessary, is it, doctor?" She spoke faster and more decisively. "Mr. Black might feel more lonely – more unhappy – in a nursing home, than in, say the London – or the Jewish Hospital. The wards are quite comfortable. And the facilities for a Jewish patient can so easily be arranged."

"And the – the treatment?"

"May have even better chances of success," said Doctor Williams. "The attention will be perfect. Of course, you can pay the hospital – all you can—"

"What exactly is it – I mean the preventive operation?"

"Peritarterial sympathectomy," said the doctor, his shrewd black eyes twinkling. "Removal of the fine nerves surrounding the main artery. I know a first-class man who's done a few lately. As soon as you decide – the sooner the better – I'll write to him."

"I suppose my father will have to remain there for some time. Can you tell me how long?"

"Oh, about six or seven weeks."

"It means – over the Passover" – Simon addressed Edith with sudden frankness. It was wonderful, the sense of ease her nod confirmed.

"I'm afraid so. It will be rather a break for your people, not to be able to celebrate *Seder* in the usual way. But I will see they do not miss it too much. A good deal can be done – and perhaps your mother and sisters will be able to spend the week very near – the hospital. They can stay at Grannie Miller's. I am sure she would be delighted."

She had thought of everything. How could one help yielding to her at last, unquestioningly? The onset of alarm and apprehension on his father's account was stayed at her hands – delicate flesh-and-blood, strong as rock. The other tide rushed back, dimming his eyes as they rested on one of those hands, laid lightly on the arm of her grandmother's chair. He dared not lift them higher. The shadow he had noted on Lady Hafod's face – it was something deeper than the shadow cast by the subdued standard lamp behind her. It merged, in some mysterious way, with the dark haze of Jani, cutting him off from the sweet brightness above. Bright – bright – too dazzlingly bright! She always spent the Passover with her Bubele – and if his own mother and sisters were to be there, too, would he not be expected to join them? This was no time to remember that he had forsworn the Seder rites. But the cool voice joined to the doctor's steadied him. He forced his own note to the level of theirs.

They remained discussing details a little longer. Then Williams rose briskly, and bent over Lady Hafod's hand in courtier-like farewell. The mixture of matter-of-fact energy with emotional flair in the Welshman's manner won Simon too, in spite of himself. He accepted an offer of a "lift" on the motor-bike to the gates of the road. Edith accompanied them to the starting point, under a high lamp, lighting the gravel where long ago the fat coachman had waited to take her from the little boy's rapt gaze.

"Then it's settled," she said to the tall man looking at her with those same eyes. "You'll talk it over with them in the morning – not to-night. No need to spoil their rest. And in the afternoon I shall call to back you up."

"It depends far more on you than on me," he said. "They believe in you."

"It is Doctor Williams they must believe in," she said. "Fortunately, that should be easy – even for them. It isn't just luck that he's keen on Buerger's. You must get him to tell you how he took it up!"

"Was there – a special reason?"

"Doctor, do tell him!"

Williams was coaxing his cold engine. He looked round at Simon with an odd smile.

"Ever know a chap called Brenner? No? A decent chap. A Jew, though he didn't look much like one. Something like you—" The doctor's voice was raised as he continued bending over his machine; his words were punctuated by the noise of false starts. "We were in the same medical school. I hadn't much to do with him until one day, when we went the rounds under Henry Lockett. H. L. wasn't a bad old stick, but he had the usual down on Jews. And he sniffed at Buerger's. There was a case in the ward, and he talked a lot of rot about it. Trouble was, he went on, to generalise. Told us not to be taken in by the fuss Jewish patients made. Squeal at nothing and exaggerate like the devil, he said. 'Those Jew things' he called them. The fellows sniggered. But all at once there was a dead silence. Brenner was standing forward, stiff and straight, rather white, with a funny look in his eye. His voice shot out like a bullet. 'What was that you said, sir?' H. L. it was who turned red and stopped, as if he didn't know what to do next. Then he said quietly, 'I beg your pardon, Brenner,' and went on to the next case. Not much in it, perhaps. Though when you know what students are – especially meds. – and what it means to challenge a prof. – Anyway, it impressed me. I like to see a fellow stick up for his race." The engine, still spluttering, began suddenly to throb with a succession of steady beats. "Brenner and I took up Buerger's together. You see it's come in useful for you."

"Yes," said Simon. Edith retired. In the shadows he had seen her eyes widen and glow, brighter than the faint stars above. They would never shine like that for him, he thought. Vaulting recklessly into position after the doctor, he nearly fell off, and for some moments clutched and swayed ignominiously; Williams would think him deuced clumsy … after he had boasted too of his steady seat with Ted…. They swerved explosively into the dark avenue of elms, and reached the lodge gates before his discomfiture waned. The doctor was in a hurry to proceed in the opposite direction. Simon set off towards the village.

The friendly dark ended too soon at the illuminated hives of the "Black Swan" and the railway station. Saturday night was in progress. Shoppers straggled the irregular pavement that alternated with cottage walls and hedges. Youths shuffled behind squat men in and out of public-houses: already some were retching too audibly and visibly, in the foul passages that opened to the street. In the "square," formed by an intersection of the highway by two stony lanes, one leading up to the Wimberry Mountain, the other down to the river, a drum was being beaten by a little fat greasy man in a red-braided uniform. Surrounding him were two others similarly garbed, a few women in poke-bonnets and a number of children who clapped their hands solemnly as one of the women shook a tambourine. The Salvation Army had commenced its weekly mission to the drunkards of Blaemawe.

As Simon came up, the drummer was beating, not his drum but his breast, and in a hoarse alcoholic voice acclaiming the Lamb of God, who had cleansed him in His Redeeming Blood after fifty years of sin. With groans and Hallelujahs, and strange confusion of Old Testament imagery, he recounted, in illiterate Anglo-Welsh the delights given up at the call of the Lord.

"The new sacrifice of Isaac," thought Simon, grinning. He knew Jepthah Isaac: the village reprobate for years had varied drunken bouts with "religion," as practised by the tolerant Salvationists: but never had his Hebrew names and debasement of Hebrew terms seemed so comic. Tragi-comic. The universal right of mankind to the spiritual store of Israel – yes. But this distortion of one's ancestral symbols! Perhaps, vulgarity apart, it was no more intrinsically funny than their perpetuation in any other church – or state…

Simon turned sharply down the lane towards the river. The essence of Edith, pervading him, suffusing his faculties in vivid beams, must surely disperse in the harsh acrid air of his wife's old home. He had not yet seen Jani's parents, and could not defer longer a visit to Ty Gwyn. His boots squelched on the muddy bank, as he followed the course of the black, soft-rushing water and his excited thoughts. It came to him in a queer fantasy of comparison, that the pebbles on which the stream stumbled and gurgled, were so many Janikins; the elusive glints of starshine, rays of Edith; and the water flowing, flowing, rising to the rays, sinking to the stones – himself, the fluid, ceaseless Jew. He stood still for some moments in a stubborn pause. Then drew his lagging footsteps up the steep cinder track towards the privet-grown white villa.

XXII

"THE FLOWERS? Yes, from Miss Miller. You know that for Shabbos she used to bring specially nice ones. And this time she has not forgotten. Just this morning came a long box for me from – what you call it, Millcom? The Sister could not take her eyes away – nor her nose. She only smells and smells. But they are *také* fine. Like Miss Miller herself, noble and fragrant—"

Simon smiled. The Yiddish terms would have conveyed no sense of poetry to him if the image had not been of Edith – and if she herself had not opened his ears to the fact that his father had a poetical turn.

"Did she write?"

"Write? What should she write? *Ungewunschen*, of course, on a little card. After all, it is only a pair of days since she is gone."

"It seems more like a pair of weeks," said Simon, but he no longer smiled. Instead he sighed unguardedly. He did not notice the glance his father gave him. He was thinking of the interminable stretch of time until September. Especially if she did not write. No doubt when his father was home, she would write there. But not to him. There was no prospect of a letter – not even a *wunsch* on a *cartel* – from Millicombe to Simon. He sighed again. His father turned abruptly towards the wall.

"But it is good that she has gone."

"I don't know," said Simon absently. "Oh – I suppose it is good work that she is doing, in Millicombe." As soon as he had said it, it flashed across him that his father might have meant something else. He sat up with a jerk.

Not until then had he noticed how still the ward had become, after the bustle of the evening ablutions. Sounds of traffic from the congested streets beat in through the windows. In this western corner, screened for comfort and not for any sinister reason, the May daylight lingered in seeming concentration. It pooled in vivid delicacy the tall white lilac on a table near the foot of the bed.

At this hour Simon was here only as a privileged visitor. Besides it was practically the eve of his father's departure from hospital. On Sunday the patient was to leave for home, convalescent, and with the assurance of renewed health. A remarkably quick and progressive cure had followed the first uncertain weeks. In mind as well as in body Gedaliah Black appeared eased of torment. Father and son had never been nearer each other, had never talked together so familiarly and unimpededly. In the soluble spirit of Edith's sympathies, many barriers had melted, as Simon was keen to perceive. But it had not occurred to him that his father's insight might reach as far. Or even further? He felt himself grow hot as he sat, perfectly still, waiting for Gedaliah's next words. They came hesitatingly, yet clearly.

"Everywhere – she will do good. For she is good. She has a true Jewish heart. But – my son – you must not think so much – about her."

The silence in the ward deepened. Such coughs and mutterings as made the background of sound behind the screen ceased, as if in suspension of all wakeful sense. He bent towards the table below the bed, and inhaled the scent of the tall white blooms, proud and graceful in their heavy glass jar.

His sniff seemed to him a loud vibration in the air. When he forced himself to look round at the bed, he saw that his father was asleep. The bearded face lay closed upon the pillow, the breath fretting lightly the inscrutable lips. Had this dry, reticent man, remote as Job from modern ideas of romance – had he penetrated his *Goyish* son's secret? Were his words a reluctant warning – an intimation that he saw, condoned, yet feared, the sweetest danger that son had encompassed?

Half thrilled, half embarrassed, Simon watched for some moments the placid form. Then he rose, tore a sprig from the clustered lilac and stuck it in his coat. Its fragrance went with him into the darkening streets, as he made his way through the broad Whitechapel area, past the little shuttered shops with the familiar foreign names, past the familiar foreign faces under shabby high hats, donned already in pious haste for *shool* (synagogue).

Outside the station he hesitated. One plunge into that roaring maw and he would leave the atmosphere which, against his will, had reclaimed him. It was Edith and not his father who had made him linger in it. But now it seemed as if they were leagued together to chain him down. His desire urged him towards Caramel Place. There, in her absence, he would feel Edith's being, vivid and more real than even Hafod gave it to him. In part it came from Bubele herself, its troubling stayed within the sphere of peace. For there was in that fragile personality, an ineffable sense, as of some inviolable quietude in whirl and din. He would have gone to it now, but for the incoming Sabbath. He turned irresolutely, let the hustling crowd push him to the ticket-office, and regretted it the moment the doors clanged behind him. After all, she would have welcomed him, in her fine unasking courtesy, even though she disapproved his overstaying the twilight hour to travel home on *Shabbas*. She was aware that he did so, in any case. But she would not reproach him. That was the marvellous thing about this ultra-*froom* (pious) old lady – rigid as were her views of ritualistic observance, she never forced them upon another, she did not harass or condemn. His mother's loud – voiced lamentations found no echo in one whom she acknowledged, with awe, her superior in piety. He had pointed out once, in a moment of irritation (and there had been many such moments, in the brief week of the family visit) that Bubele's methods were the most effective. "You see how her granddaughter carries out every religious minutiae in her house, though she isn't expected to do it." "Ah, Edith Miller," said Mrs. Black, making a Yiddish sing-song of the name that exasperated Simon further – " she heeds her Bubele as such a *koshere nashoma* (pure soul) ought to be heeded," and she added the favourite phrase that Gedaliah had used, "besides – she has a Jewish heart."

His wife could be as galling as his mother, though her spleen freed him actually from clash and yoke. She had refused the invitation to Caramel Place.

"A sort of religious service going on all the evening at the table – no, indeed! If *you* got to put up with it, *I* haven't. And I don't believe they want me, either – not asking me till the last minute. I'd rather go round to Tegwen's for supper. They are having fresh pork pies in at the dairy."

Her husband did not assure her that the "last minute" delivery of Bubele's message was due to his own half-heartedness. He knew that she was not really offended. Had she wished to go, she would have over-ridden any objection, fancied or actual. But her attitude had changed completely.

She seemed to have forgotten that she had ever played with the idea of becoming a Jewess. Her contact with his family was perfunctory, in the hospital and out. It was an accident accounted fortunate by both that enabled him to excuse her absence from the *Seder* (Passover Feast). In the morning, as she lit the gas for the breakfast kettle, Jani fainted suddenly. She recovered very soon, and appeared none the worse, agreeing with Simon that a whiff of escaping gas had overcome her – "That old gas stove wants seeing to, it's been leaking a long time" – But he did not scruple to exaggerate the incident. And curiously enough, Mrs. Black, unlike Dinah, was convinced of the truth of the plea of illness when they met at the hospital, and afterwards at the flat. Jani, she declared, *looked* ill: she was certainly pale and haggard, with the yellow tint prominent again around her cheeks. The furtive air with which she avoided her mother-in-law's scrutiny was interpreted as "sulks" by Dinah. Simon was surprised and relieved at the tolerance shown by his mother. She seemed positively to "humour" Jani, to close with tact any opening for dissension. The visit passed off well. But as soon as they were alone together, Jani burst into a prolonged fit of crying. She scarcely spoke to Simon for the rest of the day, was peevish and dolorous by turns. Sharing his sister's view, Simon made no attempt at conciliation. Indeed, he asked himself, what was there to conciliate? He ignored her moods now as completely as she ignored his. Since his return from Blaemawe she had been absent-minded, more and more neglectful, openly indifferent. At first she did not show irritability, and he was glad to be left alone, to drift back into dreams, to spend as much time as he could with his father, to concentrate on fresh studies and plans. He had felt it his duty to give a full account of his visit to Ty Gwyn, even to express, with unusual warmth, a concern for old Lloyd.

"He isn't treated properly – it's a shame to let the fools of Blaemawe make a mock of him. Why, there's something fine in the old man, though he *does* believe in a lot of nonsense. And I'm afraid he's breaking up. He wants to see you soon – so does your mother. But they won't hear of coming to town. I think you ought to go down and see them. If I can't get away soon, you might go alone." She smiled suddenly.

"Yes, I could go by myself. I would like to see my mother – and some of the others. Perhaps I'll go before very long." She tossed her head and gave an impudent look directly into his eyes. "When your people have moved away."

Simon shrugged his shoulders, unruffled.

It was during the Passover week that her easy carelessness, her gay impertinence of manner, collapsed into nervous gloom. He supposed that the presence of his family and the religious celebrations really disconcerted her, in spite of her airily proclaimed scorn. She could not by any possibility, he thought, have guessed about Edith. He had told her as little as he could; she knew already all the Blaemawe gossip of Miss Miller's doings. The revelations of a Jewish grandmother he made purposely vague. Jani was not curious enough to understand more than that an old Jewish lady in the East End had some connection with Miss Miller's nursing schemes. She had become excited, however, at the idea of Lady Hafod's granddaughter as a guest in her rooms and invited some of her Welsh friends to meet her. Edith seemed her easy, gracious self, but to Simon, with his preoccupations as host, the evening was a disappointment. He wished miserably that he had been merely her fellow-guest – then he might have had a chance to talk to her, to receive more than a cool hand and a vague glance at coming and going. Even Jani had seen that "Miss Miller didn't take much notice of you, Simon." There was a malicious note in her voice as she said it in bed next morning. She had been asleep while Simon dressed and breakfasted, and had only begun to yawn languidly when he came to the door to call out a brief – "good morning – I'm off" – But her sudden animated comments on the party detained him. "They all enjoyed themselves, after all. Miss Miller didn't take much notice of you, Simon. But she talked a lot to me about Blaemawe, and father. The girls liked her, although they expected somebody more stylish. Mrs. Howells says that's how all the big people are – very homely when they visit you and are working for your good, but grand when they are by themselves."

"By themselves?" said Simon stupidly, unable to determine how much was silly prattle, how much intentional sarcasm, yet convinced that she had no suspicion of his feelings.

"In company with their own sort of people, of course. Those friends of yours are not so grand as the Hafods, though they think they are the cleverest people in the world."

"That's nonsense," muttered Simon.

"It isn't nonsense, indeed, then." Her slightly excited voice became sharper, higher. "Of course you think the same as them – and you think I'm not clever enough for you. Oh yes, I know very well what you think. No need for you to look so black on my friends, either. I'm glad I'm like them – I'd much rather be like them, and be with them always, than with – than with—" Jani struggled for a moment with a sob, to Simon's disgust. But as she remained silent, her red head sunk back in tousled calm on the pillow, he hurried away, to forget everything about the episode, except that it marked another failure in his efforts to meet Edith on intimate ground.

The fact was that he had seen very little of her except during the Passover week. Though she spent so much time with his father, it was usually when he himself could not be present. Her visits to the hospital rarely coincided with his. After the departure of his mother and sisters he was not invited to Caramel Place. Edith never appeared where he might reasonably expect to find her, unless she was there when he was not. He had asked her to the flat several times before she finally came, and it seemed as if she accepted only because she could think of no pretext for refusing. She was very busy at her clinic, he knew; but he would have suspected her of deliberately avoiding him if she had not been so frankly sweet when they met – and if the Seder nights had never been. It was a puzzle that did not fret him deeply. Her friendship with his parents was a fact, her return to London certain – though she had announced, rather abruptly at her farewell, that her resumed attendance at the clinic would be preliminary to a longer absence abroad. "I'm taking a special course, with a special object in view. It's something I've just lately decided on." He had an idea afterwards, when it was too late, that she wanted him to ask more; but he did not. Standing beside her, at his father's bed, he had felt stupidly incurious, content with the moment of feeding his eyes on her (he had not thought then that his father observed and read those glances). It was of a piece with his general state since she had come with them to London. He had simply yielded unquestioningly to a sense of enchantment in life – to a revived and deepened sense. He knew now that his feeling for her was rooted and unchangeable. His boy's vanity had merged into a man's forbearance, readier to find savour in the reproaches of the adored, than in the caresses of any other. But she did not offer him reproaches. She too, had grown, as he had felt in the garden at Hafod, into an expanded mood of tolerance. Whether it was a general mood, or one particular to himself, he had not dared to discover. But obviously she had not changed her Jewish course of life; as obviously she had accepted his divergence from it. If her criticism was reserved or suspended, it was not because she was deceived, not even because she could not challenge his temporary conformity with his parents' wish. On those Seder nights alone she had let him see it, had opened her hands to show him her silver dagger, had pricked him so delicately and intimately that his pain was a delight to him.

Sitting next him at the crowded table, she had kept her eyes upon the Hagadah, the order of service printed in Hebrew and English in a thin book of which everyone present had a copy. He could hear her firm undertone as she joined now and again in the chanted words, while his own voice dropped and shook in agitation. A new significance attached to the famous question, asked by the youngest Miller – "Wherefore is this night distinguished from all other nights?" – to which the whole service was an answer, a recital of the trials and the triumph of Israel "when our ancestors went down to Egypt with a few persons, and became a great nation—" It was an embarrassment to take his part in the rejoinder, to intone with the competence expected of him by his mother and sisters and the other Millers – and due, not least, to his hostess. Looking across at the little pointed face, its light drawn inwards in quiet concentration, he lost something of his sharp self-consciousness. Her son and his family, his own sisters, had nothing of that still intensity. They wore easy, accommodating looks, bland, wry, or bright with gusto, as they lifted winecups, swallowed the symbols of bitterness, and sang in thanksgiving. He saw that Bubele, even more than his mother, actually lived the ancestral tribulations, herself fled from Pharaoh with the unleavened bread and paschal lamb, crossed the Red Sea in a paean of faith, and watered the desert sand with creative tears. When her low voice vibrated in the "Dayenu", acclaiming each sign of God's favour to His people as "Sufficient unto the day is the *good* thereof", he knew the cry was a natural expression of her being. Fainter or bolder, it echoed round the table. The Yiddish and broken English, Welsh and Cockney intonations of his own and the Miller families, no longer eddied separatively, but were lost in the single stream of Hebrew. And suddenly he tried to force his own aloofness, to abandon the pretence of a cross-current bearing him away from these others, of whom, miraculously or not, Edith was one. Awareness of her in her loveliness was charged with awareness of the Jewess absorbed in a common commemoration. The sacred tongue might not come glibly to her lips, but its message flowed clear to her sight from the printed English page. And knowing this, he had begun his mumble with the translation jumping confusedly in his mind: ... "the bread of affliction, which our ancestors ate ... let all who are hungry, enter and eat ... and observe the Passover. This year ... here ... but next year we hope ... in the land of Israel. This year we are bondsmen ... next year we hope to be free." But the words meant nothing until he reached the citation of the four sons – the wise, who inquired the reason of the celebration in a proper manner; the wicked, who asked only to deride; the simple, and he who had not even the capacity to inquire – each to be instructed as he deserved.

It was then he caught the first flash of her sideway glance. Deliberately she arched her brows at him, with her old smile of ironic interrogation. He smiled back, and as deliberately shrugged his shoulders. Very well: he was the wicked son, excluding himself by his formula. "What mean *you* by this service?" from the collective body of the nation, and earning the retort – "This is done because of what the Eternal did for *me* when I came forth from Egypt" – "For *me*, and not for you, since had you been there, you would not have deserved to be redeemed."

She dropped her lids, and resumed the quiet study of the page. And soon afterwards he repented. He did not want to proclaim himself the outcast from the feast, he did not desire to have his teeth set on edge. On this occasion at least he would sit beside her spiritually as well as physically, and claim the crumbs that were due to him – even the unleavened crumbs. In the instant of his effort, in the richer gush of Hebrew that came from his tutored lips, he had an extraordinary feeling of release and joy.

"This unleavened bread, wherefore do we eat it? Because there was not time for the dough of our ancestors to leaven when they were thrust out of Egypt. This bitter herb, wherefore do we eat it? Because the Egyptians embittered the lives of our ancestors."

Therefore, in every generation each individual must look upon himself, as if he personally had gone forth from Egypt … It was not our ancestors only, but us also did he redeem with them … He brought *us* from thence, in order to bring *us* to the land which he swore unto our fathers . … He brought us forth from slavery to freedom, from sorrow to joy; from mourning to festivity; from servitude to redemption. Therefore let us chant unto him a new song. Hallelujah!"

Winecup in hand, Simon threw back his head and roared the Hallelujah. Dinah looked up curiously from her corner, but she did not have a clear view of her brother. Her mother looked up, too, and though she sat opposite, she saw little through her dim, mournful eyes. Yet as she returned to her book she nodded happily to herself. Simon's glance found Edith's, a deeper curl on her lips, a higher tilt to her eyebrows. She doubted him, of course. She challenged his loud-voiced protestations. But he did not care. The sparkle of her doubt brought them closer than her serenity. The little stabs she gave were thrills from heaven. He carolled rather than chanted, he led each new strain, setting the pitch for Hyman Miller's gutterals, the strident babble of the sons, the softer chimings of the women. The meal interval hardly broke the new-found unison. There was talk of past *Sederim*, in the former homes of the Millers and the Blacks, when crime and calumny stalked the celebrant hearths. "In every generation some have arisen to exterminate us", quoted the grandmother in Yiddish, and Edith said in German, – the nearest she could manage in response, – her head haughtily erect, "But they never will – never, Bubele! We shall not remain slaves and bondsmen. We were free once, we became a great nation – we shall be free again, we shall become once more a nation, greater than ever!" – The younger people gazed at her, fascinated for a moment, and Simon held his breath. He was fascinated eternally, and everything she said was now precious to him.

He listened as she sang, in her soft undertone, adapting the English version to the closing lines,

"Rebuild Thy house, O Lord,
Rebuild Thy house betimes!
    Speedily, speedily, in our days
    Rebuild Thy house, O Lord.

And in English she repeated, suddenly leaning towards him, her rapid murmur meant, it seemed, for him alone,

"Next year in Jerusalem!"

The movement and the murmur were like an exaltation. He wished he could have scooped up Holy Earth in a bowl and presented it to her. But the impulse sank frozen in the coolness of her look as she wished him good night. He had to steady himself, to restrain his fingers in their grip of hers; for a second he wondered madly if she, too, were exercising a guard, if she had felt her probing of his soul to be as dangerously sweet to herself as to him. But the illusion faded, more quickly than the memory of the probing itself, and the Seder harmonies which surrounded it.

She had not brought herself again as near to him – or rather tried to bring him as near to her. But he had gone on watching and waiting, absorbing the casual glimpses he could get of her, in a kind of effortless continuation of his dream. His father's warning interrupted him with a jerk. But it was less a check than a provocation. It sent him forward, perhaps, more consciously, directing his thoughts, concentrating and deepening his emotions. With Gedaliah gone, and Edith away, he let his inner life focus entirely upon her.

The dream went on simultaneously with a serious devotion to work. His plans for months ahead precluded waste of time,

and he spent strenuous hours alone over his books. His neglect
of Jani made little difference to either. She seemed to accept
his preoccupations, and spent a great deal of time with her
friends. Occasionally they talked of a visit to Blaemawe, but
she always advanced reasons for postponing the trip. He made
no effort either to urge or dissuade her. He avoided, in fact,
anything in the nature of argument, since nothing now proved
easier than to fall bickering with his wife. There came a day
when they quarrelled over a card from Marjorie Newell.
Simon had learned from Edith that her friend was in France,
having accompanied her latest employer-patient abroad in
March.

"Lady Terring is an old schoolfellow of Grandmother
Hafod", Edith had said. "She isn't an exacting invalid, and
Marjorie should have an easy time with her."

"So she told me," Simon had answered, recalling the
meeting at Paddington. "But I don't think she expected to go
abroad."

"No – not then. But Lady Terring is fond of travelling, and
usually starts off at a moment's notice. Marjorie had a rush, I
believe."

It accounted for the fact that Simon had not seen Marjorie
again. It did not occur to him to wonder why she had not
responded to his invitation, or tried to see him before she left.

One Sunday in July, he was searching for an old notebook.
He had warned Jani not to destroy his student papers, though
as a matter of fact she scarcely needed the warning. It was not
Jani's habit to destroy papers of any kind. She had a passion,
rather, for storing litter in odd corners and drawers, and Simon
had a tiring hunt the evening through. The missing notebook
was not in any of the dusty piles he explored. In search of

further hiding-places, he came across a discarded workbasket, filled with soiled bits of silk rags, cottons, and household bills. He flicked a careless finger through the papers, and to his astonishment saw a postcard addressed to him by Marjorie Newell. It was not dated, and the postmark was blurred, but it seemed to have been posted in London in March.

"Dear Mr. Black", she had written in a hurried almost illegible scrawl, rendered more difficult to decipher by smudges that might have been caused by rain – "I find … leaving … week-end … would like to see … call to-morrow … have to be in Kensington in any case … Marjorie Newell;"

When Jani came in he showed her the card. At once she flew into a rage so hysterical that he could make nothing of it. She stormed at him senselessly for raking through her basket, and her explanation was confused and contradictory.

She knew nothing about the silly old postcard. Oh yes, it came when he was away in Blaemawe. But she didn't know what it was about nor whom it was from. She had thought it must be some mistake and threw it away. What right had he to mess up all her pieces. She wanted them for a little patchwork quilt for the baby" (there was a second Thomas baby) "and they were all spoilt and dirty and twisted—"

"But I've hardly touched the things, Jani. They *were* messed up, anyhow—"

"Oh, of course, I'm the one to blame – I'm the one that makes a mess of everything—" She went on shrieking shrilly, provoking retorts, until Simon, bewildered and exasperated, realised that he was still without information of Marjorie's visit.

"But surely if she called, you ought to know—" He recalled her telling him that on the Saturday of his absence, she had not gone out during the afternoon. It had rained heavily, she had had a headache, and rested until she went to spend the evening with friends. He wondered at his own clear recollection. She must have told him of it several times.

But now Jani didn't know and couldn't remember. Such a long time ago – how could she? Lots of women called, women who canvassed for orders, who had all sorts of rubbishy things to sell – sometimes she answered the door to them, sometimes she didn't. Simon might have thought this reasonable if she had not been in such a ferment about it, and added wildly – Who on earth was this Marjorie *Newly* anyway? And what did he mean by making a fuss about some woman she had never heard of and didn't want to hear of – perhaps it was someone he met on the sly and was impudent enough to think she would welcome to their home – someone he liked better than her, of course. She knew very well indeed he didn't have much liking left for *her* – he needn't shout at her and behave like a – like a – conceited bully – Jani was genuinely at a loss for a description of the attitude with which Simon stood regarding her, and the fact that he sneered rather than shouted was not likely to temper her veracity. She went on hurling epithets at him until his silence reduced her to a spluttered repetition of "*maldood – maldood –* I won't stand your *maldood—*" and flung herself about the adjacent bedroom, while he sat over his books for hours into the night. When he retired, it was to revolve more calmly his impression that Jani was not quite sane. There could be no reason for a concealment of Marjorie's visit, if indeed she had made it. But there must be something wrong with Jani to account for her rapid descent to hysteria. Her health had not been good lately. She was excitable and cantankerous to an extraordinary degree. There was no doubt her nerves had gone to pieces. His conscience troubled him for the first time. Was it enough to deny any ground for her senseless suspicions? She knew nothing, could have understood nothing, of his feelings for Edith. But though such feelings were, in his view, entirely removed from the plane of injury to Jani – still— He was uneasy. He decided to avoid contention, and to suggest to Jani that she should see a doctor. He waited a day or two before he spoke of it.

"I'm sure you need a tonic, Jani. You are run down, you haven't been out of London this summer – I'm sorry we couldn't manage our usual week-end trips – But you know I had to work. Still, there's no reason why you shouldn't have a holiday at once. Why not pay your Blaemawe visit *now* – spend a couple of weeks there, and then I'll take you to the sea for a month?"

His tone was modulated to a soothing strain. She did not answer, but stared at him sulkily from her chair near the window. The colour on her yellowing skin was mottled.

"Come, now," he went on persuasively. "Didn't you tell me the other day that one of your friends – Miss Jenkins I think – is going to play at a concert in Tavcastle on Saturday?"

"It isn't a concert. It's a garden party at the Castle."

"Well, it's all the same – if Miss Jenkins is to play—?"

"Yes. Ieuan Richards is singing with her."

He frowned a moment, but resumed in the same tone,

"I suppose you'd like travelling down with them—"

"They are not going together," she said. "Ieuan's leaving the night before. He has to be in Aberystwith first to arrange about a concert. He may be staying there until he goes on tour afterwards." There was a little more animation in her manner.

"Then you can travel with Miss Jenkins," he said. She was

silent again. He came up to her chair and patted the hand lying on her lap. "Promise you'll go, Jani," he said. "And see the doctor first."

"Oh, all right," she snapped; and suddenly began to laugh. Simon made the appointment for her himself. Her own doctor was away, but expected back on Friday.

As she would not go to another, it was agreed to wait till then.

The intervening days tried Simon sorely. Jani was in her worst mood of hysterical petulance. Though she said she had written to her parents of her coming, he doubted if she had done so, as she threw out hints of surprising them. His efforts to provide for her comfort and the care of the flat were resented as evidence of his anxiety to be rid of her. "Indeed, then, I know you'll be glad to see the back of me. Sure enough you can manage well without me—"

He had never exercised as much patience in his life. He made few retorts, humoured, and even petted her, though he had to overcome a queer new repulsion as well as reluctance in doing so. It struck him as a strange phenomenon that she was more depressed by his tenderness than by his rage. Almost it seemed as if she delighted in irritating him, in provoking bitter words that she could rend in turn. His studied gentleness merely made her mope and sulk.

On Friday he was late in reaching home. He had gone straight from his office to an address in Stamford Hill, to complete the purchase of a second-hand motor bicycle – a wonderful bargain according, not only to the seller, but to Ted Rendall and other friends. A trial run in the nearest long quiet street, ended abruptly in a flattened tube. Determined to await its repair, Simon telephoned to Jani to explain the delay. She did not snap at him as he expected. In fact, her voice seemed so subdued that he asked a little apprehensively about her visit to the doctor. "You saw him, of course?"

"Yes."

"Well? What did he think?"

She did not answer immediately, and he hurried on – "There can't be anything – serious?"

"No, no, of course not. Don't be silly. It's nothing at all."

"Nothing. Are you sure? What did he say?"

"Oh, I'm just run down, and I've got to take medicine, and go away for a bit."

"Just as I thought. So now you can get on with your packing. Don't fuss about anything. You needn't trouble about a meal for me. I'll get a snack somewhere here while I'm waiting."

He found an A.B.C. not far away, and remained there for a time. In returning to the garage he crossed the quiet street he had first run through. Night, it seemed to him, was setting in early; so many lights were showing in uncurtained windows. He looked in vaguely, and realised they were Sabbath lights. He had forgotten the Sabbath. Almost every house in this street had remembered it.

He stood still against the corner of a railing that enclosed a square of grass. Through a side pane he had a clear view of a small dining-room, its long table covered with a white cloth. On one end was placed a couple of twisted loaves, and in the centre a tall branched candlestick, holding two unlighted candles. There was nobody in the room. But Simon saw his mother standing at the table, shading her eyes with the worn, veined hands as she recited the blessing… He turned away, but irresistibly his glance went back, and again he stood still, staring at a transformed vision. A figure was near the table, but it had no resemblance to his mother. A young woman in a white silk dress was spreading an embroidered cloth over the loaves of bread. She had set down a tray of cutlery, and these she arranged deftly, laying places for two. A smile played on her lips as she altered, to her satisfaction, the position of knives and forks at the head of the table, immediately in front of the loaves; a sweet, secret smile, dimpling her cheeks, lengthening the corners of her long, downcast eyes. Standing upright before the candles, her demeanour altered. The smile trembled from her face, a look of gravity composed the round, pink cheeks. It was the moment of due meditation. "Lord of the Universe, I am about to perform the sacred duty of kindling the lights in honour of the Sabbath... Make me worthy to walk in the way of the righteous before thee, loyal to Thy law and to good deeds... Keep from us all manner of shame, grief and care; and grant that peace, light and joy ever abide in our home. For with Thee is the fountain of life: in Thy light do we see light."

She lit the candles slowly, as if in unaccustomed ceremony, her lips pursed, intent and serious. Then her eyes closed, her hands rose in arched formation to her brow, the young lines of her body showed both supple and taut. For at least a minute after her sanctification was uttered she remained motionless. In that minute Simon lived in another fusion of his dream. The lithe figure, heightened into Edith's, moved in smiling preparation of his Sabbath table: the hands, whiter and more tapering, lifted to a brow more exquisite under waves of brighter gold, blessed the Sabbath lights of his home. The wings of his vision flapped abruptly. The girl at the table dropped her arms, darted to the window, pulled a cord, and shut herself and the shining scene from view. Simon shivered in the soft warm air of the night. He jerked his shoulders, thrust his hands in to his pockets, and with eyes on the ground, strode back to the garage.

In a few moments he was swerving wildly through the streets, conscious of his machine, but all his pride and pleasure in it thrust below a sense of misery. The faster he went towards his home and his wife, the more disturbingly repellent they grew. It was as well the ride was a long, precarious one, and that its end meant a hunt for location for his steed. By the time he had settled matters and walked round several turnings to the flat, he was able to force a smile of greeting to his lips.

But Jani did not see it. She was sitting near the window, bending over a black silk stocking, the heel of which was stretched over the palm of her left hand, while she jabbed at it with a needle in the fingers of her right. A streak of daylight still lingered in the panes, which overlooked a courtyard; the rest of the room was in shadow. Even in the gloom there could be seen a general disarray. Garments were strewn about tables and chairs and floor. An open suitcase held jumbled articles overflowing its sides. Simon stumbled over shoes and hangers.

"My dear girl," he said, trying hard to keep the irritation out of his voice. "Why don't you have a light? Surely you can't see to sew – your eyes—"

"I've finished," she said, pulling off the stocking and throwing it down. "Oh – don't put the light on!" His hand had already found the switch, and an electric glare lit the confusion of the room. She turned in the chair, her back to him, her hand over her face as she bowed it. "I can't bear it! – I mean, it hurts my eyes more. I've got the headache." Jani never varied the formula of Blaemawe, where nobody ever had *a* headache.

"No wonder," said Simon, "If you've been mending – black things, too – in the dark." He looked round at the litter, then at her head. The red bunch of hair straggled untidily, and was partly flattened, as if it had been pressed a long time against a hard pillow. "You ought to lie down." He touched the settee near him in a doubtful way. It was covered with hats, underclothing, and packing paper. "If I turn the light off here, I can't read. You'd better go into the bedroom."

"Oh all right," she said sullenly, and got up. Her face startled him. The red spots stood out on sallow, drawn cheeks, more mottled than ever. The dark eyes, once bright and round, seemed filmed over and sunken. She stared back at him in a kind of scared defiance.

"Jani, were you like this when you saw the Doctor? Tell me exactly what he said."

"I told you."

"Just that you were run down – nothing more?"

She jerked her chin downwards.

"You've got a tonic?"

She nodded again, and began to move towards an inner door on her right. Simon watched her uneasily. She flung her hand out with a sudden stagger, and he sprang to her and caught her elbows, guiding her back into the chair.

"It's my head," she muttered, sitting up quickly. "It's been bad all day – and I get a bit dizzy with it. There's an awful buzzing in my ears, too. That's why I stopped packing. But I haven't much to do. Perhaps if I take some aspirins and lie down a bit, I shall be all right."

"I'll get you the aspirins," said Simon. He stood before her, still regarding her doubtfully. She did not seem able to endure the inspection. Her eyes flickered.

"I suppose you told the doctor exactly how you felt. Did he examine you?" She began to whimper suddenly.

"Oh, indeed, then, perhaps you've guessed. I suppose I might as well tell you now. It's a baby."

Simon started back.

"Good God!" he said.

He saw her stiffen, her chin go up, her lips tighten. But her eyes still blinked furtively. He made an effort to control his repugnance.

"Are you sure?" he said. "Is the doctor sure?"

She nodded, her eyes following him as he walked about the room, muttering.

"It doesn't seem possible, somehow. I shouldn't have thought – still, if you say so – but it must be a long time – how long? Why didn't you tell me before? You must have known—"

"I didn't – I wasn't certain. It's been – different – this time. And I was afraid to tell you – yes—" She cried out shrilly – "I was afraid – I knew you wouldn't like to hear it – I knew you'd say it was a dam' nuisance." She laughed hysterically.

Compunction fought with his disgust as he listened, and stared again at her haggard face. She looked ill. She was ill and after all, she was his wife, and ill of his child. He returned slowly to her side.

"I'm not saying that, Jani. It can't be helped, of course, and I – we must put up with it—"

"Indeed you must!" She laughed again. The sound grated horribly on his ears, but he had a dreary sense of her right. He put a hand on her neck and tried to speak tenderly. "Sorry, Jani, if I seem a brute. I didn't expect it in the least. And I didn't think *you* – wanted it, either – now. After the bad time you had before – but of course you needn't be afraid of *that*. It can't happen again, if you take care – didn't the doctor tell you so? And I'll look after you. If you like, I'll take you down to Wales myself, to-morrow afternoon. No need to rush in the morning. It will give you more time to get ready. Leave the things to-night and just rest. Come along, I'll help you into the bedroom—"

He lifted her gently; she obeyed with a stupefied look, and let herself be led into the adjoining room. He sat her on the bed and began to take off her shoes, talking soothingly. Her eyes rolled in a curious manner. Suddenly she pushed him away, sprang to her feet, and burst into sobs, calling out wildly,

"I can't – I can't!"

He stood a moment, perplexed.

"I wish you wouldn't upset yourself. Come – you've got to rest."

"Listen to me – you must listen to me." She stamped her foot. "I told them I wasn't a liar – l'm not – I *won't* be – nobody shall call me a liar, whatever. I'll tell you the truth now, straight out!" Deep sobs choked her speech.

"Why – were you pretending then, just now? Do you mean – there *isn't* – a baby?"

"Oh yes, yes, there's a baby, but—" she made a desperate effort to control a sob, and stood taut – "it's not – yours!"

"Jani!"

She moved from the bed as he stepped forward, then stood again, pressed against the wall. Her face defied him above her little panting bosom.

"There, then! You know now – you know."

"Who is it?"

"Ieuan."

Simon put a hand on the wooden frame of the bed. The other hand went to his forehead. He said nothing. As if unable to bear the silence, Jani burst out afresh in a torrent of words.

"Don't you say it's all my fault – or Ieuan's – it's you, you! You don't care a bit really. You didn't want a baby – and you didn't want me. You don't care about anything I care about – you can't bear my friends – and you knew quite well I wanted a baby more than anything – more than *anything*, I tell you—"

"So you went to that common lout."

"He's not common! He's better than you a thousand times! Why, what are you, then – only a Jew! I wouldn't stay with you anyway – I was a fool to go with you at all – everybody is saying – Tegwen Thomas said there was a curse on it. And you know well enough Ieuan always wanted me – Miss Jenkins would give her eyes for him, but he doesn't want her – he never went with her at all, it was me he wanted – and he said I belonged to him, not to a dirty Jew!"

Simon laughed suddenly. She stopped at the sound, and watched him sink on the bed, covering his face with his hands. But the next moment he jumped up, and she rushed backwards through the open doorway, falling into the settee.

"Don't touch me! Don't touch me!" she screamed in terror.

"Be quiet," he said in a low tone, pausing at a distance from her. "You'll bring the neighbours in. Though even *they* know that Jews don't beat their wives."

He laughed again. She shuddered, gathered herself together, leaped past him back into the bedroom, and banged the door. For a few moments he remained where he was, listening to her hysterical sobs. Then mechanically he switched off the light and went out, hatless, into the street. He had no idea for how long he walked about, but presently it began to rain, and a heavy downpour soaked his head and his thin summer suit.

He became aware that he was streaming wet. Hailing a bus, he returned to the flat. The rooms were still in darkness. As the light spread, he saw that the suitcase and the littered garments had vanished. The bedroom was unlocked and empty of occupant. Everything else remained exactly as he had left it. He stared vacantly around. Where could Jani have gone, at this time of night? It was past eleven. He was not very curious or concerned. He felt terribly tired. Was he supposed to sit up and wait, or to begin making inquiries? He knew dully it was necessary to come to a decision. Suddenly the telephone bell rang. He answered a drawling Welsh voice.

"Is that Mr. Simon Black?"

"Yes."

"Oh. I been trying to get you before. This is Mrs. Thomas the Dairy talking – Tegwen Thomas."

"Yes."

"I was thinking it only right to tell you about Jani."

"Yes."

"I seen her."

"Yes."

"She have gone away on the late train from Paddington." Pause. "She have gone away for good with Ieuan Richards."

"Yes."

"I was thinking it only right to tell you."

"Yes."

"I am sorry, mind you. And I don't say it is right, neither. But p'r'aps it had to be."

No reply.

"You aren't much surprised, now, I don't suppose?"

"No."

He put the receiver back and went to bed.

XIII

THE HON. MRS. CHARLES RACHLIN was extremely annoyed. She fluttered about her crowded drawing-room in Grosvenor Place like a wary raven, her thin olive face with the purple-black eyes, jet brows and elongated nose, strained in the effort to combine a smile with a frown. The smile was a vague apologetic diffusion over any guest who might stray into her glance; the frown was meant for a group near the piano, the most prominent members of which were a fair girl in a frock of bronze moire, a dark girl in green satin, and a tall brown-haired young man whose evening suit set off the shapeliest male figure in the room. As Mrs. Rachlin worked her way towards them, the girl in green detached herself in advance, the girl in bronze and the tall young man followed with another man, nondescript but pleasant-eyed, in the rear.

Mrs. Rachlin abandoned her smile, and poured a cascade of scathing murmurs into her daughter's ear.

"Really, mother, it's your own fault." The brilliant creature in green smiled teasingly. She had contrived to be met at an opening to a recess, which was in fact a tiny ante-room, with a window overlooking the street. She sent a significant look backwards as she led her mother in. "You insisted on having her here instead of letting the Hafods give a farewell party of their own—"

"But my evening was already arranged – I couldn't cancel it. And Lady Hafod agreed. It was you who went round to Lowndes Square to persuade her—"

"Because you thought she wouldn't listen to *you*. Confess, mother, you preferred it this way. The first time you've been able to show off the Hafods as relatives in your own drawing-room!

"A nice showing-off, with Edith in her most perverse mood. You know quite well *I'm* not infatuated with the Hafods." Miss Rachlin lifted her brows, in acknowledgement of a thrust. "But I see no reason why they should be allowed to disown us. Cynthia Lansome did marry into our family, and was the mother of a Rachlin. The stupid part of it is that she won't make any distinction between us and those vulgar Millers—"

"People never do, my dear mother."

"Never do – what?"

"Make distinctions between one sort of Jew and another."

"Lena, you're getting as impossible as Edith. I used to think it was that dreadful Bohemianism turning your head, but since you've taken up with Edith again – really, it's as well she's going on that preposterous trip. You encourage each other, I suppose. But I wouldn't have believed she'd make such an exhibition of herself – *here*! To recite some Hebrew gibberish – and then explain it!"

"Yes, that was a pity. They might have thought it was Greek – or Welsh."

"Atrocious taste!"

"Oh, come, mother! I'm sorry to repeat myself, but you *have* brought it on yourself. If you hadn't announced Edith's trip to the East as a charitable enterprise, she might not have explained anything."

"If she was bound to do it, she could have done so in private. But to make practically a speech after that awful poem, introducing *religion*, with all these Christians listening—"

"Christians? They are no more Christians than we are Jews. Only they aren't as susceptible as we are to misnomers. My dear mother, where is your sense of humour? Come along, Edith – mother's had it out with me. She doesn't really mean to blight your last hours with us by being cross."

The other three, having been detained on the way, had just appeared. Mrs. Rachlin turned, and re-captured her smile for Simon; she could never remember immediately that he was a Jew. But she discarded it again before she looked at Jack Harman. She had known him, or his mother, too long to forget.

"I'm sorry if you're offended, Cousin Beatrice," said Edith. The slight increase of colour with which she had delivered her unexpected "piece" still warmed her face. Otherwise, thought Simon, whose eyes hardly left her, she seemed even cooler than usual. "Did you think my 'few words' out of place? I hadn't intended to add to my sins in that way. It's been so kind of you to turn me into a sort of guest-of-the-evening, and everybody seems to know I'm going to Palestine. But I got rather tired of being asked if l were going out on a mission – to convert Turks or Jews or Arabs, I hardly know which or to what – by means of nursing and medicine! I felt I had to make it clear that my work had nothing to do with religion—"

"*Nothing* to do—!" repeated Mrs. Rachlin. Her tone was full of helpless exasperation. "But you talked of the religious longing for Zion – you said you were going to Jerusalem in the spirit of what's-his-name Levi—"

"Mother darling, don't speak of a great Hebrew poet as if he were a rag-and-bone man!"

"Ah, here you are," broke in a guttural voice. A heavy man

with flat black hair and very red cheeks came through the opening. "What's this about a rag-and-bone man, Lena?"

"It's mother. She talks of Jehuda Halevi like an ignorant Gentile—"

"There can't be any ignorant Gentiles left in this room, at any rate," said Charles Rachlin, "after Edith's lesson." He frowned, shrugged his shoulders, grimaced half-jocularly, and tweaked Edith's ear, to Simon's intense annoyance – and surprise. The Hon. Charles had mannerisms akin to those of old Uncle Elman. "But you ought to know, my dear, that very often ignorance is bliss. We don't wish to be regarded, in this age, as – as – hm – as—"

"As Jews?" prompted Lena, in a mock whisper. "As un-English dreamers and fanatics," said her father, ignoring her loftily. "As dangerous fools, rushing in to – er – to—"

"But, sir, it's the angels who are rushing in," ventured Simon. Charles Rachlin stared heavily at him. "Bravo, Mr. Black," said Lena, laughing. "Edith, you don't seem to realise that your champion has turned the very neatest of compliments – in addition to confounding papa! Really, papa – people who talk in proverbs ought at least to recognise them, especially when they're improved upon!"

"You make a joke of everything, child," said Mrs. Rachlin coldly. "Did you want me, Charles?"

"Yes, I think the Edgertons are leaving. They seem to be looking round for you."

"Already? They are usually the last—"

"Disgusted, probably," jeered Lena, as her parents moved away. Her mother turned resentful black eyes over her shoulder.

"It's quite possible they won't come again – they are Catholics, you know—"

"Does that make their consciences more tender? But don't worry, darling. Your Christian friends will never desert you – they love bankers' houses. I'm not so sure about the Jews, though – they can't forgive being reminded of what they are under a *Jewish* roof."

Her mother did not deign to answer. Her father shook a rotund finger at her as they passed out. She glanced drolly at Edith, and both girls laughed.

"How they can *expect* to be regarded as anything but Jews!" murmured Edith.

"It's pathetic," said Lena. "All the same, thou chip of the Rachlin block, my dear parents are not Jews in *your* sense."

"Why?"

A little silence fell between the group, filled by the loud chatter and passing of figures in the large room beyond. Jack Harman had been standing at the narrow window, one foot on the low short sill, looking abstractedly down into the street. He tapped a cigarette on his knee, and without looking at her, offered a light to Lena Rachlin, who had produced her own silver case. The others refused to smoke. Simon remained leaning against a damask panel, his hands in his pockets, his eyes on Edith, in the dumb, fixed gaze which had not varied through the evening. She showed no consciousness of it; unless by the fact that she seldom looked at him.

Miss Rachlin drew at her cigarette until it glowed, and said: "You know they don't practise Judaism. They don't believe in it, and won't be identified with it. Since you are so keen on the antiquated rites, I take it you'll agree that once they're absolutely discarded – phut!" – she blew smoke into her fingers, and waved them – "the thing's gone!"

"I can't agree, though," said Edith, in her rapid, even tone.

"I don' t see our historical past as a mere dishful of rites, or think that when you pour them out, you pour away the whole of Judaism. A Jew remains a Jew even if he doesn't practise his religion – not only to the undiscriminating Gentile, but to *me*."

"Of course – it's race you worship – like Jack here – à la Disraeli—"

"Disraeli escaped," muttered Simon.

"Did he?" For a second Edith's glance touched his. "I fancy he was dragged out by his father. But he came back of his own accord."

"Not to the ghetto, dear," said Lena.

"But does a Jew ever get out?" said Harman. "A ghetto isn't necessarily a place where Jews congregate to carry on outworn customs. It exists wherever a Jew is out of harmony with his non-Jewish fellows, somehow separated even when his life seems theirs. Even if *he* thinks he's 'out', the others don't. Disraeli's countrymen have always regarded him as inexorably 'in'. Politics, literature, society, marriage – nothing discounted the 'damned Jew' in the accepted servant of England."

"It would have been the same," said Edith, "even if he had not been a conscious Jew."

"Conscious?" said Lena, a little irritably. "Surely we're all conscious?"

"Not in my sense," said Edith. "You are thinking of the mere smart of reaction to contempt. 1 mean conscious of our racial values – an informed consciousness that makes us stand up proudly and exact respect. I'm not sure whether Mr. Harman thinks as I do. Race doesn't cover all *I* mean by Judaism."

"Your point of view seems to be the same as mine," said

Harman. "I believe in Jewish nationality. I don't think the religious side counts."

"But I *do*."

"Oh! " Harman disregarded Lena's malicious wink. "I see. You mean the *spiritual* side. It's so easy to fall into a confusion of terms when we talk of antiquated rites. Mixing up sanitary regulations with religion is rather rot, isn't it?"

"Not at all," said Edith pleasantly. "Mens sana in corpore sano. I support the holy view of cleanliness. If you knew as much as I do about domestic hygiene, you would agree that its observance is a true form of religion. As to 'antiquated' – I find an intelligent anticipation of science in our old laws of health. Medical men to-day are only just getting abreast of Moses."

"But would orthodox Jews talk of intelligent anticipation? If Moses was divinely inspired—"

"Now you're quibbling, Jack," exclaimed Miss Rachlin. "Shut up, and let Edith go on talking shop. It's fascinating when she explains sexual hygiene as a model subject of divine legislation."

She flung back her polished black head and sent out a great puff of smoke – almost into Harman's face. The emerald necklace on her rich dark skin emitted sparks of green fire. But the sparks, thought Simon, drawn to glance unwillingly at her, seemed to come from her flesh – from her eyes, too: those bold sad eyes that stared derisively at him from under heavy lids. She was queer to-night, he felt uneasily but not too surprisedly. Who wouldn't be queer when Edith was going away? But it wasn't like Lena to watch him so oddly; to make him feel – in the intervals of rapt concentration when he completely forgot her – that he was behaving like a fool. An enviable fool, perhaps. Her malice never grudged him a measure of admiration. And he was grateful for one effect of her gnat-like restlessness. It seemed as if she, who always sought and created notice, was actually trying to avoid it. She had played and been sociable as little as she could. Certainly it needed skill to screen her personality and the vivid green frock from too much attention. But she had manoeuvred, for the second time within the last hour, a temporary withdrawal into this particular recess. There was no reason why the four should keep together, or be allowed to do so for long. Yet there was a tacit imposition to that effect, which outwitted any effort of others to divide them.

"'Divine' and 'national' are interchangeable terms, as applied to Judaic law," said Edith. Her manner, untouched by Lena's audacities, was at once composed and abstracted. She spoke, Harman thought, as he had seen his mother knit; in perfect control of needles, with a rapid accuracy and skilled manipulation of stitch, while the mind was absorbed in other things. "God inspired Moses to build a nation, not simply to create a sect."

"The interchangeable theory isn't much use to me," he replied. "Perhaps because I've come back to Judaism from a different angle. Lena knows that my people are as un-Jewish in practice as hers – more so, if anything. English for three generations, and as far as I can gather, the original immigrant from Holland was excommunicated for agnosticism. Religion, spiritual or material, has given us a long miss. Yet I'm a convinced nationalist. I recognise the claims of 'Israel, a nation.' It's clear from all points that the Jewish people are a separate entity. The most heroic efforts at assimilation seldom succeed – every Gentile whale eventually rejects its Jonah. I don't know whether we can recover our lost glory in Palestine. But I agree that our problems would solved by the re-establishment of a national centre, where we can develop our special gifts, as well as relieve a widespread embarrassment. I'm just as sure –" he flicked the ash from his cigarette carelessly into a corner of the sill – "that such a centre must be based on a practical form of Judaism, in accordance with modern views."

"Which must be the traditional basis, if it's really Judaism." Edith smiled faintly. "And if it is to lead, not only to the satisfaction of the Jew, but to the peace and harmony of the world."

"The Messianic ideal," said Harman, also smiling, a little superciliously. "You come back to religion."

"Really, for two people who agree on fundamentals, you're remarkably unsympathetic!" Lena Rachlin looked from one to the other with a subtle delight. "If I didn't believe all nationalism to be vicious, I'd say that Jack's point of view is the more likely. Moses is all very well. But do you include in your 'tradition' the thousand and one ghetto accretions to the Mosaic code?"

"Why not? My Jewish grandmother finds them no obstacle to the practical life. And at the same time she has shown me how spiritual a force our 'sanitary regulations' can be. Besides, I respect everything that has helped to preserve the identity of the race."

"My dear Edith!" Miss Rachlin threw away her cigarette, and put her arm round the other's waist. "I can't make out what it is exactly that you worship. But papa is right. You *are* a fanatic!" The brilliant contrasting sheen of the green frock against the bronze, of the black and golden heads, drew a simultaneous flash from the eyes of both young men. Involuntarily they changed their lounging positions.

"Am I?" said Edith, with her grave, sweet smile. "I thought a fanatic would never yield a point. If you want to know what I believe in – what I worship, if you like – it is the Jewish Idea: the motive power of Jewish nationality, and, as I see it, a unique force for practical righteousness, that has been expressed in Jewish types throughout the ages. I am struck by the fact of its recurrence in every generation and in every environment – as regularly and unvaryingly as the condition of prejudice and hostility. When I was a child I was stirred by the list of Jewish genius set out by Disraeli in 'Coningsby'. But now that sort of thing merely depresses me. It is too sad a reminder of Jewish waste. What moves me more and more is recognition of the Jewish Idea, working through men and women of our people, obscure as well as great, often isolated and unaware of each other. My faith in the Idea goes beyond any temporary expression of it. I am convinced that much even of the ghetto way of life is sound. But if a re-established Jewry in Palestine decrees its abolition – I should say, why not? A living Jewry can afford to scrap dead laws."

"Good," said Harman. "You believe in the future. So do I. In a Jewish people working out its self-emancipation in its own sphere. And I'll concede a point to you, too. I believe in the practical nature of the old Prophetic ideals. Lena thinks nationalism is vicious. But that's what the Gentiles have made of it. I accept the Jewish view of nationalism as the gateway to universal brotherhood. Not an impossible millenium where every natural distinction has vanished. But a possible confederation of peoples – the finer energies of each released to do the work that suits it, in its own environment – pooling the stock to which each contributes. If Palestine means that, it's a real guarantee of peace and happiness."

Lena Rachlin withdrew abruptly from Edith and walked to the window. A sulky frown drew her brows together as she stared out.

"You're both crazy," she said. "It's agin human nature. Gentiles won't give a chance to each other, much less to the Jew. They'll neither eat their cake nor keep it – nor let anyone else have it. As for the Jews, they'll always prefer other peoples' nationalisms to their own." And why not, when one's *English*, thinks Simon Black—

"Speak for yourself, Lena," said Edith, more sharply than Harman had heard her speak at all.

"Very well," said Lena, as unexpectedly meek. "Even if your few colonies come to anything – a harum-scarum lot of Jews in a new ghetto isn't going to give me peace and happiness."

"How do you know?" said Edith. Even to Simon's ears the sudden change to softness was puzzling. "Perhaps – if you come to Palestine – and try your music there—"

"What? Play in the desert?"

"It won't be a desert – any more than it will be a ghetto – when you are there," said Harman. He smiled slightly.

She flashed a furious look at him. "Thanks for treating me kindly! " she sneered. "But I thought you said a Jew could never get out?"

"I merely questioned if he ever had – I don't doubt that he can. Haven't I just agreed with Miss Miller that Palestine is an alternative to the ghetto – in fact the only real escape from it?"

"You two may pretend to agree as much as you like – I

don't believe it – neither does our friend Simon." She smiled at Edith, a little defiantly. "Sorry you disapprove of my speaking for the dumb. But you know he'd say so himself – if he wasn't afraid—" she hesitated, and continued flippantly – "if he wasn't afraid that you won't let him take you home—"

"How – do you – know – I'm going to?" stammered Simon. Miss Rachlin laughed out.

"I heard Edith refuse to have the car to-night much to my mother's relief! She doesn't like the chauffeur to know that Miss Miller lives in an East End tenement."

"It isn't a tenement," Simon muttered.

"Listen to me, Simon Black. Edith or no Edith – confess! Wouldn't you rather die for England, than live for Palestine?"

"I'd die for anything – for anyone – I loved."

"Simple Simon!"

She leaned forward and laughed again in his face. Partly because he was still in a state of trance, partly because he was too used to her teasing, too much aware of the real liking beneath, to be annoyed, he merely smiled back vaguely, blinked his eyes, and continued to stare past her at Edith, who had moved towards the opening.

"I'm going back to the Hafods," she said. "I must wish them good-night before they leave—"

She stood still abruptly. A man and woman, grossly fat, swarthy, thick-lipped, had hesitated in their oncoming waddle, glanced at her in half-fearful avoidance, and drifted past.

Lena broke into another little peal, rich with malice.

"The sweet Wiffensteins – I knew you'd shocked them: I watched their faces when you hailed the new Jerusalem – they could have thrown a bomb at you. Charming dears! Mother hates to have them, but they go everywhere. They've got all the traits described as 'typically Jewish.' The fact that their habits are as German as their accent doesn't help. How would you like their company in the desert? – assuming they could be dragged there."

"Nobody will be dragged there," said Edith. "But the desert might prove a useful place in which to shed – the habits. Forty years, and the real Jew would emerge."

"The real Jew – who, of course, hasn't *any* faults!"

"At least, not the kind his enemies fasten on him, as you've implied. It's hard to know what exactly they would be, if he had progressed normally into the modern world. We know what he was, in comparison with his contemporaries, two thousand years ago. But perhaps you're right. I prefer to think of the virtues the real Jew will develop."

"Personally, I think we have a right even to our faults," said Harman. "But I suppose the important thing at present is to avoid more prejudice and hatred."

"The important thing is to trust ourselves," said Edith. Her voice shook with a sudden surge of feeling. "The adoption of other people's standards is bad enough, confusing enough, but the adoption of other people's contempt of us – that's poison. When we Jews despise our Jewishness, we don't even succeed in getting rid of it – we simply corrode the fount of our life." Simon had moved towards her, and she looked full into his eyes. "You know," she said, in a lower tone, "I've always felt that. When I first understood it, it upset me very much. I couldn't feel calmly about it – then. That was why I was so angry – with – with – everybody who seemed to me—"

"You were terribly angry with me," said Simon. A little tight burden that had been pushed into some unused corner of his mind, rolled out – rolled away. He held her gaze with an intentness in which years of suffering passed into a moment's joy. Neither thought of the two watching them until Lena cried out irritably—

"I see Sir Gwilym wandering about – he must be looking for you."

The gaze broke. Edith walked away slowly, Simon following. Harman began to move after them, but hesitated as Lena swung round, lit another cigarette, and commenced to puff violently.

"So my cousin has captured you?" she sneered.

"She has the Jewish type of imagination, with the English coolness of blood. It's a powerful combination."

"It appeals to you, no doubt. Cold – stubborn – Yes, I see it. Edith is really your type!"

He smiled, but did not answer. She insisted—

"Isn't she? Isn't she?"

"Not exactly."

"Then who the hell is?" The violence of her words was increased rather than subdued by the low tone in which she spoke. "Some charming American, perhaps? Is that why you are rushing back so soon after your last trip? Don't tell me that business demands you again after nearly a year of it."

"I certainly won't tell you anything – about business. Do I ever talk to you about the things I hate?"

"I'm asking you to talk about the things you love."

"Don't be inquisitive, my child—" He took a deliberate pace forward, but as she did not stir, he paused and smiled at her.

"You're handsomer than ever, Lena – and naughtier – and ruder – and more – intolerable—" in spite of his smile, his face worked a little oddly for a moment. A voice hailed him, and he turned to speak to a couple of elderly men. As they passed on, Lena joined him and said rapidly, "Don't come with me now. When everybody's gone, slip into the morning-room and wait for me. Mother will go straight to her room – I'll see that Papa does, too. There's something I want to tell you."

He looked doubtful, but she brushed past him before he could reply. The great room was emptying. Guests were hovering around host and hostess in farewell. The Hafods were just leaving. Edith's grandmother held her by the arm, while Sir Gwilym and his wife sauntered ahead. They were to meet next day at Victoria, where Edith's trunks had already been despatched. She had insisted on spending her last night under Bubele's roof, and it was the easier for Lady Hafod to submit, since the four were to travel together to France. Her son and daughter-in-law had been staying at Cannes, and she was returning there with them. Their visit to England had been made on business of their own, though they talked as if they had come over specially for Edith's sake. Simon, standing a little way off, watching the last eddies of the circle around her, felt able to gauge, better than Edith herself, the measure of the attentions paid her by the younger Hafods. Through her eyes their reflection showed an amiable, good-natured, if rather stupid couple; genuinely fond of her, though they thought her a little mad. Through his own eyes he saw how easy it was for them to humour her, since her schemes fitted so agreeably into their desires. Neither husband or wife cared for the Dawy Valley, where their responsibilities were carried by an estate agent and a colliery manager. Edith's philanthropies in the district added to their prestige without involving them in effort or expense: even such social activity as hinged on the

charitable was organised by her and the dowager. Sir Gwilym
and his Ann had simply to grace occasions and take the
honours. More gratifying, still, was her Jewish "craze"; since
it increased their chances of someday possessing Millicombe,
which they preferred to Hafod as a country residence. Her
decision to go to Palestine, though a blow to old Lady Hafod,
was particularly welcome to the others. They helped to
dissolve her Ladyship's opposition to what she considered an
apotheosis of folly. Convinced that Edith's determination to
assist in the upbuilding of a new Jewish commonwealth was
irrevocable, they represented it to her grandmother as a
temporary delusion. They had been to the East, and had seen
the dreary wastes and huddled insanitary towns, with frowsy
Jews and barbarians praying and idling. Nothing comparable
to Western civilisation would ever take shape there, they were
certain: still, there was no harm in engaging in charitable
enterprise, in erecting shelters and clinics, in trying to
persuade lazy beggars into the use of soap and water, – and
teaching them English instead of French and German, which
was what other missionaries were doing. The good couple
were a little suspicious of the ladies Edith had taken up with
– Jewesses from Berlin and Vienna, who came to London to
induce their sisters to share in their Eastern activities, and
called themselves a *Cultural* League. Odd word to apply to
lace and craft ateliers and farm schools, where they proposed
to turn shiftless girls into artists – artizans – dairy workers –
and similar absurdities in a land where there was no prospect
for either art, industry, or agriculture. However, Edith might
as well spend a year or two there as in the slums of England
and Wales. She was of age, and bent on wasting her modest
Rachlin income in her own special way. God's work or not, it

was a godsend to them at this particular juncture of their affairs. The doctor in London had confirmed their incredulous hope. After twelve years of marriage, and on the verge of her forties, Sir Gwilym's wife expected to produce an heir. A grandson would be a formidable rival to Edith in the old lady's heart! They could afford to placate every objection, and to oppose only the dowager's sudden desire, once she became reconciled, to accompany the girl. Since Edith herself would not hear of it, the idea was frustrated. Lady Hafod consoled herself with her grand-daughter's promise of a visit home in the following year. She accepted her son's assurance that the child would be sick of the whole business by then. There was no meaning to her in the glance he exchanged with Ann, by which they signalled to each other their belief in the permanence of the "craze."

All this was clear to Simon as if he saw it in a mirror. He who was seldom able to read the ulterior mind, developed a strange perspicacity where Edith was concerned. He had learned a great deal at Millicombe, where he had spent several week-ends; the first not long after the disaster from which he emerged with nothing worse than a mortified spirit. Old Lady Hafod (he showed so plainly that he did not regard her as old, that this alone endeared him to her!) was kind to him, – even encouraging. Edith's latest plan had startled her into welcoming any bait that might keep the girl in England. She surrendered to her liking for this handsome nobody, who looked more of an English gentleman than the aristocratic natives of her circle; and who, sharing with them a discreet passion for her pet, outshone them in evidence of favour.

With a mixture of relief and apprehension, not always clearly proportioned, Lady Hafod observed a singular situation. Simon Black utterly at Edith's beck: Edith beckoning him where she disdained to see others, yet blind to him when he approached. Her ladyship was baffled. Often she had dreaded the possibility of Edith's falling in love with the "wrong man" – "some Jew, of course" – But now she sighed with Lena Rachlin over the "child's lack of romance".

"The wretched wife probably ran off because she was neglected. No use telling me she was drawn back to her own kind. If he hadn't been thinking too much of Edith, it might never have happened. However, one can't be sorry about that. He was too good for the little hussy, and though he isn't good enough for Edith, one can't help being touched by such devotion. Besides – I feel queer about the way my instinct has justified itself." She had confided to Lena the tale of the photograph. "The little boy's eyes as he looked at her – and my instant jump into the future! Almost uncanny, my dear. I did all I could to prevent it happening. And now—" she sighed again. "After all, I can't even tell whether I interfered with Fate or not. It's clear enough on *his* side. But on *hers* – I can't make out whether she cares for him or not. Sometimes I think it isn't in her to respond to any deep *personal* love. Haven't you noticed—" She paused: not only because Lena was smiling quizzically.

It was Simon rather than Lena who had noticed how indifferent Edith was to the lavishings of her grand-mother's affection. She accepted in her most casual way the frequent caresses and endearments. But to Simon the fact did not imply a congenital lack of tenderness. He had seen, too often, at Caramel Place, Edith sitting at Bubele's knee, smoothing the little wrinkled hand, pressing it to her lips, in a spontaneous warmth she did not demonstrate elsewhere. Lady Hafod bedarlinged her with a thousand kisses. Bubele used no stronger term than "mein kind," and herself blushed shyly at a caress.

The younger Hafods did not approve the dowager's indulgence of Simon. They regarded his advent with alarm, tempered only by their construction of Edith's attitude. The hints they permitted themselves to drop when alone with him confirmed his intuition of their point of view. He was not in the least perturbed by their animus against himself. But in the end, their belief that Edith would never return struck at him like a blow. Somehow, with all his closer access to Edith's thoughts, such a conviction had never held his mind. In spite of her interest in the *Yishub*, the new Settlement of Jews in Palestine, and her practical arrangements with regard to a hostel in Tiberias; he, like Lady Hafod, had taken it for granted that her action was experimental, and would not outlast the autumn of the following year. She would not – she could not – detach herself so completely from England, from all she cherished here – from Bubele, if not from Lady Hafod and Millicombe – from – he dared, and dared not, add, *himself*. The intimacies of these last months had not reached the stage of admitting his claim. He was not yet in a position to make explicit demand. And even if he were, could he expect her to stoop to him? In spite of the familiar self-query, he expected, now, a great deal. She spared no other man as much of her attention: as far as he knew, no other man could deflect as much of her will. He was aware that she yielded more to him than she chose deliberately to yield: but it did not help him to cross a barrier that she could erect at any moment, out of the fusion of her reserves with his fear. How precious it was, how much to risk – the little that she gave, to him alone. The dismay with which he had first heard of her project –

when he understood the meaning underlying her emphasised "*Next Year in Jerusalem*" at the memorable *Seder* – was mitigated by the promise of correspondence, and, of course, by the implication of her return. For she herself had never said – "For ever."

And then, suddenly, the calm assumption of the younger Hafods sprang out, like a new element come into league against him. He did not know how to deal with it. Like a shapeless monster, it loomed and mowed in foglike penetration of his last day's peace of mind. To speak of it seemed impossible. Even Lena Rachlin, with her acute perceptions, did not see it behind the shutter of what she called his "infatuated gaze." But this evening she was coping with some demon of her own. When the three drew together in final farewell, she laughed in a kind of absent haste and exclaimed.

"Go, then, go – it's no use dragging it out! But I can't see you to-morrow because of my concert. In any case you'll ruin it."

"I?" said Edith.

"Of course. I know I shall think of you and *thump* – thump off all the worry you've given us – all the frustration you've been the cause of——"

"You couldn't thump, Lena," said Edith calmly. "And nobody's frustrated. My going away is a – fulfilment."

Lena looked at her as if she were seeing her for the first time that evening. Her excitement died. She stretched out her hands and took Edith's in a steady clasp.

"Perhaps," she said slowly.

The two girls kissed in solemn ceremony. Simon had a confused vision of green hips swaying, in an abrupt turn of figure as if it were *she* who were making a departure. And then his impatience spent itself in a delicious hustle. He was taking Edith away from the lights and the voices, from the pressure of other presences, from the footman and the great heavy doors, down the wide stone steps into the waiting cab.

"At last," he said. The velvet folds of her cloak lay softly against his arm, but she herself was turning to the window, opening it in spite of the keen, easty air. Before he could lean across to help, the sash was down, and she was resting her head in the corner. He looked at the curve of cheek under the shadowed hair and added,—

" I hope you're not too tired."

She did not answer at once. They had passed the dark hulk of Buckingham Palace. Beyond the gates of the Mall, Queen Victoria stared stonily into space.

"It has been rather tiring. Perhaps I'm ungrateful – but I almost wish the Rachlins hadn't been so kind. Of course it would have been the same at Lowndes Square. But I would sooner have spent the evening quietly with Bubele."

"If you meant to include me, I should say – much sooner!"

She laughed briefly, and drew the cloak higher round her shoulders.

"My cousin Beatrice would have been spared the outrage to her feelings! I ought to have told her how nicely some of her Christians took it. Did you hear old Sir Gilbert Wayne say he believed in the mission of the Jews? He's a bit mixed, poor dear, but it's easier to understand the British Israelites than the British Jews. He reminded me that his ancestor had fought with mine – a Lansome, of course – in the Crusades."

"I heard you acknowledge the Crusader." Simon had seen the ancient pictures housed at Millicombe. "I wonder if you feel there is some truth in Sir Gilbert's suggestion – that it is the blood of the Crusaders in your veins which calls you to Palestine?"

"*You* can hardly believe that – knowing the Crusaders spilt rivers of *Jewish* blood!"

"They left enough to flow back into you – predominantly. I couldn't very well believe anything else, now. But it seemed to me – in fact, I thought it when I saw the picture of Hugh Lansome – that in you the two strains could run together – more fitly, perhaps, than in anyone else."

"I'm glad you thought that. Though I don't know that I should be singled out. After all, there are many English people, *unmixed*, who are in real sympathy with Jews. I don't mean exceptional persons like George Eliot. And of course she came of Welsh stock!"

He smiled back into the illuminated corner. It was not embarrassing to either of them to evoke the image of old Lloyd.

"A Bible sympathy," he said. "Why not? But other nations have the Bible, without revealing the sympathy. There really must be something kin between the English and Jewish peoples. Our best types show it."

"*Our*?" He could not help a rare touch of mockery, of triumphant 'catching her out.' She moved impatiently.

"You need not think I care *nothing* for being English – as you care nothing for being Jewish!"

The bitterness in her voice was music in his ears.

"That isn't quite fair," he said gently. "You've made me care a good deal about being Jewish. Don't attack me for reminding you that I'm not half as English as yourself."

"I'm sorry, Simon." She seemed to struggle for her equability.

"I see what it is, Edith," he said, with a coaxing eagerness.

"You hate leaving England, after all. I felt sure you would – though you won't admit it—"

"I don't mind admitting it," she said, and leaned to the open window. They were crossing Trafalgar Square. The column that had grown, as it were, into Simon's retina, so that he saw it upstanding in the initial letter at every mention of the word London, was cut off by the roof of the cab from actual sight. He could see only its base, the couches of the lions, the slope of the parapet lit by an intermittent shine. The sense of spaciousness, larger for the subdued current of humanity, running low in the midnight hour, narrowed between the walls of the Strand. Outlined in the dark clarity of the sky, the old buildings pressed thick towards the river.

Edith's eyes filled with an enveloping zest.

"Are the gods kind or cruel," she murmured, "in giving me such a night for remembrance? If there was rain or fog – but no – starlight in this delicious air. I'm afraid I must have prayed to them unconsciously – my old British gods! I *wanted* it to be like this, Simon – you and I driving through the clear, cold night, in the city that has got into your bones, and is in mine, too, though I'm leaving it for one that's clearer – that belongs to us – both, even more—" She lifted her hand that had been lying on her knee, and he seized it. The falling notes of her voice affected his nerves uncontrollably. She did not withdraw from his clasp, but maintained her arm at the same rigid angle, and said, more steadily,

"Very well, then, Simon – swear it with me. 'If I forget thee, O Jerusalem, let my right hand forget its power'—"

She said it in slow, emphatic Hebrew.

His fingers loosened and fell away. A policeman near the

Law Courts looked in at them curiously. Edith drew back into her corner, and laughed, a little soft, sighing laugh. Her voice changed its timbre.

"Tell me," she said. "Was my Hebrew very bad?"

"You mean – now?"

"Oh, no – Myer Billig taught me the oath quite beautifully. I mean Jehuda Halevi, whom I'm afraid I abused. Be my honest critic."

"It wasn't *bad*. A little stilted, perhaps – I thought that might have been nervousness – though I've never known you nervous."—

"Naturally I was nervous. I knew *you* were listening."

He could not smile back now.

"Did you say it in Hebrew – for *me*?" She did not speak, and he went on – "You did not *look* nervous – but very brave – and sweet. I'm afraid I didn't listen closely. You see – as soon as you stood up, I began to think of the time I first heard you recite. You remember, the college soirée? You wore a similar dress – at least the colour was the same – this goldy stuff –" He touched the gown where it flowed through an opening of the cloak.

"Was it?" she said. "I don't wear it often, though it's my favourite shade."

"You look marvellous in it. Like a golden princess. That's what you always seemed to me, you know – from the time I saw you at Hafod. That night at the soirée I knew you – and yet I didn't, at first. I've told you, haven't I, how I tried to find out? – And how I dreamed – and it came to me?"

"Yes," she said. "But to-night—"

"I had just found you, then," he said. "And to-night – I'm not losing you, am I?"

The breath of the monster was upon him. He determined to rout it.

"You should know best," she said, "whether a Jew loses a friend – even a princess – when he discovers she is a Jewess."

"He would lose her anyway, if she went away from him." He hesitated a moment. The taxi-driver changed gear. The cab mounted Ludgate Hill with a slower, noisier motion. "Edith, you don't mean to stay away – for good?"

"For good?" she repeated. "If I did, I suppose it would really be, for *good*."

"You are torturing me," he said in a low tone. "Do you think – I could bear—"

She sat up hurriedly.

"But I mean to come back for a couple of months next year – and to write to you constantly. Why should you talk of loss? Perhaps" – she spoke less rapidly. "Perhaps we shall become far better friends than if I remained here."

A test? A promise? He caught at the suggestion, and turned it over silently in his heart. All he dared say was, "Then are you sure you will go back, after the year or so?"

"I must, if I'm to complete the course I've undertaken. It's a matter of three years at least. After that, who knows? It's quite possible I shall want to settle permanently. But I have to learn the conditions. And there are all sorts of uncertainties for people in my position, who are not actually colonisers. The need is for workers on the land. The utmost I can do at present is to help in training and caring for such workers. What else may arise, I don't know. Don't ask me more now – please. If I'm content to trust to the future – you must be, too—"

The careful precision of her speech had broken into tremor. It silenced him, with its hint of confirmation – meagre, perhaps, but confirmation. She looked out of the window at the great Bank buildings, dark, hushed, and eyeless in the city's lull, and let the crisp air strike her forehead.

"You haven't told me about the interview with your chief," she said suddenly.

"I'd forgotten. But it's all right – the transference is as good as arranged."

"It's a phenomenal jump for the service?"

"He thinks I'm keen. And it happens I've swotted up particularly well."

"I thought seniority counted."

"It does. But I suppose this is where my luck comes in. My two seniors have other fish to fry. Besides – an unmarried man stands the best chance in this case. I may have to travel about with the Secretary."

"Lucky all round, then," she said, turning with a smile.

"I don't know." He did not like her bright, detached tone. There was a time when her interest in his career would have seemed its greatest prize. But now the expression of it was unwelcome, with its effect of fending him off, of approving something that divided them. It led to a startling reflection in his mind.

The cab slowed down at the corner of Caramel Place. Edith wished to avoid the sounds of stopping and restarting at her grandmother's door. The pavement was dry, and she could walk with impunity in her bronze satin shoes and fine-spun stockings of the same hue. As he handed her out, Simon longed to lift his golden princess bodily from the step and carry her across the harmless flags. Her hair shone against his breast for a dazzling moment. But his palms could only clutch emptily at the air as she hurried on, put her key in the door, and pushed it open. Within the dark interior she stood still and waited. A very dim light showed from the curve of the stairhead. On the wall near her hand was a switch for the lower lamp. She did not touch it.

"I won't ask you to come up," she said. "It would disturb Bubele too much. So—" she hesitated. He remained in the doorway, staring out.

"This is where you cast me off, once," he said. "Are you doing it again?"

"As you're *inside*, now," she said lightly, "you can't really think so."

"Of course I can't," he said. "You wouldn't be so cruel to me again. No, no, I know you weren't cruel – I know I was a fool about it all." He had turned towards her. "When you told me to-night why you were so angry, that time, I realised at once as I had never done before – that it was because I had *hurt* you, somehow – it wasn't just anger at my not thinking as you did. You were angry with Hector Wyn, too, for thinking differently. But it wasn't the same – I know it wasn't Edith, my dear – you *did* like me then, a little more than you liked Wyn – and it hurt you more that *I* disappointed you. Didn't it?" She did not speak, and he came nearer, looking pleadingly at her. "Isn't it true, Edith?"

"Perhaps," she said. "But we were just children – there are other things I didn't understand, either, as I do now – or make allowances for – we've both changed since then—"

"One thing in me has never changed," he said – "except to grow stronger. And in you, too – that liking – if it hasn't grown, at least it's still more than you feel for anyone else – won't you *let* it grow, my – dearest?"

"I begged you not to ask me now," she murmured.

"Because – truly, Simon, I don't know – I don't know – perhaps – I shall find out – please wait—"

"I suppose I must," he said. " But not – too long. And I couldn't let you stay away from me. If you decide to remain out there, I'll come, too."

"What?" she said. Her downcast eyes flashed up, glinted blue light at him. "As a chalutz? Really, Simon, I can't see you working on the land, breaking stones, draining swamps—"

" I'm strong enough, surely. There are other things I might do better. But I shouldn't mind *anything*, if you wished it – if it proved to you, that I—"

She broke in hurriedly, deliberately.

"But if you came to Palestine because I wished it, it would prove nothing to me that I – wanted proved. It would be a mistake, believe me – for you, for me – and for Palestine. Oh, don't you see – you should not come unless you want – Zion!"

There was a little pause.

"Won't you ever – care – for anyone, *more* than you care for Zion?"

"I – doubt it."

The words were more confident than the tone, which faltered. He stood within an inch of her, his gaze hungry, absorbing, in the semi-darkness. She did not stir, only her lids drooped again over her eyes, so that he could not look into them.

The moment was magical: but he did not know it. It did not occur to him that if he took her into his arms, he might resolve her doubt. He was so accustomed to accept her judgment, to believe in her certainty of herself – and so humble in estimating his power over her. It was he who drew away, to lean against the wall, pressing his hands to his forehead.

"Edith, Edith," he said, almost in a whisper, more to himself than to her. "I don't know what my life will be without you."

She said nothing. He heard a deep breath, and the swish of her dress. When he looked up, she had ascended a few stairs, and was bending towards him over the rough banister.

"I've an idea," she said in her ordinary light rapid tone. "I want to make it quite clear that I'm not casting you off. As a proof, I'm going to ask you to do something."

"Anything."

He stood, gazing up at her. She smiled, tilting her face upwards, and seemed to listen. The only sounds were a faint gurgling of water in a cistern, the creak of wood somewhere in the dark old warehouse-office, a raucous blend of voices in the distant street.

"Come and see Bubele sometimes."

"Yes, of course. I meant to, in any case. It's always been to me a certain way of keeping in touch with you."

"But you like Bubele for herself? "

"Rather. She is a finer lady than Mrs. Rachlin."

"I'm glad you feel that."

Her voice deepened warmly – trembled. "She is – the finest lady I have ever known. God bless her – my darling Bubele!"

"Do you wish me to take care of her? "

"Thank you, no. Her son – my uncle – does that thoroughly, you know. But if you come here, sometimes – she likes you, too, and will be glad to see you. You can talk to her about – about—"

"We'll talk about you."

She laughed softly.

"But that's not the proof I mean to give you. My idea is just this. Instead of leaving you on the doorstep while I close the door on you, I'll wait here while you shut yourself out. Just draw the door, it locks quietly. Then I'll run upstairs and watch you go down the street from my window."

"Splendid!" He was childishly delighted that she could be childish with him.

She stretched her arm over the banister.

"Good-night, Simon," she said. "You'll come to the station to-morrow?"

"I'll try." He moved forward, looking up, drinking in the last time – for more than a year – that he would be alone with that dear, unyielded face. Had the banister been of spiked iron, it would have divided them less than her will, which he imagined himself powerless to infringe. He took her hand between both his, pressed it, and held it to his lips. She drew it away very gently.

"Go, now, please."

He backed slowly, returning her grave smile. The door remained ajar on his reluctant grip.

"Say 'good-night'," she urged in a whisper. "Remember, you must not keep me waiting – neither here nor at my window. Unless you go straight away of your own accord, letting me watch you out of sight, I'll be obliged to go first – and you'll spoil my idea."

"Good-night – my princess—" he said, and with a quick movement closed the door behind him. He stood on the pavement until he saw her at the window, too shadowy in the darkness to strain obedience further. With a last salute, he walked sharply away, and did not even turn his bare head as he rounded the corner where the taxi waited. A film of happiness spread thinly over his discontent. Not childishness, but womanly awareness, had eased the parting for him. She had made him leave her, but the promise of her sweetness went after him. He might have felt it less adequate, if he had seen the shadow waver from the window to a stool before a mirrored table, the falling blur of cloak melt unheeded in the floor, the white lines of arms meet over a shine of hair, while reflected gleaming eyes – gleaming with tears – told the same tale as a pair of parted lips – "Oh, my dear – my dear – why didn't you—? Have I punished myself as well as you? Have I missed something I'll never find again? Will you reach what I want you to reach – and *without* me?" The shining head sank between the lines. There was a rustle at the door. A small figure in a shawl and slippers showed in the pool of light outside.

"Mein kind, you are not yet in bed? And with such a journey to-morrow? – What are you doing?"

"Naughty Bubele – why did you get up? I'm undressing – and I'm going to sleep at once. So must you. I won't say another word until the morning, so you needn't ask…. Good-night, darling … oh, God, must I drive everybody who loves me away?"

Still less adequate, if he had seen another's cup of joy filled to the brim, at the moment when he drained his own small measure.

As the lights went out in the Rachlin drawing-room, the daughter of the house came down the wide stairs to the hall, and said something to the footman lingering drowsily about. She halted at a cream-panelled door on her left, watched the servant disappear down a long corridor, then turned the handle, and entered a softly-lit room. Harman, who was sitting over a book at a table, rose instantly.

"Sorry you've been kept so long," said Miss Rachlin. " But I had to make sure the dear parents had gone up."

"What's the mystery, Lena?"

"It's to be a mystery, or at least a secret from them, for at least a week longer. I didn't mean to tell you, either, just yet – not until Wednesday, anyway. But since you threaten to go back to America on that very day—" she paused. "You'll postpone your trip until my party's over, at least?"

"Oh, it's a party?"

"A special one. I've never had one like it before." With hands pressed behind her on the table, she lifted herself in a sinuous bound, and sat, close to him, her black head drooping to his shoulder. He stiffened himself as he stood, but did not move. A strange look hardened the pleasant eyes.

"Perhaps – it's a wedding party?"

She projected one knee above the other, clasped hands around it, and contemplated her long black shoe with its emerald buckle. A trilling chuckle came from her throat.

"I shouldn't be surprised," she said. "Should you?"

"Sorry, but I'm not interested," he said. " I'd rather you didn't tell me your secret – until it isn't one – until everything's over. I sail on Wednesday."

"There'll be another boat – *after* the party."

"I sail on Wednesday," he said. She looked at him with a smile he seemed to find maddening.

"I've told you," he said, with emphasis, "I'm not interested." He turned, and picked up his hat from a chair.

"You're a liar, Jack," she said. With a sudden leap, she was off the table, coolly taking the hat from his hands and putting it away.

"Poor thing, I'll put you out of your misery at once. Listen. I've taken a flat. The dear parents have opposed my little scheme for a year – it's absurd of them, as I'm hardly ever at home – even when I'm in town. But I can't stand rows – with *them* – so I decided not to tell them until it was a fait accompli. A duck of a flat, Jack. You'll like it enormously. I'm having it re-decorated. The nicest room will be finished by Wednesday – that's when I intended you to see it. The rest won't be ready till the week's out. Then I'll have the boys and girls in – for a warming. So now you see why you've got to stay." She fingered the lapels of his coat and looked demurely into his eyes.

"I can't, Lena. I wish you luck in your new domicile. But I can't stay to see it."

"You mean you won't."

"Very well. I won't."

She dropped the coat-edges and moved away. Her emeralds flashed as they caught the light. "I don't know why I ask you. I don't know why I *want* you to come. You and I have really nothing in common. I simply can't think why I like being with you."

The mixture of petulance and chagrin was curiously naïve. His glance relaxed on her green and olive back.

"Your cousin would say because we are Jews."

"What nonsense! Jews don't necessarily love each other."

"At least they understand each other."

"You don't understand me in the least."

"Is that so?"

"You neither understand me nor love me."

"You know I do."

She whirled round eagerly.

"Which – or is it both?"

"I don't see why I should give you superfluous information."

"Now you're an idiot – in fact, no Jew!" She laughed,

throwing up her chin. "It seems a banker's daughter doesn't really attract you."

"You told your mother it was the Christians who were attracted."

"Never mind what I told my mother. Answer what I say to *you*."

"A banker's daughter is too expensive an attraction for a poor man."

"How feeble! Scrupulous persons needn't touch my dowry. In any case I can pay my own way. You don't, by any chance, object to the brilliant musician earning her living?"

She came close to him and put her hand on his. He squeezed the fingers and threw them away.

"You extravagant butterfly – it isn't only money you're extravagant with—" His low tone hoarsened slightly.

"You won't share my Gentile lovers with me?"

"No, by God! "

Her eyes danced.

"So that's the trouble – that's why you cleared out so smartly from Dick's last week. I had one or two special friends there, and you didn't like them! But you needn't be jealous of them, you fool – not even of our dear Dick himself."

"Dick's all right," he said curtly.

"Of course. He doesn't paw and spit at the damned Jewess. You don't think I'd marry any of those – tom cats?"

"I don't know that you should marry – anybody. You want a slave, not a husband."

"A slave?"

"Do you imagine I can't guess why you're set going like this to-night? I don't flatter myself you've changed your mind – but it doesn't suit you now that *I* should change. You're all afire for a simpleton to stand adoring you – for ever and ever – no matter what you do – or where you may be—"

She turned her face away to hide an exultant smile. It was the note she wanted to hear – the note so difficult to force from this controlled, fastidious man. Rage, with the exaggeration that betrayed it—

"You're mistaken, Jack boy," she said in her most honeyed way. "I'm not Edith."

"And I'm not Simple Simon."

"You *are* like him, all the same. Simple, dear – not a simpleton. That's what I meant, you know – simple in the nice, direct English way." She poured her audacious smile upon him. "And you *do* adore me, Jack—you *do!*"

"I'm no idol worshipper."

"A real Jew, then, after all – by God!" She mocked his tone and tossed her head disdainfully. "Stiffnecked and unaccommodating – so unlike the charming Gentiles. And won't even flatter himself, in case he has to pay! Never fear, I'll take you at your word. Rat, if you wish to – rat to America. When you come back I'll be gloriously – sunk!"

She spread her arms and let them fall, in a magnificent gesture of art. But the sudden swing towards the window, the leaning of her elbows on the frame as she dropped her neck, were not quite calculated. He hesitated a moment. Then in a swift stride he was close behind, his arms around her, his hands twisting her face gently to his.

"Adorable," he murmured, "how can I help but adore you?"

He kissed her forehead, with the same tenderness that restrained his powerful grip. She stood mute within it, neither yielding nor resisting, her eyes closed beneath long, shadowed lids.

"Only I can't let you make an utter fool of me, sweet – and if I stay—"

"If you stay, we'll be fools together."

"Perhaps I'm one already – I don't quite understand—"

"Didn't I say so?"

"You bewilder me – especially now – I can't think. – Do you, or don't you, still refuse to marry me?"

"When did you ax me, sir, she said? Oh, I suppose you mean that little affair about fifteen years ago – at one of your birthday parties!"

"You remember?"

"Do you?"

"Every moment. My thirteenth – the last you came to. It should have been Barmitzvah, I suppose, if my parents had – well, it was just an ordinary birthday. Until *you* turned me into a man. I wonder if you *do* remember – how I skulked in a corner, the shyest youngster that ever was, while the others enjoyed themselves. I took no notice of them, and they took no notice of me. Then you played. All the others chattered and didn't listen. You were angry, and broke off in the middle. Still they didn't notice. I watched you go into another corner and sulk. I followed you and tried to console you. You wouldn't speak, but looked at me with those eyes of yours. Suddenly I took you in my arms – just as I've got you now – and loved you. I asked you to marry me. You *do* remember?" He gave a short excited laugh.

"I don't remember refusing."

"Not then – but years later. – Oh, but you didn't even let me ask you – you wouldn't let me touch you – you simply laughed in my face. You knew – and you went off, laughing, to dance with – with a beast—"

"He was terribly handsome," she murmured.

"The most notorious beast in London. And each time I've seen you since—"

"I hadn't learned, Jack. I hadn't found out the difference between other men's arms, and yours."

He almost released her. But she clung, and involuntarily he responded.

"Oh, Jack, hold me, hold me. I've been loved and hated so many times since you – but nobody has ever tried to comfort me. Nobody but you. And it isn't only – comfort. It's the way you are holding me now – the way—" She did not continue, but let her head sink on his breast. He put his lips to her hair and whispered over her.

"The way a man holds the woman he loves."

"The way a man holds the woman he – respects," she murmured.

"Of course. If it's the woman he is going to marry."

A little smothered laugh rippled out to him – a laugh that sounded almost a sob.

"Not Lena Rachlin, I suppose – the brilliant musician – the Banker's daughter – the handsome, rude, intolerable Lena Rachlin? Oh, no. Only the woman he wants to marry—"

She raised her head and opened her eyes. He looked deep into them and a strong sigh shook him. "Beauty," he said, "Your eyes wring my heart. If I were only sure – that I could make you happy—"

She drew his face to hers and their lips met. A few minutes later she sprang away. There had been a click as of a door. But it was only a coal fallen from the dying fire. As she regarded it, she said,

"Jack, I want to ask you something."

"Ask, my darling."

"It's rather private."

"Can anything be too private – for your future husband?"

"That's exactly what I feel." But she did not proceed immediately. She played with her necklace, and let him take her hands away to rub between his own. They were cold he declared and he went on rubbing and kissing them alternately, all the time looking at her with the air of a man smiling for joy. He was not, however, actually smiling. An inward radiation had that effect on his plain face marked always by a singular charm of expression.

"'It's just this, Jack," she said with deliberation. " Have you been circumcised?" His hands dropped hers abruptly. "You shameless creature! Why do you want to know?"

"I'm not shameless. Surely it's a question the strictest Rabbi would approve!"

He stared at her for a moment. A sensitive disturbance darkened his look.

"Possibly. There's no reason to object. Well, then—" He half sat down on the rolled arm of a divan chair, and folded his arms – "I wasn't originally. My parents didn't care, as you may have guessed. But two years ago – when I was in Switzerland—" he hesitated, and seemed to reflect – "Didn't I send you a card, telling you I was attending a congress of nationalist Jews at Basle?"

"Perhaps. Wasn't that the time when there was an accident to your party on the Mer de Glace? … I heard of somebody being detained in a nursing home."

"I wasn't in the accident. But I was detained in a nursing home, a little later on – on my way back through Germany."

"I see. You had it done – then?"

He nodded.

"Because of what you heard at Basle?"

"Not altogether. It gave a kind of culmination to an idea I had before – that I ought—" he hesitated again, as if with a difficulty of expression – "that I ought to seal myself to my people."

"What! Not even a medical-hygienic – reason? And you're a *rationalist*! " She shrugged her shoulders and smiled in a peculiarly wry fashion. "Oh, Lord! How extraordinary! Mother's convinced I'm a little demented – but compared with Edith – and you—" She came and kneeled on the long wide seat of the chair – "Jack, Jack, I didn't believe you had any surprises for me!"

He put his hands on her shoulders.

"Well, – are you satisfied?" he said.

"I'm satisfied that I'm marrying – a damned Jew," she said, and laughed against his breast. There was another click. This time they did not move apart. But the door had actually opened. A voice articulated in thickly harsh tones – "Lena!"

She raised her head and saw her father.

Harman relaxed his hold. He had been caught prematurely, and showed it. Lena's eyes flashed back to his. Her hand touched his arm.

"I love you, Jack," she whispered.

Harman's head went up. He pressed the hand, smiled at her, and advanced towards the forbidding visage at the door.

XXIV

THE YEAR passed, less slowly than Simon expected. His work became more varied and exacting; his friendships widened for a time, then narrowed and deepened: the messages from Palestine spanned gaps of fertile thought. At first he had made a false step. Edith had no sooner left than he sent her a reckless letter. It was an outpouring of love in all the sweet and ardent terms he had never uttered. No reply came. When he found that Lena Rachlin and Bubele were receiving epistles, while nothing followed the card addressed to him from Egypt, he was more than chagrined. Inquiry brought a brief response. He must not write to her in such a strain, she said, or it would be impossible for her to reply. He thought her hard and evasive, but did not say so. His expression of penitence – not too meek, but free of endearment – was rewarded with a description of her journey and surroundings, lengthy, light and charming. He was pleased, yet surprised. He had anticipated something solemn and impressive, if not ecstatic. She might have been writing of a trip to Morocco. Even Jerusalem was dismissed rather coolly. "The approach was wonderful. But the city itself disappointing … of course it isn't Jewish any longer, except in a backwater sense. I liked best the view from the mountains…"

There was no further break in the correspondence, but the intervals were longer than Simon liked. Often he sent two or even three letters to her one. She excused herself on the plea of work… "You have no idea how the days fly. We have, of course, a regular routine… Up before dawn, the girls carry on a series of duties in kitchen, dairy, garden, and field – until sunset, when indoor lessons go on. There are set tasks for everyone, practical and technical instruction according to hour, season and necessity. We study the scientific preparation of food, human, animal, and vegetable physiology. There are cows and poultry to tend, thousands of young trees to foster, crops to cultivate. The staff is small and overburdened; the pupils are keen and industrious, so deeply imbued with a sense of their importance as colonisers that the responsibility of teaching increases daily … I care mainly for their health, but I cannot help but join in tasks outside my special province … We have walks and talks together, we try to understand and improve each other … Here is a spirit of camaraderie such as I have never experienced before … In the winter I may have more leisure, but even then … if I am free, I mean to do some hospital work where it is urgently needed – in Haifa – or Jaffa—"

Her accounts continued, on the whole, rather colourless, and strangely lacking in enthusiasm. He suspected her of writing under restraint, and wavered between satisfaction and anxiety. Was she homesick – heartsick? – He decided to be piqued, discovering her letters to others had more fervour. "Why is she afraid to let herself go – with me? " he wondered. But he found it was to him that she gave most information. She managed, after a time, to explore every part of Galilee, to visit Judea and Samaria, and see all the scattered settlements, old and new, of North and South. The beauty of the Lake of the Harp, from which the Jordan flowed over plain and valley, of the purple hills ranging from their snow-crowned king round a natural garden of profuse wild bloom, came through even her curbed allusions. Set in the scene of the last Jewish patriots, where Hebrew culture withstood Roman, Greek, and Christian for centuries after political power had gone, she must have been stirred beyond the bald account she gave of Tiberias and Safed – "dreary, now, and depressing, in structure and life. Western tourists go into raptures over all they see – dirty Arab, ghetto Jew, hovel and plague heap – everything's 'quaint' and 'picturesque' – how I abhor the silly, patronising words! Slums on the site of the golden age – oh Death, oh Ruin, where is thy dignity? But it is Life we must have here, not Death in Life, – so we want roads, pipes, ploughs – the paraphernalia of prosaic but vitalising civilisation."

And yet she did not rhapsodise over the colonies with their flourishing groves and meadows, their crops of wheat, barley, grapes, olives, oranges, their superior sense of the domestic and communal arts. She stressed, rather, the hardships that surrounded success, describing in detail the toils and perils of the pioneers. Parched hills refertilised, lowland swamps drained and rid of mosquito pest, trees planted to suck up poisons and shield hard-won land from constantly drifting sand at the cost of crippling disease, of lives lost in the ramp of malaria. More, even, was needed than idealism on the heroic scale, to cope with abused nature, with sluggish and hostile man, in the fetid trance of the East. Often despair and ruin followed broken health, pillage, inexperience, lack of implements, medical aid and sanitation. To the difficulties of a neglected soil were added the handicaps of development under the Turk, who hindered every constructive effort; harassment from the Arab, who raided and destroyed, or baulked from sheer superstition ignorance. "They don't understand as yet true fellowship, either with Man or Nature. Even when they cultivate the land they impoverish it. And then their notions of hygiene are too appalling." She related tales, half comic, half tragic. " But they are good souls when you get to know them. As in everything else, we need patience as well as zeal. Since we must live together, we have to raise their moral and mental status, win them from hostility to friendship, and make them share in the benefits we bring to this dear land … Particularly we encourage their children to come to our schools and clinics. As I write I see through the window an Arab woman with her child, coming to me from her village … I had a hard struggle to get her to believe I wasn't poisoning the tot, but saving it for her … Now we're fast friends…"

By the summer Simon was living again in "digs" – more comfortably than of old, since he was quartered with a pleasant family in Westbourne Grove. The acquaintance came about through Jack Harman. The Vannicks' antique shop in the Queen's Road had once belonged to his father, and there was a probability that the name of Harman, still retained, might again signify actual partnership. Simon had learned the story of Jack's recall from Oxford when the family fortunes crashed. He had been going in for law, though not ardently enough to regret it for the commercial life he was forced to enter. What he disliked, he told Simon, was not the antique business, but the form in which he was obliged to conduct it. For years he had been employed by agents in the purchase and transport of European objects to America. Now that he was in a position to buy back a share in the old family business, with a chance of ultimate control, he meant to undo some of his own recent work. Lena laughed at him for a sentimentalist.

"You wouldn't think so, to hear him drive a hard bargain," she told Simon, one evening after dinner at her flat. "But he'd sooner lose money than let some dingy sticks and stones leave their native shores – in fact, he'd sooner let them break his bones." And swinging on the piano stool, she sang to an improvised accompaniment:

"Sticks and stones will break my bones,

But names will never hurt me—"

"I'll see that the name of Harman won't," said her future husband.

"You've got to make papa see it," she retorted, "And turning down American orders won't help you, dear idiot."

Simon was in the secret – too much so for his peace of mind – of their relations, which were not acceptable to the Hon. Charles and his wife. They professed no personal objection to the son of Mrs. Rachlin's girlhood friend, but their ambitions for Lena were higher. Her parents' views however, had never yet dominated her. As in her professional career and in the minor matter of her flat, she hated their disapproval without forgoing her right to earn it. She met Jack's suggestion that she should give up the flat in order to conciliate them, by pointing out that her retention of it would be a more powerful argument in his favour. "If they think I'm leading a loose life," she said coolly, " they'll agree to my marrying anybody. Even a Jewish husband is better than a leman—"

Jack, too, though he would have preferred an amicable family understanding, was not deeply concerned. His arrangements for marriage hung on a necessary final trip across the Atlantic, and completion of the Vannick-Harman deed; though Lena declared it awaited her fulfilment of her season's tour. She was leaving London for an absence of some months.

"By the way, Jack – ," her long, powerful fingers uncurled over the keys – "what's happened about the Queen Anne service? Did it turn out to be your mother's?"

"The identical one. Came in from Christie's this morning." There was a smile on his face as he cut across her eager exclamation. "And the great 'I wanna' has already sent an offer for it."

"Then he can go on wannaing."

"He's offered – enough to pay your wedding expenses—"

"I'll be married in tissue paper." She slipped off the piano stool and perched on his knee. "Why Jack, you know perfectly well – your mother meant it to go to her son's wife. Your father told me so." Her arms were round his neck, in complete disregard of Simon. " Darling, I remember it so well – on that old Anne sideboard—"

"It's your wedding-present, you – sentimentalist."

Simon strolled back into the dining-room. To his relief, guests began to arrive. He liked being alone with either Harman or Lena. As a third, he found them unendurable.

As usual at Lena's parties, there were many strangers among the painters, musicians, writers – men and women he had not met before. Some of them had not even been invited, but were brought along by friends. Dick Partingdale was accompanied by one such stranger, whose name gave Simon a thrill of pleasure. There was a mutual exchange of satisfactory observation as they were introduced. George Westerley was one of Dick's college friends who had drifted out of range for years – he had travelled widely, secluded himself when at home, studied and written. His reputation as a fastidious literary artist was beginning to grow. Through Dick's talk Simon had been induced to read an early book of essays and a novel, and found them unexpectedly to his taste. He told Westerley so rather shyly. The author made no comment, but his eyes looked pleased. Unlike most of the men present, there was nothing shaggy or picturesque about his appearance. He was neatly dressed, his hair brushed smoothly over a wide forehead. He looked round with observant eyes, but hardly moved, and was almost conspicuously silent. Simon's fear of finding him either bored or supercilious vanished in the quiet friendliness of his regard. They chatted, casually and intermittently, throughout the evening.

Once they stood together in a general silence, while Lena played. A screen cut sight of her spread white skirts, the corals dancing in her ears and on the rippling breast; but it was not for that reason that the music, for once, obliterated thought of the player. The Handel Sonata floated out in rounded rhythm, pain-gathered sweetness moulded to perfect sound.

"Fine, wasn't it?" said Simon, as his companion did not speak.

"She's improved," said Westerley.

"All the critics said so after her last Queen's Hall. Were you there?"

"No. I was in the Balkans."

"Oh! Among the discords."

Westerley smiled.

"It's pretty bad out there, isn't it? Do you think there'll be serious trouble?"

A pause. " It might be avoided."

"Dick worries about it. He thinks the little wars may lead to a big one."

"Possibly."

Simon laughed. "Only way to settle it, perhaps. But it isn't likely to concern us much."

"I don't know."

Westerley left early to keep another appointment. He found Simon in the narrow corridor outside, where several men lounged and smoked or passed through to the other room, less hot than the crowded studio. A dark, ill-kempt fellow lurched by with a cup of coffee. He hailed Westerley with a flourish which upset his cup over the saucer and splashed the other's spruce sleeve.

"Filthy brute! " muttered the victim, taking out a silk handkerchief and mopping the stains. The swarthy fellow guffawed, made some jest about his empty cup, and passed on.

"Accident," said Simon – "but he might have apologised."

"What can you expect from a Jew?" said Westerley. "Ill-mannered, like all his tribe." There seemed unnecessary venom in the quiet voice. Ted Rendall had strolled up with young Vannick. A look in the latter's eye told Simon he had heard.

Westerley replaced his handkerchief and held out his hand. Simon took it and said,

"Our hostess is Jewish, you know. And so am I."

"Really?" There was no change in the smooth, cool face. "Ought I to beg your pardon? You're different, of course. Always pleasant to find the exception. Good-night. We'll meet again, no doubt."

Simon watched him go without a word. Ted Rendall was hunting for a match to light his cigarette.

"Damned cheek," said Vannick suddenly.

"Hallo!" said Ted. "What's up? "

Simon leaned against the wall and offered him a light.

Vannick began to mumble explosively, repeating Westerley's remarks.

"What about his manners, I'd like to know? Thinks he can get away with it by making exceptions – that prove the rule, of course! Oh yes, I know these anti-Semites. You can always spot 'em by the same old tag – 'Bless you, *I'm* not an anti-Semite – why, my dearest friend's a Jew!' naturally, quite different from the rest of the tribe, and all that."

"Rot!" said Ted uncomfortably. "Westerley's a decent sort. Dick thinks no end of him. Humanitarian and so on."

"A Jew isn't a part of humanity, I suppose," said Vannick.

"Chuck it," said Ted. "Westerley didn't mean anything. Had a right to feel annoyed, hadn't he? Eisenberg *is* a clumsy brute, though Dick says he paints like an angel." He glanced at Simon. "Now the worst of you chaps is – you're so damned sensitive. It don't seem reasonable to me. Can't you forget you're Jews, sometimes? I don't go about thinking I'm an Englishman all day long."

He moved forward to the studio and the others followed. Vannick recovered his easy spirits and forgot the incident. Simon brooded on it. It's lack of novelty made it no less galling, no less a slur on his admiration of Westerley. But Ted's remarks made him ponder most. He agreed with Vannick's protest – and once he would have replied to it with Ted's. But he had long since realised the impossibility of a *reasonable* adaptation to an unreasonable set of circumstances. Of course it was easy for an Englishman to go about England without thinking of the fact! But wasn't he likely to be conscious of it every moment when he was abroad? A Jew in England, even if he wanted to forget, was not allowed to escape constant reminder. And when the reminder was insolent – wasn't one even justified in feeling aggrieved? He had read a novel once where a Jew was jeered at for being impervious to insult. Funny thing how Jews were always being condemned for mutually exclusive attributes – for being at once too rich and too poor, for being fanatics and atheists, for being too sensitive and – too thick-skinned. The latter, perhaps, was most wide of the mark; unless there was such a thing as a Jewish fool. He remembered the Talmudic saying – "a fool does not feel an insult, neither does a dead man feel a knife."

No, Jews were not fools. Neither were they dead. If they lived again as a nation, as Edith believed – it might at least resolve the unpleasantness of duality. For duality there must continue to be, since not all Jews in the world could or would go to Palestine. The idea was to create a home, a motherland, which would be to the Jew what the mother-country was to the colonial Britisher. A centre from which every member of the race would draw dignity and self-respect. He himself would, in spite of everything, prefer to remain an Englishman – or, at any rate, an English Jew. Edith had shown there was virtue in the position, when she described herself as a link between his mother, whom she understood so well, and Marjorie Newell, whom she understood equally – while neither of the two understood the other, though each to some extent herself. It was even truer, in their case, than in that of Bubele and Lady Hafod, where the physical relationship proved as much a bar as a bond. And he, himself, – wasn't he just such a link between Ted Rendall and his own father – still more, between George Westerley and Eisenberg? He knew Eisenberg's type pretty well. If he disliked and despised him, it was an antipathy modified by knowledge – not so much of the individual, as of the conditions that produced him. A considerable span between Eisenberg's ghetto indiscipline and

Westerley's ordered life! The humanitarian, with his intellect and philosophy, not to speak of his romance, ought perhaps to have moved across himself. It was disconcerting to stumble on a block of prejudice in such a limpid pool of thought. But even this block might melt to the warmth of contact, established by one who could stand, in healthy circulation, with one foot in the icy pool, the other in fiery mud. Heat the snows, and purify the flame! Simon knew his metaphors were mixed, but his idea was clear to him, and satisfying. He had found that the condition of double existence, which had been such a misery to him, could turn into a precious advantage.

Another aspect reached him through Dinah, when she came up at the end of the month. It was the first time she had accepted her brother's invitation to spend a holiday in his charge. Mrs. Miller's offer of hospitality delighted both. Dinah had the privilege of occupying Edith's room, and it was sweet to Simon to escort his sister to and from Bubele's roof.

After a week of outdoor jaunts, the weather changed, and Dinah sated a passion for museums and galleries. They wandered through the great pile in Russell Street, worshipping the marbles, the potteries and bronzes, the petrified arts of antiquity. In the little Gem Room Dinah was fascinated by the intaglios, the tiny figures of nymphs and goddesses in jasper, sard, onyx, lapis lazuli and amethyst, and by the lovely Portland Vase, miraculously reconstructed after being smashed to pieces by a maniacal visitor. But the Graeco-Roman charms were overpowered in the Egyptian halls. Dinah stood awed before the bodies and hieroglyphics of the land of Rameses.

"Oh," she said, "Doesn't it make the Bible *real*?"

"That's what Edith – what Miss Miller used to say."

"Did you come with her here? You needn't mind calling her Edith. We all do at home – though mother and father say 'Edis'—"

"So does Bubele," said Simon. "The Askkenazic 's' is prettier than the 't.' Edis—" he added lingeringly. "It sounds like a pet name."

"It belonged to mother's grandmother. Don't you remember hearing of her? – a very froom, charitable old lady, who used to feed half the town in secret, though she fasted herself most days of the week – just like old Mrs. Miller."

"Then mother and Edith each had the same sort of grandmother. Dinah – do you really think – they have much else in common? "

"Edith understands mother wonderfully. Better than I do! Having things in common doesn't always make one – sympathetic. And it isn't only intelligence, or just living with people. Edith and I talked about it, when I asked her how she came to know the Welsh people so well. She said, what helps most is *wanting* to understand."

Dinah's halting speech was eloquence enough. Flowing and limpid with Edith's thought. To his sister, as to himself, she had given something precious – something greater than love itself. But it was love he needed: not the impartial rain of sympathy, however generous its fruits. If only Dinah had the means to sluice that need! With all their exchange of confidence, she had not even shown that she perceived it.

When he called next day at Caramel Place, Dinah was in bed with a cold. The skies were dark with rain and Bubele insisted that she should remain in her room. Simon had no objection to staying with her there, while Bubele went out shopping.

Miss Smithson chattered to him in the kitchen as she prepared a tray. He was a favourite now, and familiar in the queer old premises. This part of them, he had discovered long since, was Bubele's real sanctum. It held familiar household goods, separate cooking wares and two sinks, a huge Menorah on the mantelpiece, an embroidered Mizrach below a patch of frieze, disfigured to symbolise the ruin of Jerusalem. Among engravings of Rabbis hung a linen print, of Jewish soldiers in opposing armies solemnising Yom Kippur, together.

Simon stood and looked at the historic Yom Kippur scene, as he had often stood looking at it before. There on the plain before Metz, with the dark firs standing like sentinels on the hills, thousands of Jews in uniform worshipped around a holy Ark, surmounted by the Tablets of Stone. The Hebrew commandments towered above the men, in this unique armistice of their deadly trade. "Thou shalt not kill." What was in the hearts of the tragic multitude, brothers engaged in slaying brothers? The folds of their *Talithim*, the vestments of prayer, seemed to Simon's gaze to quiver suddenly over their incongruous garb of war. Life moved in the bearded faces, in the figures doomed to unwilling fratricide. "Have we not all one Father?" they asked, in the Hebrew-German text printed above, "Did not one God create us all?" What answer did the Shofar give on that Day of Atonement. – on that sanctified field of fate?

A cold breath passed over Simon, and he turned his eyes away. Extraordinary incident, that. He had never studied it closely before. Why should it touch him now with a sense of reality, – with anything less than the fantastic remoteness of the pictured past? 1870 was a deuce of a way behind. That kind of thing wasn't likely to recur, in spite of the splutterings of some Frenchmen about a war of revenge, and a lot of German bounce. He shrugged his shoulders, and smiled as Miss Smithson said – "Nah, then, Mr. Black, I'm ready." She preceded him fussily to the only door in the house through which he had never passed.

"Hallo, Di! Nice way to spend a holiday!" His cheery casualness was belied by the swift turn of his head to right and left. It was the sort of room he had expected to see – simple and fresh, harbouring unobstrusive treasures. There was a delightful paper on the walls; a ground of flat white on which blue ribbons hung from a yellow bar. Fastened to each strip in irregular spacing was a golden daffodil, deliciously real on its vivid green stalk. The only accompaniments were a few etchings of Devon, and a map of Palestine. On the mantelpiece was a small photograph in a silver frame; a postcard reproduction of Theodor Herzl. There was little furniture. Dinah sat up in a narrow bed, propped by a huge down "puff" that did not belong. (Bubele ever brooding over Edith's refusal to supplement her own small pillow, was gratified by Dinah's acceptance of the enormous thing.) There was a small dressing-chest in the window, a chair or two, a cupboard with a white-enamelled door, and a low bookcase. Simon read the titles of the books as he sat talking to Dinah. A complete Graetz, Essays on Jewish Nationalism, a History of the Welsh People, some English poets, George Eliot, Olive Schreiner, Hardy, Zangwill, college texts manuals on nursing, medicine, domestic science. There were gaps in all the shelves. She must have taken many volumes with her. The book lying on the bed was a modern novel brought by Simon for Dinah to read. Dinah confessed herself uninterested in Edith's collection.

"What's this?" asked Simon, suddenly. He had picked up an album, and was astonished to find in it a drawing of his sister, done with a certain crude power, and unlike the delicate sketches signed "E.M."

"It's me," said Dinah ingenuously. She was already flushed with the feverishness of her cold. Simon did not detect embarrassment.

"Yes, I see that. But who did it?"

"Gershon," said Dinah unexpectedly.

She answered her brother's expression of incredulity with a hurried explanation. Gershon really had a talent for drawing, and had exercised it secretly but continuously. He had left her a number of things, including several reproductions of herself. Edith had seen them, and taken this one away. She – Edith – had obtained expert opinion on it, and declared that when Gershon came back, he must be trained. With a knowledge of technique, he might do very well.

"Often he makes little sketches in his letters," added Dinah. She had pushed away the tray, and sat nursing her blanket-covered knees. "He isn't much good at writing, and his illustrations give me a better idea of what he is describing."

"I hope he hasn't forgotten to *speak* English," said Simon. "By Jove, isn't it nearly three years since he went away? Why, he'll be free to come back soon—"

"In September," said Dinah.

Simon stared hard at her. She shivered violently.

"You ought to be covered up more," he said. "Haven't you a wrap or something to throw over your shoulders?"

"It's in the cupboard – but I don't want it, really. I'm ever so hot." She leaned back on the pillow – and began talking again of Edith, her last visit to the family at Dawport, her meetings with Billig at their new home. Simon was diverted. He had heard most of it before, but he could listen endlessly.

"I hinted that Billig wasn't in love with her now," he said, grinning. "She declares someone in Dawport has supplanted her. Have you any idea who the girl can be? Not Sylvie, by any chance?"

Dinah ignored the question.

"It seems you suspect every man of being in love with Edith," she said, a little pettishly. "I've heard about them all – from Doctor Wyn down to Doctor Williarns. Of course it was true about Mr. Billig – once. He told me about it himself."

"He appears to have told you lots." Simon's grin became rueful. He had realised the source of her knowledge about Edith and himself.

"Of course – we are great friends. He has rather a hard time in Dawport. You know how our congregations treat their ministers. It's no wonder they get a bit 'pappy.' But he really has some good schemes for carrying on and making good. He's a dear, isn't he? Only – oh – so solemn!" They laughed together. "Still, he's given up pining for Edith. So it's not true of him now."

"And isn't it true of Doctor Williams?"

"I don't think so. He's engaged to a girl at Tavcastle."

"That's nothing. It was true of Hector Wyn – and he – perhaps you know? "

"Yes, Myer Billig told me – he did – very much what you did."

"Oh – not quite! "

"He married a hospital sister a month after Edith refused him. I don't know what happened to them – or rather, to her – but Myer says he's living with his mother in the flat. I suppose that's why she wouldn't go to the Rachlins', after all the trouble Edith took to get them invited – and wouldn't meet Edith anywhere else."

Simon was silent. He knew Edith had been disappointed at the rebuffs to her friendly overtures. It was a disappointment he did not share.

"Do you think," said Dinah, "that *she* was in love with Hector Wyn – at first?"

"No," he said curtly, " I don't believe she was ever in love, with any man who—who was in love with her—"

"Not even with you?" said Dinah, to his amazement.

"I – don't – know" – he stammered.

"Oh, Simon—" She sat up again, clasping her knees and leaning forward eagerly – "I'm sure she is."

"How on earth do you know, Dinah?"

How indeed, could Dinah know what Edith herself did not?

"Well, it isn't exactly *knowing* – but I just feel sure – it's difficult to tell how – by little things I remember. Of course, when we first became friendly at Blaemawe I had no idea – but when I look back, I realise—"

He could persuade her into nothing more definite, more revealing than her obvious desire to be very sweet to him. She began to sneeze again and to shiver violently, and agreed that he had better fetch her wrap from the cupboard. But when he opened the white enamelled door, he forgot his errand. There, in front of him, was the golden dress that Edith had worn on her last evening. The silk hung in firm graceful folds, almost as if shaped by a lovely body. His heart began to beat more quickly. He glanced round at Dinah, and saw her lying back, her face turned from him. He did not know that she was staring at his reflection in the mirror of the dressing-table opposite. His hands reached out swiftly, caressed the gleaming stuff, and drew it to his lips. His nostrils breathed the faint aroma that haunted his memory of that inadequate farewell.

"Oh, fool, why didn't I?" he thought in a flash, his mouth pressed to the empty gown. It was as if he saw her sink down, here on this bed of hers, restless, unsatisfied, as he himself had been. Why, indeed, had he not taken her in his arms, and made her listen? He would have been sure now, and so would she. Letters – what were letters!

He sighed, came back to Dinah, who did not remind him of the wrap, but snuggled down and asked him to read to her. He missed words and stumbled, but she heard nothing, busily concocting in her mind a letter to Edith, giving a full account of her brother's behaviour. If he was so silly enough to be afraid of Edith, *she* wasn't. She wanted this glorious sister-in-law – she wanted her mother to have, in overflow of compensation, this glorious daughter-in-law. Before the fever of her cold abated, she forced her laconic pen to picture Simon, secretly kissing the frock. But she never knew whether it availed. Edith's letters, friendly as ever, made no allusion to her tale. Simon remained in ignorance both of his sister's effort and Edith's lack of response.

His own epistles, however, grew ardent again. A meeting with Marjorie Newell heightened the flame. Marjorie had come back to England early in the year and he had seen her once or twice, before his own work kept him away for months from town. Their first conversation proved somewhat embarrassing. In answer to his chaffing reproaches, she felt compelled to tell him the story of her call at Baron's Court. She had arrived at the flat in due sequence to her card, knocked, and failed to get an answer. Finding the front door unlocked, she had gone into the hall, and rapped at an inner door. This was not only unlocked, but stood ajar. She could hear voices, but saw nobody. As she hesitated, a further door leading from the room was flung open, and a man came out, half dressed. They stared at each other, his answers to her inquiry for Simon were confused. Jani appeared for a moment, snapped out something, and retired. Marjorie excused herself hurriedly, and collected her wits outside. She left England with Lady Terring, deciding she could do no good by talking or writing. If it helped Simon now to know such details – he shrugged them aside. In view of Jani's admissions, her flight with Richards, nothing more seemed necessary. He was satisfied to know that Marjorie was still his friend. They had seen little of each other since, but a week after Dinah left, Marjorie came back to town. Simon took her out one evening, and confided in her. The very magnitude of her ignorance of Edith's "Jewish side" made her assurances comforting.

"I never understood about all that," she said frankly. "It had nothing to do with our friendship. But I feel sure she cared for you. Of course, one could never tell with Edith!" Her eyes twinkled merrily at him. "She was so angry with you that I thought you must have done something really dreadful, and it upset me. But when she began to scold *me* for being horrid to you, I guessed she had – well, changed, and yet *not* changed, if you understand. Of course you were married then, and out of the question – or so it seemed. But the way she talked of you – or rather *listened*, especially when Miss Rachlin came – and the fuss she made of your people – well, you know, it put ideas into my head. She was touchy about you, not a bit like what she was about Dr. Wyn—" Marjorie sighed. She had not got over her own sentiment for Hector Wyn. "It's my firm belief, she cared for you from the beginning—"

Marjorie had nothing more definite to tell him than Dinah had. And she was – so much less subtle that her intuitions were not as sound. But she had been with Edith a good deal at a time when he was what she called "off the map." Her reiterations, therefore, were the more encouraging. But what more encouragement did he need than his own heart gave him? He found himself infringing Edith's prohibitions – with impunity. If she did not respond, at least she no longer checked. After all, she would be home in a couple of months. She must know how he ached and hungered for her. His thoughts grew bold. He schemed ways of meeting her for the first time, alone, so that he might surprise the welcome in her face before it cooled, keep it warm with an embrace she could not deny, with kisses that must draw her sweetness irrevocably to him.

By Jove, she couldn't stop him now! Hadn't he done everything he possibly could to please her? Rankling below, was the knowledge engendered by her cry – "Not for my sake, but for your own." Only thus could she be pleased,

But if it rankled, it was more because he would have liked her unconditional surrender, than from any fear of failure in himself. He was conscious of a growth in racial stature, of arrival at a point where they could meet more nearly, if not as toweringly, as she might desire. No, it was she who must, ultimately, yield the little space that remained between them.

Meanwhile, he could respect the sobering emotion of her own latest letters. If she seemed to ignore the appeal of his advancing love, it was because she was still absorbed in reaction to Zion, and for the first time letting him share it freely.

"If you haven't taken my stay here seriously," she wrote,

"it must be that my method of impressing you has been wrong. I didn't wish you to be carried away by what *I* felt or thought out here. Above all, I was afraid of exaggerating my delight in it, of misleading you in any way as to the character of the life and the necessity of vocation in those who dedicate themselves to it. I've tried to make you see how hard it is. It must be years and years before a solid Jewish centre can be reared. I've more reason than before to know how much has yet to be done, in education and science, building, commerce, developing the agricultural basis by the purchase of more land and equipment. What, after all, are forty colonies and the beginnings of a few townships? And yet – how much, when one considers from what they sprang, the toil and sacrifice that have gone to make them what they are, in the brief space of thirty years. If in God's sight a thousand years are but as a watch in the night, what are a paltry thirty in the rebuilding of a nation? Surely one may look forward with confidence to generations of progressive work...

I have at times a peculiar feeling that some critical period is at hand, that there may be some great sweep of events which will hasten the consummation of desire, and dispose of the need of decades of patience. It's absurd, of course, and just arises from one's dreams... Besides, it might be bad for a people, as for an individual, to have so much granted too quickly."

Simon read the letter one evening before dinner, and felt impatient with the slowness of the meal. He was anxious to rush to his room and begin a reply. Miss Vannick dallied with the service, however, because Jerry was late. When the boy came in, his face soapy from haste, he apologised with a little tinge of excitement.

"Seen the news?" he said. "Assassination of the Archduke Francis Ferdinand at Sere-Sarajevo—"

"Yes, yes," said Miss Vannick. "Your father brought the paper. The Archduchess; too. Horrible. Now sit down, Jeremiah, do."

"Looks as if there'll be a jolly old scrap somewhere after this."

" Huh," grunted his father. "What's it got to do with us? Your soup's cold, boy."

Simon got to his pen and pad at last.

"Surely you don't mean that the time isn't ripe for the restoration of the Jews to Palestine?" he wrote. " Even if l am unable to participate, I can at least see the necessity of an early return. With Judaism weakening its hold everywhere, only some splendid alternative will bring the stray sheep back into the fold. The more you talk of hardship and difficulties, the more certain it seems that those who endure them for love of a cause, will succeed in it. Why, it must be *easy* for the Jews who have turned their backs on countries that abuse them, to toil and suffer for what they feel their very own. What is hard, is to abandon a country one loves and that has treated one well. Something very big must take possession of one first, don't you think? My dear, I understand. You wanted that to happen to me. If it hasn't, you won't blame me? But I can't agree about having too much, too quickly. When one has waited and suffered so long, it's safe, as well as right and just, to be rewarded in full measure. 'Speedily, in our time, O Lord'. Don't be more niggardly than our Rabbis expect God to be. As far as I'm concerned, I want my great good fortune as quickly as I can get it – and I'm very sure it will be good for me! Dearest, be generous…"

"Since you understand so much," she replied, "don't spoil it by imagining that I lack faith and trust ... If I have any doubts left, it is only of my own place in this marvellous *Yishub*. The sort of service I'm rendering is useful and necessary, Heaven knows. But I'm thinking of a great deal more than that ... Do I *belong*, as the real Chalutzim belong? Sharing aspirations isn't enough. One must belong wholly to Zion, or one isn't accepted. It isn't even a question of the fierce idealism that burns like a furnace, driving one from comfort and security, making one glad to suffer and endure, to give oneself in utter contribution. One may will and will, yet the heart's blood that came into being elsewhere cannot forfeit first allegiances. Can it be that I am not as completely Jewish as these colonists from West and East, or are we divided merely by crusts of upbringing and tradition, the routine of different spheres? Their ways are not my ways, though country and God are ours alike ... Possibly, they are just heady with the strong wine of freedom, while I don't feel their terrific sense of release. And, of course, all the formulas that have ruled my life have come from settled sources, an established order of things ... Here there is nothing settled, nothing established – all has yet to grow. Perhaps that's the answer, the thing to be really confident about. Ultimately we shall evolve a new generation from the present mixtures; the links in common will be welded, the rest rejected, for the issue of the New Judean. The difficulty just now is to discriminate. That is why I'm so anxious to find my exact place, my *special* place, – if I have one. And to avoid making mistakes. You see, I came with certain ideas of the value of my English blood. I had at least as much pride in the contribution it could make, as the French and German Jews here had in theirs. But it has turned out that these elements, so far from helping, have been *detracting* from the standards of the pure Hebrew ideal. Consciously and unconsciously, they have worked towards a French or German system rather than a Jewish ... That kind of error I do not wish to make. So the problem is, how to set my English brick into the Palestinian edifice, in order that a genuinely *Jewish* Home may result ... As you have found out, duality has its advantages as well as its handicaps. It is even more important to distinguish between them here, than it is in England ... We'll talk it over when I'm home." With a rare touch of response to his tender phrases, she added, "I'm almost afraid you won't know your golden princess when you see her – she's become more like a brown peasant maid; and, inside, too – perhaps I'm not quite the same ... But you'll try to understand, won't you? I want to tell you so much, Simon. It's hard to write of everything, clearly not knowing what sort of expression you are wearing."

"You shall tell me anything you wish, darling," he thought, but did not quite dare to write in full – "you shall tell me, while I hold you in my arms; and you'll like my expression – if you can see it—" And he felt his lips press down the white eyelids. Even if they had turned brown, they would be as sweet. Passionate evocations were taking possession of him, exceeding the limits of his normal cool self, and the old vague dreams of the ideal Edith. The flesh-and-blood girl, real and attainable at last, submitted to his mastery. With the mounting temperature of his love, went a clearer grasp of the workings of her mind.

"When you get this letter," she wrote in July, "it will be near the ninth of Ab. Will you take Bubele to the old Sephardic shool, where I used to go on the eve of Tisha-b-ab? I shall like to think of you both there – though I'm beginning to feel the Black Fast is no longer necessary. Surely it will be abolished soon, now that our days of lamentation are giving way to days of rejoicing, and the prophecies are being fulfilled before our eyes – 'The ransomed of the Lord shall return … sorrow and sighing shall flee away … I will rejoice in Jerusalem and joy in my people: and the voice of weeping shall be no more heard in her. And they shall build houses and inhabit them: and they shall plant vineyards, and eat the fruit thereof!'

"Will it surprise you, I wonder, if I tell you that the religious side of our history now moves me profoundly? I used to think I was not susceptible to it, that while I could feel it with my mind there was no response in my soul. Neither in church nor in synagogue, did I ever experience an emotion that was not a *community* sense, the feeling that came from human sympathy and kinship. That's divine, too, of course, but it isn't the religious absorption in God one is told is proper to a place of worship. Sometimes when I was with Bubele I seemed to catch it for a moment but I knew it came *from* her, and was not in me … I thought I must be deficient in it, but now – it's hardest of all to explain, Simon, but Palestine has given me the most wonderful conviction of religious truth. At first I imagined it was just an extended sense of satisfaction in our historic land – the pride of beholding our ancient shrines, seeing, walking on ground trodden by our ancestors, visualising them in life on the actual spots. (You remember Hampton Court? I'm sorry if I teased you too much about that!) But even apart from this – beyond it all – there is something evoked by Erez Israel that I can only call a feeling of spiritual presence. In the evening when I look up at the stars, or in the morning when I turn from the girls at their tasks to the brilliant blue sky – so blue, Simon, clearer and purer than the skies of Italy – I know there is a force here that is nowhere else. I believe that it speaks to the soul of the Jew and drives him to great things. That instinct for righteousness which is inherent in our people – it comes from a power that has its dwelling here. I kneel to it, it pervades me like an essence, it lifts my being to the heights. I am thrilled with joy that Jewish blood runs in my veins to meet and acknowledge it. For I feel now, more than I have ever felt, that Israel will receive again the messages of God, and interpret them to the world."

On the eve of the ninth of Ab, Simon hurried down to Caramel Place. The city streets were hot and airless under the cloudy dark setting in. He was anxious about Bubele, knowing she abstained not only from meat, according to rule, but from most other food, during the whole of the nine mourning days. She looked, indeed, very frail in her black "sackcloth", void even of the heavy gold brooch she customarily wore for shool. Her usual brisk movements lagged, and as he adapted his step to hers, Simon felt as if they were two ghosts, creeping with other ghosts into the shadowed courtyard, the gloomy unlit entrance to the old sanctuary. For hundreds of years had such living ghosts crept here, to lament the destruction of more ancient cornerstones, the massacre of less ghostly dead. Inside was a pitch-black cave with a floor of dancing lights – or else the universe turned upside down, the earth stretching black above, the starry skies twinkling below. As the eye adapted Itself to shade and gleam, outlines of the building came into focus. Great chandeliers hung unlit from the ceiling; the only ornamental note in a severity of washed wall and dull wood. The high grill of the women's gallery lay across stone pillars, looming up from narrow benches. On the backs of these benches, in sockets fixed to the ledge were the candles that illuminated the cave with such eerie effect. Row upon row, the tiny rays hardly penetrated the corners and upper hollows of dark space.

Across the ark a black curtain was drawn like a pall. Before it stood a shrouded cantor, intoning the Lamentations of Jeremiah. The sparse congregation sat motionless or rose, flickering shadows, to join the dirge in a low, sighing mutter of response. Then came an interval of profound silence.

It was unlike any pause that occurred in any other service. Simon had experienced the stillness of a Quaker meeting. He had gone there with Ted Rendall, whose grandmother was a Friend. The meeting-house had impressed him with its simple dignity, the prayers with their broad human appeal. But the silence had merely embarrassed him. He had had hard work not to fidget, not to indulge a cough or other untimely sound. Artificially spurred to meditation, he could not meditate. What, he wondered instead was Ted thinking of? – What were the thoughts of the others?—

But in this gloom of night and occasion, weighed down by knowledge of his forebears, the intense pause came logically from reflection on their griefs. Much – too much – matter for the mind to busy with; the long sombre history of disaster and persecution, rayed by invincible heroism and hope. Was it, then, coming to an end at last, this unwinding scroll of woe? Would one actually read with one's eyes the words – *Sof Galuth* – End of Exile – at the bottom of the stained yellow strip; actually watch the Finger write upon a fresh unspotted sheet – *Shav* – Return?

"Comfort, O Lord our God, the mourners of Zion, and the

mourners of Jerusalem, and the city that is in mourning, laid waste, despised and desolate; in mourning for that she is childless, laid waste as to her dwellings, despised in the downfall of her glory, and desolate through the loss of her inhabitants; she sitteth with her head covered like a barren woman who hath not borne. Legions have devoured her; worshippers of strange gods have possessed her; they have put thy people Israel to the sword, and in wilfulness have slain the loving ones of the Most High. Therefore let Zion weep bitterly, and Jerusalem give forth her voice. Oh my heart, my heart! How it grieveth for the slain! My bowels, my bowels, how they yearn for the slain! For thou, O Lord, didst consume her with fire; and with fire thou wilt in future restore her, as it is said, as for me, I will be unto her, saith the Lord, a wall of fire round about, and I will be a glory in the midst of her. Blessed art thou, O Lord, who comfortest Zion and rebuildest Jerusalem."

To-morrow was at hand, when these things would be said; a great To-morrow, when they would be done.

"I will be a glory in the midst of her." Already that glory was resting, not on him, but on Edith. He saw her hair radiant in the halo of divine light. She stood upon the holy soil, scattering seed – while he still crouched, impotent, in the gloom of the Diaspora. Incredible that he could so remain! "A wall of fire around about." Rise, spring through it, towards that shining sun! The image stirred his mental sense, it pricked fibres of response in heart and soul. He almost strained to see her closer, but what flashed next was the Rachlin drawing-room, the gold-robed figure standing, calm and sweet, a slight hesitation in the first notes of her voice. He had looked, then, and hardly listened: now the vision dimmed, to make the hearing more acute; the Hebrew words came clear – the words of the incomparable Jehudah, chosen to supplement Jeremiah on the Black Day of memorial.

> "Zion! wilt thou not ask if peace be with thy captives,
> That seek thy peace – that are the remnant of thy flocks?
> …
>
> To wail for Thine affliction I am like the jackals,
> But when I dream of the return of thy captivity,
>   I am a harp for thy songs.
> …
>
> Happy is he that waiteth, that cometh nigh and seeth the rising
> Of the light, when on him thy dawn shall break
> That he may see the welfare of thy chosen and rejoice
> In thy rejoicing, when thou turnest back unto thine olden youth."

Spanish names on the board outside – Spanish faces passing. The stock outcasted from glories, forsworn voluntarily by the poet-physician of eight centuries ago. How marked the diversity of the unit, Jew! Canuto, Zacutta; Warshawsky; Kolnowitz; Eisenberg; Vannick; Rachlin; Wein-Wyn; Harman-Hyman-Chayim; Milner-Miller; Schwartz-Black: the names testified to far flung exile, colour and shape to variety of habitat. Race, indeed! It was not even pure. What strange admixture of physical tissues had combined with suns and winds to mould the scattered children of Israel? "As the stars in heaven, as the sand upon the seashore, shall thy seed be," was fulfilled not only in numbers but in types. The stupid goy thought he had simply to draw a hook nose, to pillory the world-tossed Semite. Yet by inexorable law, the same spirit stamped the black eye and the blue, the short nose and the long, fair product of the West and swarthy son of East; stamped, and bound them each to each, by the natural piety – of their common mother Zion.

Simon guided Bubele carefully into the lane, his hand slow and steady on the delicate frame. But within, his heart swelled and vibrated. The sense of brotherhood. had rushed upon him strong as the flow of a deep, resistless river. Not ghosts, but living souls were round him, joined by invisible throngs. Near, familiar, no longer foreign or alien neither Russian, German, Dutch, Spanish, English; simple Jews, of whom he was one, to whom he belonged, whose claims he could never again deny, any more than he could shake himself free of their despairs and hopes.

Linked with them by the past and the present, irretrievably linked with their future.

A newsboy darted across the angle of the streets. Waving his papers he shouted stridently,

"Litest News! War brikes out! German troops marching into Belgium!"

XXV

Dream – nightmare – dream.

The stark horror of the war did not overwhelm Simon as it did Dick Partingdale, who resisted it, spent two years in prison, and was sentenced to death in France; Ted Rendall, who enlisted in high enthusiasm, sapped as much, to his shell-shocked ruin, by the bestiality of the civil "patriot", as by the filth and carnage of the trenches; Harman, who might have remained in America, where Lena went to him, but came back to join the Egyptian Expeditionary Force, blasting more than their immediate hopes; the Vannicks, crushed by the extinction of their last bright young life at Ypres; and others in their circle, which eddied round sinking bodies, like every circle spread from human groups in those tragic years.

The first shock of learning that Edith would not or could not return to England, was dulled in the fresh excitement of day to day. He offered himself with Ted to the Officers Training Corps, but his department would not release him. The depletion of staff was complete, and he was needed for important service at home.

Intimations of nightmare came with urgent family claims. In October he was summoned by telegram from Ruth. "Father ill". Why Ruth? Dinah, it turned out, was ill also. Though in her case, a fainting fit was followed only by unobtrusive nervous disorder. The collapse of their father was more serious. A heart attack followed receipt of fatal news from Russia.

Gershon, due for discharge a week after the declaration of war, had been sent at once to the Polish Front. He was among the first casualties.

"But you are not to blame – Good God, you are not to blame," Simon cried to his prostrated family. It was a cry that failed to ease the consciences of those who had let the lad go, to fulfil an apparently riskless duty. It failed utterly to erase from Dinah's mind her sense of final responsibility. "Why didn't I agree to his plan of escape?" she moaned to Simon. "I was a coward – I wanted to save myself the trouble of his coming back – I was afraid of the pain of refusing to marry him. And now I've done worse than hurt him – I've killed him." Nothing would lessen her anguish, the keener for concealment of its main cause from her parents. From Myer Billig, too, whose efforts at consolation, welcomed by Simon, might have proved more efficacious had he known. But Dinah pledged her brother frantically to silence. Her terror of Myer's censure seemed ludicrous, though as illuminating as Myer's tenderness to her. The sword of remorse was double-edged. It was as well she had to assist her mother in nursing Gedaliah, and bringing the sick man back to the endurance of his burdens.

"No worry," the doctor said, conscious of irony. Simon was helpless in face of the new chapter of harassment that opened on his people. Death – illness – the major griefs were attended by a series of minor pricks, that threatened at any moment to grow wounds.

Gedaliah Black had never been naturalised. The fact that he was a Russian and not a German or Austrian subject saved him from arrest and internment, but not from constant police supervision and mob hostility. In Dawport he had not even the sense of friendliness that came from the familiarities of Blaemawe: yet Blaemawe itself, as the war progressed, grew bitter and malicious, as toll was taken of its sons and the resources of those at home. Humanity's lowest passions flared higher, if anything, where prosperity rather than deprivation came. Favoured colliers, profiteering tradesmen, journalists, officials in their dress of brief authority, held it a patriotic duty to make the lives of aliens, even of the "friendly" order, microcosms of hell. The Blacks could not escape the suspicion that every accented Jew was a Hun. In corollary, every dissenter from the patriotic creed was at least a "pro". And prominent among the Blaemaweites, Meurig Lloyd fell into the last category, since he sympathised publicly with both Jews, German or otherwise, and with those execrated if indubitable natives who refused to participate in the war.

"In the sight of Christ," he said blasphemously, "it is not *'the* war', but 'war', in which man is commanded to kill his brother. Why do ye torture His disciples, who will not take upon themselves the blood of their fellows? Why do ye mock the Master's orders, to love your enemies, do good to them that hate you, and pray for those that despitefully use you? Our nation it is that has most reason to know the folly of opposing force to force. And shame it is to every Welshman to join in the persecution of conscience. Let us grant the right of every man to follow the call of his soul – and for Christ's sake, let us cultivate the spirit of brotherhood and forbearance, in this time of sorrow to all."

Almost all the chapels denounced Meurig Lloyd. He had always been a renegade; now he was a traitor. Fit associate of German Jews!

The two fathers became more intimate than at any time

since the family break. It was the final and most disastrous phase of their friendship.

The Blacks' trade had fallen off in both Dawport and Blaemawe. At the latter place, the young man installed as manager had enlisted and had no successor. One day when Gedaliah paid a belated visit, he found the shop windows smashed and goods removed. At his protests an abusive crowd gathered. Meurig Lloyd's appearance was the signal for threats to both, and they retired for safety to Ty Gwyn. But the hooligans were not satisfied. Stones hurtled through the privet hedges, and window panes, and Mrs. Lloyd bolted doors in a scolding rage. Her husband unbolted them, and came out to meet insulting epithets with vain appeals. He was tripped up on his own doorstep and fell fatally, striking his head.

Once he had saved Gedaliah Black's life. Now his death on Gedaliah's behalf led to the other's. Simon's father reached home to succumb to his weakened heart, and Simon's response to a second telegram was several hours too late. Almost before he left the training camp where he now belonged, Gedaliah had passed away.

Hardly was there time for a last sight of the still form to which he owed – how much, how little? So often in his boyhood he had felt only that Gedaliah was not the father for him: now he asked himself, was he the son for Gedaliah? Had he not been as saltless a disappointment? They had never shared a moment – a mood – in common, except, perhaps, through Edith. Late enough, she had held the mirror in which the son, for a space, had perceived his father…

"I was dumb, and kept silence, I held my peace, and had no comfort: and my sorrow was stirred… Surely as a mere semblance man walketh to and fro… Hear my prayer, O Lord, and give ear unto my cry; hold not thy peace at my tears; for I am a stranger with thee, a sojourner, as all my fathers were. O spare me, that I may again be glad, before I go hence, and be no more."

The mourning week was nightmare unrelieved. His mother's hair was white, and his uniform added despair to her grief. She implored him not to destroy her utterly by entering the army.

"But it's done, mother. I am a soldier. And I must serve England."

"Have we not served enough? Must I lose all? Even Russia takes not the only son – Gershon's mother has others to comfort her broken heart… You need not go, I know it. You can work for the Government here in England. Perhaps it will end soon, this terrible war… At least – at least – stay for the year of kaddish – let your father's soul find rest—" She broke into harrowing sobs, continuing to plead in the midst of them. "Simon, you must give me your word. Swear that you will not go – as your father would have made you swear with his dying breath—"

" Mother, I can't – it's impossible – it's wrong to ask such a thing—"

"Was I wrong when I asked you to swear – once before? You came to see how right I was. Do you not want, now, to have Jewish children?"

A nerve tingled through him. Edith's children would be Jews – inevitably, desirably.

"You were right there, mother," he muttered. "But this is different – it's not in my power—oh, mother, don't – I'll do my best – I'll hang it out as long as I decently can. But – listen. I'm training for Egypt. I shall go to Palestine."

He had not meant to tell her yet. The announcement, to him of such tremendous soul-easing import, had a contrary effect upon his mother. She, like Edith, could only feel appalled at a Judea soaked in blood.

"Not that way, surely, oh Lord?" Edith had exclaimed, in the horror that governed her short, infrequent notes. Revulsion settled into wretchedness at the dislocating confusion of the Turkish broil. But Simon's chief concern was with her safety: since that seemed assured – as assured as anything could be in a world turned insecure for all – he was not greatly disturbed by her views. Looking now into her mirror, he saw not only its reflections, but its limitations as a mirror. Was not every woman a mirror to the man who loved her, and who therefore saw things as she reflected them? Such a mirror might be true or false. Even the crystal truth of Edith's could not increase its natural orbit, or defy the stains of atmosphere. It was but a mirror: and the eyes of man are made to look direct at the universe of God. With tender deprecation, but a sense of power and independence of judgment, Simon turned deliberately from that flashing glass, from the lovely hands that held it, the lovely eyes that guided his gaze…

She was safe with her friends in Jerusalem. Nothing that he could say, or Lady Hafod do, deterred her from remaining at her post, serving those who needed skill and comfort, in the land most lacking in both. "Must Jacob wait another seven years for Rachel?" he wrote, and she answered briefly, "If he is Jacob, he will."

She, like his mother, did not want him to fight. The photograph of himself in bright new officer's uniform covering his remark – "You don't think me a coward now – despicable?" did not seem to balance her charge of long ago.

Events deflected her into the rejoinder – "I don't think Dick Partingale is, either" – which might console Dick in his outcast cell, but was not fair, Simon felt, to himself. She did not see, as he did, the virtue of striking a blow for the possession of something dear. The desire for sacrifice in a man was not like that in a woman. She *yielded* up; he must *break* up. He might break himself, but others must break with him…

Was not Judea necessary for the life and honour of the Jew? Then, when England endorsed the necessity in a time of danger and crisis, there was surely but one thing that an English Jew, who loved both England and Judea, must do…

Dream and nightmare blended together.

On a last day of leave spent with Lena Harman, he told her of his transfer to the new-formed Jewish Battalion.

"As a private," he added.

"As a damn fool," she said. "But so is everybody else, these days." And she kissed him like a sister. Jack was in Cairo after a Gallipoli wound. She thought its effect a blessing in its securance of a 'back-line job', not foreseeing it was to stunt their lives for ever.

"I want to keep this a secret from Edith."

"Why, in Heaven's name? Have you lost all your wits? She's changed her tune since the Balfour Declaration, and must have kissed every British soldier in Jerusalem—"

"Not she," he said tranquilly. "And anyway, she disapproves of Jewish Regiments. Says Jews are already too heavily bound to the gods of militarism, and it's their function as Jews, the primary Peace Apostles, to keep free of the curse. All the same, I don't think she'll be sorry to see me, with the Magen David on my arm –" He grinned, then became very earnest. "But please don't tell her yet. I'll send my letters to you for forwarding. She needn't know until I'm there."

"You can't be sure of meeting – for ages."

"I'll find a way."

"But supposing – anything – happens?"

"Oh God – don't speak of it!"

She raised her brows at the sudden violence. He looked down, shamefaced.

"It's not that I'm afraid," he said. "Do you remember asking me once if I'd rather die for England than live for Palestine? Well, I feel now that if I died out there, I should be doing both. Of course, I – I don't *want* to die—"

"I should think not," she said, her gaze admiring his stalwart body, his bright open-air face. "You're far too healthy and vigorous – too full of rich life—"

"All the better for Palestine, perhaps. My rich life, as you call it – all this blood and bone" – he flung his arms out, his muscles tightening – "would feed the land as well from below as above." She shuddered. "What's it matter?" he said, recklessly. "A living chalutz – or a dead – if each can serve? It's not *that* I'm afraid of, Lena. It's – oh, don't you see – I can't die until I've – until Edith—" His voice failed.

"You'll see her soon, of course you will, idiot," she said hastily. "You'll give her the gorgeous surprise you're so keen on, get married on the spot, and bring her back. If the war's not over, you'll have to get leave the same time as Jack, and all come home together for my son's Bris Milah" – She laughed her old audacious laugh, in spite of her brooding eyes, a curiously pinched look about nose and cheeks. "It'll be a show more to her taste than the Hafod christening—"

It was strange to think, on the burning sands of the

Mehallah, that their letters were still being exchanged through Lena, while actually they were so near together, that at any moment they might be walking towards one another – walking into that supreme moment when all the agony and devilry around would be lost in the heaven of their embrace. Always his dream strove towards that moment of culmination... He was prowling round her quarters, awaiting her appearance – she would catch sight of him – stop, transfixed, gaze uncertainly – he would make one stride and draw her to his breast, gently, powerfully, triumphantly. He would hear her voice, but not her words, because he himself would be the master of speech, pouring sweet phrases into her conquered ears...

It was stranger still to think that for some time after crossing the border from Sinai, he had forgotten her. Forgotten Edith! He would tell her, and she would let him hold her closer for it. Yes, because the influence that had dominated him was the influence of Zion. He had not known it would clutch him so quickly, so entirely. Bloodcall and brain-call echoed over the historic tracks from Gaza to Nablus. Beersheba and the Philistine plain, blue hills of Ephraim and Judea, groves of ancient Ludd – then the trumpet of the new life, the colonies of Rishon and Rechoboth, clarion in welcome, in banners, processions, lusty-youthed outriders. It stirred even the unregenerate, fellows of coarser fibre not strung for high notes, who grumbled and cursed the march in scalping heat, the flinty defiles that alternated with sucking sand, the incessant futile toil, the pests, the lack of sleep, food, drink, the thousand inhospitalities as well as dangers of what they called – "this God-forsaken country." God-forsaken! Simon laughed to himself in the midst of their common miseries, and soared, intoxicated, to presumptuous heights. God-steeped, rather, manifest even in plague and desolation, in ravage and unholy slaughter. Sons of Israel, the unease that racks your bones is stern reminder – If ye be not of the elect, rid Me of ye! As for me, thought Simon, footsore and perspiring, I am Joshua. I am Maccabeus – I am Bar Cochba – I am the servant of the Lord come to chasten the Gentiles, and set His people in the crown of His Holy Places…

Edith came back in rushing lure as Jerusalem approached. The occasion of which news had come, through her letters and otherwise, was at hand. There was to be a great ceremony on Mount Scopus, when the foundations of the Hebrew University would be laid. Simon meant to be in the party of officers and men selected to attend. But an accident from barbed wire, through which he had crawled the whole of one long dark night, kept him prisoner with a swollen knee.

The second disappointment fell some weeks later, when camp was struck outside the Holy City on the way to Jericho. At last Simon saw Jerusalem at leisure – but Edith not at all. She had gone to meet some friends at Jaffa. He raged and cursed his own ban, which kept her ignorant of his whereabouts, and caused absurd delays in correspondence. Yet he did not lift it in the letter he dashed off to Lena, nor suspect that the bitterness of his complaint led her to assume that he had. With savage obstinacy he would not change his scheme. Surprise her he would – he must. If he could not get early leave, he would take it – front or no front—

He reckoned without the pestilential hosts of the Jordan Valley. Here was nightmare each broiling day. From the Turkish trenches came continuous shelling, but the lesser enemy could not complete in deadly effect with the denizen

armies of the swamps. A new psalm might have arisen in
Israel. "The Turk has killed his tens, but the Mosquito his
hundreds of tens." Nets, precautions, antidotes, all the
armoury of gigantic man, failed to thwart the puny insect's
onslaught. It battened on bodies strained by terrific heat,
heavy cannonade, relentless patrolling, lack of water, and
surfeit of sand-gritted food.

Simon suffered, but did not realise how badly his nerves
were sapped, until his collapse on sodden soil. A move to the
hills took place in torrential rain, and with other malarial
victims, he tossed in agony in his steaming wraps. By some
muddle there were not enough tents, and what was worse, not
enough hospital accommodation. Sick men had to wait their
turn literally upon dangerous ground.

In this spell of nightmare he was conscious dimly, at what
seemed year-long intervals, of brisk, moving figures, officers,
doctors, nurses, baling him about, giving orders which he
struggled in vain to obey, even when he realised some were
not meant for him. He swallowed drugs, felt and did not feel
the prick of injections, his body swelled away from him or
dropped like an iron chain, in vast fits of shivering, in jellied
heat or ice-chunked cold. He was half aware, somehow, in this
vague world of unreflection, that he was being conveyed to a
house in a narrow street, utterly strange and unescapable.
Scorching devils of pain chased between its walls, until he
sank into the blessed cool of linen sheets. Doctors and nurses
flitted here, too, but soon silence and oblivion wiped them out.
He forgot at last to struggle with them, to struggle, rather, with
the vexed half-knowledge of them, with all they did and said
and expected of him. When he fought once more, it was with
figures of delirium, translated from the world he had known

before the war. There came a phase when he imagined he was his grand-uncle – old Elman – lying there helpless and inert, muttering brokenly to a vision of himself in the careless vigour of young manhood-muttering, "Bleib nor a Yid, Shimke, bleib nor a Yid" – and then that nurse would approach – the nurse with Edith's hair but incongruous face, nod and wink, turn cross, and raise her hand as if to slap – a slap that became tender in touch like a caress. He would complain through lips parched and feeble – "Where's Edith? Why aren't you Edith?" And she made answer in her prim, faraway tones – "I am Edith – don't you know me, darling?" Helplessly he would try to push her from him – " Go away – I want Edith" – and keep his burning eyes closed in weak vexation.

Then one morning he woke as if from a healing doze, and knew that he was himself – Simon Black – lying on a hospital bed in the dawn of a Jerusalem day. He lay there conscious, but hardly daring to breathe, in case the feeble action of his mind should cease. Hours seems to elapse in the minutes that revived his sense of connection and effect. He dozed again, dozed and opened his eyes, clear if languid, upon a white-aproned figure standing close to his bed. "Nurse," he said, "can I have some water?" He thought she said something as she handed him a glass, but he could not hear – there was still a slight drumming in his ears. "Thank you," he said, and tried to laugh. "I expect I'll need lots more presently – for a good old wash. I feel as if I've been lying here for years. How long, nurse? "

Again the indistinct reply. He raised his languid head slightly – his gaze travelled up, and was caught in the bluest eyes that ever looked from a delicately tanned face bound in stiff white.

"Edith," he said, and remained utterly dumb. He fell back, colour that was not of fever flushed his dry cheeks. The throbbing in his ears grew loud and thundery. Oh God, how cruel, how devilishly cruel! That his dream should stand there waiting, and his arms powerless, his lips mute, his head too weak to leave the cursed pillow. Hot tears spurted in his eyes and rolled shamefully down. Suddenly she was seated on the bed, stooping over him, raising him from behind in a firm, tender movement of her hands. His hair felt the softness of her breast.

"My dear love," she said, and laid her lips on his.

In the garden of the house which Edith and her friends had turned into a nursing home, and to which Simon had been brought as a result of her search – following a message from Lena – the lovers spent their hours of farewell.

The tall, broad-shouldered man in shabby uniform was no longer patient, but soldier, due for return to camp. His face, still pale but vivid with joy, was a lamp lit by the presence, not of a nurse in starched white, but of a graceful girl, thinner than he had known, whose milky skin showed sunstained against her light silk dress.

"Not for long, dearest," he was saying, drawing her arms round his neck as they sat together. "It's coming to an end – I'll be demobbed before you know it—"

"I'm to know everything at once, please, Simon, now—"

"Yes, my darling. But we aren't waiting for that. You'll be my very own before you – there, I was going to say it again!" They burst into simultaneous laughter. "The colonel's an awfully good sport – he'll let me fix things up at once – and whatever happens, I'll get lots of leave, or you'll come to me

– oh, darling-beloved—" He kissed her so fiercely that she drew away and put her hand on her mouth. He coaxed her fingers and pleaded, in the vibrant Hebrew he knew could charm her. "'Let him kiss me with the kisses of his mouth; for thy love is better than wine'."

She yielded, but in a little while was saying,

"So it's I, then, who am black but comely? And I was afraid you wouldn't admire my tan! Do you know, sir, I've rehearsed that part of the Shir Hashirim for your especial benefit—" and she pretended to hide her face again as she added, in her more clipped, demure accents – "'Look not upon me, because I am swarthy, because the sun hath burnt me'—"

He tilted her chin upward, and answered – "'Behold, thou art fair, my love; behold, thou art fair; thou hast dove's eyes'." He kissed the lids as he had dreamed of doing, "'My love, there is no spot in thee… Come with me from Lebanon, my spouse, with me from Lebanon; look from the top of Amana, from the top of Shenir and Hermon, from the lions' dens, from the mountains of leopards'. It fits, darling – it fits most marvellously! Do you know it all by heart as I do? The Hebrew used to be mechanical with me. I've been saying it over and over to you – in Hebrew and English – for months. How intensely real it sounds in Palestine! 'For lo, the winter is past, the rain is over and gone, the time of the singing of birds is come; and the voice of the turtle is heard in our land. The fig-tree putteth forth her green figs, and the vines with the tender grapes give forth fragrance. Arise, my love, my fair one, come away. O my dove, that art in the clefts of the rock, in the covert of the steep place, let me see thy countenance, let me hear thy voice; for sweet is thy voice and thy countenance is comely." He held her closely in a long pause, which he broke only to say,

"I ought to have sent you the *Shir* instead of that dud letter long ago – perhaps my princess would not have been as hard on Solomon, as she was on Simple Simon—"

"That letter?" she said. "It was sweeter to me than even Solomon's song."

She slipped her hand swiftly into the front of her dress, and drew out a crumpled note. As she held the page before his eyes, Simon read the ardent words she had refused to answer.

"But Edith—" he cried, astonished. "I thought you had torn it to pieces."

She smiled; instead of speaking, she put the letter back in her bosom, and offered the voluntary caress that meant more than any yielding to his.

"Dearest—dearest" – he murmured. "Why – why – have I had to wait so long?" She did not answer, and he continued, – "I know I'm a frightful brute, my Edith. Instead of being satisfied with what you're giving me, I'm trying to get all you wouldn't give before!"

"I was a brute to myself," she said. "Your dear letter – it made me want to send a cable – 'Come.' Would you have come?"

" Of course."

"Yes, to me. Not to Zion – then." She sighed, and leaned deliciously on his breast. Her free hand stroked his coat. "This uniform – I love and hate it. You know why I hate it – for the havoc and despair that all war brings. And yet I must love it, because it's British, and has brought Zion and you – together. Oh, darling, I'm still not sure of many, many things. But I knew – long ago – that I loved you – and now I'm sure I was right to wait for you." She resisted his pressure, and freed herself to add, with the grave smile that always made him attentive.

"You know, my dear, it's all in the *Shir*. Shall I tell you the part I know best of all?" Her voice deepened into a rich, tender chant – "'I sought him whom my soul loveth: I sought him, but I found him not … The watchmen that go about the city found me, to whom I said – Saw ye him whom my soul loveth? It was but a little while that I had passed from them, but I found him whom my soul loveth: I held him, and would not let him go, until I had brought him into my mother's house, and into the chamber of her that conceived me'."

She stood up, and he stood with her, deeply moved, looking into her face, noblest as well as fairest sight in the world to him. They stood a little apart, only her hands rested in his. "'My dove, my undefiled'," he whispered, "'Who is she that looketh forth as the morning: fair as the moon, clear as the sun, and terrible as an army with banners? I went down into the garden of nuts to see the fruit of the valley. *Or ever I was aware, my soul set me among the chariots of my princely people'*."

She smiled – a flower opening to the sun, with fresh beads of dew in her eyes. Her quest had been older than the mere quest for his body. And in his response, interpretation was complete.

"Dear love," she said, trembling exquisitely.

"My Edith – mine – my own—"

His head sank down over her firm, frail hands.

The small party of men whom Simon and a companion were seeking had exceeded the limits of their reconnoitre. When found, they seemed to resent the instructions for which the two had been specially despatched. Simon turned back in relief. He would be glad to have done with this last duty. The sun was going down in its swift set, and Sabbath was nigh –

his Sabbath. It grew large and bright with meaning, like all the old forms in this blessed land.

L'choh dodi

Likras kolah.

He would have chanted it high in the heavens, but for his sulky companion. The fellow had not wanted to come. He was nervy, and had made some plan of his own for the day. The suspicion that he might deviate was responsible for the double choice. The colonel could trust Simon... He hummed his paean softly.

"Come, my friend

To meet the bride—"

The blood leaped in his veins in a divine ecstasy. His bride waited, precious as the Sabbath, "crown of her husband."—

"O sanctuary of our King, O regal city,

Arise, go forth from thy overthrow...

Arouse thyself, arouse thyself, for thy light is come ...

Thy God shall rejoice over thee,

As a bridegroom rejoiceth over his bride...

Consummate image! It flashed in apotheosis in the hymn of the Sabbath of Sabbaths, when the high priest issued from out of the Holy of Holies with a countenance bright—.

"As the celestial blue in the thread of the fringes

(Oh heavenly blue of the sanctioning eyes!)

As the diadem set on the brow of a king

(Crowned with the choice of his golden quem!)

As the radiant grace of a bridegroom's face

(As he comes forth from the bridal chamber, from his sanctuary, his temple of love!)

"Hell!" squeaked the fellow suddenly. A bullet had whizzed from the opposite slope. Another – another. The two men dropped flat upon the earth, at a little distance from each other. Simon thought he heard his neighbour groan. He crawled towards him, listened, and raised himself to sling his knapsack down. The sniper began again at the same moment. A bullet struck sharp and low. Simon's head dropped back. He rolled about, then lay face upward. The other man continued to groan.

Nightmare was over. The dream – had it ended, or begun anew?

ABOUT HONNO

Honno Welsh Women's Press was set up in 1986 by a group of women who felt strongly that women in Wales needed wider opportunities to see their writing in print and to become involved in the publishing process. Our aim is to develop the writing talents of women in Wales, give them new and exciting opportunities to see their work published and often to give them their first 'break' as a writer. Honno is registered as a community co-operative. Any profit that Honno makes is invested in the publishing programme. Women from Wales and around the world have expressed their support for Honno. Each supporter has a vote at the Annual General Meeting.

For more information and to buy our publications, please write to Honno at the address below, oi visit our website: www.honno.co.uk

Honno
Unit 14, Creative Units
Aberystwyth Arts Centre
Aberystwyth
Ceredigion
SY23 3GL

Honno Friends
We are very grateful for the support of the Honno Friends:
Gwyneth Tyson Roberts, Jenny Sabine, Beryl Thomas.
For more information on how you can become a Honno
Friend, see: http://www.honno.co.uk/friends.php